D0391141

THE
MESSIAH

Other books by Marjorie Holmes

Three from Galilee—The Young Man from Nazareth
Two from Galilee
To Help You Through the Hurting
God and Vitamins
Lord, Let Me Love
Hold Me Up a Little Longer, Lord
How Can I Find You, God?
Who Am I, God?
Nobody Else Will Listen
I've Got to Talk to Somebody, God
You and I and Yesterday
Love and Laughter
As Tall as My Heart
Beauty in Your Own Backyard
To Treasure Our Days
Writing the Creative Article
World by the Tail
Ten O'clock Scholar
Saturday Night
Cherry Blossom Princess
Follow Your Dream
Senior Trip
Love Is a Hopscotch Thing

THE
MESSIAH

by

MARJORIE HOLMES

HarperSanFrancisco
A Division of HarperCollinsPublishers

THE MESSIAH. Copyright © 1987 by Marjorie Holmes. All rights reserved. Printed in the United States of America. No part of this book may be used or reproduced in any manner whatsoever without written permission except in the case of brief quotations embodied in critical articles and reviews. For information address HarperCollins Publishers, 10 East 53rd Street, New York, NY 10022.

FIRST PAPERBACK EDITION PUBLISHED IN 1988.

Designer: Lydia Link

Copy editor: Marjorie Horvitz

Library of Congress Cataloging-in-Publication Data

Holmes, Marjorie
　　The Messiah.

　　　1. Jesus Christ—Fiction.　2. Bible.　N.T.—History
of Biblical events—Fiction.　I. Title.
PS3515.04457MM4　1987　　　813'.54　　　87-45056
ISBN 0-06-015808-5
ISBN 0-06-064011-1 (pbk.)

92　93　94　95　96　MAPLE　18　17　16　15　14　13　12　11　10　9　8

*To my wonderful husband, Dr. George Schmieler,
whose patience, confidence and encouragement
spurred me on at times when the task seemed impossible, and whose keen insight and suggestions
were a genuine contribution to this book.*

Acknowledgment

I want to acknowledge the invaluable help of Dr. Roy Blizzard, former instructor in Hebrew, Biblical History and Archaeology at the University of Texas. Dr. Blizzard studied at the Hebrew University in Jerusalem, has worked on archaeological excavations throughout Israel, speaks fluent Hebrew and is the author of *Let Judah Go Up First* and coauthor of *Understanding the Difficult Words of Jesus*. It has been my privilege to accompany him on several historic and archaeological seminars in Israel. He is one of the few Americans licensed to guide in Israel. Dr. Blizzard has been my constant consultant for accuracy in writing this book. His knowledge of the Hebrew language and the current research he is conducting in Israel with the Jerusalem School for the Study of the Synoptic Gospels has enabled me to understand more perfectly the life, words, and teachings of Jesus. If there are any errors, they are not his, but mine.

Author's Note

This book is a novel, a work of fiction. I do not pretend to claim that this is the way things actually happened; only that, given the facts of Jesus' life and times as we know them, this is the way they *could* have happened.

It was written humbly, with great reverence and love and conviction. I can only pray that most people, Jews and Christians alike, will read it as a believable and dramatic retelling of the story we all know so much (and so little) about.

As John, Jesus' favorite apostle, wrote in concluding his own account of his Master's remarkable life: *And there were many other things which Jesus did, which, if they should be written down, every one, I suppose that the world itself could not contain the books that should be written* (John 21:25).

THE

Chapter 1

*M*ARY tiptoed to the doorway, pulled back the drapery, and gazed in on her sleeping son. How beautiful he looked, lying there breathing so deeply, face down, one long arm flung over his curly head. Though it was shocking to see him so thin. His usually strapping body barely rippled the bedclothes. But oh, to have him home at last! Mary gripped the cloth, almost faint with this flood of thanksgiving. There had been times when she wondered if she would ever see Jesus again. For never had he been gone so long, without a word. Never had she been so worried. Night after night she had awakened from troubled dreams about him. Dreams that haunted her till morning and tormented her by day.

As always, she had done her best to hide her worry from the rest of the family, especially Josey and Simon—those two were so quick to criticize their brother anyway. Not Jude so much; nor James—he and Jesus had always been close; nor his sisters—to Ann and little Leah, their oldest brother could do no wrong. But Mary knew that they in turn were only trying to spare her; that all of them shared her growing alarm.

True, some people from Capernaum, passing through Nazareth on their way back from their own trip to hear John the Baptizer, had said they had seen Jesus. But they had disagreed about just when, some insisting it was three or four weeks ago, others less, they couldn't be sure, they'd gone on to Jerusalem. In any case, his mother had never been so relieved and overjoyed to see anyone as when at last, yesterday afternoon, Jesus came trudging up the steps. Sunblackened—his smile was a white flash in his gaunt face, eyes burning from their deep sockets—but holding out his arms.

He hugged her in the old way, half lifting her off her feet. He crouched to wrestle about with Benjamin, who was in a mad frenzy of welcome; the dog, mourning, had eaten so little these past weeks, he was almost as thin as his master. But in a flash of awareness, Mary realized that Jesus had changed. There was something different about him, beyond the fact that he was so haggard, weary and travel-stained. Some startling, inexpressible difference.

He was followed by three young men. Rough, husky, sun-bronzed young men, very pleasant and enthusiastic, also on their way north to Capernaum. Their names were Andrew and Philip—fishermen there, she believed. She wasn't sure about the other one—Nathanael Bartholomew—but then she had been so excited, and they had stayed only long enough to refresh themselves with milk and some of her cakes. They said they must press on—they would spend the night in Cana.

They embraced Jesus with fervor as they left. Especially the long-limbed, sandy-haired one, named Andrew. "Join us as soon as you can, Master," he said eagerly. "I must tell my brother about you. We both will count the days until you come!"

As they stood together, waving to the men, Mary looked up to study her son. And again it came over her—the overwhelming sense of something different about him. He seemed taller than ever, towering above her there on the step. His shoulders even stronger, somehow, no matter how thin. And his eyes . . . the look in his eyes as they watched the men go down the hill. Those dark, liquid eyes had always shone with a special light. Now they wore an expression she had never seen.

Mary caught her breath. She knew—every sense told her—that Jesus had suffered, and triumphed over, some bitter but profound experience. She could feel it, as poignantly as if she had been with him. Whatever it was, it had prepared him. He was ready now. His time had come. And it would take him away from her many times again.

She patted his arm, over and over, simply rejoicing in her son's return. She would ask no questions. In time, perhaps he would tell her. It didn't matter. Right now he was so tired. All that mattered at the moment was getting him to bed.

In all the confusion Mary had quite forgotten Cana. Suddenly, gathering up the linens, she halted, stricken to remember: The men were heading for Cana, where cousin Deborah's daughter had been married only yesterday. If only she'd thought to tell them about it; assure them they'd be welcome. The festivities were still going on. Half of Jesus' own family was still there; the rest were coming shortly to take Mary along. She'd forgotten even to tell Jesus! Mary hesitated, torn. Lydia was so fond of her cousin, she reproached herself: the girl had been asking for weeks when he would be home. But it was so late now. And Jesus needed rest.

Resolutely, his mother made up his couch. It would be unthinkable even to suggest that he journey any farther tonight, no matter how important the celebration.

She had tried to keep the others quiet when they swarmed in later—Joseph and Simon and their wives and children; daughter Ann and her husband. Mary's heart soared, even as she shooed them into the garden. What a handsome lot they were, resplendent in their finery, and radiant with their news of the wedding the night before. They said James and Jude—and Leah, who'd participated in the ceremony—had been having such a good time they decided not to leave!

"Why aren't you dressed?" they asked. "Aren't you coming with us?"

"Jesus is home!" she told them.

They stared at her, then cried out, in surprise and relief. Ann and the daughters-in-law rushed up to hug her. The children were prancing about, delighted. If only Josey—yes, and Simon . . . Mary braced herself. Beneath their outward show of welcome and thanksgiving, she could feel their impatience even now; and the resentment that Josey, at least, was never quite able to conceal.

"He's very tired," she said. "He's sleeping. I don't want to leave him."

Josey laughed shortly, a big brusque man, and exchanged glances with Simon, who looked uncomfortable. "Where has he been this time?"

"Somewhere near Jericho," she said with some reluctance. "He went into the desert to see John."

"That fanatic!"

Ann frowned and shook her head, indicating their mother. "Try not to speak so, Josey. Remember John is our cousin."

"That makes it worse," Simon broke in dryly.

"He's a very dedicated man," Ann persisted. "They say crowds are following him."

"Have you also heard what John is telling those crowds?" Josey demanded. He turned to Mary.

She stood, chin uptilted, heart pounding, loving but adamant. They had been through scenes like this so often; dreaded them, ached for each other, but once started, Josey seemed powerless to stop. . . . Poor Josey, if he could only know how precious he was to her. How she had rejoiced at his birth. He had been her gift to Joseph, the beloved. His own first son! Yet Josey had been far less like his father than Jesus was. Truculent, aggressive, insecure, ever since childhood tormented by jealousy over Jesus, feeling himself less worthy, and no matter how they tried to prove otherwise, less loved. Yet she knew that beneath all his belligerence was a curious loving passion for his brother, and a genuine concern.

"Mother, please, can't you do something to stop it? Talk to Jesus, try to make him realize such talk is dangerous. You're the only one he will listen to."

"Josey, please—" Ann pleaded.

"Talk to John himself, or Elizabeth—*somebody*. Claims like that could be signing our brother's death warrant. For that matter, John's own. We all know what can happen to people who get the idea they're the Messiah—"

"Don't say it!" His wife, Eve, clapped a quick hand over his mouth. She was a very tall, lively girl, pleasant but often strong-willed. "We're on our way to a wedding, remember? Come with us, Mary. They were asking for you last night—Deborah and the bride and groom, all of them were asking when you would join us."

"They were asking for Jesus too," said Josey, suddenly contrite. He patted his mother, smiling, trying to make amends. "Let me wake him up. We'll wait for you to get ready; it will do you both good."

"No. No, don't wake him! Not now. Maybe later, maybe tomorrow."

"People will be tired by then," Naboth, Ann's husband, warned fondly. "They'll be serving the cheapest wine."

At last, with a clatter of hooves on the cobbles, they were off, singing, in a good mood despite her refusal and the harsh words that had been said; they didn't return until nearly morning. . . .

Through it all Jesus slept. Now, today, Mary slipped in from time to time to feel his brow or smooth his thick black curls, so tumbled, and slightly damp to her fingers. And now that it was long past noon, she hovered, hoping he would smell the stew she had prepared to tempt him: lamb with mint and dill, the way he liked it. She longed for his company; she was sure he must be hungry.

At last, sensing her presence, Jesus stirred and sat up, rubbing his eyes, astonished. "How can I have slept so long?" he groaned. "Forgive me. I wish you had called me. My brothers—" he asked anxiously. "Do they know I've returned?"

"Yes they were here yesterday."

"Then how lazy they must think me!" He cocked his head, puzzled at the silence. Though pigeons crooned outside the window and carts rattled by on the street, the house seemed unusually still. No whine of saws or pounding of hammers. The shop just down the steps must be deserted. "It's so quiet. Where is everyone?"

"Probably sleeping too, most of them. For two days the family has been going back and forth to Cana, celebrating Lydia's wedding."

"And you were not with them?"

"I couldn't bear to leave. I kept hoping you'd come; and when you did, I wanted to stay with you."

"But *Lydia!*" he protested. She was cousin Deborah's youngest girl. "Deborah would never forgive us—to miss this last daughter's wedding." He sprang up, pulling a robe about him. "Did you say Cana?"

"Yes. It's where the bridegroom lives. He's built a nice house for them there."

Jesus hesitated. But only for an instant. "Come, then. If there is still time, I will go with you."

Mary was overjoyed. She, too, had been distressed about disappointing Deborah; no small thing—the cousins were very close. But now to arrive, however late, with Jesus, whom they all adored . . . Jesus had always loved weddings. Josey was probably right—it might be just what his brother needed.

They set off in late afternoon, Jesus leading the donkey which his mother rode, protesting, albeit in high spirits. "We'll be tired," he reminded her. "It will seem a long way back."

He was touched by her obvious delight at being with him, just the two of them together. She was merry as a sweetheart, making the responses to the wedding songs he sang to her as they went. She was wearing her best dress, pleated in the Greek manner at the sleeves; once a brilliant pomegrante pink, now faded and a bit frayed. A pink shawl, fastened with a tiny gold pin, was about her shoulders, and in her curly dark hair, now threaded with silver, she had wound ribbons as pink as the touches of rouge on her cheeks. How pretty she still was, like a girl. He tried not to notice how worn and shabby were the doeskin slippers on her tiny feet, dangling below the dress. They too were frayed and faded, and long ago had lost most of their jewels; yet she clung to them, for they had been a betrothal gift from Joseph. She insisted on wearing them to weddings. Her son sensed that in some secret way they comforted her; did they perhaps help compensate for the fact that she herself had never had a proper wedding?

The sun was beginning to set, as they approached the tiny village, transforming the mud huts and fences and surrounding hills with its golden light. Through it, ahead of the donkey, Jesus strode, singing: "Who is this that makes her way up by the desert road, erect as a column of smoke, all myrrh and incense, and those sweet scents the perfumer knows?"

"Your mother!" Mary reminded him, laughing. "We will soon be there. Hadn't you better save your songs for the bride?"

"You are more beautiful than any bride," he told her, singing on: "Behold, thou art fair, my beloved, behold, thou art fair, thou hast doves' eyes within thy locks. Thy hair is like a flock of goats that appear from Mount Gilead, thy teeth are like a flock of—"

Suddenly the words broke off. They seemed to have frozen in his throat. He halted.

Crossing the road ahead of them was a mixed flock of sheep and goats. The golden haze of dust kicked up by their hooves obscured them—and their shepherd; but through it came the pleasant tinkling of their bells, the light pounding of their feet, their gentle bleating and blatting. Mary tensed, sat gripping the bridle. A sudden dread claimed her, a shocking possibility, however unlikely. What have I done to bring him here? she thought, appalled. This place so filled with his raw and recent memories.

For it was here among these hills that he had found his first and only love, the shepherd girl Tamara.

Jesus had gone white. They waited, staring. Not until the first sheep began to climb the grassy slope on the opposite bank did they see that the person leading the flock was a woman. A very old woman, quite bent.

Mary leaned forward. "We can turn back," she said. "We needn't go on."

"No." Jesus shook his head, pulled firmly at the bridle.

"But I don't want to hurt you. Please don't go to this wedding for my sake."

"Mother, hear me out," he said as they moved ahead once more. "And then we will never speak of this again." He trudged on in silence for a moment, while the beast labored behind, making little chuffing noises, its heels a hollow tapping on the stones. "I have to face things. Even the possibility of seeing her sometime. If not in Cana, somewhere. I have to face up to my own pain."

His gaze was following the flock. All of them were ascending the hillside now, their bleating and the sound of their bells growing fainter in the swiftly falling dusk. And seeing him so, Mary remembered how he had come to her, eyes shining, bursting with his news. "It's what my father Joseph always wanted. If only he had lived to see it. And you will love her too, Mother. She is so like you!" Wanting her to share it; to rejoice with him that he was not to miss it. That at last he too should experience this beautiful miracle, the greatest gift God could bestow on man.

He had brought his happiness to her like an offering, a priceless treasure. And she could only be the one to tear it from him. Her own words seemed too cruel even now; Mary sat bewildered, protesting. Yet she knew, blindly, that she had had no choice but to say them: "No, Jesus, *no*, this cannot be. You must remember—you are not as other men."

"Oh, but I am!" The anguish of that cry would haunt her forever. And how he had stood before her, fists clenched at his sides. "The one who sent me did not make me a graven image, Mother. Would that he had! He gave me a body the same as my brothers. The same senses, the same feelings . . . I am not made of wood or stone, Mother, I am flesh and blood. I hurt, I long, I yearn!"

Mary couldn't bear it. She had gone to him and gathered him against her breast, tall as he was, and tried to comfort him, even as she cried: "You must not do this, Jesus! You were meant for a greater love. For her own sake you must not do this. Don't let the sword plunge through her heart, as I *know* it will plunge through mine. . . ."

His voice brought her back to the present. He was saying almost the same words now, as he strode along ahead of her. "God will not spare me. Why should he?" he demanded, turning abruptly to face her. "If I am human—as you, of all people, should know I am"— Jesus laughed shortly, with a touch of irony, and squeezed her hand— "I have to suffer like other men. How else can I know people's pain? Why am I here, if not to endure all that God's people must endure? How else can I help them?"

"I don't know," Mary said sadly. "I am only your mother. But oh, if only *I* could spare you."

It was almost dark now. The first stars twinkled; only a banner of orange lingered on the horizon. But in the distance, as they approached Cana, a glow of torches lit the sky. Faintly, they could hear music and the sound of voices shouting.

"Look, Mother, listen!" Jesus exclaimed. "This is no time to be troubled. It's a time to be happy. The house of the bridegroom must be that way."

Cana was much smaller than Nazareth, and poorer. Though it had its synagogue, and several fine stone houses, surrounded by beautiful gardens and cypress trees, most of the homes were but whitewashed huts, squatting among the olive groves. With rising spirits, they made their way along its short dark streets. Few lamps burned in the windows; most of the people were already at the celebration, or hurrying eagerly toward it. There was a contagious excitement in the air, a joyous sense of release from work and cares. People called out to mother and son, pointing the way to the house, which was on the edge of town. Though it would have been impossible to miss, so bright were the lights and so merry was the noise, which grew louder as they drew nearer.

David, the bridegroom, came out himself to greet them: a slight, nervous, but very attractive young man, with proud eyes, anxious to please. Fervently hospitable, he led them into the torchlit courtyard, where other guests were swarming. But despite that fresh and beaming face, they sensed his agitation, and something else—some bewildered hurt and disappointment that seemed strange in so new a bridegroom.

Deborah, conferring with the musicians, waved wildly and hastened to them. "Mary, where have you *been*?" She flung her arms around them. "And Jesus! You have broken your cousin's heart. Lydia, poor child, has been weeping her eyes out because you were not here to attend her groom!"

Tall, angular, catlike, she chattered on, a woman harsh in her judgments but fierce in her affections, as radiant as her jewels. They flashed on her hands, her throat, and in her elaborately piled hair.

"Let the servants wash your feet, then come inside. You must see Lydia's house."

They followed, listening to her usual stream of exaggerations. "It isn't at *all* what we expected," Deborah confided, as they moved about. Cupping her hand, she nodded toward the unfortunate bridegroom. "He promised Lydia a balcony, and a guest chamber, and heaven knows what else." Her voice was scornful. "And just *look* at those walls—"

Mary was uncomfortable. Two walls indeed were not yet plastered. "Such things take time," she said. "I'm sure in time—"

"Time? He had plenty of time. I kept urging him either to finish it or postpone the wedding. But no, he couldn't wait; no, no, the wedding must go on. And then—would you believe it?—he was so late in coming for Lydia, some of the virgins got so tired they fell asleep!"

"Not Leah, I hope."

"Oh, no; no, not dear little Leah—such a joy to have her. Where is she?" Deborah's sharp eyes darted, in some distress, about the noisy crowd. "Oh, yes, helping prepare the food. Pray heaven there will be enough to go around."

"Don't worry," Mary tried to soothe her. "Many people eat early, before they come."

"They still want wine. Just pray the wine holds out."

Suddenly remembering, Deborah turned her attention to Jesus. "Jesus, some of your friends are here. They were on their way to

Capernaum, I believe. David invited them. Along with everybody else." She laughed suddenly, still a bit impatient, but contrite. "Our daughter's husband may be shortsighted, but he tries to be a generous man."

Surprised but pleased, Jesus excused himself and went to find them. In the courtyard, people were still singing and dancing and milling about, toasting the bride or waiting for someone to bring them wine so they could. A few, exhausted, seemed to be leaving; but even more were crowding through the gate. Jesus thought, with some concern, of David. Poor man—he'd probably be glad when all this was over.

Jesus made his way down to the grassy slope behind the house, where Deborah had said the men were playing games. Here the moon shone white on the open fields. Only a few yellow torches still blazed fitfully on their poles; the rest had been stamped out and lay smoking, their acrid smell mingling with the fragrance of earth and trampled grass. The music from the courtyard rained down, a merry, faint sweet pulsing of drum and lute and timbrel. Ahead, two men, stripped to their loincloths, were wrestling—grunting and panting, their naked limbs entangled—to shouts and cheers from the circle surrounding them. Another group squatted around a dice board; dice rattled in the cup, there were whoops of triumph or groans of disappointment as they fell. Backs were slapped, cups were drained and tossed aside, or held aloft for more.

Farther down the hill, another jovial group had gathered near a lone pomegranate tree, where someone had nailed a target; boasting and trading insults, they vied amiably with each other in their attempts to hit it with their bows and arrows. The trunk was too fragile for its burden, and its branches were in bloom. Each time an arrow struck, the small tree seemed to wince as if in pain, reluctant to spill even a few of its lovely blood-red petals. Most of the shots sped harmlessly past, however, for the men were tired with their day's work, and inaccurate with celebrating.

Jesus was amused to recognize the two awaiting their turn: Andrew—tall, sandy-haired, ungainly; his arrow went so far astray it couldn't be found. Philip was next; he was shorter and stouter, but when he had pulled back the bow in his slow, careful way and taken aim, the little tree shook violently, its petals showering the ground.

Jesus was the first to shout applause. He strode forward into the cheering crowd. It seemed that so far only a few had even hit the target, let alone its bull's-eye.

"Master!" The two embraced him joyfully, although obviously astonished to see him, and somewhat dismayed. They had no idea the bride's people were his kinsmen. It was embarrassing to be found here, having such a good time they'd gotten no farther home.

Please don't think ill of us," Andrew said. Hastily he put down the cup from which he was about to drink, and drew Jesus aside. "I am anxious to get back to Capernaum," he insisted. "I can hardly wait to tell Simon Peter—"

Philip, too, cast a furtive glance at the empty goblet his admirers were clamoring to have filled. "We meant no harm," he said.

Arms folded, half smiling, Jesus stood regarding them. "Where is Bartholomew?"

"Home sleeping," they admitted. "He lives nearby."

They stood there, his first disciples, humble, apologetic, distressed, with respect and adoration in their eyes. "We want so much to follow you," Andrew pleaded. "Please don't lose faith in us."

To his relief, Jesus reached out to grip his shoulder; he gave it a little shake. "Listen to me, Andrew—both of you. When I came up out of the river Jordan, didn't you give me your own cloak to keep me warm? And when I came down from the wilderness, you were waiting, with Philip, your friend. You didn't ask where I had been so long; or why I looked as I did—dirty and ragged and starved. You swore allegiance to me even then. And you did not desert me. Three days I spent with the holy men at Qumran, changing my garments, being cleansed, but you did not run away. When I came out you were waiting, all three of you—you had even brought Nathanael Bartholomew. And you have walked with me ever since, paying careful attention to all I have said, during the journey home. We have come only a little way together—why should I lose faith in you now?"

"We want to be worthy of you," Philip blurted. "We are very weak and human, but we want with all our hearts to follow you. And we hope it will be soon."

Jesus threw back his head and laughed. "What are you talking about?" he asked. "It is no sin to share in the joys of a wedding feast.

And if you do follow me—and it will be soon—I warn you, there will be little time for wedding celebrations."

Despite his show of merriment, the bridegroom was perspiring. More people were arriving: friends, relatives, strangers. Where did they all come from? And though he greeted them warmly, he saw with alarm that this, the final night of the wedding, was going to be even more crowded than the others. Rested from their previous night of celebration, earlier guests were returning. David mopped his brow. In the flush of excitement and anticipation, he'd invited too many people, he'd had no idea they would come back every night and stay so long! New faces were appearing, for word had spread.

The courtyard was overflowing, and so was the house. People milled about, waiting for the feast. It must surely be ready; there was a succulent odor of food in the air. But where was the wine? he knew they were wondering. How could the feast begin without the wine?

Even such poor stuff as might be left.

Smiling to cover his desperation, David made his way to the wine steward, who stood, politely intimidating, beside the door.

"The wine, the wine!" he whispered. "People are getting restless—where is the wine?"

The steward shrugged, bowed slightly. He was a large, life-weary and rather insolent man who usually worked for one of the few wealthy families in the village. He had condescended to come here only as a favor to the bride's father, Nathan, his employer's friend.

"As I told you before, Sir, the wine is almost gone. Barely enough left to fill a pitcher."

"Then water it!"

"We have already watered the wine as much as we can to make it go further." The man's lip curled faintly; David shrank before his ill-concealed contempt. "The wine is already pallid and tasteless; I'm told the guests are complaining."

"Then send out for more," David ordered. Though his own words made his heart hammer. Where would he get the money? He had already spent more than he dared on this house; gone into debt for it, in fact. How many dinars were left in his purse? Certainly not enough for such an emergency. Where could he borrow some? he wondered frantically. Not from his father—he was barely able to scrape up the marriage fee; though his father was here, and had drunk more than his share of the wine. David winced. Nor his brothers; they were poor farmers themselves, actually envious and ill at ease in this house they thought so fine. (They hadn't heard his mother-in-law!)

Not from Lydia's parents. The very thought made him ill. He would rather die.

"It's late, Sir," the steward reminded, "The wineshops will be closed."

David nodded bleakly, feeling a fool. He tried to regain his dignity, to assert himself. But for the moment he could only stare through the man, tasting the bitter dregs of his disappointment. He had striven so hard to please his new in-laws: Building the house to Deborah's specifications. (Not Lydia's, no, that precious girl had had little to say about it; it was her mother who kept insisting on changes, even at the last minute. He couldn't possibly get them all done before the wedding. David was just as embarrassed about those walls as she was!) Hiring a steward recommended by Lydia's father—a kind man, very understanding, who'd even offered to help. David had assured him no, no, he was amply prepared with food and wine. It was a matter of pride. . . .

And now to be shamed before his bride and her family, this final night of celebration. To have *them* shamed before all those people. That they should choose a son-in-law so poor, inept or stingy. An object of their disgust and disdain.

The music had stopped. It left a curious emptiness behind it, a feeling of silence, despite the babble of voices drawing nearer. People seemed to be drifting toward the long feast tables set up on the lawn. He could smell the threatening fragrance of the food. Lydia was hurrying toward him, holding up her skirts. Even in his desolation, he marveled at the beauty of his bride. Not angular, like her mother, though she had the same green uptilted eyes—but soft and warm and shining. He could think of no bliss greater than for everyone else to vanish, that he might fall asleep forever in her arms.

"David, what's keeping you?" she cried. "The feast is ready; the servants can't wait much longer. You must come now and sit with me at the table."

Scarlet with humiliation, he drew himself to his full height. "There will be no feast."

"No *feast*?"

"There is no more wine."

"But there is plenty of food."

"There can be no feast without wine to toast the bride." She was staring at him in disbelief. But her eyes were tender. She reached out to take his hand. It was clammy; she pressed it to her breast. "Dear David, it's all right, truly," she tried to comfort him. "We cannot turn the guests away hungry. Come, we will sit together with our heads high, and pretend it doesn't matter."

"If that is your wish," he said. Either way, he could not spare her. Walking as jauntily as he could, he accompanied her back to the people, who were laughing and calling lavish compliments, which only made his misery worse.

Mary was among them. She had been seeking him. Almost from the moment she first saw him, her heart had ached for this young man. For the past hour her concern for him had increased. She could restrain herself no longer. Smiling, she stepped forward to block the couple's path.

"Wait," she urged quietly. "Tell the servants to delay the feast. I believe my son can help us."

In all the commotion, David could not place her—this small, dark-haired woman in the pink dress. He was only aware that he had never seen a face more lovely, or filled with such sympathy and reassurance.

"Jesus?" Lydia asked, puzzled. "Cousin Jesus?"

"Yes. Just give me time to find him."

David remembered now; she had come with the young man from Nazareth. He gazed at Mary, incredulous. Surely her son didn't own a wineshop in Cana; and there was no earthly way he could have brought such a supply. Yet he knew she was not joking; such a woman would never make light of anyone's predicament.

"Tell the musicians to keep playing," Mary said confidently. "Urge the people to keep on singing and dancing. We will—" For the first time she hesitated. "I feel sure we will soon have wine."

Mary pushed resolutely through the crowd. Breathlessly scanning the moonlit hillside, she noted that the men had left their games; a few were beginning to ascend. To her relief, she saw Jesus striding toward her, well ahead of them. He had sensed something wrong.

Mary ran to meet him. "Hurry!" she ordered before he could ask. "You must help them. They have no wine."

⟨ 14 ⟩

Her son halted. He stood regarding her, dismayed. "Please don't ask this of me," he said quietly. "You know I cannot . . . not yet."

"You can do whatever you will to do. Nothing is denied you. Don't deny your cousin this."

They could hear the music, livelier than before, hear the merry, expectant voices. Over the smell of trampled grass and smoking torches drifted the succulent odors of the feast. Jesus drew a hand across his stricken face. He stood shaken, awed and shaken before the terrifying sense of power that began to rise in him. . . . For he realized now the enormity of what the tempter had revealed to him on the mountain: He could do far more than turn mere stones into bread. He could multiply the food on the table. He could increase the wine until it flowed in the streets. His mother . . . Jesus stared at her in anguish. He could dress her this instant in silks, transform that poor little pin on her breast to diamonds. *But this must not be,* he realized. Never for material goods—not even for Mary. And never for personal glory.

"Mother, no," he said. "My hour has not yet come. What has this matter of the wine to do with me?"

"These are your people," Mary said. "They need you. You can help them."

Jesus looked away, toward where the men were trudging up the hill, Andrew and Philip among them. They had already pledged their faith in him. The very thought of proving himself to them was abhorrent.

Something within him was crying, *Not yet, not yet. Surely not like this.* Surely, when his time came, it would not be for such a paltry thing as wine. Would his power not be manifest for something significant? It must be used for healing. The blind would see, the lame would walk, he would cleanse the lepers. He would restore them, make them whole. . . . Those people out there: beneath all the cheerful singing and shouting and cavorting, he could feel their afflictions, he knew how many were suffering. He longed to help them. When his time truly came, he would stretch out his hands and heal them. Not only their bodies but their sick souls.

It was not wine they needed but healing of the spirit. He would show them the way to eternal life. He would give them living water!

"Mother, don't ask this of me," he pleaded.

"I have asked very little of you, Jesus," she said, gently determined. "But I do ask this. Your hour *is* upon you. I can feel it, for you are part of me." She turned, beckoning. "Come with me."

She had noticed a number of large stone jars standing on a rise of ground behind the house, left there by the land's former owners. Usually they had held water for rites of purification, some thirty gallons each. The new owner had put their contents to more immediate use, with all the foot washing to be done for a wedding, and the demands of the wine. Mary marched firmly toward them now. And reluctantly Jesus followed.

But as they skirted the crowd still milling about—tired and hungry and thirsty, but still cheerful, expectant—a strange exhilaration came over him: a compassion so complete it was akin to joy. In love and joy and pity, his heart went out to everyone: To his cousins in their embarrassment. To the eager, proud young bridegroom, so anxious to please, yet cringing before his mother-in-law's belittling, and so piteously overwhelmed by the unexpected horde of guests. And to the people. The people most of all. These people who were so poor, so cruelly taxed, working so hard for so little. Whose lives held so much pain and worry, so little pleasure, that they would come miles and stay as long as they could—for a wedding!

A wedding was no place for anyone to be hurt or embarrassed or disappointed. If he could give them pleasure—even another hour or two of simple pleasure . . .

Several servants were gathered in some confusion beside the jars. Mary halted. Eyes flashing, she gestured to Jesus. "Do whatever he tells you," she ordered.

She wheeled to face him.

Mother and son regarded each other for an instant. Then Jesus covered his face; for a long moment he stood in silence, praying. When he opened his eyes he was smiling. He drew a deep breath then, and strode forward to grasp the rough stone rims of the jars. He saw that three of the jars were empty; a little water glistened in the cool, dark depths of the others.

He turned to address the servants—two men and a maid. "Go to the cistern for water," he said, "and fill the jars."

They exchanged astonished glances. Was this a joke? Yet the man spoke with authority. Summoning others to help, they rushed around to do his bidding. And while Mary and her son watched, they filled the jars to the brim.

"Now draw the wine from the jars," Jesus said. Firmly he put his arm around Mary's waist. Never had he felt such exultation. For the liquid in the vessels had turned the color of rubies; its rich, sweet scent was beginning to perfume the air. "Take it to the steward to be tasted, then serve it to the guests."

The awed servants said nothing. Striving to repress their excitement, they replenished the pitchers and went about refilling mugs and glasses. The guests were exclaiming over its quality. "You rascal!" Lydia's father rushed up to accuse the bridegroom. "What did you mean, making us think you were running out of wine?"

"That's right," others cried. "Did you think to drive us away early, that you might be alone with your bride?" Beaming, they lifted their glasses. Never had they tasted such rich, delicious wine. "You sly one—you have saved the best until the last!"

Chapter 2

$\mathcal{M}$ARY could hear the grandchildren playing in the garden. Good—
for a little while at least, they didn't seem to be quarreling.
Josey's son was inclined to bully the younger ones; and Simon's little
girl always seemed to be running to her, crying. But now, before it
would be time to start their supper, she would stretch out on her pallet
for a little rest. She lay smiling, wondering if it had been thus for
Hannah during those years she kept their children while Mary and
Joseph set off so merrily for the Passover Feast.

For several years now, like her mother—in fact, like most grandmothers in Nazareth—Mary had been content to stay behind. She had
come to dread the trip, which seemed so lonely without Joseph; so
much longer and harder. Although she was torn (for she missed those
precious visits with Elizabeth), keeping the grandchildren was a perfect excuse. And she did enjoy them. But as the week wore on, she
found her strength and her pleasure in them waning. Again Mary
smiled, wondering if Hannah had been as glad as she would be when
the parents returned to claim them.

A grandmother. Mary lay regarding the length of her own arm
on the pallet. Still small and supple. I don't feel like a grandmother,
she thought. Oh, *Joseph*! She pulled his pillow toward her, buried her
face on it. *I need you. There is so much I want to tell you.*

A warm breeze blew the curtain across Mary's face. Beyond the
window, bees droned, drunk with the blossoming flowers; doves
crooned, and from the garden drifted the voices of the children, still
peaceful for now. They seemed to be making mud cakes. They would
be dirty when they came in. . . . Drowsing, Mary dreamed of Joseph.
That he was down there with them now, his own children; she could

hear them shrieking as they always did when their father appeared, see him swinging them over his shoulder. The dream was almost too sweet to release; she clung to it as the voices grew louder, more excited.

"Cleo, Cleo! Uncle Cleophas!"

Startled, Mary sat upright. She pushed her feet into their sandals, brushed at her hair; her breasts still ached with the dream. Even so, it was comforting to see that large, handsome, always vibrant and colorful figure charging up the path, tagged by the eager youngsters. "Go now, back to your games," his rich voice boomed. "I must talk to your grandmother." He squatted to tousle their hair, and with deft movements of jeweled fingers produced for each of them a coin. When he lifted his square dusky face to Mary's, he was smiling. But as he stood up, she saw that he was very tired. His eyes, heavy-lidded but usually bouyant, were bloodshot and dark-circled; his fine clothes disheveled from traveling.

Mary cried out her joy at seeing him. "But you're alone?" She was scanning the street below in surprise. "Where are the others?"

"Miles back. More than a day's journey, I'm afraid. I rode on ahead of the caravan." Head low, Cleo spanked dust vigorously from his striped robe; his face was flushed. "I have something to tell you."

Mary sensed that it was urgent; his voice and his manner warned her. She didn't want to hear it. She was glad when he dropped to the sunny stoop and patted the place beside him. "But first tell me what's troubling you."

"Am I then so transparent?"

Cleo grinned faintly. "You've always worn your heart in your eyes, Mary. You should know that; you may as well tell me."

"Well, then, come inside. I must start the evening meal, and you must eat with us."

"I can't stay," he said, though he followed her, and sat listening, watching her as she moved about in her quick little way, taking the loaves from the sill, bringing curds and fruit from the cupboard. Such times were precious to Cleo; as if this were his own house and Mary his wife preparing the table. He had been Joseph's chief rival for Mary, best friends though they were. Everyone enjoyed the dashing, lighthearted Cleo, and his father was wealthy, he was considered a catch. Reckless, headstrong, comical, spoiled, he had been astounded (and so had most of Nazareth) when Mary's parents gave her to Joseph ben Jacob, son of the carpenter, instead.

His own marriage had been a sad one; his wife had lost three babies before fleeing in disgrace to her parents in Ptolemais. Cleophas had gone after her repeatedly. And though he had pleaded with her fervently, in his heart he knew it did not matter. He had never loved her.

It was Jesus' brothers, Mary told him. They had been upset that he would set off early for Jerusalem with some new friends from Capernaum. "Josey's the worst, always. 'Mother, who are these people?' he wanted to know. 'Why does he prefer to travel with them instead of his own brothers?' It isn't that, I tried to explain. They have important matters to attend to. They may seek out John again."

Cleo's thick black brows were frowning. "I hope not," he said bluntly.

"I do feel sorry for James," Mary plunged on. "James was disappointed; he had wanted so much to be Jesus' companion on the trip this year. But James never criticizes—he loves Jesus too much." Mary moved back and forth from the cupboard, setting mugs of milk on the table. "The others resent him. True, they are concerned about Jesus' safety, but they resent him. There's no hiding the fact—they consider him an embarrassment, and in some ways a threat. They don't realize the importance of what he must *do*." Mary lifted her chin. She felt better. It was good to unburden herself like this. "Oh, Cleo, they don't understand about Jesus. And I must not blame them. How can they, since I have never had the courage to tell them?"

Cleo leaned forward, startled. His frown had deepened. "Understand what, Mary? Tell them what?"

Mary turned quickly from the cupboard, her face almost as dismayed as his own. "Why, who he *is*!" she said, after a minute.

"Mary, dear Mary, no—no, please!"

"But you must have *known*. Surely you must have known!" Mary groped blindly about in the cupboard. What had she come for? Oh, yes, a vase; the children usually picked flowers. But though she kept rummaging, it no longer mattered. She walked slowly back to the table, empty-handed, and sat down across from him. "I thought surely Joseph must have told you. You were so close. You were like brothers."

"Told me about what, Mary?"

She could not believe it. Was he being deliberately obtuse? Cleo had many faults, but he was not stupid.

"About Jesus," she said softly, in wonder. "About his birth."

Cleo flinched and looked away, but she had seen the pain in his eyes. "Must we go into that?"

No, no, he was right; there was no need to hurt him. Any explanation, even the true one, would hurt him. Any reference to those days when she and Joseph were the talk of Nazareth would only open old wounds. And despite Mary's bewilderment, she realized: Joseph had considered this secret too sacred to share with anyone. If he hadn't told his own mother (this much Mary knew), how could she have assumed he would confide in his best friend? Mary felt a surge of admiration for her husband, so proud and private, unwilling to discuss their love. She could do no less for him now.

"No, no, that isn't necessary," she said. "Only that . . . Jesus is not the same as other men. You've always been so close to him too, Cleo. Ever since he was a little boy, I thought you knew, or at least suspected—"

"I love him," Cleo said. "I couldn't love my own son more—if I had a son."

"You have been like a second father to him. He needs your support more than ever now that Joseph's gone; you, of all people, must believe in him."

"Of course I believe in him!" Cleo insisted. He sounded almost angry. "Jesus is special, very special—don't you think I know that? I'm proud of him. I wish you had let me send him to Jerusalem to study; he could have been a rabbi as great as Hillel. Still could be, if he'll settle down—" Cleo caught himself before he said, *and stay away from John.* "I will still help, if you let me."

"Oh, *Cleo!*" Mary reached across the table to take his big hand, where the black hairs bristled, holding it so tight his rings bit into her fingers. "Don't you realize? Jesus is destined to be far more than a rabbi, no matter how great. More—even more than a prophet. I really thought you knew. That much, at least, Joseph might have told you— or certainly prepared you for."

Cleophas was staring at her in distress. There was a moment of charged silence between them. They could hear carts rattling by on the street below. Men were going home to their suppers.

"A messiah?" The word burst suddenly from Cleophas. "Are you talking about a messiah?"

For a second Mary was taken aback. She was still surprised and confused, trying to think how she could possibly convey this to him. "Not just a messiah, Cleo. *The* Messiah. The One we have expected so long."

"Mary, I beg you—no, Mary, please—!"

"It's true, Cleo. You must believe me."

"How do you know?"

Mary released his hand. "We were told," she said simply. "The Lord himself told us—from the very beginning. Sent messengers to us, both of us. The child I carried would be . . . the One. And this was true. Jesus was born in Bethlehem, as the prophets predicted."

"Many babies are born in Bethlehem."

"It was why we had to leave. Herod suspected something and ordered that terrible slaughter. It's why we fled to Egypt."

Cleo's square jaw was set. He kept shaking his head.

"Don't you believe in the king that was prophesied by Zechariah?" Mary challenged. "All our life we have heard nothing but predictions of his coming—our only hope of release from our problems, our poverty and pain, these terrible persecutions from Rome." She flung out her hands in despair. "We've been taught to expect him, and according to the prophets it will be soon." There were sparks in her eyes; she gripped the table's edge. "Don't you believe that, Cleo? Or is it just a false hope?—the Messiah is never really coming; our wait will always be in vain."

"Yes, of course I believe," he said impatiently, "but not—"

"Not now, not in our time, he can't be one of us." The words were familiar; almost the same ones she had once cried out to Joseph.

"No. Not Jesus," Cleo said stubbornly. "Why, I watched him learn to walk; we've ridden the hills together; I taught him to ride horseback—"

"Always somewhere else, sometime in the future, to strangers, someone we don't know yet. Only then will it be believable—and safe!"

Cleo nodded miserably. "Yes, that's right. Safe. Mary, I fear for him—and for you. I'm sorry, but your other children are right. Their brother will not be the first messiah—if, heaven forbid, he takes the course you think. And he won't be the last." His face was grim. "Those men are taking an awful risk. They're watched like hawks by the priests. And heaven help them if anybody even thinks they blaspheme. Please try to keep him from this, Mary."

Mary scarcely heard him. "Don't you think Joseph and I were worthy to have raised such a son?"

"Never have I known any two people more worthy," he said wretchedly. "But oh, Mary, I couldn't bear to have you mistaken, to have you go through what it could mean."

Mary gazed at him, breathing hard. He loved her, he had always loved her, and this fact was dear to her. She needed this knowledge now; unfair as it was, it comforted her, sustained her, for she knew he would support her, no matter what his own convictions, or what happened to her son.

"I'm sorry," she said. "I didn't mean to burden you with all this. It was hard for us to discuss it, even between ourselves. But you and Joseph meant so much to each other. I thought—I really thought he must have shared at least this truth about Jesus with you years ago."

Cleo got to his feet. "He shared his family with me," he reminded, with a show of his usual cheerfulness. "That was enough."

"We all love you. You are like one of us." The dog was barking; she could hear the shrill voices of the children swarming up the path. "Please stay," she urged. "They will be so disappointed if you go, and it would truly help. Wait, I'll fill the basins for you to wash—"

Cleo was hesitating, his face again heavy with concern. And with a fresh stab of guilt, Mary remembered. "Oh, dear, you must forgive me. You had something to tell me."

"Not now, later. Yes, it's something you should know, but it can wait."

The youngsters were already hurling themselves at him, clamoring for more of his magic tricks. Merrily, in the mock-bullish way that always charmed them, Cleo fought them off, rings flashing as he produced coins from the air or the ends of their noses, before they sat down. And it was all so pleasant for a time, to be here with Mary, who was scurrying about—the children were very grubby from playing in the dirt—she must get soap and towels. But she was patient and amusing with them, as she had been with her own. Yes, they could serve Uncle Cleo their little mud cakes. She flashed him a smile. Yes, of course she loved the flowers; never mind their short stems, she would find a vase. Then she must quiet their laughing and chattering long enough for the "Hear, O Israel" and the blessing of the wine. The evening sun slanted peacefully across the white cloth; outside, birds were twittering; the bread was crisp to his nervous fingers.

If only he could just enjoy this for a little while, then escape. Cleo wished desperately that he had said nothing. His news, which had seemed so urgent, could wait. Despite his qualms, during the hard, fast ride back from Jerusalem, telling Mary had seemed quite simple. All that had seemed important was to prepare her before the others came bursting in. But now, stunned by what she had told him, he regretted his haste.

Mary had enough to worry about. The thought of adding to her burdens, especially right now, filled him with dread.

Cleo climbed to the roof and waited impatiently, cursing himself, while Mary put the children to bed. An interminable job, it seemed. The first stars shone. Behind the willows, in the direction of the mountains, the sky was bright with the rising moon. He strode about, shaken and confused. Preposterous! His common sense protested. He would not have it. Not Jesus, his friend, his almost son. Not Mary, please not Mary! She had been widowed only a year, and she had taken Joseph's death hard; could it have affected her mind? She was at an age when women sometimes imagined things. He must help her. He must not add to her delusions.

It was not true. Even if it were true, he would not have it! But it simply was not true.

Cleo was not a particularly religious man. Although he faithfully attended the synagogue and all the festivals, and performed all the rites and duties of his Jewish heritage, they had little reality or significance for him. Cleo understood things he could feel, touch, smell, devour.

His father was a wealthy importer. Since boyhood Cleo had traveled to the markets—Egypt and Greece, Persia and Rome, Tyre and Sidon—to choose elegant things and have them brought back on the caravans. Scarlet and purple velvets, sleek silks and satins, pure linens and woolens and rich brocades. He took a sensuous pleasure in the fabrics—in selecting them and speading them out before customers in the store. And the exotic Egyptian rugs and tapestries with their lovely colors and their lavish imagery, forbidden to the Jews. Such things excited him. Since pagans outnumbered the Chosen People here in Galilee, there was plenty of sale for them. He enjoyed the heady perfumes and unguents in their beautiful containers. And the jewels— even the poor ones, like that little blue stone he had once polished and made into a ring for Jesus to give to some girl. And high time, Cleophas remembered rejoicing—sorry only that Joseph was not alive to see it. Joseph had been so distressed about his son, nearly thirty and still unmarried. . . . What had become of the girl? Cleo often wondered, disappointed that nothing had come of it.

And now—what Mary had just revealed. No, no, it didn't make sense. That her son, that beautiful son, no matter how brilliant a scholar or how devout, should go traipsing around the country like his mad cousin John. Preaching, exhorting, talking like a prophet—or worse! Inviting trouble.

It was getting late. Twice Mary started up the ladder but had to turn back; one of the little girls kept crying. Mary looked disheveled when at last she joined him. It touched him to see the little dew of perspiration above her lip; a curly tendril of her hair had fallen down. Smiling, Mary pushed it away with the back of her hand. "Probably my own were just as obstinate when we left them," she speculated fondly. She was brushing crumbs from her skirt. "And no matter how my mother pretended, I'm sure she was just as anxious for us to get home." With a sigh of relief, she sat down beside him, and patted his knee. "And now, Cleo, that we have a little peace and quiet, I'm ready for your news."

Cleo gazed at her, his dark face troubled. Then suddenly, decisively, to his own surprise, he crouched by the bench and took her hand. "Mary, listen," he said firmly. "I'm sorry to have to tell you, but I feel you should know. There is talk in Jerusalem that John has been arrested."

"No!" Mary returned his gaze, aghast. One hand flew to her mouth. "Oh, no. Poor Elizabeth! If this is true, I must go to her." She half sprang up, but he pulled her down again.

"Please listen. Not yet. It may be all a mistake. You know how rumors fly, especially during Passover."

"If it's true, then John must be in prison!"

"Yes, probably."

"Why?" she gasped.

"As you know, he has been denouncing the goverment—the Pharisees, the priests, the whole hierarchy of the Temple—"

"John means no harm. That's nothing new."

"Don't be too sure it's harmless; John is very much feared and hated—especially by the high priest's family. If old Annas and his sons have been lenient, pretended to look the other way, it's probably because of his mother. They respect Elizabeth. But when John goes too far, when he attacks Herod Antipas—"

"The man is a monster, as bad as his father was."

"He's also our ruler, authorized by Rome. John has done the unthinkable, Mary. He's not only calling Herod the usual names; he's accusing him of *incest*."

Mary gave a little cry of disbelief.

"Because of taking his brother's wife," Cleo said with disgust. "The queen, of course, is furious."

"Oh, dear, poor John. How foolish!"

"Worse than that—reckless, irresponsible. If John is mad enough to risk his own life, that's his business, but he ought to consider the risk to others." Cleo had gotten to his feet, stalling for time. The moon was visible now, huge, radiant, beaming. The stone parapet glistened, chill and damp with dew. Cleo went to lean on it, bracing himself. Finally he turned back to her. "It isn't really John that concerns me so much," he said carefully. "It's Jesus."

Mary's face paled. "Where is he? Did you see him? Does he know about this?"

"He must have heard. No, I didn't see him. I looked everywhere, but you know how it is at feast time—there was such a mob. But I did hear about him, Mary. There are people who are linking Jesus to John."

"Why, not?" she reasoned. "Of course! They are cousins."

"I'm afraid it's more than that. There were rumors at the Temple— I heard them again at the inn where I stayed. Some people have been claiming they were at the Jordan the day Jesus was baptized. At first they didn't know who he was. Only that John had been predicting someone important was coming—they'd better repent, get ready, a king was coming! You know how John exaggerates. The very lamb of God! And when Jesus appeared—" Cleo bit his full lips; he didn't want to offend her.

"Please, Cleo, tell me."

"John pointed to him and began to carry on. He even ran to greet him, crying out, 'Behold, this is the one I was talking about!' Something like that. A few people may have recognized Jesus, but most didn't know his name, not until later—he was just someone from Galilee, they thought. But now they're claiming strange things happened that day. Voices. Heaven opening." Cleo laughed impatiently; he couldn't help it. "Ridiculous things," he blurted, despite the fixed look in Mary's eyes. "The kind of things people are so ready to believe."

He had been pacing about, miserable at this mission so alien to his nature. Now he stopped before her. "What all this will lead to I have no idea. Only that it's dangerous talk. And right now," he declared, "it's expecially dangerous to have anything to do with John."

"But John is our cousin," Mary protested. If he's in trouble . . . !"

"That's what I'm afraid of. Mary, talk to Jesus when he gets home. I was hoping he might be here already—I thought he might have taken a shortcut through Samaria."

"I hope not!"

"All Samaritans aren't cutthroats, Mary. They worship the same God we do. I've ridden though Samaria many times; there are a lot of good Samaritans."

Mary smiled faintly. "Yes, but you were on horseback—they probably thought you were a Roman."

Cleo gave a short laugh, grateful for the diversion. "Mary, Jesus must be warned," he went on. "Under no circumstances should he try to see John. As you said, Herod Antipas is a madman, as bad as or worse than his father. Jesus' name is known now—you can be sure Herod knows it. And being John's cousin only makes things worse."

Mary sat rigid, white and still.

"I'd give anything to spare you," Cleo said. "And pray heaven I'm wrong." He straightened a lock of her hair, longing to comfort her, to somehow make amends. "I don't know what Jesus is trying to

⟨ 27 ⟩

accomplish," he admitted bluntly. "Maybe because I do love him so much and know him so well, it's hard for me to understand. But I do know this—it could lead to serious trouble. Prophets and . . . holy men"—he could not bring himself to use the word "messiah" again—"are under greater suspicion than ever in Jerusalem right now."

In the garden below, night-blooming jasmines were beginning to open, their fragrance drifting up. Nearby, where it had been tied, Cleophas' horse was whinnying. "Hyksos!" Cleo exclaimed suddenly. He strode back to the parapet to whistle reassurance. "It's late, and he hasn't been fed."

Mary rose and came to join him; they stood for a moment looking down on the white Egyptian steed, beautiful in the moonlight, pawing and shaking its mane. Cleo owned several horses, a rarity in Nazareth. "Poor Hyksos," Mary said. "I shouldn't have urged you to stay. Go now; he needs you."

Cleo gripped her hand, reluctant to leave. She seemed so small and so alone for such a burden. He was worried about her. He felt almost guilty—as if the bad news he had brought was somehow his fault. At least his own report of it seemed to him now so clumsy, foolish and tactless he winced. It could only have made things worse.

"Mary, forgive me. The last thing I want is to alarm you unnecessarily, or to hurt you in any way."

Mary returned the pressure of his hand. "I know that, Cleo. Your concern is precious to me."

"You will let me know when Jesus gets home? And you will talk to him? Or would you like me to?"

Mary nodded. "Naturally I will talk to him about our cousin. And you—dear Cleo, you are welcome to tell Jesus whatever you wish. You are his friend. But surely nothing we say can influence him." Mary lifted her small, firm chin. Leaf shadows were flickering across her face. She looked strangely luminous herself, standing there in the moonlight, a part of the night's soft radiance.

"Jesus has a wisdom far beyond our own. Jesus will know what to do," she said.

Now that she had him home again, she did not want to let him go. She must, she knew that she must—it was written; yet every aching sense protested, for Mary knew that this time would be final. Jesus belonged to others now; he would never again be so completely her son. So during the few days he lingered, preparing, she cooked for him—all his favorite dishes—and with special care washed, mended and packed his few clothes. He would begin his mission in Capernaum.

He had already been preaching to the crowds along the Jordan, while his men baptized on behalf of John.

"I knew John would want me to," he told her. "I could not go to him, of course. It would only have made things worse for him. But that much I could do for him. At least then." When the crowds became too great, he knew he must move on. "That, too, John would want— that I fulfill his prophecy. That, above all!"

Listening, Mary was consoled, though they grieved together over the tragedy of John. And the family grieved with them; on this at least they were united. Madman though their cousin might be, John was their kin—and the hated enemy was even madder. A cruel tyrant who, in imprisoning one of their own, had also insulted and deviously imprisoned them. They felt frustrated, their outrage shackled; they had no release for their anger, they could only discuss it, gravely or stormily, among themselves—all the family—not just Mary's sons and daughters, but aunts and uncles and the two grandmothers, Hannah and Timna.

In a curious way, their unity created a different attitude toward Jesus. To Mary's great joy, his brothers' furious criticism—for Jesus' own safety, they supposed—had given way to something protective, trusting, almost proud. They treated him with surprised respect: that he had had the courage to go out to that river and preach, after John's arrest! Even Josey expressed a grudging admiration. Foolhardy? Yes, but there was something grimly satisfying about it. That one of them had dared to thumb his nose at Herod, and escape.

As for now, Jesus was safely home, thank God (not only for his sake, but for their mother's); leaving again, but this time going only as far as Capernaum. Nothing much ever happened in those fishing towns along the lake. He couldn't get into too much trouble there. True, Herod's summer palace was pretty close, in Tiberias. But John would be miles away. That was the main thing. And Jesus was no fool. He'd be careful not to say or do anything that might antagonize the king and make things worse for John.

Privately, Josey was glad—and he was sure the others were too—that Jesus didn't intend to start preaching in Nazareth.

This too Mary had discussed with Jesus. He was right, he must leave; she was wise enough to know that. Yet she could not stop her heart's longing, and it was hard for her to keep it out of her voice when they spoke of his going, or its pleading from her eyes.

"I can't stay, you know that, Mother. People here know me too well. To Nazareth I'll always be just a carpenter—or a vagabond shepherd." They were in his chamber, sorting his things. His scrolls were piled around him on the floor. Jesus examined another one, then put it back in the old wooden chest. He looked up briefly, eyes twinkling. "A prophet is not without honor—save in his own country."

"Many people here admire you," Mary insisted. "Cleophas, the rabbi, your brothers. Lots of people! They have told me so, those who know about it; they are proud of what you did for John.

Jesus said quietly, "It wasn't only for John."

"I know that too. And so will they, in time." Mary paused in her simple task. She was trying to fit necessities into the worn leather sack on his bed. His comb and brush, his soap and oil, his garments. How would he keep clean if he didn't take more underwear and tunics, and at least another robe? How would he keep warm? True, he must travel light (he refused to take the donkey, knowing the family would need it), but he would be gone a long time. "Oh, my darling, they will, even the people of Nazareth—all of them in time!"

"Not here, Mother. Here there will always be doubt about me, and I can do nothing where there is doubt. Capernaum is the place for me." The Sea of Galilee. He had loved it ever since Joseph had taken him there as a boy. To swim there, work with the fishermen. Strong, tough, loyal men, he told her, most of them very devout. "They can help me. Andrew and Philip and Nathanael already have. They were born around there, they have friends in all the fishing villages—Bethsaida, Magdala, everywhere. They will tell others. Now that they've been with me, seen for themselves—" He broke off. Mary's heart pounded.

"Miracles?"

"Yes. A few. There will be more."

For a time there was silence between them as Jesus went on sorting: Books, writing materials, keepsakes from childhood . . . An old robe of Joseph's that Mary had cut down for his own first appearance at the

Temple. It had never quite fit him— at first it had felt too big, and then so quickly too small, almost skimpy, yet he had worn it loyally, not wanting them to suspect his discomfort. There were so many children to care for, and so little money. Now it hurt him to see it, so faded and worn; it was a part of all of them, and he loved it. . . . His first rod for protecting the sheep; he remembered how proudly his grandfather Joachim had led him into the woods to select just the right sapling and dig the root. And how far Joachim had hurled it to demonstrate its power—beating even Joseph and Cleo, who were competing in their own eagerness to show the boy. Jesus held its small, dark weight a moment, remembering. . . . The lopsided clay lamp his little sister Leah had once made for him; at first he had used it to please her, but it had become dear to him—a welcome flame beside his bed. . . . What to discard, what to keep, and what to take along? His needs were few; he would have carried nothing if it weren't for Mary. His own throat was taut with the significance of this parting; an awareness of change so painful neither of them could speak of it.

"Miracles!" Jesus got to his feet. He was still holding the little clay lamp. He made a troubled gesture. "People want miracles. Signs and wonders. If only they will continue to listen to me anyway, and believe."

"They will, Jesus," Mary said. "Have no fear of that. Are you not God's own? And it is his words you speak. Yes, miracles will help. People are so weak and human; there are times when our faith grows dim. Be glad that this power can rekindle that faith!" Mary looked up. She had been trying to get another sandal into the bag. "But rejoice in the sheer wonder of miracles, too!" she exclaimed. "The happiness they can bestow. Remember the wedding at Cana—and the wine? That had nothing to do with anyone's faith; you did it only to help, to provide pleasure, to be kind."

Her face was filled with awe. "And the healings. Oh, Jesus, the healings you will perform! The help you will be to those who are suffering. How I wish I could be there with you to see it."

"You will be with me wherever I go," he told her. "As the Father will be with me."

Jesus left that evening. He wanted to walk after sunset, when it was cooler. He would spend the first night in Cana with his cousins. Mary stood on the doorstep watching him go, the heavy bag across his shoulders, Benjy bounding triumphantly ahead. All day the dog had tagged at their heels, or lain anxiously beside them, suspecting something. And after supper he was not to be restrained. He too sensed that this time was different. Twice he escaped the pen where Mary usually kept him until Jesus was out of sight, and raced down the steps to await his master.

"Let him go," Jesus decided, at the urgent barking. "He must know I need him."

"Won't it be a hindrance? The way people feel about dogs?"

"Not all people, Mother. And he's my dog; I love him. He'll be a comfort to me."

"God keep you," she whispered, as he slung the bag across his back. "Send us some word when you are settled. If you need anything, we could—one of your brothers could bring it."

With a little groan, he adjusted the straps under his arms. "You have already packed enough for three sons," he chided, smiling as he bent to kiss her.

"Be careful," she said helplessly. "Rest if you get tired. Give my love to Lydia and her new husband. Oh, Jesus, I pray this choice is right for you."

He held her against him with both hands, and looked deep into her eyes. "I must go to Capernaum, Mother. I *have* no choice. It is written."

Eyes closed now, Mary nodded, unable to reply.

She waved until he disappeared down the deserted street; then waited until she could see him again on the road around the bend, beyond the synagogue. A tall figure, walking backward, arm upraised, but already small and growing smaller in the distance. Frantically, standing on tiptoe, Mary kept waving until he had vanished in the blue dusk.

The night was cool and sweet. A heavy dew had fallen. Lights were coming on one by one; in their glow the wet leaves and grasses glistened. She stood a moment, not wanting to go back into the empty house, yet glad that Jesus had told no one the time of his departure; thankful they could be alone when it was time to part. Except for Grandmother Timna, whose lamp burned in her quarters behind the shop, the rest of the family were nowhere about.

Mary trembled, and gripped the wooden handrail Joseph had long ago put up to help his heavy mother negotiate the steps. All day she had guarded her emotions, refused to acknowledge them, put them away to be dealt with later, if at all. Now she felt them beginning to stir, to claim their right to assault her, in a way she had not imagined. Waiting there under the first frail stars, Mary steadied herself; not so much in fear that she might submit to this incredible anguish, but more that she might examine it.

Why? she demanded of herself. Why now? She had said goodbye to Jesus many times: more often than to any of her children. Except for trips to Jerusalem, the others were content to stay close by. Why did it hurt so this time? "You will be with me wherever I go," he had said. And now, for an instant, it was as if he had literally taken her heart with him. She felt . . . empty. Gouged. She pressed her hand against her breast, felt its rhythmic beating. And her womb—there was an actual aching in her womb. As if unseen hands had reached into her very body and plucked its first fruit from her.

Mary swayed and held on to the rough, damp rail. To the northeast, beyond Mount Tabor in the direction of the Galilean sea, the sky was strangely bright for such an hour. Perhaps an early moon was rising; she hoped so, for it would light his way. . . . Why now? she continued to implore. She had borne other children, and for years her womb had been empty. Why should it ache so now? Yet she must remember: It was the Father himself who had placed her precious firstborn there; and it was for this her son had been delivered into the world. And despite Jesus' wanderings, they had had him for themselves all those years—she and Joseph, and then she alone. Now finally the time had come for the Father to claim his own. Jesus must go forth into that world.

If it had been otherwise, she would have failed them.

Mary knew that. She had known it always. Humble and fallible though she felt herself to be, she was honored above all women. She had been chosen to bear this wonderful child and nurture him, and she had done her best. She could let him go with pride. Surely no mother on earth ever had such cause to be proud. The realization came over her, comforting and triumphant. Absently, Mary touched her body again: She felt whole; the pain was gone. A peace that bordered on joy came over her. She stood gazing at the strange light in the northern sky.

It seemed even more brilliant now, and vast. How beautiful—and puzzling. It was past the season of the full moon; and surely no moon could create such a fire.

Fire. Could it be, she wondered uneasily, that the forests on the far side of Mount Tabor were on fire? If so, she should rouse someone. She wished some of the men—Josey or Simon or someone—were about. They often cut lumber there; they would know. But no, this strange radiance was not confined to the sky above a single mountain; it had spread as far as Mount Hattin and beyond. Mary thought of running down the steps to alert Timna, if only to share the spectacle. Yet something held her rooted to the spot. She could only stand frozen, awed before the sight which seemed to be hers alone. Else why didn't people come running from their houses, exclaiming? Why didn't the few on the street even bother to look up?

And now as she gazed came the revelation: Jesus must indeed carry the light to Capernaum! For it was in the land of Zebulun and Naphtali, sons of their forefather Jacob, as the Prophet Isaiah had decreed: *"Toward the sea, across the Jordan, Galilee of the Gentiles"*—the words were chanting in her head—*"the people that sat in darkness saw a great light. And to them that sat in the region and shadow of death, to them did light spring up. . . ."*

Mary clutched her throat. She watched exalted as the light held for a time, then began to change, dispersing . . . thinning . . . dissolving . . . until it was but a silvery fog which finally drifted away. Darkness blanketed the mountains once more, and the stars bloomed again in the heavens.

Mary groped back into the house. It must be late; the streets were vacant, Timna's lamp was out. . . . She lay awake a long time, still in a state of rapture.

She would tell no one. It would never be recorded. But it was true, this sign and wonder.

Chapter 3

*A*ND now Capernaum.

Andrew had rented a small whitewashed house for him, not far from the synagogue, beside the sea. It was furnished only with a mat for sleeping, an outdoor oven, and a cupboard for his few utensils and his scrolls. Here Jesus cooked and cleaned for himself, and washed his garments in the water. The house was perched on a shelf of rock. From here he could watch the fishermen casting their nets—graceful as dancers as their burly arms whirled the broad weighted circles, vigorously hurled them and then carefully drew them in. Or seining— the boat drawing close to shore, where most of the crew sprang into the water to pay out the ropes as it drew away. Then gently, gently, while the boat glided in semicircles, the vast weighted net was lowered, to be pulled to shore by the men there, until the boat was once again beside them.

Often, unable to restrain himself, Jesus ran down the path, Ben barking wildly behind him, and waded in to help, as with jubilant shouts and singing the catch was harvested.

At night he could hear the waves lapping or sometimes lashing at the banks. For this beautiful body of water had as many moods as its names: Lake of Gennesaret . . . Lake Galiel . . . Sea of Chinnereth . . . Sea of Tiberias. Or, more poetically, it was known as the Jewel, the Silver Woman, the Blue Harp. This last it most resembled, seen from the hills behind the city. The elegant white limestone pillars of the synagogue quivered in reflection on its glassy breast. Morning and evening, the trees were mirrored there, and the endless pageantry of the encircling hills—ribboned and prancing with color during the flowering of spring: yellow and scarlet and blue; then a brief bright green, which the fierce suns of summer burned to the golden brown of a lion's skin.

Along the northern shore, when Jesus climbed to his rooftop, he could see the city of Tiberias, which Herod Antipas had been rebuilding on the site of an ancient cemetery, to the horror and disgust of the Jews. Famous rabbis were buried there; it was not only unlawful it was a desecration. Yet the king had made this unclean place his capital. And now, to add to the insult, he was erecting another lavish colonnaded palace, to honor Herodius, the wife he had taken from his brother. A glimpse of its gleaming white marble mocked him from above the trees. Jesus winced at the sight, remembering that John was still in prison. It brought back the terrible pain of John.

Yet even this could not destroy his fascination and delight in the lake. He loved it, whatever the hour—ablaze under the merciless noonday sun, paved with jewels at sunset, or lying like a polished silver platter under the full moon. He loved it best just before daybreak, when he and Ben would rise and run down the narrow path to plunge in.

Often a white mist blanketed sea and sky, so that to merge with it was like swimming through a dream. Sometimes a pale shell of moon still hovered, even as the first pink light began to bloom. The water was usually bitterly cold, despite the merciless heat that would come later in the day. A fiery baptism, making his blood tingle, his spirits soar: comforting, cleansing, refreshing, giving him courage for the day.

At times Philip, Andrew or Bartholomew joined him; sometimes all three, clambering over the rocks and hallooing as they spotted Jesus far from the shore, with his dog chuffing along beside him. They were all strong, tough swimmers, as fishermen had to be. The lake was treacherous, they warned him. Smooth as a good sail one minute, the next, a sudden squall could churn up waves as savage as those of a mighty ocean, whirling and sucking like a pack of demons. "Be careful," they pleaded. "They can whip a boat over and drag a man down in a second!" Until he knew it better, they worried that he should swim out so far alone. It was one reason they went out to find him.

Yet they also came for the pleasure of his company. Reaching him, they would wrestle and dive and cavort, as carefree as youths on the street. Then, racing each other, they would all strike for shore, to take up again the serious business of making a living, or serving him—their master, their teacher and their friend.

They were proud of him, and basked a little in his glory. For were they not the first to know him? This remarkable man who soon packed the synagogue, and whom crowds left their work to listen to whenever word went out that Jesus would speak beside the sea. He could drive out evil spirits—it had happened that first Sabbath right in the place of worship! He could heal. Word had spread. Now crowds followed him wherever he went, pressing so close to him at times he almost fell.

To Andrew's dismay, Simon Peter was not among them. It was a bitter disappointment. After all his proud assurances to Jesus! Outwardly, Andrew went about as confident and cheerful as before, but inside he was stricken. He adored his much older brother, who had been like a father to him. Peter was a curly-haired ox of a man, fearless, stubborn, brash, but none better with a boat and much respected in Capernaum. He prided his independence. Let other people flock to the synagogue—the law didn't say you had to, he would worship as he pleased.

Toward Andrew's innocent religious enthusiasms Peter had shown a kindly tolerance, mixed with an affectionate concern. He tried to guide and curb his younger brother as best he could. For despite his brusque front, Peter writhed to remember the troubles his own somewhat naive and impetuous nature had gotten him into at times, and still could if he wasn't careful. He had not actually rebuked Andrew for traipsing off to follow that radical, John the Baptist, but he had advised strongly against it. And when news of John's trials began to circulate, though Simon Peter was not a man to gloat, he felt his judgment confirmed. And now, to have Andrew return as a convert to another unknown rabbi—worse, a cousin of John's! Peter was disturbed. While he listened patiently to Andrew's supplications, he refused to encourage him.

All this Andrew suffered in silence, too embarrassed even to try to explain the matter to his Lord. He could only wait, with a kind of blind beaming faith, for the time, sure to come, when Peter would actually see and hear for himself. And then . . . !

By day Jesus wore the usual striped garb of the tradesmen, or a faded blue tunic, tied with a frayed rope or a worn leather belt. But toward late afternoon, when the heat-wilted people would be rousing from their naps, he clad himself in a pure white robe that he had washed in the morning, still smelling sweet from the sunny rock where he had dried it, and wearing or carrying his father's fringed *talith* or prayer shawl, he set off for the stretch of shoreline nearer the town.

And the people were already running to meet him. By word of mouth or some knowledge that moved like a fresh wind over the city, they knew he had appeared. They dropped whatever they were doing—the mother preparing supper, the maker of shoes at his last, the carpenter, the smith—they put down their tools and extinguished their fires and joined the streams of people moving toward the lake, where they knew they would find him. Young, vigorous, beautiful, his dark curls blowing, his rich musical voice calling out in the manner of John, whose fame had spread to the far reaches of the country. Yet with a poise and dignity and authority that surpassed anything they had witnessed or dreamed. He was tall and fervent, yet smiling; gentle and friendly; the stories he told them made sense.

He was like the voice of their own hearts speaking.

Something was happening here, something important. Who was he, this mysterious stranger? It was said that he cast out demons: He had delivered a tormented man from a demon the first time he spoke in the synagogue; at his command the horrible thing had come out, convulsing and screaming, "Leave me alone, Jesus of Nazareth. *I know who you are—the Holy One of God!*"

He had come, he had come, this holy one. And they all had evil spirits in their souls—hatred, jealousies, fears, guilt, anxieties about tomorrow. His words wove a sweet enchantment; by his words he could deliver them. They had only to forgive each other and love each other, as the heavenly Father loved them. He told them they need not worry about tomorrow, but rather to thank and trust the bountiful Father who first gave them life, and he would provide all their needs. Some of their devils possessed them outright, body and soul; they lusted, cheated, committed adultery, stole. Jesus said to rejoice, for if they sincerely repented and made amends, there would be great rejoicing in heaven; their sins would be forgiven, and every one of them made clean.

He promised them victory over pain and poverty and even death itself. And in Capernaum these days, nothing mattered much but to hear him.

Jesus and his dog had swum alone this morning, for his companions were still fishing. The catch had been poor these past few days. Zebedee, who owned the business in which they all participated, had ordered the boats to stay out all night. Jesus was aware of them out there in the gray dawn, tiny black silhouettes rocking gently on the glassy swells. A broad circle of boats, not just those of Zebedee. How patient and persistent fishermen had to be. There was something lonely and touching about it.

But now, at midafternoon, when Jesus set off, most of the boats had come in. They were lined up along the beach, huge storm-battered hulks, mostly blue-gray like the water, rocking rhythmically at anchor, or lying like weary giants on the sand. Broad, sturdy, sound, like the men who rowed them. A few men squatted, sorting their miserable catch. Others were sloshing out the boats with buckets of water, or scrubbing the barnacles and seaweed from their massive, curved sides. Jesus had left early, hastening up alleys or little-used back streets, hoping to arrive unnoticed before the crowds reached the banks, sometimes pushing and shoving in their eagerness to get near him; struggling to touch him, beg him for healing, holding up their children to be blessed.

Today it occurred to him that one of those boats could help. Shielding his eyes, Jesus looked about for his friends. None of them were in sight. But in one empty boat sat a huge man, mending his nets. And Jesus recognized him at once. With a shout of joy in his soul, he knew him, and his whole being reached out to him, this giant who was destined to walk so many miles with him in the time to come. For a moment he stood regarding him—the thick cap of tightly curled hair, bleached almost white by the sun. The big ruddy rawboned face, bent over his task, but lifting before the intensity of Jesus' gaze. The keen, sharp, ice-blue eyes.

And, with a start, Simon Peter recognized Jesus as surely the prophet Andrew and his friends had been proclaiming. For an instant they stared at each other, those two.

Then Jesus asked simply, "How's fishing?" And Simon Peter responded bluntly, "Terrible, as you can see." He indicated the empty hampers in disgust. "We have caught nothing worth keeping." Surprised, excited, troubled, vaguely amused, with a kind of heavy, unhurried grace, Peter got to his feet. He was so tall that when he stood he towered even over Jesus. His shoulders were a trifle hunched from bending down to others. "So you're the rabbi my brother has been talking about. What can I do for you, my friend?"

Jesus gestured to the people already beginning to pour down the bank. "If you could row me a little way out onto the lake," he said, "I would be most grateful. I would like to try speaking to them from the water."

Simon Peter squinted, his keen eyes surveying the situation. The crowd, like a mounting wave, would soon be upon them. "Get in." Quickly rolling up his net and heaving it into the rear, he extended a hand. With a rattle of chains he hauled up the anchor, while Jesus grabbed an oar and helped shove off. "Ever row a boat before?" Peter asked, as Jesus strove to fit it into the lock.

"No, but I'm willing to learn."

"We all have a lot to learn," Simon Peter said. "But later." He reached over and took the oar. With a few strokes of his hairy arms and massive shoulders, they were soon a proper distance from the shore. There, in the still, glassy water, he dropped anchor.

And waiting for the last of the people to arrive, Jesus covered his face and sat in silence, communing with the Father. And when it was clear no one would be disappointed, he rose and spread his arms to answer the crowd's eager greetings. Then he bade them sit down, there on the sand or the rocks and the grassy slopes, and bow their heads while he blessed them. The water nibbled against the boat, herons waded in the shallows, and the little ruby-throated swallows dipped tiny beaks into the brilliant sun-stars exploding all about. There was the rhythmic squeak of wood and chain, the twittering music of the birds, but the whole world seemed to be hushed while Jesus spoke to them in a voice as clear and strong as a sweet bell chiming. Even the usual racket and babble of the city beyond seemed to have quieted.

Simon Peter sat listening, with his chin propped on his fists. So this was what Andrew had been talking about! Never had he heard such words of love and hope and forgiveness. Or such almost frightening promise. The kingdom of heaven was at hand, the man claimed.

⟨ 40 ⟩

The prophecies were being fulfilled. Their injustices would not last forever. But no man knew the hour; they must get ready.

"Make peace with your brother, go to him this very night and settle your differences. Your offerings on the altar will mean nothing until this is done, for they will only be poisoned by the resentment in your heart. Don't postpone your good deeds, do them now. Sell what you have and give to the poor. Feed the hungry, comfort the sick, visit the lonely and those in prison. For inasmuch as you do it unto one of the least of these, your brethren, you are doing it unto the king who will remember you when you are called. Verily I say unto you, take heed, listen, believe! For this teaching is not mine but that of the Father who sent me. . . . "

Peter lifted his finger to warn the occupants of another boat, which had drawn up beside them: James and John, twin sons of his boss, Zebedee, high-spirited and inclined to be noisy. They had gone back out fishing, but now they had pulled up their nets; they, too, wanted to listen.

The sun was slanting through the trees, sending little snakes of light across the gently swaying boat, blazing a golden roadway from the shore to the place where Jesus sat. His white figure was at its crux, its very heart, as if he and not the sun were the source of all this light. And when he stood up once more, to finish his message, the sun seemed a halo behind his head and the sight of him was so dazzling Simon Peter rubbed his eyes.

Now go to your homes, Jesus was saying, for it would soon be dark. Wives, cook a good supper for your husbands and children; men, cherish your wives. Love each other and keep the commandments, pray, turn your worries over to God, sleep in peace. . . . Smiling, he turned to Peter, whose big, rugged face was staring up at him as if in a trance.

"Now let's do some fishing!" He clapped his hands smartly together. "Row out farther, where it is deep, and cast your nets."

"But, Master!" The word sprang unbidden from Peter's open mouth. "We have toiled all night and taken nothing."

"This time we're going where the fish are," Jesus said. He was taking off his prayer shawl, and carefully folding it. "With faith we'll find them."

Peter shrugged. "Well, Sir, if you insist." Suppressing a grin, not wanting to be rude, he reached obediently for the oars. Bracing his big bare feet, he pulled with his powerful shoulders in the direction Jesus was pointing—a dark glassy area where springs bubbled deep below.

On the shore, dusk had fallen swiftly, but out here the sky was still light. Behind the Syrian hills an impish half-moon tilted. The water, a silvery lilac color, reflected the trees, the jutting quays, and their own figures standing in the gently rocking boat. Jesus had tucked his white robe up about his waist. An excited anticipation claimed him as Peter handed him a round weighted net. Leaning back, he hurled it vigorously and watched it sink, as Peter cast out another.

For a few minutes all was still. The sky deepened its color, the first stars began to twinkle, the water murmured, shining. The smell of fish and the sea was strong. Then suddenly, incredibly, there was a sense of weight and lively stirring in the nets. Both of them came alive, heavy with bodies, dragging down. "Bring it in, bring it in!" Peter ordered as Jesus struggled. Then, whooping for joy, he turned to his own. No time for baskets; they dumped their flapping, squirming treasures on the floor and cast again.

For now all about them the whole sea was exploding, giving birth to silver bodies, a teeming population, jumping, darting, swarming, piling on top of each other in such layers they were like a living pavement heaving and thrusting against the boat. The men felt it lurch and sway.

"Look, look, look!" Simon Peter was jubilant, shouting and singing in his bluff and hearty way, even as he groaned, "We'll never be able to hold them all!" To his relief he saw another boat approaching and waved excitedly to James and John. "We've struck a shoal!" he yelled. "Come help us! We'll have to use the seine."

Quickly the brothers drew alongside and dropped anchor. Young and fair, agile as nymphs, they dived into the water and caught the ropes of the great seine Peter and Jesus tossed out to them. Then they swam shoreward as the net was unfurled, drawing it together while Peter circled with the boat until the seine was bulging. Crouched on the prow, Jesus joyfully helped haul it in. Both boats were soon calf-deep in the slippery, gleaming, wildly drumming fish.

And still they came. A mad multiplication of bodies, overhead now as well as below, for the sky was suddenly a riot of birds screaming and croaking for their share. Kingfishers and pelicans, striking like thunderbolts, so thick the men had to duck and try to drive them off with oars. While a little higher the cranes hovered, waiting to risk their turn.

At first to Peter's consternation, then to his delight, other boats were approaching, rowing as fast as they could. He hallooed his welcome and beckoned them in. Enough fish for all! For had he not found them with the help of his new friend? He felt like a bountiful host. It was wonderful, terrible, glorious, the water splashing until they were soaked, the din of the birds, the shouting and singing, the fish like cascades of heavy jewels as they poured from the nets into the groaning boats. A kind of enthralling madness of sea and sky and greedy birds and men.

Simon Peter sloshed about, huge, ruddy, beaming, drenched, singing at the top of his lungs. Jesus too, working feverishly beside him, was having a wonderful time. But the boat was filling too fast, the nets could not meet the strain much longer. Even as they struggled to haul in one final catch, they could feel the seine giving way. It broke just as they dragged it over the side, spilling half its riches into the lake.

The boat shuddered under the weight of even the remainder of the shining avalanche. "Stop, stop, that's enough!" Peter bellowed. There was a dread sinking sensation beneath his feet. Nearly knee-deep now in cold threshing fish, he saw that the waterline was level and spilling over the vessel's rim. In horror, he realized that some of the other boats were also in trouble.

Peter turned his shocked and striken face to Jesus. This strange authority on fishing who had never even rowed a boat. Suspicion pierced him suddenly, a thought almost too hideous to believe. "Who are you," he accused, "that you should bring us here?" His voice, so joyful a moment ago, was now the piteous wail of one betrayed. "Is it only to perish?" he pleaded. He made a dazed, helpless gesture. "The boat is sinking—we will lose all our fish, and our lives as well."

Jesus, too, was astonished. Caught up in the sheer adventure, he had actually forgotten its reason. Pity overwhelmed him. He reached out to steady Peter as he staggered. But a wave broke over the side, sending him sprawling. In his terror, Peter scrambled to his knees, hugging those of Jesus. "Depart from me, Lord, whoever you are!" he moaned. "For I am a sinful man, I don't want to drown!"

Jesus bent to embrace him. "Don't be afraid," he cried. "Peter, dear Simon Peter, believe me. God has sent us even more fish than I had dreamed. But we are not sinking, I promise." Firmly he pulled the shaking man to his feet. "And all the boats will reach shore safely. See, some are already on their way." Jesus reached for the oars. "I will help you row. We will go back to land together. And there you will unload your fish and follow me."

Peter stared at him, bewildered. "Do you mean you know more such fishing grounds?" he gasped. "We will fish together for more such hauls as this?"

"Not only more but better," Jesus told him. "You are a great fisherman, Peter, the best in Galilee. But from now on you will be far greater—for I will make you a fisher of men."

His wife, Adah, was still asleep when Peter rushed in the next morning. She groaned when he shook her, and sat up, not wishing to believe her eyes. Her husband was soaked, his ruddy face streaming, and he was more excited than she had ever seen him.

"Wake up! Listen," he panted. "I've found him, I have found the Messiah! I was with him half the night."

"Hush, please be quiet," she scolded. "You'll wake up Mother. She's worse, she has a fever—"

"The man can heal her—wait until I tell you: He performs miracles. I've just seen one!"

"Oh, no," she groaned. "Not *you*." Adah crawled out, a rugged woman almost as tall as he was, her hair a skimpy tangle on her freckled shoulders. She yawned, stretched, and patted him fondly, trying to quiet him. "Please, Peter, not you. If Andrew wants to believe such things, all right. He and his friends. They're young and impressionable, but you're steady, you've got more sense, you have a wife to take care of. Not you!"

"Adah, Adah—" He was charging about like a caged animal, stumbling over things. His wife blocked his path lest he hurt himself, also to stop the racket. She put her arms around him, and he stared at her, but dazedly, as if he didn't see her. He stank of fish. His still-damp garment was smeared with blood and entrails, scales glittered in his beard and hair, but he was smiling; there were sparks in his usually chill blue eyes.

"This is different. A wonderful thing has happened! Life will never be the same for us again."

"Go to bed and rest," she urged, soothing. "But no, first you must bathe. I will fetch some water. Wash and I will give you breakfast, then you must sleep. We will talk of this later, when you wake. When you feel better."

"Never in my life have I felt better. I have *seen* him, I tell you. He is here with us now, not just another messiah—no, no, no—the Promised One, sent down from heaven, the giver of life and health eternal. And now that I have seen him—!" Peter choked suddenly. "I should have listened to Andrew. I was wrong not to see him before. And you must see him too. Oh, Adah, once you have seen and heard him, you will understand."

Trembling with anticipation, James and John rolled up their nets that afternoon and hurried home. Their father, Zebedee, was as unpredictable as the lake—one minute calm, the next a raging storm. Though apprehensive about his reaction, they could hardly wait to tell him. They hoped he was back from his business trip to Tyre. What a shame he had to miss all the excitement: last night's drama on the water; and the madhouse of the marketplace this morning. Merchants, peddlers, wholesalers, dealers from the caravans, women with their baskets—all clamoring for attention like those screaming birds above the lake. The bright tide of money changing hands. (This night, for the first time in their life, many a fisherman would go to bed feeling rich.)

And everywhere the amazement at the incredible catch. The biggest ever brought into Capernaum. Even with extra help it had taken most of the night just to sort it in time for the morning's sale. A miracle, people were saying. Although few if any of them realized—actually realized, the brothers marveled—what had happened. While they . . . now that they had been alone with him, the man called Jesus, spoken with him these last two hours . . .

Still awed, they loped along toward the spacious house—two very fair young men with cloudy golden hair, heavy brows and radiant smiles. They were not identical. James was a trifle taller, more animated in manner, and some people thought John had a gentler, sweeter face. Even so, they were enough alike to confuse people, and it amused them sometimes to switch roles. Venturesome, reckless, daring, they had become known as Sons of Thunder. From boyhood they had loved to launch their boats when the lake was at its wildest, or to ride out its fiercest storms. They also rode their father's fast horses and drank too much at sheep shearings and other feasts. Zebedee was always thundering at them, in a voice that could be heard almost to Bethsaida.

The brothers were loud, friendly, flirtatious, the best dancers along the coast. Around them parents watched their daughters, half fearing, half hoping for a request from Zebedee on behalf of his sons. For Zebedee owned a winepress, a pottery and a prosperous string of fishing vessels. James was considered the wilder of the two. "James leads John on," his parents fretted. Yet though Zebedee and his wife railed at them, both adored these madcap sons and chuckled in private at their antics. For the twins were also very devout, at heart good boys. And like their friends and co-workers Philip and Andrew, they lived in expectation of the long-promised Messiah. Fortunately, they did not go chasing off after pretenders and dreamers and would-be prophets, the way Andrew was prone to, but they fully believed he would appear—a kind of swashbuckling deliverer king, who would somehow sweep them up in his magnificent adventure. Or so it seemed. It had become, in its own way, a kind of family joke.

Unable to repress their enthusiasm, James and John burst into the kitchen. "We've found him, we're sure we have found him! And he has asked us to join him!"

Their mother looked up from the pot she was stirring on the fire. She was a plump, skeptical, but amiable brown-eyed woman named Salome. "Who?" she asked scornfully, but with a little laugh. "The Messiah?"

"Yes, yes!" James hugged her and tried to whirl her about. "I know you don't believe us, but it's true."

"How do you know? Did he tell you this himself?" Their mother laughed harder, and appealed to her husband, who had indeed returned from Tyre and was just coming in from the garden, carrying a handful of onions for her stew. The aroma of vegetables and bubbling kid filled the room. "Listen to them," she said, "they've got great news. They've just been talking to the Messiah."

"The Messiah, ha?" Grinning, Zebedee bit into an onion, chewed it thoughtfully for a minute. He was a short, bright-eyed man, with a shrewd, gaunt face. He drove a tough bargain, but he was well-liked, he and these prankish sons. "And I suppose he promised you the kingdom and urged you to join him?"

The twins exchanged startled glances. "Please don't tease about this, Father," said John. "This is serious."

"How do you know *who* he is?" their mother repeated. "Did he actually claim to be the Anointed One, son of David, sent by God?"

"Not in so many words; he didn't have to," John said earnestly. "It's in his face, in his eyes."

"It's more than that," James insisted. "It's what he can *do*! All those fish last night. If only you could have been there—or even at the market this morning. Everybody's talking. Have you heard, Father?"

"Yes, yes, I've heard."

"Never has there been such a haul. And within an *hour*, Father, every boat on the lake!"

Zebedee threw back his bald head and laughed, a deep rumbling chuckle in his throat. "Don't tell me he's trying to take credit for that? Surely you aren't such fools as to think anybody had anything to do with it? Our luck changed, that's all. Or let's say our prayers were answered."

He looked up to acknowledge the presence of Simon Peter in the doorway, with Andrew and Philip just behind him. "Come in, come in, sit down," he welcomed them. "I hear there was a lot of excitement while I was away in Tyre." Zebedee turned his attention back to his sons. "Listen," he went on, "I've known this lake a lot longer than you have. I've seen it hold back its fish for weeks, when suddenly"— he smacked his hands together—"lo, they come swarming, thick as pudding, so thick you can't work fast enough to bring them in. Right Peter?"

Peter looked agitated; his deeply burned face had an odd pallor. "Yes, but never like last night," he blurted, though he hated to contradict his employer. "Your sons are right," he said, in a voice still hoarse from last night's shouting. "I was there when it began. He was in my boat with me, this man Jesus. He told me precisely where to find them." Even now Peter's big red hands were trembling. "Like you, I wanted to laugh at him, a rabbi from Nazareth who'd never even rowed a boat—that he should try to tell *me*. Yet there they were, so many we could barely drop anchor. And more and more—beyond any this lake has ever seen!"

He broke off, plunged his face into his hands, unable to continue. James and John took up the amazing story, with an occasional comment from Andrew and Philip, who, hearing the commotion, had rushed their own craft onto the lake the night before. Zebedee sat listening dubiously, pinching his narrow lips, occasionally shaking his head. His wife, with the help of a servant, was ladling out the stew. Zebedee was puzzled. The young ones' fervor he could understand, but not big, bluff Simon Peter's. Peter was independent, yes, ardent in his convictions, but always rational, in control of himself, at least in recent years. Zebedee had never seen him like this.

"We met him again this afternoon while we were mending our nets," said James. "We've talked it over, and we know we must go with him."

"Go with him *where*?"

"Wherever he leads."

Zebedee appealed to John, who had more sense. "Is this true?" he asked bluntly.

John nodded, his eyes shining. He left discussions like this to his brother.

"Father, Mother, don't look so disgusted or amused," James rushed on. "Don't you realize what this means? He is the King, I tell you. The prophesied King. He will establish his kingdom right here on earth."

"When?" Zebedee demanded angrily. "Are you talking about overthrowing the Romans?"

"Well, yes, in time—how else can justice be done? He will free us all. Yes, yes, it will take time," James cried. "He's only beginning. But those who recognize him *now*," he insisted, "those he chooses *now*, those of us willing to follow him *now*, surely we'll be rewarded when he comes into power. We'll be honored, we'll have influence—"

His father could tolerate no more. His fist banged the table. "Stop. Enough! That's dangerous talk. I've heard of him, this person you're raving about—he's a rabble-rouser, a troublemaker. The man has a price on his head!"

"Not this one." Andrew spoke up anxiously. "You must be thinking about John the Baptist."

"Whoever. Not the one you and Philip, and I guess even Nathanael Bartholomew, were chasing after until it got too hot for him? All right—now this one. Anyway, they're all alike, stirring people up, getting them into trouble, and I'll thank you not to influence my sons, not if you expect to go on fishing for me."

"But we don't," Andrew said quietly. "Do we, Peter?" he addressed his brother. "We are going to fish for him." And, as Zebedee gasped at this treachery, "He will make us fishers of men."

It took the rest of the evening. Zebedee's wife insisted they all stay for supper; and when they had washed and prayed, they were at it again even as they noisily dipped their bread. "What's the matter with you?" Zebedee kept demanding. "You have a job and responsibilities here. You all make a good living on this lake—three meals a day and a good place to sleep. Simon Peter, you've worked for me for years. Haven't I treated you fairly? Don't I pay you well?"

Peter nodded miserably.

"What about your wife? Have you told her? What does she say about this mad scheme, taking up with some impostor you don't even know? How will she manage while you're away? Not only your wife, but your mother-in-law, who's been so sick, I hear."

Simon Peter sat baffled but stubborn, staring straight ahead. "I haven't told them everything yet," he admitted, "but they will understand. They must. The way will be provided somehow."

"And you—" Zebedee turned his fire on his sons. "You'll inherit this house, the whole partnership, someday. Do you want to break up the family business, throw everything away?"

"Father, listen, we've got to, we must. And as I've tried to tell you, in time you'll be proud, we'll be handsomely repaid."

Zebedee snorted. "Let him start blaspheming or upsetting Rome, and you'll be nailed up with him, that's what! You must be out of your minds. It's dangerous to follow such a man, and it will be damned uncomfortable. Why, why, why?"

Peter's big head went back. "Because he is the Christ," he said.

"How do you know?"

"His miracles. All those fish last night. Trout, carp, perch, every kind—it wasn't just the quantity but the kind. Thousands and thousands of fish of every kind . . . " He paused. "Except the unclean."

Zebedee gasped. "I don't believe that. Do you mean to tell me there were no shellfish among them, no crabs or clams or anything without scales?"

"Not so much as an eel."

Zebedee was incredulous. "Is this true?" he barked at his sons.

"Father, believe us. We have never seen anything like it."

"The man must be a magician." Their father wadded his napkin and got to his feet. He strode about, scowling, pinching his lips again. This, of all they had said, impressed him most. His mind was racing. To dispense with the long, tiresome, disgusting business of sorting and disposing of the unclean fish; be rid of the stuff that could be sold only to the heathens.

Suddenly, almost merrily, Zebedee threw up his hands. "Go then!" he exclaimed. "But first bring this magician to me, that he may show me how he does it."

To his surprise, there was absolute silence at the table. He could feel all the eyes upon him, some of them still uneasy, confused, but all quietly protesting. Finally John spoke, his earnest young voice not quite steady. "Jesus is no mere magician, Father. He is far more than that. He is the true Deliverer, and he has performed miracles far more important than fish. That official, Reb Zadok his name is—the one who has charge of the gates—swears Jesus cured his son. Without even seeing him, just with a word. The boy was on the point of dying, he said. And that man possessed of a demon . . . "

"Were you there?" Zebedee pressed him. "Did you see either of these things?"

His sons exchanged embarrassed glances as they shook their heads. "What about you, Peter?"

"No, those I have not witnessed."

"I have," Andrew said quietly. "I was present at them both. I can vouch for them. I saw the boy later, myself. And the thing in the synagogue, screaming and frothing on the floor—a terrible sight."

Zebedee was startled. But he shrugged in disbelief. Andrew had a good imagination, like a lot of other people. Even this matter of the fish could probably be explained. "Then let him heal Simon's mother-in-law," he said. "Simon Peter, I challenge you—go get this wonder worker right now. Take him to your wife's mother, see what he can do for that fever she's had so long. If he makes her well, then perhaps I will believe."

With lumbering dignity, Peter got to his feet. "He is the Christ," he said solemnly again. "He can do anything."

Chapter 4

*A*T last there were twelve.

More than six would be needed, that had been evident during those first months of his astonishingly successful ministry beside that beautiful inland sea. Then in a northward sweep through Galilee, teaching and preaching in the synagogues; and when the crowds became too great, from the hills and fields. Teaching, and healing every infirmity.

Like wildfire his fame was spreading. Throughout all Syria, from as far away as Jerusalem, the Decapolis, beyond the Jordan, from Tyre and Sidon and Idumea, people flocked to hear him, bringing their children to be blessed and their tormented bodies to be made whole. For never had there been a prophet of such power or such compassion.

He cared, he really cared: he was not afraid to touch them! With his own spittle he bathed the eyes of the blind, and they saw. Gently he drew the paralyzed, the hopelessly crippled, to their feet. He even embraced the lepers.

At first his men came charging up in horror. "Master, no! She's unclean," they cried one day. "Stand back, stand back, you can bless her from a distance." For this was the method of other holy men who sometimes went about healing.

To their astonishment, Jesus rebuked them sternly. "Get out of my way," he ordered. And moving toward the heavily veiled woman, he drew her to him, and held her like a frightened child, murmuring softly to her until her tears had stopped.

Carefully, gently, then, he lifted her face and pulled aside the veil. In concern and love he regarded it—scarlet, inflamed, puffed, riddled with running sores. "My poor daughter," he said, "you have suffered.

But don't be afraid." The rest of her body was in similar torment, he knew, but he did not embarrass her further by asking her to bare even her arms. "Quiet, now, quiet," he was soothing, "it is all over. You must return to your home and bathe. A tub of warm water will be sufficient. Bathe yourself in love and joy, thanking God for your healing.

"Don't be afraid of her," he told those who were drawing away. "She is well now, she is healed. When she comes to us tomorrow she will be clean."

And on the next day the woman returned, rejoicing. She was beautiful, he saw. So radiantly beautiful that people gasped. Her husband and some of her relatives were with her, astonished and elated.

Jesus waved aside the money they tried to press upon him. Somewhat to the consternation of Peter and several of the others. The purse was always low, and these people were obviously able to pay well. It seemed only fair. There was no avarice in any of them, but it hurt them to see Jesus being without the comforts he deserved. Why shouldn't such a miraculous physician be compensated?

After that the lepers came in droves. So many that sometimes the multitudes were afraid to come near. Yet he healed them every one. And those who were possessed by demons, wild-eyed, writhing, some of them in chains—Jesus knelt, and with his own strong, tough hands he unloosed their bonds and furiously flung them away. Then, when he had commanded the evil spirits to be gone, he told the tortured victims to lie quietly a moment, in the love of the Father, before they rose. And when they stood up, though at first bewildered, they were filled with his precious peace. And they kissed his hands, or bowed down, together with the families or friends who had brought them, and weeping, kissed his feet.

And although he always warned, "Now tell no one, but go straight to the priest as the Law commands, make your offering and have your healing confirmed," people could not wait. They ran from him rejoicing, many of them proclaiming, "Surely he is the son of God!"

Though such things could be dangerous.

Every crowd also had its critics and skeptics, as well as agents from the Temple, alert to report any suggestion of blasphemy or conflict with the Law. This was not unusual. Wandering messiahs were always under surveillance, though most were considered harmless. But this one! Jesus was not only related to John; he had multitudes at his heels. Already they had challenged him about healing on the Sabbath.

Crowds followed him everywhere, so great he and his little party sometimes dared not enter a town but must sleep in the fields. The people were frantic to get near him—or even the six young men who traveled with him. Begging them to come for supper or to spend the night, for such an honor would bless their homes.

Eager eyes followed them, so young and attractive they seemed (even the eldest, Simon Peter) to be so serious, so dedicated—and yet so merry, their eyes shining with the joy and pride of serving such a hero. His aides, his bodyguards and companions, able to witness his miracles every day. Jesus smiled to think of them: Andrew and Simon Peter, Philip and Bartholomew, James and John. Never had these simple fishermen enjoyed so much attention. And they knew that others envied them. For as the followers multiplied, many begged to join their ranks.

"Master, Master, I will give up everything for you. Take me!"

Jesus listened to each one carefully. For however fervent and loyal his band, there just were not enough of them to handle everything. And the word must be carried farther. Especially now, with John in prison. Jesus thought with anxiety and pain of John. So much to do and so little time. But few of those who came to him were really ready: "I must first go bury my father." "When I have finished my harvest." "Must I really sell all my possessions? I am a very rich man."

"Now go to your homes and rest," Jesus told Peter and the others the night they returned to Capernaum. "But come to my house tomorrow. I will have important news for you."

Peter lingered, there on the lakeshore, where they were parting. He was thirty-four years old, not much older than Jesus, but as the eldest he had assumed the role of father and protector to this man who offered the bread of life to others but himself sometimes forgot to eat. "Promise me you, too, will rest," Peter said. His burly face was anxious. "You need it most of all."

Jesus drew a deep breath. Peter was right. Every bone in his body ached; he felt drained. Yet there was something that must be done before the avalanche swallowed them up again. "I must first go into the hills and pray," he said. "Only the Father can help me with the decisions I must make now."

"But you are so weary. Let me go with you and watch."

"No; go home to your wife." Jesus pressed his heavy shoulder. "All I ask, Peter, is that you support me when I tell the others . . . for that is what I must pray about—the new men we must have to go with us and do our work."

Simon Peter swallowed. He had seen this coming, known it was inevitable, yet he couldn't help a pang of disappointment. They had been so close these past exciting weeks, the chosen few, like a proud family. "Lord, Lord," he declared stoically, "you know you can depend on me to stand by you, whatever you do."

It was late afternoon when the six gathered, to perch uneasily on the rocks that surrounded Jesus' house. There had been much to tell their families, and many things to attend to; they were also very tired. Rested now, they were bursting with curiosity. Peter, unable to keep his counsel, had warned them, and like him they were taken aback at the news. They had come to feel possessive of Jesus. To share him with the multitudes was one thing, but to share their intimate circle with newcomers seemed somehow an invasion.

Arms folded, Jesus stood before them, his hair blowing about his shoulders from the wind across the lake. He sensed their expectancy and their apprehension, and as he spoke, his heart went out to them. "I have chosen our new fellow workers," he told them. "From now on there will be twelve of you."

"Twelve!" Philip gasped. He exchanged astonished glances with Andrew and Bartholomew. "But why so many? We, here"—he made a dismayed little gesture that included the twins and Peter—"have we not served you well?"

"None could have served me better. Or will ever become as dear to me. But the fields are ripe and we must have enough laborers for the harvest. All night I have prayed, and the Father was revealed them to me. Soon I will tell you who they are. But first I have called you here to thank you. Jesus turned to each one then, addressing him by name, to reassure him.

"You, Andrew, my friend, my first disciple: Except for you, Peter and the twins would not be here. . . . Philip, Bartholomew, Andrew— I will never forget our first journey to Jerusalem together. How bravely you baptized for me after the arrest of John. You even risked coming home through Samaria with me. And you won the hearts of the Samaritans on the way!"

Andrew's heart raced. He was trying to keep his composure, pleased, yet with a wistful sense of envy and loss. Yet it is my brother Peter you most often walk with, he thought as Jesus praised him; whom you confer with at night as you once conferred with me. And it's those scalawags, the twins, that seem to give you the most delight. He harbored no resentment, however; his long, pleasantly homely face was resigned.

"And what a treasure you brought me in your brother Simon Peter," Jesus continued. "Peter, you live up to your name: You are truly a rock. And James and John"—Jesus was smiling—"you have brightened every mile we have taken together. But now we must have help. The message I have been sent to bring the world is too important to be confined to so few. You will be twelve in number, like the twelve tribes of Israel. And, like the patriarchs before us, you will be empowered to establish the new kingdom of God on earth."

Jesus paused. "I know this sounds awesome, and it is. But you will suffer many hardships," he told them, "and your responsibilities will be great. From now on you will be called apostles—messengers. For in time you will be sent forth, in pairs, to carry the word. By then you too will be given the power of healing."

There was a moment of stunned silence.

"All of us?" John exclaimed. He felt suddenly young and vulnerable, unworthy, almost alarmed. "Even the newcomers like James and me?"

"With faith you will be able to do all I have done, and more. All of you," Jesus said firmly. "It is a power that cannot be given lightly. That is why my Father and I have chosen so carefully those who will join us. So that you, all of you, will be worthy of such a gift. And strong enough," he reminded them, "to meet its demands."

The men were staggered. They stared at him, incredulous—suddenly ashamed of their selfish misgivings. *Healing?* Had Jesus actually said they, too, might one day have such power? To be able to perform miracles, such as they had witnessed! Shaken, they exchanged astonished glances.

Now, slowly, clearly, Jesus gave them the promised names. Some they would recognize. He invited their honest reactions. "We will discuss them together, for you are my family, and there must be no secrets among us."

Thomas. Peter, Andrew and Philip all could vouch for him; they had played and fished together along the wharves as boys. Thomas was careful, took nothing for granted. "Like Bartholomew," Peter said, grinning. "But once he's convinced, you won't find anybody braver or more loyal."

Thaddeus. A musician, born in Edessa but living in Jerusalem when he was first attracted to John. Andrew remembered seeing him among the crowd along the Jordan the day Jesus was baptized. And now that John was in prison, he had followed Jesus to Capernaum. He was merry, fluent and fervent; some of them had heard him playing his lute and singing in the inn. His songs would enliven their journeys.

Simon the Zealot. Simon Peter was troubled at first. The Zealots were a radical bunch. "Anyone who would join them could get us in trouble." And there was the problem of having a similar name. "Hereafter we will always call you Peter," Jesus said. "As for having a Zealot among us—we are zealots too, in our own way. We can profit by his experience."

James, the younger son of Alpheus, a greatly respected town official. Of James there could be no question. His reputation was above reproach. He was fair and slight of build, with a kind of eternal innocence in his rosy cheeks. He could be identified as James the younger; it was fitting, and it would avoid confusion with the other James. Like his parents, James was very devout. And like them, he was deeply ashamed that his older brother Matthew should have become a despised tax collector.

Matthew, sometimes known as Levi, the publican. And *Judas Iscariot.* These were the only two who roused their actual concern.

"But, Master, a tax collector?" There was a mass gasp, a long, horrified silence. "Would you ask us to eat at the same table with such a vulture?" Peter finally blurted. "A Jew who robs his own people to work for Rome?"

"Matthew has repented," Jesus said gently. "He has closed his booth at the customs, and is even now preparing to make amends before he comes with us."

"But to be seen with such a sinner," Andrew protested. "To make him one of us!" He couldn't believe it. Dismayed, feeling responsible, he looked about at his friends, at his own brother—so willing to follow this man, give up so much. Jesus was right; except for him, they probably wouldn't be here. It seemed imperative that no mistakes be made now. For their sake, as well as that of the Master, he must speak up, hard as this was for him. "Forgive me, I know we're not perfect, any of us. But if we are to preach," he faltered, "if—if we are actually even to *heal*! surely we must set a good example. How—forgive me, but I must ask—how can we afford to consort with sinners?"

Jesus listened, nodding his understanding. He couldn't blame them. Yet his voice, however compassionate, was firm. "Pray heaven many sinners *will* follow us. Those who are well have no need of a physician, but those who are sick . . . We must not shun them, we must make them welcome, no matter how we are criticized. Remember, it is not the righteous we are called to save. Matthew needs us," he went on. "We can help him. And Matthew can help us."

But of all the names, it was that of Judas Iscariot that caused the most consternation. Especially to James and John. They had known Judas in synagogue school. A brilliant scholar, yes; but vain, aggressive, determined to surpass everyone else. And sly, very sly, always trying to ingratiate himself with the teacher. He was also very handsome, with a quick, sharp wit that charmed people; yet his very greed to excel, be praised, put a kind of torment in his long dark eyes. He did not deserve this honor; he could only cause trouble.

Both brothers felt apprehensive, threatened, almost stunned. How could Jesus be so blind? And Jesus was theirs. They had found him first. Their claim had been established. Ever since that night they first heard him speaking with such fiery affection and wisdom to the crowds from Peter's boat. And later, during the mad hours of fishing—to find him singing and whooping as joyously as Peter, helping to throw the nets and haul them in. How they had admired him even then.

And to have him seek them out the next day! The two would always marvel at this. The instant rapport between them, the sense of some deep recognition of spirit that went beyond mind or body, anything they had ever dreamed. They knew, with a kind of blind finality, that they would follow him through hell if he asked. For they loved one another, these three. True, Jesus loved them all, and was particularly close to Peter. But the brothers knew they were special to him.

And the sense of some sublime communion was keenest between Jesus and John.

In the heat of their discussion, the men had gotten up from their rocky perches, or the places where they had been squatting on the sand, and were meandering about the little yard. James had braced himself against one of the few palm trees, gesturing with one hand. The sun was going down, the breeze was stronger. Behind his words the palm leaves clashed their patient rhythms. As usual, John stood back, wearing his enigmatic little smile, and let James do most of the talking. But a nameless fear clutched his heart. Some strange, chill sense of foreboding.

And when the others began to trudge down the hill toward their homes, he told James to go on without him. "I want to speak with him alone."

He went to crouch beside Jesus, who had gone to sit on the big rock Peter had occupied. He was gazing out upon the water. It was blue-gray but sparkling, and ruffled with white as the waves rolled in. The dog lay alert at his feet.

"Master, I beg you to reconsider." Absently, to relieve his anxiety, John stroked Ben's smooth brown coat. "I have a strange fear for you. I know Judas too well; I really don't think he's to be trusted."

Jesus roused, turned to regard him, but it was a moment before he replied. "I am well aware of Judas' faults," he said. "But he needs us. We can help him, as we will help Matthew . . . And we need *him*. Both Matthew and Judas can help us, John. Both of them are good writers, and skilled with figures. They can help us manage what little money we have."

"It's only because we love you so much," John said wretchedly. "We feel we must warn you."

"I already know," Jesus said quietly. A dark pain clutched his heart. He, too, bent to pet the dog. "Judas is still my choice, and for me it is the right one."

Chapter 5

*P*ETER squatted on his heels. His feet were hurting, he was sweating profusely, and hoping desperately that after this little rest, Jesus would dispense with his usual sermon and simply dismiss the crowds.

The morning had dawned cool and clear. But by the time they had reached this grassy hillside the sun was already fierce, and by noon it was a forge, its heat growing more insufferable during the long hours of trying to control the people, all of them struggling frantically to get near the place where Jesus was healing. The Master, patient and caring as always, had seemed impervious to the terrible heat; although Peter, occasionally carrying a cup of water to him (he refused to eat even a morsel), noticed that his white garment was drenched.

Peter mopped his streaming face with his sleeve. The crowds still spilled up and down the hillside and the adjoining slopes, like a vast colorful field of flowers. They were quieter now that the healings were over, but sitting expectant, reluctant to leave. Grudgingly, feeling puzzled and surprised, Peter had to admit that Judas had been one of the most effective in keeping order. All twelve had helped. (The Master had been right; they had reached a point where today's events might have been impossible without them.) But Judas! While the rest of them had to charge about, physically holding people back sometimes, this intense young man with the dark burning eyes had simply circled among them, somehow charming them into awaiting their turns. Never mind that Peter found him personally obnoxious; for now he had to acknowledge this arrogant newcomer's usefulness.

Judas, squatting on Peter's right, was shaking his head in amazement. "Where do all these people *come* from?"

Peter stiffened, until he realized that the voice, pleasantly nasal, had not been mocking. Judas answered his own question. "Why, that man with the epileptic son—clear from Damascus, he told me!"

"It's that way wherever we go," Peter said with satisfaction. "Sometimes we have to put out in a boat lest he be crushed."

With one accord they turned to regard Jesus. They had persuaded him to rest awhile in the shade of a cypress tree a little way above them. He sat bent forward, his head in his arms.

"All those healings." Peter fretted gruffly. "He's done enough; he should send them home now. I hope I can persuade him."

"I have never seen such a man," Judas marveled softly. "I never dreamed! The way he touches them—are you sure it's safe? He embraces even the lepers. Isn't he afraid of contamination?"

"He is afraid of nothing," said Peter.

"I couldn't do it."

"You," said Peter curtly, "are not the son of the living God."

He rose, striving to repress or even understand his feeling of hostility. Their eyes held for a second. Peter marched up the slope then, to crouch beside Jesus. "Here, I have brought you more water." He was pouring a cup from the bag at his girdle. "Master, it is so hot, even now when the sun is lower. You have healed them all—every infirmity among them—they are claiming. Even those who couldn't get near you!" he exclaimed, still astonished. "Never has there been such a miracle. You have done enough; they expect nothing more. Only to see you again and to have your blessing. Please dismiss them now and come home with me to eat and sleep. Adah will have our supper waiting."

Jesus had cast off the white mantle that covered his sweaty tunic. It touched Peter to see it so rumpled and stained where it lay on the grass, Ben's head resting blissfully upon it. It was soiled with tears and sweat, even the blood of some of those Jesus had pressed to his heart as he healed them. Peter's throat ached suddenly. He must have Adah wash it. She would want to . . . . At first there had been a terrible row with Adah, even after the curing of her mother; but finally his wife had yielded. Now she couldn't do enough for Jesus. She fussed over him, the way she still did with Andrew; in some ways they had become the sons she'd never had.

Jesus straightened, gulped the water gratefully, and held out the cup for more, to splash on his face and hands. The murmuring of the crowd came to them, like a gentle humming of distant bees. The leaves trembled, flakes of light danced across his countenance. Jesus was smiling, looking not only rested, it seemed to Peter, but radiant: even more vigorous than before he began his arduous labors this morning.

Jesus had been meditating. Now he rose, stretched, and hot as it was, picked up the long white mantle with its fringe of blue tassels; he shook it and began to tie it at one shoulder. Once more the dignified rabbi, handsome, serene.

Peter watched proudly, despite his concern. How broad Jesus' shoulders were; and his arms, with their heavy hairs, so brown. Yet for a second Jesus seemed to him like a child, fumbling with the cloth. Wordlessly Peter stepped forward, and with his own big rough hands retied the knot. "Master, please—" he muttered.

Jesus embraced him. "Peter, can't you understand?" His voice was affectionate even in reproof. "How can you ask me not to speak to the people today? For it isn't their bodies I have come to save, but their souls. Now more than ever they must be made to realize that— yes, and you too, Peter. And certainly the new apostles. Oh, there is so much I must teach you."

A wheel of butterflies—lake ladies, they were called—danced about him as he strode down the hill a little way, to the chosen spot. Peter saw Jesus raise a white-sleeved hand, reaching out to them with a kind of whimsical love and joy, as if to caress them, or even direct their dancing as he walked. The dog bounded eagerly beside him, and when Jesus reached the place, settled down at his feet. Here a rock outcropping formed a platform that faced the natural amphitheater of the surrounding hills. Here the acoustics were so perfect that no matter how far away the audience, every word could be distinctly heard.

The lake sparkled in the descending sun. The hills were turning to violet. The low humming of the people's voices ceased; a great silence had come upon them, a sense of awed expectation. And it was like the miracle of all-pervasive healing that had touched and cleansed them earlier, every one. For now, though they spilled down to the very water's edge, most of them simple people with their families— fishermen, farmers, laborers, tradesmen—each one could see Jesus vividly—his tall strength, his great beauty, his garments dazzling white and stirring faintly in the breeze that blew up fresh and cool now from the lake—and hear the words that fell like notes of music from his lips.

Lifting his arms and smiling, Jesus began to bless them. For the Holy Spirit was upon him. And all sat rapt, enthralled.

"Blessed are the poor in spirit," he told them, "for theirs is the kingdom of heaven.

"Blessed are those who mourn, for they shall be comforted.

"Blessed are the meek, for they shall inherit the earth. . . . "

The people leaned forward, excited, instantly recognizing the scriptures to which he was alluding. Yes, yes—hadn't Isaiah said the same? They nodded their heads in agreement. That God would look with favor on him who is poor and of a contrite spirit. . . . And the thirty-fourth Psalm of David: *The Lord is near unto those who have a broken heart, and saves those who have a contrite spirit.* . . .

To be poor in spirit, they knew, was to turn to God, repenting of their sins, and he would forgive them and welcome them joyfully into his kingdom. And to mourn meant much the same: Brokenhearted, at the end of human strength, crying out to God in despair, yet the Father would accept them no matter what their failures; he would comfort them, he would save them.

As for the meek: "the meek" meant "the righteous." Jesus was reminding them of the psalm that said: *For yet a little while, and the wicked shall not be* . . . *but the meek shall inherit the earth and delight themselves in the abundance of peace.* . . .

To mourn for your sins, to be meek and poor in spirit, all really meant the same—to be *righteous.* In Hebrew, *tsedakah,* "right with God, living an upright life"—and one that was not merely holy but also generous and giving.

"Blessed are those who hunger and thirst after righteousness," Jesus continued, "for they shall be filled.

"Blessed are the merciful, for they shall obtain mercy.

"Blessed are the pure in heart, for they shall see God."

The apostles had formed their usual semicircle around him, both to observe him and to protect him from the crowd. Jesus focused his attention on them now, particularly James and John. His eyes twinkled. Despite their own first objections, they had done their best to reconcile Peter and Judas. "Blessed are you who are peacemakers," he said, "for you shall be called the sons of God.

"Blessed are those who pursue righteousness, for theirs is the kingdom of heaven. Blessed are you," he said, still primarily addressing the twelve, "when men revile you and persecute you and utter all kind of evil, lying tales about you because of me. As they will, you can be sure. Rejoice, consider it an honor; remember that is exactly how they persecuted the prophets before you."

Jesus' eyes and his words went back to the hushed crowd. "You are the salt of the earth," he told them. "You give it flavor. You are the light of the world."

The sun was setting, pouring its gold across the sky before it sank into the sea. The mountains were deeper in shadow. Jesus gestured toward the north. "Look up there, toward Zephath. A city set on a hill cannot be hid. Watch, soon we will see the lights of Zephath come on, as the women light their lamps. Not to hide in a closet—that would be foolish—but rather to glow in the darkness for all to see. Their lights will help and guide others. Let your own life be like that. Don't hide your lights. Let your good deeds shine as an example for all to see. Not to glorify yourselves but to glorify the Father, who wants us to light the way through the darkness for each other."

His tone changed, his words rang out now, no less friendly but firm. "You must not think I have come to abolish the Law and ignore the warnings of the prophets. No, no—despite all you may have heard of me, that is not true! Everything I say and do is based on these things. I have come to fulfill that Law, in the way the Father intended. Every one of God's laws is sacred; the commandments must be taught, and obeyed.

"But don't be misled," he warned. "Unless your goodness far exceeds the hypocrisy of the scribes and Pharisees—even the *priests*—" he cried scornfully, "you will never enter the kingdom of heaven!"

The people had been sitting transfixed. Now for the first time they stirred and glanced uncomfortably about. For there were always religious leaders among them—rabbis, scholars, heads of the synagogue—some of them genuine admirers' but others deliberately planted by the Sanhedrin to report such remarks. The apostles nudged each other and frowned, indicating a little group standing apart from common people. Conspicuous in the headdresses and black robes that marked their status, and carrying slates and scrolls to be consulted, these judges, scribes and interpreters of the Law were making no secret of their mission.

Jesus plunged on. "Now let me tell you what our heavenly Father really means by the laws we have tried so hard, but often so mistakenly, to follow. The blind leading the blind!" he cried. "Because our judges and even our teachers understand the letter of the Law—yes, but not the great spirit behind it." And for an hour or more, Jesus named the laws, elaborating on each, while the people and the authorities listened, dismayed or thrilled or shocked.

"The law of Moses said, 'You shall not kill; if you do you are in danger of the judgment.' But I say unto you that anyone who is even angry with his brother and insults him by calling him *raca*—fool—is in danger of hell."

Again his audience quickened, remembering the words of the psalm: *The fool has said in his heart, "There is no God."*

"For one who makes such a libelous statement is assuming the role of God," Jesus went on to explain. "And condemning that person to judgment. . . .

"You have heard that it was said, 'You shall not commit adultery.' But I say to you that anyone who even looks at a woman with lust—an ungovernable desire to possess her—has already committed adultery with her in his heart. . . .

"And what does the Law of Moses say about divorce? That if a man wants to get rid of his wife, all he has to do is give her a bill of divorcement. Dismiss her with a letter—a piece of paper!" Jesus' voice shook, remembering the agonizing experience of his mother's sister, Aunt Salome. "He can do this even if she has never been untrue to him. I say unto you, whoever divorces his wife except for the cause of adultery is committing a grave sin. And it is cruelly unfair to her, for she is still his wife in the sight of God."

The first stars were beginning to sparkle. On the slate-blue lake some of Zebedee's fishing boats were being launched. The lights of Zephath could indeed be seen now, as well as the lights of Capernaum, where suppers were being cooked. Yet no one moved. They would never remember all that this amazing man was saying—not even those closest to Jesus—but the primary points of his message would be engraved on their hearts forever.

"The law of Moses taught, 'An eye for an eye and a tooth for a tooth.' I say unto you, God does not want us to repay evil with evil, but rather to counter it with good. If someone strikes you on one cheek, turn to him the other also. And if someone steals your robe, give him your cloak as well." Demonstrating as he spoke, Jesus untied his own long, tasseled garment and tossed it to James. "And if the soldiers order you to carry their gear for a mile, carry it two. This is not only kindness, it is common sense, for they will treat you better in the long run. If we examine the laws of our Father rightly, we will find they are designed not to repress us but to free us. Share what you have, give generously to the needy. Yes, this pleases our Father, but it will give you great happiness as well. . . .

"You have heard it said, 'You shall love your neighbor, and hate your enemy,' but I say unto you *love* your enemies, *pray* for those who treat you unfairly! The Father who made us loves us all, we are his children, good and bad. He sends the sun and the rain on both of us. For if you love only those who love you, what reward have you? Isn't that what sinners and pagans do? You will be no better than they are. No, God wants us to be like him, to love each other as he loves us, no matter what is done."

Again, in tones of gentle indignation, Jesus attacked the hypocrites. Beware of their example, he warned—calling attention to their good deeds in order to be praised by men; praying loudly in the synagogues and the Temple and on the streets. Even disfiguring their faces when they fast, in order to be seen. Why should God reward them? "Truly I say to you, they already *have* their reward!

"Don't lay up treasures for yourselves on earth, where moths and rust destroy and thieves break through and steal, but lay up treasures in heaven. . . . For where your treasure is, there will your heart be also.

"The eye is the lamp of the body. So if your eye is generous, your whole body will be full of light. But if your eye is stingy, mean and selfish, your whole body will be full of darkness. . . . "

Some of the things he was saying were familiar, based on ancient laws he did not challenge. "Judge not that you be not judged. . . . Do unto other people only the things you would want them to do to you. . . . " John the Baptist had preached them, and so had the Essenes. Yet in the magic of Jesus' voice ringing out there on the hillside, where night had fallen so swiftly, sweet and cool under the stars, everything seemed new and thrilling, under a spell. The lingering band of scarlet across the horizon, the dew, the damp fragrance of wild flowers and earth and trampled grass, the children asleep in their parents' arms—all, all had a quality of freshness and discovery, as if none of this had ever been seen or sensed before. The man's words came thrilling into the people, stirring their blood, generating new life.

Peter sat with his chin in his hands, listening as intently as he had that first night in his boat.

"No one can serve two masters," Jesus was declaring. "For he will hate the one and love the other . . . you cannot serve God and money." It seemed to Peter that Judas winced; all those hints about his father's wealth. Peter looked at him sharply—at the bold yet secretive olive face beside him. For the first time he noticed the scar that branched mysteriously from Judas' mouth; oddly, it only made him more attractive. Peter was jolted. He must try to love this man, as Jesus said. And who's to judge? Hadn't the master just said we must not judge?

"Therefore, I tell you, do not be anxious about your life, what you shall eat or what you shall drink; nor about your body, what you shall put on. Is not life more than food, and the body more than clothing?"

Peter was jolted. It was almost like an echo. He'd said almost the same things to Adah, or tried to, during those long arguments about what they would live on if he left. And James and John—he'd heard them pleading in the same way with Zebedee. Not as eloquently, of course . . . He gazed down on the water. Some of Zebedee's boats were halfway across the lake now; he'd taken on other partners. Peter could see their lights. The fish were jumping . . . it would be a good night for fishing. Peter swallowed; his eyes strayed to his other companions. The words applied to them too. They'd risked it, given up everything they depended on, to throw in their lot with Jesus, and it would work out, it had to. Don't worry, as Jesus was saying, don't be anxious. . . .

Insects were singing and chirping in the grass; cranes waded in the weeds along the shore, night birds were dipping. Jesus paused a moment, his hands on his hips. Two great white herons lifted slowly from the rushes, flapping their magnificent fanlike wings. Head back, smiling, Jesus watched, and as they coasted off, he lifted his arms to wave at them. "Look at the birds of the air!" he marveled. "They neither sow nor reap nor gather grains, and yet your heavenly Father feeds them. Are you not of more value than they?" he asked. "Which of you by being anxious can add one minute to his span of life? And why are you anxious about your clothing? Consider the lilies of the field. In the spring these very hills are covered with such colors as even Solomon had never worn. Flowers toil not, neither do they spin, yet even Solomon in all his glory never was arrayed like one of these! Surely, if God so clothes the grasses, which today are alive and to-morrow are only thrown into the ovens for fuel, will he not much more generously clothe you?

"Oh, my children, have more faith! Ask and you shall receive, seek and you shall find, knock and the door will be opened to you. But seek first the kingdom and God's righteousness, and all these things shall be yours as well. . . . "

Jesus said many more things that night, but at last it was over, concluding with a little story the first six recognized. For they had stood with him one stormy night, watching helplessly as a flimsy house that had been built on the sands collapsed and was swept out to sea. While the house they had found for him, built on the shelf of rock, stood fast. Andrew and Philip exchanged pleased glances. "Be like the man who built his house upon solid ground," Jesus warned. "Heed the words I have spoken to you, and follow them. If not, you will be like that foolish man who built his house upon the sand, and all that you possess and hold dear will be swept away."

Then, spreading his arms like the majestic white wings of the herons, he sang out the beautiful blessing.

Quickly the apostles surrounded Jesus.

For these first few minutes the people were still in the thrall of his words, too amazed to move; never had they heard anyone speak with such authority, especially a rabbi so young. But soon they would be pouring down the hillsides, eager for another glimpse of him, ready to besiege him, even to follow him home.

"This way, come with us!" James and John scurried ahead, break-ing a path through some thickets along a little-used trail that led down to the water. With Andrew, they had come earlier and chosen it for Jesus' escape.

Peter tramped close behind them. The path was strewn with shells and shards of pottery, which glittered in the moonlight filtering through the trees. Nearby, some ancient pagan temple had collapsed; broken columns and paving stones lay ghostlike among the shadows. They skirted an abandoned wooden boat, overturned, rotting, half overgrown with vines. There was the acrid smell of ferns and weeds, and from below, the tang of fish and water. Descending, they could see the moonlight white upon the sand.

Jesus followed docilely, feeling their concern for his fatigue. Yet he felt wonderful. The day's long hours of healing had actually given him strength. Each act of healing seemed to regenerate him, relieving him as it did of his own agony at people's suffering. When the crippled rose up astonished, he rose up too, in delight and affirmation. When the blind saw, it was as if a new world was born to his own vision, vibrant with color and clarity. The leaves had never been so sharply honed, the flowers so vivid, the faces of children so beautiful. He felt a little bit guilty that Peter, the twins, and even the new men, particularly Judas, were so solicitous of his well-being, urging him to rest, bringing him figs or cups of water all day.

They didn't realize that when he sat beneath the tree, or lay supine upon the grass, he had been communing with his Father. That a great sweet spirit had invaded his being, stirring him to impassioned words for the multitude that blanketed the hillsides, together with an inordinate sense of aid and compassion. Now, with a kind of bemused but gentle obedience, Jesus followed Peter and the others, so eager and proud to protect him. Part of him sang with the joy of the day's accomplishment; another part longed only for the sweet oblivion of sleep.

The plan was to hasten Jesus along the deserted beach to Peter's house. The apostles were all tired and hungry, drained from the day's work and excitement, yet, like the people, still under the spell of his words, and elated at being his guardians, spiriting him away.

"My wife will have a hot supper for us," Peter told Jesus. "All your favorite foods. You must keep up your strength—you've eaten almost nothing all day."

Peter halted abruptly, startled to see the two figures that stepped from behind some rocks on the beach ahead. He moved in front of Jesus, lifting a warning hand to the others. There would be no avoiding them; they were already approaching, one man tall and gaunt, in a hooded cloak; the other younger, of mid-stature.

"Peace! Forgive us." Both appeared apologetic, yet determined. "We know your Master must be weary—"

Peter opened his mouth, but before he could respond, Judas sprang forward, briskly officious. "Our Lord is indeed! He has been serving the people all day, healing, preaching. Surely whatever you have to ask can wait until tomorrow."

"We have little time," the older man said with great dignity. "For we have come from John. We have come all the way from where John is imprisoned."

"John!" Jesus cried out. He pushed past Judas to embrace them. "John the Baptist? Then you are his disciples."

The two men nodded. "John has sent us here with a message for you, Master." Their names were Daniel and Rapha, they said. "We were among the first to be baptized by your cousin. And we were with him when they arrested him. We found out where they were taking him—to the fortress palace at Machaerus, near the Dead Sea—and followed him there."

"Then you have seen him!" Jesus exclaimed. "Tell me, how is it with my cousin John?"

"John isn't well," said the older man, Daniel. His long gentle face was grave. "They feed him very little and keep him in chains. You wouldn't know him: that great body of his starved and chained—chained to the bench on which he must sit, chained to a wall. That wild spirit—" His voice broke; he had to look away.

"We fear John is getting discouraged—and confused," his companion, Rapha, said. "Herod visits him almost daily. Partly to bait him, we're convinced. Sometimes pretending to repent of his sins." He gave a bitter laugh. "But he will never give up his brother's wife, Herodias, as John insists."

The other men had crowded around, appalled at what they were hearing, especially the four who had been among John's first disciples.

"John would never compromise," said Jesus. "Even if his life were in danger."

"As it may well be." Daniel had regained his composure. "We think Herod is really afraid of John. The things John preaches about God's judgment. And his claims about the Messiah. How the true

Messiah will change everything, bring everyone to justice." Daniel hesitated, concerned. "Jesus, we must tell you—Herod repeatedly questions John about you."

"John must say no more," Jesus said quickly. "Warn him—not for my sake, but for his own safety—to keep silent. But tell me, why did John send you here?"

The two men looked at each other uneasily. The older cleared his throat. "Remember, John is not himself," he pleaded. "So you must try to understand—forgive him for the question that he could ask only in weakness and despair."

Jesus gasped. "John has no need to be forgiven by anyone," he protested. "I tell you, of all men born to women, there is not one greater than John."

The two were gazing at Jesus soberly, still hesitant, not wishing to utter the question. For they, too, had been in the crowd since morning, awed before his miracles, deeply moved by his sermon. Finally, lifting his chin and throwing back his narrow shoulders, Daniel said, "This is the question that is troubling John the Baptist. These are the words he has sent us here to ask: Are you the one who is to come, or need we go on looking for another?"

Jesus plunged his face into his hands, then, turning abruptly, he walked to the water's edge. The vast harp-shaped lake was molten silver; its waves lipped the sand. For a time he stood there with his back to them. . . . John, oh, my poor cousin—you who have known me best, you who are dearer to me than my own brothers. How have they broken you that you should doubt now? . . . And he saw again the bold, bright boy at Ein Karem, striding the chamber, informing him so fervently, to his own astonishment: "You *know*, you must always have known—*you are the Messiah!*" And all the pronouncements later at the river; at the very hour of his baptism, the sweet impassioned words of confirmation: "The one of whom I speak is here among you now. Behold the lamb of God!"

John, who had dedicated his life to this. John, the child of prophecy, his forerunner, the "voice crying in the wilderness"—to think of him now, defeated, discouraged, no longer certain, groping out like a disillusioned, bewildered old man. Asking, in essence, "Are you truly the *Habah*, the king that is to come? The Messiah will have salvation in his hands. Are you truly the Messiah?"

Jesus' shoulders shook. Never, despite all the human misery he had seen—never had he felt such pity for anyone.

At last he came back across the glittering sand. His eyes were still wet, but he managed to smile. Kissing Daniel and Rapha on each cheek, he said, "Take this kiss of love back to my cousin. Go and tell John his predictions are right, all the things he has done to prepare for me have not been in vain. Tell him in the words of Isaiah what you yourselves have seen. The blind receive their sight, the lame walk, the deaf hear, lepers are made clean. The dead, too, are raised up."

Both messengers nodded. They had heard excited talk of this last astounding miracle. The only son of a widow in Nain, actually on his bier, being carried to the grave!

"The poor have good news preached to them. And blessed are those who hear what I say and believe in me. Go now and tell these things to my beloved cousin, that he, too, may have the comfort of believing."

The apostles also embraced the men as they prepared to depart, walking along the beach with them and sending words of encouragement to John. Those who had known him so well—Andrew, Philip, Bartholomew and Thaddeus—asked to be remembered to John by name.

"If only you would stay longer, tell us more," Peter urged. "Won't you at least consider coming home with us for food before you leave?"

No, their mounts were waiting, they said. They could ride a few hours tonight; the quicker they reached John the better. Relieved, but still deeply concerned, they turned again to Jesus. "Your words will mean so much to John. He must have them—while there is still time."

Anxious, frustrated, deeply concerned, the little group stood a few moments longer beside the water, watching the two climb the hill. There was a neighing sound from the thickets; presently two mounted figures emerged, and waved as they rode away.

Chapter 6

PETER'S wife, Adah, was childless, to her sorrow, but not to her disgrace. Adah was independent; she refused to accept blame for that which the Lord had willed. She loved Simon Peter, and he seemed to love her none the less for her barren state. In a way that was unusual to most couples, they were very close. They "matched," she sometimes thought, to her own amusement. Both very large people, both forthright, a trifle impetuous, yet with their feet on the ground.

This thing now—this incredible thing that had gotten her husband so aroused . . . The *Messiah*? The true Deliverer at last? That thought was too staggering; she dismissed it. Never mind, no matter really; Jesus had captured the heart of her husband, and that was enough. She would follow them both—what choice did she really have? To live alone with her mother? No, no, she could not bear the thought of having Peter's great body apart from hers another night. She had let him go thus far, not willingly but unable to voice the terrible pain that tore her.

Now that Peter had proposed it himself, she would simply go with them. Wherever the strange path led.

"Mother, I'm leaving," she announced one morning. "They are setting forth again tomorrow. I must be with them."

Her mother, Esther, looked up from threading her loom—a surprisingly dainty, fine-featured little woman, compared to her husky daughter. "Is it your husband you are following?" she asked sharply. "Or—that man?"

"Both," Adah told her. "Men!" She laughed, on a note of disdainful good humor. "I will cook and mend for them. His garments—

did you notice the tears?—and those broken sandals. And him a rabbi! He's like a child—worse than Andrew was. No, no, I cannot have it."

"Ha! He is as old as Simon Peter."

"He needs me. They all need me. Yes, you need me too, but not like this. You're well now, stronger than ever, thanks to Jesus. Better than I've ever seen you. It's the least I can do for him and Peter."

"But you—alone with all those *men?*"

"I won't be alone, Mother. Mary, the mother of one of the new men—James the younger, they call him—will join us in Magdala. And soon, if all goes well, the twins' mother."

"Not Zebedee's wife? Not Salome! No, no, I can't believe this. Zebedee would never stand for it. Who will cook for him?"

"The servants. Zebedee . . . you'd be surprised: He's concerned about his sons, actually relieved that their mother will be along from time to time to look after them. And there is some talk about a woman named Joanna. She has money, I think; she wants to help. There are sure to be others."

"I don't like it. Decent women don't go traveling around the country with men."

"Times have changed. The old order is passing, Mother. Jesus is bringing about a new order. Peter is convinced of it. He doesn't think things will ever be the same."

"How will you eat?" Esther worried. "Where will you sleep?"

"Mostly in the homes of believers. Peter tells me people beg for their company, wherever they go. It's an honor to associate with such a prophet. Mostly common people like ourselves, yes, but some of the rich people too, sometimes even the Pharisees."

Adah's mother was shaking her head. "I don't know, I still just don't know."

"But Jesus *healed* you, Mother. I don't believe you realize how sick you were, even now. You had a terrible fever, you hardly knew us, you were out of your head! He had only to kneel beside your couch . . . I can still see him, how he took your hand—oh, it was so hot, your whole body was like an oven; I'll never forget. Yet he had only to say a few words to you, and in a few moments you sat up! You were smiling, your brow was cool—I felt it. We all did. And then—surely you remember what happened?"

"Yes, yes, I remember. I got out of bed. I even got dressed and cooked your supper."

"We tried to restrain you, all of us. Even Jesus urged you to rest— but no, you were determined. It was good to see you so spirited again." She laughed. "That alone proved you were well. You insisted on showing us you could. And what a supper that was."

Her mother sat, arms folded, nodding in reluctant agreement. "Yes, yes, yes, it happened, it must have happened—look at me now," she exclaimed, amazed but frowning, still confused. "How do we know where such powers come from?" she fretted. "The evil one—it is said that Satan has strange powers too."

Adah was shocked. "No, no, *no!* How can you say such things?" she gasped. "That beautiful man. 'By their fruits you shall know them,' he has said. His fruits are good. He must be . . . such a man can only be . . . " Words failed her. What did she really think? What was she trying to express? Adah drew a deep breath: "A very gifted prophet," she managed.

"Well, I can't stop you. And if I were younger—" Her mother sprang up, smiling brightly, in a sudden change of mood. She even held out her arms: "I think if I were younger I might go with you!"

"Master!" Judas was bending over Jesus, breathing hard. His olive cheeks were flushed, his dark, narrow eyes excited. "Would you like to see the stoning of a woman?"

Jesus woke from his nap, startled, for an instant bewildered. Where were they? Oh, yes, Magdala. It was a hot afternoon; from the open windows came the redolent stench of the city, and the rising murmur of its voices. Then he was reaching for his clothes, springing to his feet.

"*See* it?" he shouted. "We must stop it!"

"But she is an adulteress, caught in the very act. You know the law about adultery. You'd better hurry," Judas flung over his shoulder, for he didn't want to miss this. "They have already dragged her into the street."

"And the man who was with her?" There was no answer from the departing disciple. But now from below Jesus could hear the voices growing louder, an angry clamor mixed with laughter, all male. He could hear no sounds from the woman.

Fury possessed him, blind and terrible. He looked helplessly around for a whip, anything he could piece together—he wanted to lash them, drive them away like the snarling dogs they were, although such a comparison was an injustice to Ben, who lay anxiously beside him, growling.

"Don't go," Andrew warned. He had roused up from his own pallet. "I know these people here. There are spies among them. I have heard talk; they may be trying to trap you. This could be a trick."

Jesus paused only to pat the dog and snatch up his mantle. Then he, too, was rushing down the steps.

It was a winding street of shops and stalls selling fruit, leather, jewelry, spices and the heavy perfumes favored by the city's many prostitutes. Its rich, fruity odors mingled with the smell of food, offal and animals from branching alleys. The shops and stalls were just reopening; sellers and customers stood on the sidewalk, curious, shielding their eyes, discussing the excitement. A crowd of men had gathered in a little circle at the end of the street. Others were scurrying to join them, some squatting to grope in the gutters for rocks. A few women, looking frightened but somewhat righteous, peered from doorways or windows.

Jesus ran. Reaching the group that surrounded the woman, he gave a little start of recognition. At its front was Abram, a prominent and portly judge, who'd traveled some distances to hear him, pretending interest. Beside him, grinning, were several Pharisees and other officials.

"Stop!" Jesus shouted.

He pushed past them. The woman had been flung face down in the dust. Only her long black hair covered her naked back. Someone, in a gesture of decency, perhaps another woman, had thrown a towel across her hips. Silently, Jesus unfastened his mantle and handed it to Andrew, who had raced behind him and now went quickly forward to cover her.

Her limbs were long and slender, her flesh dusky, smooth, albeit covered with small cruel marks. The men stood leering, hungry for blood yet reluctant to destroy a body made for pleasure, or even to have it hidden from them first. The men were shoving, trying to see over each other's shoulders. Even lying their mute, prone, helpless, disgraced, she gave an impression of great beauty.

"But, Teacher," one of the officials challenged, toying with the stones in his manicured fingers. He was tall and suave, a wrinkled, clever-looking man. "Would you break the Law of Moses, who commanded us to stone such a woman? Caught in the very act!"

"Yes, Rabbi, what do you say?" The judge winked at the others and chuckled, his round belly jiggling. "Speak up, advise us. You seem to know all the answers. Would you contradict this ancient law?"

Andrew had been right, Jesus realized. It was not righteous indignation that had moved these men to drag this poor woman here. They knew her well, had patronized her themselves. She was but the tool of his entrapment. They knew that he who had preached, "Blessed are the merciful" would never condone this savagery. Yet if he ordered them to break that law he would be guilty of the crime of heresy. They would have the right to lay hands on him instead.

For a long moment Jesus stood considering, as the jibes and taunts continued. Dogs were barking, there was the clatter of donkeys' hooves as two scared but thrilled boys rode by, big-eyed. "Stone her, stone her!" somebody yelled from a neighboring roof. Some people were laughing, but he could hear an old woman crying. A breeze stirred the dust. The woman herself made no sound and lay as still as if she were already dead.

Jesus regarded the men, who were growing impatient. His eyes burned into them, reading their secrets: That fat Pharisee, their spokesman, holding the biggest rock—only last night . . . And that clever fox beside him—for years he had betrayed his wife. . . . All but one or two of them—the maids they had ravaged, the loose woman with whom they had lain . . . The whole storm of their sins assaulted him, shook and sickened him. The smell of their lust, the taste of their desires. Their hypocrisy, their guilty fears, the lies they had told, the sly and jaunty boastings, the sacrifices to compensate, the secret torments in the night.

Man's nature. Jesus felt the tragedy of its evil, lacerating his own flesh. For was he not also a man? And for a moment, despite his outrage, he pitied them.

Jesus drew a long painful breath. Leaning over, to compose himself, he began to write with his finger on the ground.

"Come on, tell us, what shall we do with her?"

The crowd pressed closer, curious to read what he might be writing.

You shall not commit adultery.

Then slowly, with great dignity, he rose to face them. "First go find the man who shared her shame and bring him here to be punished. That, too, is the Law of Moses," he reminded them. "Then attend to this woman."

The men gasped; there was a rumble of angry astonishment. "I have not come to destroy the Law but to fulfill it," Jesus said sternly. "When the man has been executed, you who are sinless may deal with this woman. Those of you who are without this sin, remain. If they return, any one among you who is without this sin may cast the first stone."

Without further comment, Jesus turned his back and, crouching, began to write again. He could hear the men's voices, shocked, protesting, laughing nervously, or arguing hotly among themselves. A few still strove to see what he was writing; a horrifying possibility had struck them. The way this man had looked at them! How much did he really know about them? What else might he be putting down for all to see?

Finally, still grumbling, or joking to cover their embarrassment, one by one they walked away.

Jesus was aware of the woman, who stirred at last and sat up, wrapping herself in the garment he had brought. When he raised his eyes, she was standing before him. Her makeup was smeared, her face tear-streaked; even so, her beauty was overwhelming.

"What has happened to your accusers?" he asked. "Where are they? Is there no one left to condemn you?"

"No one, Lord," she muttered.

Rising, he took her hand. "Neither do I condemn you. Go, and do not sin again."

She hastened off, clutching the big garment around her. It was almost dark, lamps were being lit; more people had rushed onto the street. Fingers pointed; curious eyes followed her; there were whispers, laughter. Head hanging, she hurried past them, desperately hugging the garment, trying to hide herself.

Jesus' heart ached for her. Yet, though he had saved her life, and he knew there was more, far more, he must do for her, at that moment he could only stand there feeling helpless.

Then suddenly he saw Adah descending from the rooftop where she had watched. Huge, clumsy, amiable, kind, she almost bumped into the fleeing figure. But she held out her arms and caught her, this stranger, this sinner, and enfolded her. Sheltering her, shielding her. Head high, impervious to the stares and comments, Adah steered her through the arch leading to the courtyard of the small house they were using. "I am one of his followers," she was saying. "Come now, my darling, my poor little bird—you must not go back to your home just yet. Come with me, come to rest at least this night where you will be safe with us."

Jesus could not hear the words of comfort Adah was murmuring. He only knew that a woman had been sent to do and say what no man could right now. Not even himself . . . Only another woman.

The woman, who was known as Magdalene, ate with them that night. Her black hair was piled decently high now, her face scrubbed clean of the paint that had encircled her eyes and her full sensuous mouth.

In stubborn silence she had submitted to Adah's ministrations, Adah clucking and crooning as she bathed the beautiful body, careful of its bruises and lacerations, and rubbed it with oil, then brushed and arranged the flowing black fountain of hair.

"There now, don't you look the queen? See, here are some fresh underthings. Mine are much too big for you, ox that I am, but Joanna is slim like you, lucky thing. She has even lent us a dress that will become you."

Only then did Magdalene speak, and her voice was bitter. "Aren't you afraid I will sully these garments?"

Adah paused, the ghosts of pain haunting her cheerful face. "We are all sisters in need of forgiveness," she said. "And have we not all suffered at the hands of men?"

"*You?*"

Adah did not miss the note of contempt. She nodded, shuddering. . . . Her own father. Never told her mother; it would have killed her. Shrank at the sight of him. Never told anyone, not even Peter. Who'd have believed it? Awkward, overgrown—not pretty like her sister, who was really her father's favorite, but Fava would have told. . . . All the men who had rejected her . . . an embarrassment to her parents until finally Simon Peter's father made an offer of marriage. Peter, she knew sadly—defensive for him, wanting to comfort him—had been rejected several times himself. How they had needed each other, she and Peter; how they had learned to love each other. But sometimes even Peter! Stubborn, opinionated, given to sudden furies—or he had been until Jesus came along.

"Even me," Adah acknowledged shyly. "But none so lowly or ill in spirit that Jesus cannot heal and cleanse and make whole. You must speak to him," she urged. "Whatever has happened, or whatever is troubling you still, Jesus can resolve."

"How do you know this?" Magdalene demanded. Her eyes were hotly suspicious. "Who is he? Why should I trust him? True, the man saved me, but what are his motives? You here, you women who seem to belong to him—this woman whose dress I'm supposed to wear—" She snatched it from Adah's arms and regarded it cynically. It was of fine silken stuff, gold and green, imported from the Orient. "Who is she—his concubine?"

"No!" Adah protested. "He has no women, not like that. He is a man of God."

"Then who is this woman?"

"Her name is Joanna, wife of a steward of Herod."

"Herod? The monster who has put John the Baptist in prison? What is she doing *here*?"

"Yes—Herod. She has fled the palace. She has given up everything to follow Jesus, though it may mean the death of her husband as well."

"But why—*why*? I don't understand."

"You will," Adah promised. "Just listen to him. His message, the life he says we can live to find the kingdom of heaven right here on earth. And his message of forgiveness and salvation for the life to come. Oh, my dear Magdalene, tell him what is on your heart. Dress now; supper is almost ready, and when you have eaten with us, stay so that you may talk with him. I will arrange it."

Thus Magdalene sat dipping her bread with them, though keeping herself remote from them, silent and sullen, eyes downcast. Armed only with her incredible beauty. Still suspicious. These kind, decent people, what did they want with her? They knew what she was—a bitch rescued from the pack in the streets. These women who, to her surprise, had cooked and served the meal and then sat down as equals beside the men. Strange. They were like a big, cheerful family, praying together, singing the psalms. Then discussing their plans for the coming days as they ate.

It seemed some of the men were going out in pairs to neighboring towns. While their leader, with a few others, stayed behind. She stole a glance at Jesus, leading the discussion at the end of the table. They were to take no money, he told them, to her astonishment, and to receive no pay from anyone. A matter seriously questioned by two of the men, Matthew and Judas. And no wonder, she thought. Everybody had to have money. "Heal the sick, raise the dead, cleanse the lepers, cast out demons. You have received this gift without pay, you must give it without pay," Jesus insisted. Evidently they had been told all this before, but now he was making sure they understood. Magdalene was astounded. It didn't make sense. They would need money, no matter what he said; some people must help them. *I have money, I could help!*

Then she caught herself. What have I to do with them? I must leave as soon as I can. Yet she was tense, and heavy with dread . . . The men who might accost her on the street, the men who would surely be waiting at her door . . . This night friend or foe? How would she know? How could she ever trust another man? Men—ugly, loathsome, trying to devour her, crush her, kill her . . . Oh, she was sick unto death of men.

The windows were open onto the courtyard, where Peter had lighted a bonfire, for the night had turned cold. A breeze stirred the tablecloth, and brought the acrid-sweet smell of the fire's burning into the room. Jesus got up to shut the windows, then lifted his arms to lead the final prayer. Magdalene mumbled it with them, wondering miserably what to do.

The meal was over; the men began to disappear, the women were about to clear the table. She would help them, she decided, rising. But to her surprise, Jesus came to stand beside her. She had felt his gently encouraging eyes upon her from time to time all evening. Now he was smiling.

Adah was suddenly there too, holding a cloak.

"Come with me," Jesus said. "We will sit by the fire and talk."

"Go with him," Adah said, as Magdalene hesitated. Firmly Adah wrapped the cloak around her shoulders. "Go with him!"

They were still by the fire long after it had turned to ashes and the others slept.

"This was not the first time I have been saved from death by stoning," Magdalene told him. "Once, just outside the Temple, when I was very young. Still a bride, barely fourteen. My husband's parents were ashamed of me, for I had become pregnant by their son before the time of our marriage. We were both very young, and in love, we thought, and betrothal was hard on us. I confess we didn't wait. When they discovered my condition, they accused me of adultery. This was untrue—I swear it now, as I swore it then!"

"I know," said Jesus quietly.

"They pretended to believe my denial, and we all went together to the Passover in Jerusalem. I was quite happy, looking forward to having my baby. But once we were there, they changed, they tried to frighten a confession from me. When I wept and continued to deny their accusations, they dressed me in black and dragged me to the Temple to be tested by the priest."

Jesus covered his eyes. He already saw it all—every detail of degradation that she was about to reveal.

"I was terrified. The humiliation, the awful humiliation. That priest—that fat priest! I can still feel his pudgy hands yanking the pins from my hair that it might fall down loose. Loose, loose," she mocked, "like the loose woman I am now!"

"You are a loose woman no longer."

"I can feel those hands tearing open my dress," Magdalene rushed on, "so that my bosom was exposed." For the first time her tone of defiance changed. Closing her eyes, she hugged her breasts, began to rock back and forth, like a sorrowing child. "Then he forced my mouth open—I was fighting—and made me drink it to test me. "The *bitter water*. You know what it is?" she cried fiercely, "Water from the sanctuary, holy water mixed with dust from the Temple floor and ink from the scroll where they'd written their terrible accusations!

"I gagged, I choked, but I was forced to swallow it. And it *worked*, just as they expected. I became deathly ill, I sickened, I retched, I fainted, my eyes bulged. I could feel the blood bursting in my veins. And I lost my child. No angel came down to proclaim my innocence. I miscarried. My babe, my poor little baby, tore itself from my loins in a torrent of blood. They had to drag me quickly away lest it stain the priest's vestments—the floor was desecrated. When I looked back as they were dragging me away, they were *mopping up my baby!*" Suddenly she broke down and began to cry hysterically, flinging her arms around wildly, clawing at her breasts, her womb, her hair. Her face was distorted, her teeth were bared; horrible noises came from her open mouth.

Reaching quickly forward, Jesus touched her. "Begone!" he ordered. Immediately the noises stopped, her threshing body quieted. She stared at him a moment, bewildered, then in wonder. With the hem of his gown, Jesus wiped her clammy brow and cheeks.

Presently, holding tight to her hand, he asked, "And then?"

"Thus was I found guilty of adultery," Magdalene said simply. "And according to the Law of Moses I should have been stoned. I could hear my husband and his father discussing it. The other men, the priests and those who had witnessed my shame, were eager for the penalty to be exacted. But now that the terrible thing was actually upon us, the family weakened. My husband"—she sneered faintly— "was afraid of the gossip; it might hurt his chances to remarry. My husband's mother, though she refused to speak to me, attended me until I was recovered. By then it was time for them to leave. She even pressed a few coins into my hands before she turned her back on me and walked away."

Magdalene was gazing beyond him, into the dying fire. She bit her lips; her eyes were wet. This seemed to trouble her most. "She said nothing, not a word, not even goodbye."

"Where were you?

"On a busy street. It was almost dark. I was all alone there in Jerusalem, somewhere near the Sheep's Gate. I was frightened, I didn't know where to go, I was still weak. Men were going by, men with animals, camels, donkeys, goats, men carrying whips. Some of them saw me, some of them were drunk. One of them came up to me and grinned and said an obscene thing. One of them grabbed me, then another—I don't remember, I don't remember!" She covered her mouth with her fists and began to sob hysterically again. "Only they hurt me, forced me to do terrible things—the men, the beasts! They came into me, I was forced to drink them like the bitter water. Even when they let me go I was not rid of them; their ugliness was still inside me, growing inside me like my baby—"

Her voice broke; the sobbing turned to screams. Her black hair had fallen down. Now she hurled herself about so violently it whipped her face.

Jesus sprang up. Grabbing both her arms, he shook her. "Begone, begone!" he said grimly. "All of you—come out!"

Magdalene began to belch, and a strange odor came from her. Jesus recognized the vile stench. Once more she quieted, her whole body went limp against him. Crouching, and murmuring words of comfort, he held her gently a few moments while she slept. Once more he wiped her streaming face.

In a little while she stirred and gazed at him. "Where am I? What have I been saying?"

"You are quite safe; you are with me. You are being cleansed."

"Cleansed?" Magdalene smiled. She sat up, giving a little shrug. With cynical calm she resumed her story. "After the loss of my child I began my life of shame. In the Holy City!" She laughed. "I had learned that all men are demons, or demon-possessed. A woman must have demons of her own to destroy them. Mine came unbidden, but they have served me well. With their help I found a camel driver willing to bring me here to Magdala, a city known for its wicked women. I was more beautiful than any of them," she boasted, stretching her arms over her head. Her eyes had grown seductive, her full, rich mouth slyly flirtatious. "And I determined to make the most money. Why not? Since the God who could have delivered me failed me. I am quite rich, and if you hadn't come along I could be even richer—"

Another laugh burst from her, this time bitter and wild. Her dark, velvety eyes were different—mocking, triumphant. There were beads of saliva at the corners of her lips.

Three more, Jesus realized. The most difficult of all to uproot: vanity, greed and lust. "Stop!" He clapped a hand over her mouth. "Hush, you evil ones, say no more. You no longer possess this woman. In the name of the God who created her, I command you, come out! Be gone from her forever!"

The retching was more violent than before, the stench more over-powering. And this time for an instant he saw them, writhing in ugliness, and hissing, before they were consumed by the coals.

She collapsed now completely in his arms. Her eyes were closed, her face peaceful, restored to its beauty. Gazing upon her and holding her lovely body against him while she slept, Jesus thought of Tamara. His eyes filled. Never had he cradled the beloved like this, never had he gazed upon her dear face sleeping.

Looking up, he found Peter and his wife coming toward them. "Let her rest a little while," he said, "but stay near me. When she wakes, we will carry her into the house. I know you will be gentle with her, Adah, for never has a woman needed a woman's comfort more."

Chapter 7

---

*T*HE news of John the Baptist devastated him.
    He had known it was coming, seen it, sensed and experienced it in some secret layer of agony within his own being. Still, when the apostles began returning from their first missions, anxious to report their experiences, yet restrained, heavy with the burden of the awful confirmation, it seemed at first that he could not bear it.

After weeks of warnings and admonitions, he had sent eight of them out in pairs, keeping Peter and Andrew, James and John behind to help him. The women, too, remained in Capernaum, making their headquarters at Peter's house. Magdalene and Adah had become inseparable. And Esther, Adah's mother, took delight in mothering them both.

Magdalene had never known such contentment. It puzzled her; there must be some mistake. At times she felt so unworthy it seemed she should run away. How could they want her? How could she help them? Didn't they realize people still looked at her askance?

She stared at the blue tassels she was sewing back on Jesus' garment one day. Who was he, this man whom people clamored to touch, so frenziedly sometimes they threatened to tear the very clothes from his back? A rabbi? She shuddered. She had had enough of rabbis: hypocrites who sneaked to her door sometimes in the night—or had. No more, no more. But this particular rabbi walked alone—if you could speak of it so when the mobs dogged his footsteps wherever he went. And never had any mere rabbi possessed such powers.

Magdalene thought of that woman with the flow of blood, thrust about by the crowds, struggling to get near him. She and Adah had sensed the problem at once—the woman's pallor, the subtle odor.

Adah had elbowed people aside. "Here, let this woman through," she ordered. Magdalene helped too. Even so, they could clear the way only so far; the woman was able to get only close enough to reach out, in her desperation, and touch his garment. And Jesus had halted, turning about with that special expression on his face. Magdalene remembered the night when she had first seen it, beside the fire; she had seen it often since. A beautiful, half-startled expression of loving, restoring forgiveness.

It must have been that woman, or someone like her, who had ripped these dear blue tassels. Magdalene held them for a second against her cheeks. A sweet peacefulness filled her, pure and clean, surpassing desire. Who was he? It didn't matter. She knew only that he had stripped her of anguish, and she was here now, safe in the house of Peter and Adah, waiting only to serve him—and them. All of them. For they were dear to her too, her first real friends.

James and John, that merry pair—they had taught her to laugh again. And how wonderful it was to hear Jesus laughing with them, especially after long, strenuous hours of healing and teaching. They would gather sometimes at the home of Zebedee and their mother, Salome, a chubby woman with a dry wit. She was ardently committed to Jesus, thanks to her sons, for whom she was obviously ambitious. The whole family put a twinkle in Jesus' eyes, a smile on his mouth. He adored them all, but John was especially dear to him. Peter and his brother Andrew were more serious. Peter was plainly the sturdy rock on which Jesus depended.

But Jesus—how much longer could he go on like this, with only the four to work with him? Despite their best efforts to protect him, people besieged him day and night, giving him scarcely time to eat or sleep. And no matter the hour or the provocation, Jesus was too kind to turn them away.

Only a few days ago, when Jesus was due to return from Chorazin, Magdalene and Adah had slipped up to clean his little house. What a beautiful day, the wind brisk, just right for airing his bedding, shaking the mats, laying fresh reeds on the floor. Salome and Joanna had joined them later, bearing lamb to be roasted. But their very ministrations—the linens drying on the rocks, the smell of the fire—had signaled his coming. Word spread. By the time Jesus and the four came toiling up the path, it was already choked with people, the yard swarming.

"Send them away!" Adah pleaded with Peter. "Tell them Jesus can't see anyone tonight. He's tired and hungry—all of you are. You must get some rest."

Her husband shrugged, knowing it was hopeless. Too many parents, thrusting their children upon the Master, asking him to touch them, bless them, protect them from disease. Jesus was already kneeling to examine the eyes of a little blind girl. Blind from birth, her anxious parents told him. He picked her up and cuddled her, talking whimsically to her until he had her laughing. Then he kissed her and gently touched her eyes. The child blinked, gasped, and began to cry; shocked by all she was seeing, she burrowed into his shoulder. Smiling, he cradled and comforted her before handing her back to her ecstatic mother and father.

The women were anxiously waiting to serve supper. It was hard to keep the flies off the platters of fruit and cheese. The lamb and the crisp little fish cakes would have to be reheated. Children always added to the commotion, and that night whole families tried to follow him into the house. This was too much for Adah and Salome. At a signal from them, Andrew and the twins began courteously but firmly asking the people with children to leave.

Discovering this, Jesus exploded. "Why, the children are the kingdom of heaven!" He had been washing; he threw aside the towel and strode to the door. "Come back!" he shouted to those departing. "Suffer the children to come unto me. Forbid them not," he told the others. "Let them through." And he pulled the children onto his lap, as many as he could, talking to them and stroking their hair. Then, with the wide-eyed, newly sighted toddler on his shoulder, and leading the others by the hand, he took them outside to see the sunset, pointing out the birds to them, and the beautiful colors on the lake as the boats came in.

He returned then, and prayed, and bade the people be patient while the men tried to eat their supper. But even as Jesus broke his bread, he spoke to them: "Children are good and pure, as you must be pure if you are to make up my kingdom. I warn you, don't cause any of these little ones to stumble, or lead anyone who is pure astray.

He who does will be severely punished; better for him to have a millstone hanged around his neck and be thrown into the sea!"

That must have been the night—Magdalene wasn't sure, there had been so many—that several men actually tore a hole in his roof, so determined were they to reach him. They were carrying an uncle, a paralytic, on a pallet. Unable to get through the door, they had slipped around behind the house to a rise of ground. From there it was quite easy to crawl onto the roof and claw aside some of its branches layered with palm leaves and mud. The house was so crowded, nobody knew what was happening until dust and sticks began raining down. And looking up, they saw to their amazement the quilt bearing the sick man dangling from the ceiling, then slowly being lowered to where Jesus sat.

Some people howled with laughter, others were indignant. Peter charged forward, waving his hands. Before he could get there, however, Jesus was standing, reaching up to help guide the paralyzed man down. Instead of upbraiding those overhead, he was actually smiling, commending them on their ingenuity and their faith. Then, kneeling beside the man, he took his hand and gazed with compassion on his suffering face. "Your sins are forgiven you, my son," he said. He stood up then, and drew him, with great force, to his feet. "Rise!" Jesus' voice rang out. "Take up your bed and walk."

And the man did, Magdalene remembered vividly. He not only walked, he pranced about in triumph, carrying his bed above his head, shouting praises to God, as the people made way for him, applauding.

But not all the people, even then. In every crowd the spies and skeptics lurked. That night, that very night, she had spotted some of those who had tried to use her to entrap him. She had stepped outside to get a little air, and to feed Jesus' dog some scraps from the meal. The stars were bright; light poured from the windows. There was a low, angry rumbling from a little group of men. "Blasphemy!" She could hear them. "Who is he to forgive anybody's sins? Only God can do that. The man's making himself equal to God—that's blasphemy!"

Her heart pounded wildly, for now they recognized her too. Abram, the thickset judge, beckoned to her, and when she did not move, charged up to her, breathing hard. "Well, if it isn't Magdalene!" His eyes glistened, leered up and down, as if to strip her. "So you're one of his women now?"

BETHLEHEM LUTH. CH. LIBRARY
101 E. 38th, Tacoma, Wash.

"How *dare* you?" she blazed. Amused, the other men sauntered up to listen. "You—all of you! You've witnessed miracles tonight. Because of him a blind child saw the sunset and the boats coming in. Because of him a paralyzed man leaps for joy and runs away carrying his own bed! And all you can do is sneak around like rats, sniffing at reasons to condemn him."

"Who is this woman?" one of them asked coldly.

"A common prostitute," Abram sneered. "She's alive because of him. The man broke the Law of Moses to defend her. No wonder she defends him—and now shares her favors with him."

Oh, hideous, intolerable, the memory of their laughter.

"Oh, yes, now I remember," said another. He snapped his fingers, discussed her as if she weren't present. "She must be the one who embarrassed my friend. Simon, a Pharisee—you may know him—a good man who had the decency to invite the man to supper, even after that disgraceful scene on the street. Simon wanted to question him, he told me, judge for himself. They were talking, when some woman broke in and hurled herself at his feet, kissing them and crying and anointing them with precious oil. Even drying them with her hair." The man snickered. "And even knowing what she was, when Simon reprimanded him for not stopping her, the man actually turned on Simon and scolded *him!*"

The horror of that moment would haunt Magdalene forever. She had wanted to die. That act of blind, impetuous devotion soon after her deliverance. Foolish, yes—she saw that now—but honest. Never in her life had she performed such a pure and holy act for any man. That they should use and defile it thus, not only to mock and shame her but to vilify him. Uttering a bleak little cry, she ran from them. And later that night, at Peter's house, Adah's mother heard her moaning.

"You'd better go to her," she advised her daughter. "I've never heard such sounds."

"Hush, my love, my precious pet," Adah soothed, sitting beside her bed. "Of course you will be reviled because of him, persecuted, made to suffer. He warned all the apostles of that, from the very beginning. But those who believe in him will be richly rewarded."

"It's not me, it's not me—I don't care what they do to me!" Magdalene cried. "It's Jesus! To have them say such things about him, I must destroy them, hurt them, tear them to pieces. I want to kill them!"

"No, no, no—remember what he teaches." Adah stroked her hair. "That we must turn the other cheek, we must even pray for those who treat us badly. He is the way, the truth and the light," said Adah serenely, for this she now believed. "The Father who sent him will not let anything happen to him, or to us. There will be hard times, yes, but nothing we can't overcome. God's eye is on the sparrow, Jesus has said, and we are far more dear to him than any sparrow. How dear Jesus must be then to the Father! No, no, we must not be afraid for him. . . ."

Nonetheless, they were all concerned. Jesus' great dark eyes were haggard from loss of sleep. His magnificent body, still brown from the sun and strong-muscled from swimming, had grown thin.

"He gives everything to others, never thinks of himself," Peter worried to Adah. "He can't go on like this much longer."

"Or you either," his wife said flatly. "All of you must get away somewhere and rest."

"It should be easier soon, in a few days now, when the other apostles get back. Especially if they bring some word of John the Baptist."

Adah stabbed at her sewing. . . . She had heard rumors at the well this morning. A story too hideous to believe. A nude girl dancing, a head on a golden platter. Impossible, too vicious and ridiculous to repeat. Why did women seem to relish such things? The bloodier the better, it seemed. No, her husband was already troubled. "But if the word is not good?" she ventured.

To her amazement, Peter shot to his feet, glowering. "I'm afraid for John," he said grimly. "If only he—if Jesus had just let us form an army, go to the palace and free him. I can't pretend I'm not afraid. I didn't want to tell you, but I have heard—"

Adah put down her mending; their two big hands locked tight. They stared at each other a moment. "So have I," she said. "If it's true, it will surely go hard with Jesus."

Jesus sat in the garden of Peter's house, his head in his hands. All day the apostles had been arriving, spurred on by the terrible news. First Matthew and Judas, then Philip and Bartholomew. Later Thaddeus and James the younger. And finally Thomas and Simon. Appalled and shaken, all of them, but solicitous for their master, and so restrained. After a few brief words of greeting, they withdrew, that he might be alone.

Jesus was aware of them, talking in low voices among themselves, matching experiences—where they had been accepted or rejected, the baptisms and healings, what they had said: reports he knew they were anxious to share with him.

At last, toward sundown, Peter came to crouch by his side. "Come, Master," he urged. "We have a large boat waiting." It was a sturdy sailing vessel, the prize of Zebedee's fleet. He and the twins had gone to their father to ask for it the minute they were sure. Without hesitation, Zebedee had agreed, even personally seeing to it that it was anchored out of sight around the cove. "All the men are here now—the last two have just arrived. All are very weary. We will put out to sea. Come with us; we will find a quiet place apart, where you can be alone with your grief."

Jesus lifted anguished eyes. "But the people are waiting. Listen to them." Dimly from the distance came the sound of singing. People were cheering themselves, passing the time, as they often did, with psalms and songs. They had been gathering on the hills and banks for hours.

"Dismiss them" Peter pleaded. "Give them your blessing but tell them you cannot speak to them this night. No, let me do it for you. Once they see you, no telling what will happen."

"Peter is right," barked Zebedee, marching toward them. He was followed by his wife, carrying a basket of provisions. Small, tart, bridling with authority, he took over. "But you, Peter, go on with the men. I will handle the people. They know me and trust me; I will get rid of them. Go quickly," he warned, "lest they find you. Down the back way. The sails are already hoisted."

Jesus had no strength to resist. He felt drained, despondent, a leader now able only to follow, grateful for their guidance, stumbling along through the thickets until they reached the shady inlet where the ship rocked placidly on the jeweled water. From it, James and John waved to them, shielding their eyes from the glare. Blindly Jesus let himself be led aboard, to a place to rest, on a wooden pillow just below the stern. The ship smelled of rope and tar; he was conscious of women's voices on the shore.

Several women, carrying food for the voyage, had also scrambled down the path, and stood there now among the trees to watch them depart.

Adah and Magdalene were among them. Adah scanned the sky. A beautiful evening: The sun was thrusting blades of rose and gold on the horizon, a vast fan of light. Yet thick white clouds were coasting; she could feel a sudden chill wind from the mountains. She shivered. "God go with them," she murmured.

Behind her, Magdalene was staring fixedly toward the craft that was carrying Jesus away. "God *is* with them," she said quietly, to Adah's surprise.

Jesus lay in a stupor of exhaustion and sorrow. There was the rattle of chains as the anchor was hauled aboard, the creak of oars, then the whine of wind and the snap of sails. The boat rocked rhythmically, plowing forward, putting distance between them and the people waiting with such hope and trust onshore. Concern warred with his lassitude. He should not have fled from them; they would go away disappointed, unhealed, still sick in body and soul. He should rise up even now and go to them—if need be, plunge overboard and swim back to them. Yet he had not the strength.

God had willed this grief upon him, and he must give himself up to it. How could he help others when it was not the Father's will that he save his own cousin?

John. That bold, bright youth who had so fervently announced and confirmed his mission. A host of memories came flooding, as if to postpone or deny the hideous fact of his death: Their merry forays among the bazaars and along the streets of Jerusalem, often with giggling girls trying to follow. Even the inviting eyes of older women, for John's charm was like a magnet wherever he strode. *Had John ever loved a woman?* Had his cousin died without at least the comfort of that memory? Surely somewhere, sometime, that vigorous loving heart . . .

The time—they were both about fifteen—John had slipped him into the inner Temple at midnight to witness the night watches. The doorkeeper had let them in through the Fire Gate. The companies of priests marching east and west around the court to see that all was in readiness for tomorrow's services, the smell and glow of their torches, casting shadows. The cries of "All is wellll . . . all is wellll!" echoing through the marble emptiness of the corridors. And the mysterious aroma of meat baking somewhere: the meat offering for the high priest, John explained . . .

John, who had scorned the privileges of the Temple, to live in the desert and emerge to proclaim what he so passionately believed: "Repent, for the Messiah is coming!" Jesus remembered the day of his own baptism. The rocks, a fallen tree aslant, the sun bright on John's tempest of corn-colored hair. The tears running down that fervent, sweet young face as, in solemn triumph, John led him into the water. And how joyfully John had looked up toward heaven, the first to hear the voice and to see the white dove descending!

Vividly, in all its beauty, Jesus relived the scene, before the full horror of John's fate assailed him. That magnificent head slashed from the once strong body . . . rolling away in blood . . . served up on a golden platter to a drunken king . . . Again he was shattered by that last plaintive plea that was brought to him from John. Did my cousin die disappointed in me? he tortured himself. Thinking I failed him? For I was not—I am not—the kind of messiah John expected.

And although Jesus knew many things, that one question he could not answer.

Once, during Jesus' anguished reverie, he roused to find James kneeling beside him. "Master, take a little wine. Try to eat a little something. They tell me nothing has passed your mouth all day."

To please him, Jesus sipped from the jug James held to his lips, but the boat was now lurching so much the wine spilled. And he did not want it, he could scarcely swallow a mouthful of the bread. "No, please, let me rest. I need only to be alone now, and to sleep."

The storm struck swiftly. The water, at first like a bolt of silver cloth covering the gently heaving body of a woman, was suddenly seething, as if the woman herself had risen up in a violent temper, screaming and snarling, yanking at the sails. Peter, steering the ship in a diagonal course across the lake, was not at first concerned.

He grinned, as Judas came reeling toward him, pale with alarm, grabbing at the rails. "Don't worry, I know these squalls. We can ride this one out and be on shore within the hour. She's unpredictable," Peter went on, even as a huge wave pitched the ship suddenly into a foaming trough. "Only a woman could be so contrary," he yelled into the wind, recovering. "Like my wife's mother, or even Adah herself sometimes, before they were gentled by—" He was about to say, "Jesus," when a blast of wind nearly tore the rudder from his hands. Instead, he began to bark orders.

The waves, swollen to glistening monsters, were bearing down upon them, snarling at the fragile craft. James and John were already darting about like monkeys; the other men, drowsing below or on the deck, threw off their cloaks and came running to help. Even Judas, who knew little of wind and canvas, sprang to the task, no longer the vaguely bemused manipulator but obediently following commands.

Thunder crashed, lightning nearly split the sky, whipped fire across the black heaving water. The wind roared, there was the steady lashing boom of the waves. Where is Jesus? Peter worried. Is he all right? James, coming back with the tray, had reported that he was sleeping. At least lying supine on his pillow. How can he? Peter protested. How could anyone lie peacefully sleeping, as if this were a night of calm seas?

Judas, drenched to the skin and terrified now, was suddenly at Peter's elbow, asking almost the same question. "Where is our Master? We're only here because of him. Why isn't he up here with us?"

"Say no word against him!" Peter bellowed. "I'm the one who got this boat and urged that we sail." Yet his own fear had begun to poison his heart. Jesus, their leader—the one they trusted. Have I misjudged him? Why am I out on such a night when the lightning strikes at us like flaming spears and the waves snarl? Why am I not safe at home beside my wife, holding her in my arms, knowing I will taste her warm bread in the morning? What am I doing following this man who has promised us the kingdom, yet lies sleeping like a baby while the waves are like whales threatening to devour us?

"We must remember," he gasped, "our Master has not often sailed these waters."

"Neither have I," cried Judas, "yet I have at least tried to help!"

A glassy mountain, huge, dark, glistening, was suddenly upon them, bashing the boat, its white crest exploding over the bow; all were sent skidding and crashing into one another and against the rails. At the same instant there was another blast of lightning. Half blinded by the light, stunned by a blow on his head, Peter found himself crawling on his hands and knees. "I will go fetch him," he panted. "He will save us."

Peter began fighting his way toward Jesus. Another blast of light revealed the still white form, the curly head propped peacefully against the wooden pillow. So utterly still he lay, undisturbed by the pitching and rolling, he might have been a statue—or a corpse. New terror struck Peter. "Master, wake up, wake up!" he screamed. He was grateful to find Andrew and Philip just behind him. "Help us," he begged, as Jesus stirred and opened his eyes. "You must help us! Don't you care what's happening to us? This terrible storm—we will drown. Don't you care that we perish?"

Jesus sat up, blinking, and gazed at them, for an instant bewildered. Then he, too, felt the pitching and rolling, heard the furies. Springing to his feet, he pushed past them, leapt the single step, and strode to the rail.

They saw him standing there for a moment, feet apart, bracing himself with his hands. His head was back, his chin outthrust, his face lifted to the storm, as if to welcome its cold wet torrents, and the wind that so wildly blew his hair. There was power and dignity in his stance; it was as if he were embracing its very assault, that it might wash and beat and free him from the agony of John.

He lifted his arms then—a gesture of both authority and release. "Peace, be still!" he cried out in a loud voice.

The men could feel the boat shuddering under their feet. They staggered and clung to each other as it gave a final lurch. Looking up in amazement, they realized the avalanche of rain had stopped. Only a few scattered drops still fell. The wind had ceased. The angry sea calmed, the very skies began to clear. Only a few clouds remained, scudding across the face of a placid moon. Soon, though the deck was still awash, the men were soaked, there was only the gentle undulation of the ship and the lapping of the water, which was once again a deep blue-silver under the stars.

Jesus turned and beckoned to them. "It grieves me that you were so troubled," he said kindly. "But oh, Peter, don't you remember the night you first rowed me away from the shore? Have you forgotten the great haul of fish where there had been no fish for days? And the boat that was sinking? You too, James and John," he addressed them— and all the others who stood shivering and astonished. "Have you not yet learned there is nothing to fear so long as you are with me? Why does it take you so long to believe in the Father who sent me? Where is your faith?"

Awed, they went back to mop up the deck, repair the battered sails. The night was far gone. They discussed it among themselves until nearly morning. Marveling at this man who could not only heal the sick and raise the dead but command the storm. Who was he that even the winds and the raging seas obeyed him?

Chapter 8

*T*HE place, they had felt sure, would be deserted. A remote, heavily forested clump of hills between Bethsaida and Gerasa. Even the shepherds did not graze here, for there was little grass, and lions and wolves prowled the dense woods. Few people ventured here from the settlements nearby. Yet when they landed at daybreak, they were astonished to find the banks swarming. People began running down to the water's edge, waving and shouting, "He's coming, he's coming!" Men even waded out to greet them and help pull the craft toward shore.

One by one the apostles climbed over the side and stood regarding the crowds, dismayed. The ship had been seen leaving, they were told. Word had spread, along both sides of the sea. All night the people had been coming, walking or running, desperate to see Jesus, fearful of missing him.

All night they had camped, some of them, huddled together like sheep for protection against the selfsame storm. Even now their cloaks and blankets were being spread out on rocks or from trees to dry. Mothers were nursing their babies, or holding them close for warmth until the sun should be higher. Men were crouching, trying to encourage reluctant fires. The sick were being carefully tended on their litters, cold and miserable, too weak to rise. But the faces they lifted to the apostles, who were walking in consternation among them, were shining. He had arrived at last—he would help them!

A very old man, shaking with palsy, perched half naked on the trunk of an oak that had crashed. The wind had literally torn the clothes from his back; they dangled now almost merrily from roots and branches. Yet he was weeping for joy. "Don't forget me!" he yelled, reaching an eager hand to grab at Judas. "When the holy man starts the healing, find a place for me."

"Sorry, old man," said Judas, striding past in his casually arrogant way. "I'm afraid there will be no healing here today." He paused, however, to pat the stricken face. To be that old and ugly! he thought with a shudder. He would almost linger to help the man himself.

The apostles strode about, offering such comfort as they could, but knowing they must be firm. "You must leave," they insisted. "Go back to your homes. Jesus can't take care of you now; there are too many of you, for one thing, and he is under a great burden himself. Be patient," they urged, as wails of protest went up. "He will see you another time."

People began milling about, witless in their disappointment; others remained, stubborn and defiant. Arguing, weeping, a few shaking their fists.

Baffled and frustrated, the apostles gathered around Peter to confer. He was exhausted from last night's struggle, and stricken at this unexpected failure of his mission. "Plainly, there will be no rest for Jesus here." He made a helpless little gesture toward Judas, who was better with crowds than any of them.

Judas nodded. Smiling and waving his hands, almost amiably he began to shout: "Look, if you don't leave, we will have to! All right, farewell, and bless you!" He wheeled about. "Come on, Peter, let's go. Since they won't listen to reason, we will have to put out to sea again."

Regretful but determined, the men began trudging back toward the boat. The sun was rising now, a golden disk on the gray horizon. Jesus was standing on the deck in his white robe, bathed in its glow. He stood surveying the teeming multitude, his face composed from prayer but poignant with compassion: their misery, the terrible hope and faith that had driven them here, like sheep who will travel miles for a blade of grass or a drink of water. They were frantic now in their disappointment; they were like sheep without a shepherd.

Tucking up his tunic, Jesus threw his mantle to John and sprang over the side. Then he fastened it about his shoulders and came to them, holding out his arms. "Peace, be still!" he commanded them in his rich ringing voice, even as he had commanded the wind and the waves. And like the elements, the apostles and the people were suddenly quiet. The fretting, the wailing and the angry questions ceased. A great hush fell upon them; in the silence they could hear the lapping of the waves and the sweet trilling and chirping of morning birds. The night of travail was over; the day was newborn.

"Hear, O Israel!" Jesus led them then in the Shema, and when it was finished, Thaddeus, whose eyes were sparkling, played his lyre and led the singing of the psalms. They were all rejoicing now, at peace, refreshed, eagerly awaiting all that was to come. Jesus blessed them then, and again entrusting his mantle to John, went to the water to wash himself before the healings.

"Go among the crowd and find the worst cases," he ordered the apostles. "Bring them to me first. But watch over all the others; stand close by to be sure no one is left out."

"But, Master," Peter worried, "what about your fatigue and your grief?"

"I will serve John best by doing the work the Father has sent me to do," Jesus said. "Now that John's voice is still, now more than ever I must go on."

All that day he gave himself to them, finding surcease from his own pain as he cured them; and when the healings were finally over, he taught them, ministering to their souls. And the people sat enchanted, watching and listening, fascinated. For though he taught in the manner of the rabbis, alluding to familiar scriptures and demonstrating his truths with parables, he brought to the form an originality, a freshness of authority and conviction they had never heard before. No one left, and with every hour new ones stole onto the scene, eager to partake of the rich spiritual feast he was spreading.

"Come unto me, all you who are weary and heavy laden," he comforted, out of his great compassion, "and I will give you rest. Shoulder my yoke and learn from me, for I am gentle and humble in heart, and you will find rest for your souls. . . ."

Sometimes sitting, sometimes striding up and down the bank much as John did, he told his parables, many of them tales from his own experience—and theirs. "What is the kingdom of heaven? many of you have asked me. It may be compared to a man like my grandfather, who sowed good seed in his field. I know, because in my youth I helped him. Yet Grandfather, good man though he was, had some neighbors who were jealous of his crops. One night they sneaked in and sowed tares in his field."

The farmers were leaning forward, nodding. This was a not uncommon trick. "When the new wheat sprouted and ripened, there were the tares as well. Those of us who had helped him sow the good seed went to ask him where the tares had come from, and what did he want us to do? Should we pull up these weeds? No, he told us, because we might pull up the wheat as well. Wait until the harvest, when he would have us collect the tares and tie them in bundles to be burned; then we would gather the wheat into the barn.

"The field is the world," Jesus explained. "And you are the good seed, being sown. So it will be when it is time to reap the good souls for the harvest of heaven. The Son of Man will send his angels to gather up those of you who have done no evil. You who live virtuous lives will shine like the sun in the kingdom of heaven. But those who break the commandments, those who serve Satan, will be gathered up like those tares and thrown into the fire!"

On and on he spoke, loving them even as he warned them.

"The kingdom of heaven is also like a mustard seed, from which springs the largest shrub we have. Once I remember my mother showing me this tiniest of seeds. Then she pointed out the enormous mustard bush, so big the birds were nesting in its branches and singing their little hearts out for joy in their Creator. I tell you, you must have faith in yourselves and in your Creator, and in me, the one he has sent to guide you. Faith, no bigger than a mustard seed, will give you power. With such faith you can move the very mountains! . . .

"But you are lost, some of you will say. You have sinned, there is no way back for you into the kingdom. Wait, listen: God loves you as the shepherd loves his sheep. How many of you have sheep?" he asked. "You know how stricken you are when one of them wanders. How you will leave the entire herd until you find it, as I have often done when I tended the sheep for my grandfather and my uncles. What man among you with a hundred sheep, losing one, would not leave the ninety-nine in the wilderness and go after the missing one?" Jesus was striding up and down to illustrate. "And when you found it, would you not joyfully carry it home on your shoulders and call together your friends and neighbors to tell them—" His voice rang out the glad words of the shepherd: " 'Rejoice with me, for I have found my lost sheep!' "

Jesus sat down again on a rock beside the sea. Behind him the boat swayed gently, the silver-blue water washed in. He sat resting for a moment, considering. And another experience came to him.

"Let me tell you another story that illustrates this very lesson. About a young man I knew and loved. How he tired of his life tending sheep and helping his father on the farm. One day he took his inheritance from his father and ran away to a distant country with a friend, who soon abandoned him. There he spent all his money on riotous living, and found himself with nowhere to go and nothing to eat. He was so desperate he hired himself out to another farmer, who put him to feeding the pigs. At times he was so hungry he would willingly have eaten the husks on which they fed. Finally he came to his senses and said to himself, 'Why, my father's paid workers have more food than this, while here I am dying of hunger. I will go to my father and confess how gravely I have sinned. I will tell him, "I no longer deserve to be called your son; just treat me as one of your hired men." '

"So he set off home. But when his father saw him coming, instead of being angry he was filled with pity. He ran to the boy with his arms outspread. I was there, I saw this myself—how he kissed his son and wept for joy! And he ordered the family to bring out his own best Sabbath robe and put it on him, and a gold ring for his finger, and sandals for his feet. What's more, to kill the calf they had been fattening—they would have a great feast. 'Because,' he cried, 'this son of mine was dead and has come back to life; he was lost and he is found!' And they began to celebrate," Jesus said.

"The other son—and I knew him too, very well—this son who had remained, faithfully working the fields, heard the music and dancing and was so shocked and angry he refused to come in, even when his father came out to plead with him. 'How unfair of you!' he accused his father. 'Look at all the years I have obeyed you and slaved for you, but you never rewarded *me* with a party. Yet when my brother, who deserted you and squandered your property on women, when he comes back, you kill the fatted calf for him!'

"And his father told him, 'My son, you are with me always, and you know that all I have is yours. . . .' " Jesus' voice was filled with

emotion, remembering it all so well; it was as if his grandfather
Joachim stood beside him now, uttering those very words to Uncle
Amos. " 'But how could we *not* celebrate and rejoice? Because your
brother here was *dead* and has come to life; he was lost and now he is
found!'

"So don't weep, you who have wandered. You are like the lost
sheep, or the lost son, or the coin my mother once lost and looked for
for days before, to her great joy, she found it. You are still precious
in the sight of God. Don't be afraid to come home to him!"

He told them many other stories that day, answered many questions. Earnest, loving, indefatigable, sometimes joyous, sometimes
stern, his voice rang out for hours. Yet no one moved to leave; and as
the afternoon wore on, more people kept arriving. Several thousand,
the anxious apostles calculated. What to do with all of them? they had
begun to wonder. The sun was setting, drenching both sky and water
with gold, yet dark would fall fast. Many families had a long journey
home; they would be hungry, they had better start. Quietly Judas and
Philip began moving about among them, urging them to leave; while
Peter went to squat beside the rock where Jesus was speaking.

"This is a lonely place," he reminded him. "And the time has
slipped by. Hadn't you better send the people away now, before it's
too late to go to the villages and buy themselves some food?"

Jesus looked up, concerned. Reluctantly, people were getting to
their feet. Most of them had eaten little all day; the food in their hampers was gone. Hungry children were whimpering, a few crying.

"But there is no need for them to go," he said. "We must feed
them."

Peter gasped. "Master, we have barely enough for our own supper!" His ruddy face was dismayed. Biting his lips, trying to hide his
impatience, he jerked his head toward Matthew. "How much food do
we still have?" he muttered.

Matthew leaned forward in the confidential way he had, a large
man with thick black brows and dark, defensive eyes. "Not more than
a few loaves and a couple of fishes," he admitted.

Jesus overheard. "Bring them to me," he ordered. Then, to their
amazement and horror, he called out cordially to the crowd. "Wait,
don't go yet! We can't send you away hungry. Sit down; we will see
that you have plenty of food."

The people hesitated, relieved but incredulous. Puzzled, exclaiming in surprise, they scanned the lake. Where would the food come from? Had another ship, laden with supplies, arrived while they sat, too enthralled by his words to notice? Now only the same small ship rocked at anchor, and only two men were trudging toward it.

Apprehensive but obedient, Matthew hurried back to the boat. Once he would have thought this madness, but no more. Not after all that he had seen—the sick healed, the dead raised. Not after last night—the quieting of that storm-tossed sea. And with a kind of blind, dumb, shamed amazement, he remembered how he had once doubted an earlier story of fish miraculously multiplied in that sea. Heard it first while he sat coldly collecting taxes: excited claims of boats so full they almost sank, the biggest catch ever brought into Capernaum, and every fish clean! Laughed at it, considered it crazy until he heard it confirmed by both Peter and the twins. . . . Not long after that incredible day, the man called Jesus actually beckoned him from his booth, and uttered the quiet command, "Follow me."

Me. To think he would summon me! Matthew gave a little astonished shudder, climbing aboard. Before the miracle of his own experience, even those others paled. None that he had yet witnessed, nor any miracle to come, would ever compare. That he should be transformed—from a despicable cheat, a loathed tool of Rome—to this! Loved and followed now, himself. He thought of the weeks just passed, working side by side with Thomas, teaching, baptizing, even *healing.* These grubby, ink-stained hands healing, actually healing. But even more important, he was trusted. Worthy to serve Jesus.

It annoyed Matthew to find Thomas trotting just behind him, his blue eyes more anxious than ever. "This is ridiculous!" Thomas protested. "We'll only look foolish. That bread, what little was left, was soaked this morning. And how far will two fish go?"

"That's not our problem," Matthew said curtly. "We were told only to fetch them." He strode on to the hold, where the food was kept. A discouraging sight. The fish, so crisp last night, were hard and dry. Only five loaves of bread, most of it still sodden. Even so, he put them into a basket. "Were you not listening when Jesus spoke of the mustard seed this afternoon? Or the pinch of leaven that could make the flour rise and multiply it into many loaves of bread? This is surely a test of our faith, Thomas."

Nonetheless, Matthew's heart was pounding as he returned and handed over the meager supply. He could feel the eyes of the multitude upon him. And those of the other apostles, who had quickly gathered around him. An instant of the old craven defensiveness smote him, as if it were somehow his fault that there was so little. I swear, it's all there *is*! he was tempted to declare. I didn't cheat, I didn't steal—

Jesus took the basket calmly. It seemed to Matthew that his eyes were twinkling as he turned and gave orders that the crowd, still milling about, to be seated once more on the grass. "Go among them and see that this is done," Jesus ordered. "Gather up as many empty baskets as you can and bring them back."

There was the murmur of voices, the smell of trampled grass. Children bounced in their mothers' arms, no longer fretting but confident of food to come; the people didn't question, they only waited gratefully. A sense of awed anticipation prevailed. In a few moments all was still, except for the sound of the waves rolling in and the birds chirping and twittering in the trees.

Then Jesus took the five loaves and two fishes, and lifting his eyes to heaven, blessed them. And facing the apostles, who stood waiting in suspense, he began to break the loaves and hand them to the men, along with the crisp savory fish. Enough to fill all the baskets they had brought, which were then distributed to the crowds. And the multitude feasted, men, women and children. And when they were finished and were rising to leave at last, happy and filled in body and spirit, the apostles went about collecting the scraps that were left over.

"Twelve baskets full!" Thomas marveled, wiping his furrowed brow. "I don't believe it."

"Faith," said Matthew, kneeling beside him and crumbling a piece of bread between his fingers. . . . Bread enough, and more to feed the birds and fishes.

Jesus was suddenly tired, unutterably tired.

Dismissing the people, bidding them goodbye, blessing them as he urged them to return safely to their homes, he felt a waning of his first great joy at feeding them. For he knew that their enthusiasm now was not for the things he had said—no, all that he had been telling them seemed to be forgotten before this glorious miracle of food.

Manna from heaven! Their bellies filled. Some of them were saying that he was Moses, a powerful new Moses who could easily feed the world. Such a man could overthrow Rome!

A small group of men, feverishly excited, had accosted him as he strove to make his way back to the ship. A few politicians, but mostly husky fishermen and farmers, with eager, desperate faces, insisting that he come with them that they might make him king. Except for Peter and the others who rushed to protect him, they might have seized him by force. He had to reprimand them, warn them, "You are proclaiming me for the wrong reason—because you had all the bread you wanted to eat. Do not work for food that cannot last, but work for food that endures to give you eternal life."

Pitying them, for he knew their hardships, he spoke to them for a time, trying to make them understand. And when he had calmed them and the place was finally cleared of people, Jesus knew he could speak to no one else that night. Not even his own twelve.

"Go back across the lake," he told Peter. "I am going up into the hills to pray."

"But will you be safe?" Peter worried. "Shall we not wait for you, to be sure?"

"No. This is a time when I must be alone."

John spoke up, his affectionate young face troubled. "But when will you join us, when will we see you again?"

"I will come to you later. Go now, don't worry about me," Jesus assured them. "And don't be afraid."

Chapter 9

CLEOPHAS surprised Mary in her garden. She was bending there, toward evening, pulling weeds from the bed of roses. Their fragrance mingled with the smell of the earth on her hands and the fresh bread cooling on the windowsill. She was startled at the urgent pound of his footsteps behind her and, looking up, shocked at the expression on his square dark face.

"Mary, you had better sit down," he warned, breathing hard. He reached for her hand. "Again I'm the bearer of bad news . . . terrible news."

"Jesus?" she cried, white and shaken.

"No. His cousin John. Word has just reached Nazareth. A runner who is one of his followers. It's the talk of the marketplace. I came as fast as I could." Mary was staring at him, still clutching a fistful of weeds. Birds were singing. A moment passed before he could bring himself to say it. "It's over for him, Mary. John's work is finished. Herod has had him murdered."

Mary swayed, eyes wide with horror, one fist pressed to her mouth. "Oh, Elizabeth—poor Elizabeth! I must go to her at once."

"Wait, not yet. Mary, listen." He held her slight body against him, fearing for a minute that she might crumple. "Come, let's sit here on the bench." Cleo led her to it, the small wooden bench where she and Joseph had sat so often, hand in hand. It was covered with leaves; he made a clumsy gesture of brushing it off with his handkerchief. "It's your own son you should be thinking about right now. I think we should find him, persuade him to come home."

Mary could only continue to stare at him, aghast. "The story of what happened is too ugly to tell you," Cleo went on. "Besides, I don't know all the details. But that *beast*. If Herod could do that to John, he'd have no qualms about Jesus. Especially since—" Cleo floundered, not wanting to offend her. "Forgive me, Mary, but . . . all those claims of John's—that Jesus would be the savior of Israel, king of the Jews. It's not safe for him out there now, Mary."

Even as he spoke, two of her sons came running down the path: Josey, tall and flushed, looking angry as well as concerned; James, his warm loving eyes big with distress. Cleophas left her for a moment to confer with them, while she sat locked in her own arms, swaying back and forth. "Don't upset your mother any more than you can help," Cleo was telling them. "Just help me make her realize what we must do before it's too late."

Nodding, they came to her almost meekly, hovering, solicitous. James knelt at her feet. "We must help our brother," he pleaded. "We must save him if we can." As soon as possible, both sons agreed; it would be madness to wait. "People from the Temple are after him too," Josey said. "Surely you realize—" It was hard for him to contain himself. "He's being accused of a lot of things. Wine bibbing, for one. It's a motley crew he seems to be with—tax collectors, even prostitutes."

"No, no, no!" Mary cried.

"Yes. Of course it's probably exaggeration, but I have heard women are traveling with them—" Cleophas was frowning at him, shaking his head. "Perhaps only wives of some of the men," Josey added hastily, "as if that isn't bad enough. But they are saying some of these people don't even wash before eating, they're not fasting the way we are ordered, they are breaking the Sabbath—"

"Your brother is the cleanest, most devout man I have ever known!" Mary said indignantly. "He would never consort with sinners, he would never break the Sabbath." Yet would he? she wondered, in an astonished, secret part of herself. "And it is not the Sanhedrin we have to fear," she reasoned, "only the king—"

"I'm afraid it is the Sanhedrin too, Mother," said Jude, who had just joined them, sweaty and disheveled from felling trees, as well as from his own alarm. "I've heard they have their spies everywhere, reporting his attacks on the scribes and Pharisees." He disregarded the warning glances of the others. "Also his heresies. Heresy is a serious crime."

Mary shivered, though she felt half suffocated by the day's heavy heat. She is so tiny to breathe so hard, Cleophas thought.

"He's forgiving sins. Promising people who believe in him *eternal life*. Claiming that he has secret bread to give them, secret waters— he, our brother! They have only to believe in him and they will never be hungry or thirsty again."

"To put it bluntly," Josey broke in, "Herod has some reason to fear him. They think he's claiming to be the son of God."

They stayed for supper, but left at last, Josey to go home to his family, James to seek out his betrothed, a strangely colorless girl named Tilma, whom he seemed to adore. Mary looked up from where she was cleaning the plates and cooking vessels. She could not remember the troubled gathering around the table, any of it. She knew only that Elizabeth must be mad with grief, and there was no way to comfort her. She was a little surprised to find Cleophas still lingering, regarding her with his heart in his eyes.

"Mary, let me help you," he pleaded in a low tone, totally unlike him. "Let me take care of you. You know how much I have always loved you. Marry me. Let me help you in this matter of Joseph's son."

"You don't believe," she whispered, after a stunned moment. And again the words were almost exact echoes of those she had spoken so long ago to Joseph himself. "You still don't *believe* my son is what he claims."

"I know only that I love you. Whatever you believe, I accept for myself."

"That is not enough!" She thrust him from her when he would have taken her in his arms. Tempted, but appalled. Yet she needed Cleo. And he was right. The threat to Jesus was real. "I'm sorry," she said, "forgive me. I can think only of Jesus right now—and John, poor John! The outrage to John. And Elizabeth . . ." Helplessly, frantically, Mary began to weep for them. "If only we could be together this night, to comfort each other, think how to help each other. I must get word to Elizabeth, go to be with her as soon as possible. After we find Jesus."

Cleophas stood rigid, fighting his longing to hold her, but relieved. "Then you are taking my advice? You will send us after him?"

"I will send no one," she told him. "He is my son. I will go myself to persuade him."

"You can't go alone. Be reasonable, Mary. No one is sure just where he is right now; it might take days. Let me go. Send me, along with Josey or Jude or Simon—any of your sons."

"He would never listen to you," she said. "Nor to his brothers; they are too hostile," she said wearily. "I am his mother. Surely I can convince him."

Mary slept little that night. The nightmare of John haunted her, and the anguish Elizabeth must be suffering. It was like a sword plunging repeatedly into her own womb. Helplessly, hopelessly, she wept for both of them. And for Jesus. Never had she felt such fear for him. Unable to rest, she got up and began making preparations for the journey, laying out a few things, deciding to wash her hair.

The water she dipped from the cistern was brackish. She stood in the moonlight straining it into a pitcher, and discovered she was shaking uncontrollably. The water spilled, splashing its coldness on her bare feet. God, dear God, she prayed, where can I go to find him? Help me to find him and bring him safely home. He could not, would not, refuse her; he loved her too much to worry her so. He would see how much she needed him to comfort her in her grief for John. And she would comfort him in the agony of his loss. As for his brothers— surely this tragedy would bring them all together.

By morning, when James rose from his bed and her older sons appeared to see about her, they found Mary seated by the table, dressed and ready, her still-damp hair tied under a fresh white kerchief. She looked almost like a child, but her voice was firm with authority. "Bring up the donkey," she ordered, but warmly, almost as if this were to be a pleasure trip. She lifted her face for their kiss. "The sooner we start the better."

Like Cleophas, they were shocked. They had come prepared to go after Jesus, bring him back by force, if necessary. Hopefully, to get her consent. It had not occurred to them that she would so easily agree, let alone insist on going with them. And, like Cleophas, they tried to dissuade her. No telling what might happen; it could even be dangerous. "It may take time even to find him; they say he and his men"—Josey's dour mouth tightened, biting back the words *and women*—"that they wander all over, sometimes on foot, sometimes by sea."

"We will go straight to Capernaum," Mary stated simply. "We will make inquiries. People will help us, tell us where he lives, where he might be."

They set off, in a surprisingly good mood, for it was a beautiful day. Last night's angry shock, making their emotions run high, had changed. Once more they felt curiously close to each other, united in the tragedy. They felt that strange near euphoria that often sweeps the living after death has struck down someone close to home. They were alive, seeing the sunrise, hearing birdsong and barking dogs, the clatter of hooves and carts, the sound of their own sandals on the dew-wet paving stones.

Mary's sons found themselves reminiscing, almost merrily, about John, for though not as close to him as Jesus was, they remembered him with affection and a kind of amazed admiration. Madman that he seemed to be, John was famous. People had flocked from all over Judea—and beyond—to hear him. A man important enough to be slain by a king! And they were his kinsfolk. The very manner of their cousin's murder lent a dark fascination to their own role.

It was the subject of discussion in every settlement they passed through. People rushed out to greet them, begging for more details. Rumors were rampant. Was it true Herod had now left his wife for his niece, the dancing girl? John had come back to life! Had they heard? He had been seen walking over the waves on the Sea of Galilee! No, no, it was the man called Jesus, others excitedly corrected—only last night, a woman from Capernaum claimed. A prophet surpassing John or even Elijah, or Moses himself, for he was healing all manner of sickness—the lepers, the crippled, the blind.

"My neighbor's daughter—I knew this child myself, from a baby—they took her to the best doctors in Jerusalem, in vain, bathed her in the springs, then they heard of Jesus and took her to him. Her sight was restored; she sees as well as you or I!"

It was said he had even raised the dead. Perhaps it wasn't too late, even yet he might raise up John. "Since you are related to John, do you also know this man?" they asked.

Mary's sons had been listening with mixed emotions, torn between astonishment, disbelief and uneasy pride. Now Josey threw his broad shoulders back. "We are his brothers," he announced. "We are on our way to see him."

His brothers . . . his brothers . . . The news ran through the little crowd. "And this must be his mother!" the women exclaimed. "To be the mother of such a man. How proud of him you must be!"

"I am proud of all my children," Mary said quietly, anxious to be on.

"But you must have seen him perform these wonders."

"He has not been home to Nazareth for a long time. We are hoping to bring him back for a visit." For her sons' sake Mary was trying to be patient; they seemed to be enjoying the attention, however dearly bought, and it put some of her earlier fears at rest. But she was jealous of every moment that kept them from their destination. *Jesus, Jesus.* To see him again, hold him safe against her heart. And oh, he would be so happy to see *them.* Surely, knowing the danger and their terrible concern—yes, and just because he loved them so much—Jesus would *want* to come home.

The long miles passed, Mary sometimes riding, sometimes trudging along beside the men. A second beast clopped behind them, brought along at the last minute to carry the bundles she insisted on bringing in case Jesus needed anything. Mount Hermon beckoned them, white-capped in the distance, and at last the glittering lake, rimmed round with its now parched hills. With all the interruptions (Cana had taken the longest, for Lydia and Deborah, her mother, frantic to discuss the situation, insisted they stay for a meal), it was late afternoon before they were skirting the lakeshore. They were tired and beginning to feel nervous approaching the busy city where Jesus was so at home.

The water was almost too dazzling, blinding them. The smell of fish, the softly clashing palms. Docks, a noisy shipyard where boats were being built. Hammers rang out; two men, naked to their loins, paused to stare at them. Dyeworks, potteries, great sour-smelling vats for the pickling of fish, and then the confusion of streets.

But all would be well once they found him. Pray heaven he would be at the little house he had rented. It was somewhere near the synagogue, they were told, when they paused in the marketplace to inquire. The man pointed in the direction from which they had just come. They would have to turn back; but they couldn't miss it, the man said. "The most beautiful synagogue in Galilee. He preaches there often, though I can't say I've heard him myself. His house, they tell

me, is up a path just behind it, overlooking the sea. You'd better ask
someone, once you get nearer."

Exasperated and feeling foolish, Josey jerked at the donkeys; they
began to retrace their steps. Never mind—Mary smiled reassuringly
at her boys—she had determined that they would find their brother
quickly; he would be there, and how he would welcome them! She
could hardly wait to see his face. How wonderful that they were all
here together (all except Simon, whose wife was ill): Joseph's family
united on this mission of love.

But again, in their fatigue and eagerness, they got lost. Again they
had to ask directions before they found the synagogue, huge as it was.
They paused a moment to admire its soaring columns; then their eyes
began searching the slope behind it. So many paths among the vines
and weeds, and there were several houses. An old rabbi, hobbling out
of the building on a stick, saw their bewilderment and approached
them.

"Looking for Jesus?" he inquired. "Everybody comes here looking
for the miracle worker." He was bent and bald, a very loquacious old
man, not belligerent but rather amused. "You folks looking for healing?"

"No, but it's important that we see him," said James. "Would you
be kind enough to point out his house?"

"That little one there—you can see it from here." The rabbi waved
his stick. "But I can tell you, you won't find him."

"Why not?"

"Well, he moves around. And when he's back, the whole town
knows it and gives him no peace, poor man. If he was there, that path
would be so crowded you'd be lucky to get through. Healing," he
scoffed, "magic—that's all people want anymore." The old man
whacked at a weed. "Not to hear the Law and the prophets preached.
Let those claims of special powers alone, I say. Once they get started,
people go crazy. They're claiming now he can walk on the water—
some people think they saw him last night, on this very sea."

"Then you don't believe these stories?" Josey frowned.

The rabbi's withered pink face was almost merry. "I am a sensible
man. An apparition—yes, that's what they saw, if they saw anything.
There are cemeteries nearby; everybody knows how a ghost might get
out of his grave and do such a thing, but a living man? Never! And

listen to this—they're saying he's the new Moses, raining bread from the trees. That he fed four or five thousand just yesterday—somewhere up the lake. Just by casting a spell over a few dead fish and a couple of loaves of bread!" He made a good-humored gesture of dismissal with his stick. "Now, everybody knows you have to carry plenty of food along when you go out to hear a prophet; some of those fanatics preach all day. The people had enough bread left in their own baskets, that's all; you can't tell *me*. Not that I blame him, mind you; I have nothing against him. He may even be afraid of these exaggerations—talk like that is dangerous. Could get him in trouble with the authorities. Big trouble—look what happened to John! I just thought I'd warn you."

"Why are you so sure this man is not what people think?" Jude challenged. This was an elderly rabbi speaking; he must listen with respect. But he resented the man's derision.

"A neighbor boy from Nazareth? Son of a carpenter, or so I hear. Ridiculous!"

"We, too, are from Nazareth," Josey told him brusquely. "And wherever he is, we must find him."

"Sorry, no offense." The man was taken aback.

"We are his family," Mary said quietly, yet on a note of pleading. "Do you know anyone who could possibly tell us where to look for him?"

"Forgive me." The rabbi bowed, all apologies now, filled with curiosity, and honest concern for them.

"You might try the house of Simon Peter," he told them. "It's just down the street, only a few paces from the beach." Peter was a prominent fisherman who traveled everywhere with Jesus now. "Somebody there is sure to know." The rabbi even limped a few paces beside them, leading the way. They seemed so lost, and yet so determined. He felt sorry for them. He wondered if they had eaten, if he shouldn't have offered them food and shelter somewhere. He wanted to know more about them and about this preposterous brother and son they sought.

They came upon the small stone house suddenly, behind its cluster of palms. At first their hearts sank, for it, too, seemed silent and deserted. Only a single lamp burned. Then, as Josey kept knocking and calling out, a woman appeared in the door. So unexpected was she, and so beautiful, the men were for a moment startled.

Magdalene had been brushing her hair; it was not yet bound, but fell in a black cascade around her body, voluptuous even in a simple white dress. Her dusky arms were bare, holding up the lamp. They saw her long velvety eyes, rich with experience, the ripe full seductive lips. Even innocent of the makeup that once marked her trade, the aura of all that she had been was still about her. And instantly, with one accord, the brothers felt a thrilled, uneasy stab of recognition.

Magdalene's face was guarded, unsmiling. Three men. She had not seen Mary waiting in the shadows. "What do you want?" she asked.

"We must be mistaken," Josey blurted, flushing. "We were told this is the house of Simon Peter. And that we might learn the whereabouts of the man called Jesus here."

"This is the house of Simon Peter," Magdalene acknowledged. "But Jesus is not here."

"It's very important that we find him," James said anxiously. "We are his brothers and his mother, come all the way from Nazareth today."

Magdalene had drawn a sigh of relief. Now she was searching their faces in astonishment. A little cry escaped her. Then, without a word, she pushed past them, down the flat stone steps, seeking out Mary, who was perched on one of the donkeys, patiently holding the reins of the other. Mary saw her coming and, prodding the side of the little beast, rode forward to meet her.

"His mother, his mother!" Sobbing, Magdalene fell to her knees and began kissing the hem of Mary's garments. "The mother of my Lord!"

"Oh, my poor child, don't, don't," Mary pleaded. "Please rise." Reaching out, she drew Magdalene to her feet. For an instant she, too, was stricken by her beauty. "Where is my son? Only tell us where to find him."

"He is preaching in the house of Zebedee tonight. It's the largest in Capernaum; no other would hold the crowds. Wait, I will take you there myself. I was just preparing—" Magdalene was suddenly aware of her fallen hair. "I was just binding up my hair. I will soon be ready, wait for me!"

In a few moments she emerged, to stride joyfully beside Mary as she rode, holding Mary's hand as if never to let go. "Your son saved my life—you will never know what he has done for me!" The voice was husky, rich and sweet and comforting, pouring out exclamations of praise and wonder, but Mary scarcely heard. She was too tired, weak from hunger, and a little dizzy with the excitement of knowing they would soon see Jesus. Her sons marched vigorously along, renewed in spirit, murmuring to each other. At least he was safely in the city; they would not have to set out again.

They were not prepared for the imposing house of Zebedee, brightly lighted, set upon a hill, with its gardens and terraces and dancing marble fountain. Or for the crowds that swarmed the lawn, striving to hear, or patiently waiting for servants or messengers to bring Jesus' words out to them—at least as much as they could remember of all that he was saying inside. Jude and Josey lifted their brows in surprise. This was no ragtag band of followers; mostly common people, yes, but there were obviously Pharisees among them, rich merchants, rabbis, scholars, doctors of the Law. That their brother should command such an audience! Nothing else impressed them quite so much. This miracle, at least, they could confirm.

Mary's very pride made her anxious. For the first time she realized how poor and travel-stained they must look, with their bundles and their donkeys. Magdalene beckoned to a boy who was standing near the street, and asked him to hold the beasts.

"Follow me," she told them. "I will try to break a way for you to get near."

She was so beautiful and confident, people made way for them, almost to the front. Mary and her sons followed her eagerly, but feeling shy and self-conscious; she paused to speak with a servant stationed there. The two conferred a moment, nodding and pointing to the house.

"Wait right here," Magdalene said. "We'll try to get word to Jesus that you are outside."

"Perhaps he shouldn't be interrupted," Mary said nervously. "We don't want to embarrass him."

"He will want to know." Magdalene smiled. "I will have the servant lead the way."

The two disappeared. Hearts pounding, Mary and her sons

waited, taut with anticipation. But as time went on they began to glance at each other, mystified. What could be taking so long? "He may want to finish his sermon," James whispered, squeezing his mother's arm. She was trembling. . . . Yes, that must be it. If only they could *hear* him! Mary stood on tiptoe, trying to see over the other people. Finally there was a little stir, and she realized, to her great relief, that at last the two must be returning.

But her heart sank at sight of them. Magdalene's face was strange—surprised, upset, almost angry. She seemed to be arguing with the servant, a large, awkward, big-eared fellow, who looked embarrassed and refused to meet their eyes. He halted before them, stood stiff and scowling, obviously struggling to remember the exact words, but in dread at having to say them. He stole one quick commiserating glance at Mary.

"I—regret to inform you," he stammered, the sweat rolling down his face. "It—is my unpleasant duty to report—"

"Please," Mary implored, gently encouraging. "Don't be afraid. What is it you must say?"

"The Master has just stated—that he *has* no brothers!" the man blurted desperately. "No brothers and sisters and no mother."

"No, no, Jesus couldn't have said that," Magdalene protested impatiently, as Mary gasped. "Why, Jesus *loves* his mother. Sometimes he speaks of little else. Think now, try—what else did he say?"

To her distress, others were pressing around the astounded family, trying to hear this latest message from inside.

"He pointed to *me*," the servant claimed, "and called me his brother. I swear it. Then the Master lifted his arms, something like this—" Clumsily, the youth demonstrated, miserable before the attention he was receiving, fearing he would not be believed. "He held out his arms and said, 'Behold! *You* are my brothers and my sisters and my mother, all of you who do the will of God. You women here, you are just as much my mother as—as the one who bore me in her womb.' "

Mary's sons were listening, appalled. Josey's fist clenched. "I don't believe this," he said furiously, and turned in a flood of pity to Mary.

The color had drained from her face. She had covered her mouth.

Her eyes were huge, staring at the man. But to Josey's astonishment, even now she spoke as if to defend him.

"I believe it," she whispered. "For it is true."

Mary dragged her gaze from the speaker, from her sons. A part of her was dazed, another part unusually alert. She gazed in wonder at the people, all these people swarming about. They were his family now, and she must look at them. Rich and poor, old and young. Those children romping in the fountain—where were their parents? Was it safe? they might fall in, catch cold. . . . Young mothers hastening to their rescue, fathers and grandfathers huddled in earnest discussion, or listening to other servants reporting the words of her son: *You are my brothers and sisters and my mother and father, all of you.*

It was true. It was written. Was that not why God had sent him—to gather up the human family and somehow make them one? . . . She had always known this was coming, must have, it had to; she was but the vessel chosen, and Joseph, her beloved, another instrument. Their private memories and emotions didn't matter. Jesus' precious babyhood, childhood, first day of school . . . sawdust fights in the carpenter shop, his dog, the flowers he always brought her from the fields . . . And the strange bright wonderful years of his youth, growing, growing, in beauty and strength and wisdom and compassion, taking upon his own young shoulders every burden he could carry for anyone, man or beast. All this, even as he prayed and studied, drawing ever closer to God and his greater mission as the son of God, sent to save them all.

And then, toward the end, his single experience of loving a woman. The shepherd girl Tamara. So pure and beautiful, and brief. And though Mary's heart broke for him—for both of them—she rejoiced that he had not missed it, that the Father who had made her son human in every way had not deprived him of life's most sacred and glorious experience.

Mary's eyes were suddenly flooded. She blinked rapidly, embarrassed, trying to deny her tears, and the assault of other thoughts. But now—what had happened to this man whose life had started at her breast? Who were the people really closest to him now? That woman, Magdalene, so exceedingly beautiful with her exotic perfume—what did she mean to him? Jesus had been away so long, and no word of him ever came except from strangers. She remembered, with an ironic pang of amusement, how she had learned to read against the day when his letters would come. (He himself had taught her.) *He could have written!* At least a few words. No, no, that was like the accusations of her own mother, Hannah, when they first brought him home from Egypt. Mothers don't understand. "Mother, why can't you *understand?*" she had begged. Now it was her turn.

I knew he was born for the masses. What did I expect?

Not this, not this! Suddenly the pain struck, like an avalanche, blows from a terrible sword. Mary's knees buckled; she sagged. She could feel Magdalene's arms about her, and her sons'. . . . They seemed to be back on the street, for she could smell the donkeys. The poor things were braying; had they been fed? She couldn't remember. . . . She was aware of James and Josey supporting her, trying to lift her onto one of the little beasts, but she struggled against them. She must stand upright, keep walking. Her face was ashen. She was unable to look at the woman, who was trying to help, trying to comfort all of them, pleading, "Don't be hurt. *Please* don't be hurt. . . ."

Mary submitted; she was on the donkey after all, for she found she could not stand. "We must go." She made a feeble groping gesture toward her sons. "We shouldn't have come."

"Let me try to explain," the woman kept begging as they began to move. "That stupid servant put it badly; what Jesus said is not the way he made it sound!" In desperation, Magdalene appealed to Josey and Jude, whose faces were set as they strode indignantly along. "Jesus *loves* his family; he would *never* forsake you. Some of his finest lessons are phrased in such terms. He was only trying to illustrate a larger truth—that we all are brothers and sisters, one family, children of the Father who loves us, if we will do his will."

"He refused to see us," Josey reminded her bitterly. "He failed to acknowledge us."

"No—oh, no! That is not what he meant to convey."

They had reached a corner. The street was almost deserted. Still shocked and bewildered, they halted a moment, wondering where to go. "Are you all right, Mother?" James asked anxiously. "We must find food; we must find lodging and get you to bed."

"You haven't eaten?" Magdalene exclaimed, dismayed. "Why didn't I ask you before? Come home with me to Peter's house. Jesus and some of his men will surely be there soon."

"We don't want to see him," Josey informed her grimly. "He is no longer our brother."

"Don't say that!" Magdalene cried. "It's all a mistake. Those messengers don't always get things straight. How can they? Even the best of them can't remember his words exactly in the short time they have to listen. They get confused, they often forget, misinterpret." Magdalene appealed to Mary. "I myself am often astonished at what I have heard them report—it is sometimes so different from what I know Jesus actually believes and says."

Josey sneered. The knowing look he gave her stung. "I'm sure you have good reason to defend him."

As Magdalene flinched, Mary held out her hand. "Forgive us," she said. "We are all very tired. Perhaps it would be best if we accepted your hospitality some other time."

They turned then, startled by the frantic familiar barking of a dog, a voice shouting, "Wait! Wait!" The crowd before Zebedee's house was dispersing. They saw Jesus running toward them, both joy and consternation on his face.

Benjy got there first, barking and lunging, mad with joy at the sight of Mary. The frightened donkey shied and kicked. Mary lost her balance, felt herself spilling from the saddle into the strong dear arms, felt the curly silk of his hair and beard against her cheek. Jesus hugged and kissed her, then held her a little apart that he might study her face.

"Where are you going?" he cried, astonished. "Surely you're not leaving! I came as soon as I could."

He attempted to embrace his brothers. James submitted stiffly, but both Jude and Josey struck his arm aside. "Don't touch me!" they said.

Shocked and stricken, Jesus turned back to Mary. "Don't cry, Mother. Why are you crying?" he pleaded. "What's wrong?" And when she could not answer, his eyes went to Magdalene. "What message did that servant bring? Didn't he tell them that I was anxious to see them, and I would join them soon?"

"No. He only brought word of what he thought you had proclaimed: that you had no family, save those who do the will of God. No mother and no brothers and sisters—"

"You hypocrite!" Josey accused. "To deny us in public, humiliate us like this. You who accuse the *Pharisees* of hypocrisy and cheating their own widowed mothers."

Even James joined the attack. "To turn your backs on us is one thing," he said, though it cost him dearly to do so. "We are only your brothers. But to reject your own mother—!"

Jesus listened with an aching heart. "I meant no such thing," he said. "I also told them how much I love my mother and the memory of my father, but the love of the Father in heaven is greater—"

They refused to let him finish. "You are out of your mind," Josey lashed on. He was glaring, his plump rosy face more truculent than ever. "It's why we came—to bring you home, where you will be safe. All this fame and attention must have driven you mad; you are demon-possessed. People say you cast out demons. By whose power? I ask. The devil's? Well, whatever devil possesses *you*, let him come out!"

"Oh, no, no, no," Mary was moaning softly. This quarreling, her own flesh and blood in battle . . . it had always hurt, but never, never like this. And repeatedly now she felt the merciless stabbing of the long-predicted sword in her breast.

"You are a disgrace to our father's memory, a shame to us in Nazareth. . . ." The charges and denunciations rained on until Mary could bear no more. Suddenly, with the spunk of her own mother Hannah, she sprang toward them, once more a woman whose word was law. "Stop this," she ordered. "Stop it!" And though Josey towered over her, she grasped his shoulders and shook him. "I command you, say no more. You too, James and Jude." She paused to get her breath.

She stood breathing hard for a moment, while her children watched, alarmed, their eyes almost pitiful now, in their sympathy and remorse.

"Oh, my son," Mary said to Jesus, "we all love you. Our hearts are sore with fear for you. Please come home to Nazareth with us."

"Our mother is right," Josey said gruffly, ashamed. "This terrible thing that has happened to John . . . We need you. It would be a great comfort to our mother."

"We are not ashamed of you," Mary insisted softly. "Indeed, we are proud. We want you to come home to Nazareth, where people can see and hear you for themselves. Once they witness some of your wonders, once they hear you preach in the synagogue—"

Jesus smiled at his brothers, and gave a little laugh. "I'm afraid I can perform few wonders in Nazareth," he said. But he held Mary close and kissed her. "Of course I will do as you ask. Surely you know I would never say or do anything to hurt you. Of course I will come back for a time to Nazareth."

Chapter 10

*H*E was home, he was back home in Nazareth once more. And it seemed to his grandmother Hannah almost more joy than she could bear that he had chosen to spend these first few days in seclusion with her at the farm.

Mary slipped up too, of course, to be near him. Hannah smiled to hear their voices in fervent or quiet discussion, sometimes far into the night. A cozy peace enveloped Hannah as she drifted into sleep. A sense of some ultimate in her life achieved. If only his grandfather could be here to share it. Dear blunt, stoical Joachim, who had never once doubted, even in the beginning. Her husband had studied the scriptures, and he almost worshiped their daughter, to a point that angered her sometimes, leaving her out. Stubbornly, saying little, she knew Joachim had lived for the day when his adored grandson would fulfill every prophecy. While she . . . not that she was cynical, rather that her dry, cryptic, practical nature neither comprehended nor cared much about spiritual things. Leave that to the men. No, no, her passion for Mary and this blessed child was more one of blood, pride, possession.

They had vied for the boy's affection, she was ashamed to remember, quarreled and quibbled over many things. But oh, how they had loved each other, and how she missed him, and now if only . . . if only Joachim could be alive to see their grandson in his triumph, and herself—how much she had changed, how blindly she, too, now believed. But no—Hannah cut herself off sharply from futile grieving and regrets. Some things could never be corrected. On the other hand—Hannah blinked rapidly into the darkness one night, jaws tight with the old pain—sometimes some things *could*.

The family had joined in a conspiracy to protect Jesus. Once Nazareth got word that its famous son was here, he would have no peace. James and his uncles Matthew and Amos had met him after dark on a little-used road, and led him directly to the farm. Jesus needed rest; and he would be too conspicuous in town. They would say nothing. They would try to hide his whereabouts, at least until the Sabbath, when he would have to appear, of course. Perhaps to speak in the synagogue.

Hannah was torn. She could hardly wait for that victorious hour; yet she clung jealously to every minute this special grandson could be with her. Hers once more to pet and scold and spoil. To sleep on her fragrant linens, and devour the tiny raisin and nut studded cakes he had loved as a little boy.

"Stop now, you'll be sick—remember how your mother used to berate us both?"

Grinning, Jesus reached for more: one to pop into his own mouth, the other to feed to Ben, who lay eagerly watching.

Quickly, smartly, Hannah's little claw slapped his big brown hand. "How dare you feed that creature at my table?"

"Hannah, dear Grandmother Hannah—" Jesus pulled her onto his lap—that spindly body so shrunken and brittle with age he almost feared to crush it, those mischievous, fretful, loving eyes burning ever deeper in their sockets. "Live forever," he cried. "Don't ever change!"

Some days he slept late; others he rose before daybreak and went off to spend the day in the hills with his uncle's children and the sheep. Mary and her mother drew together while he was gone, speaking of him as they worked.

"Oh, it's such a joy to have him here," Hannah declared. "If only we could keep him, if we just didn't have to share him."

"We mustn't be selfish, Mother. He can't be ours much longer. He belongs to the people."

"Well, at least the people of Nazareth will see what he can do while he's here." Vigorously Hannah shook the skin of butter she was churning. Her eyes were snapping. "He'll show them. All those rumors, all the criticism—I've heard it, and so have you. People are jealous, that's all; they don't want to admit he's . . . who he is, because he comes from *here*."

Mary smiled to herself and went on with her mending. She had brought a big pile of it with her, mostly for her grandchildren. "It doesn't matter what people say or think, Mother."

"Well, it matters to me. And those other things they say. Cora was telling me just the other day—depend on your aunt to keep me well informed," she added testily. "They're saying Jesus thinks he's too good for Nazareth. That if he can really do all those wonderful things—feed the crowds, heal the sick, even—" Hannah caught her breath; she could not bring herself to utter "raise the dead." "Whatever it is he does, he ought to do them here!"

"People are only human, Mother. There are sick and hungry people in Nazareth too. A lot of them would like to believe."

"Not according to Cora."

"I'm sure Aunt Cora has a good answer for them. After all, she must have known about the wine at her granddaughter's wedding. I don't remember seeing her there that night, but surely Deborah or Lydia or someone must have told her."

"Yes, yes, the wine at the wedding feast." Bleakly Hannah inspected the contents of the skin. The milk was pale and watery, only a few clots were forming; she sniffed and it didn't smell right. In disgust, Hannah went to the edge of the roof where they were working, and pitched it, skin and all, over the side. The reminder of what she had missed by not going to Cana made her feel like that milk, weak and sour. To think she had stayed home to nurse a headache that night, of all nights, when it was to happen—somehow Mary had let it happen. *Jesus' first miracle.* And, ironically, in the home of Cora's kin, relatives only by marriage.

Hannah was hurt, and ashamed of being hurt.

"Cora really loves us, Mother. She's a valuable ally."

"Oh, yes, maybe *now.* But not in the beginning, not during your betrothal. Not when we needed her most, you and I. Me, her own sister-in-law; you, her own niece! Your aunt had the sharpest tongue in town."

"Mother, don't. That was all so long ago." Mary put down the small torn tunic she was patching, and went to stand beside Hannah, who was gripping the parapet with both hands, staring forlornly into the mountains. "We must forgive and forget. No matter how many times we are offended, Jesus says. If we expect the heavenly Father to forgive us, we must forgive."

"Oh, I've forgiven," Hannah insisted stubbornly. "I've put it all away, buried it, been nice to everybody, you know that. But forget? Does a mother ever forget the aspersions cast upon her daughter? Never!"

In love and pity, Mary contemplated her mother.

"How sad to carry such bitterness so long."

She put her arms around the intense little body then, comforting Hannah as if she were a child. "And it is all so trivial," Mary said, "compared to the pain and suffering in the world." Her voice broke. "Compared to Elizabeth. The agony Elizabeth must surely be going through right now."

Hannah winced. Once again she realized how grievously she had fallen short in her daughter's eyes. "Yes—oh, yes," she groaned in self-despair. "I'm the one that needs to be forgiven." Helplessly, in little strangling sobs, Hannah began to cry. "Thinking only of myself, when my own sister has lost her son! Oh, poor John, so viciously murdered. And Elizabeth, the sister I used to envy, so ill with grief— she may be dying, and I can't go to her. To think of her going through all this while Jesus—your son, my own grandson—is succeeding. Living up to all of John's predictions!"

Suddenly, buoyed up by the prospect, Hannah rallied. She blew her nose and wiped her eyes. She could not resist; almost against her will, she found herself declaring, "And Nazareth will soon realize it too, once he appears in the synagogue."

Mary was troubled, filled with apprehension. "Oh, Mother, please don't put so much stock in this," she warned. "Just remember the influence Jesus is having all through Galilee, in cities like Capernaum, and even north to Tyre and Sidon and beyond. The crowds that follow him—I was astounded when I saw them. Nazareth is just a little town, Nazareth isn't important."

"It is to me!" Hannah flashed back. "I don't care how many people follow him anywhere else—I'm not there to witness his wonders. It may seem trivial to you, but not to me. It's Nazareth I care about. It's Nazareth I want to pay him homage."

Despite their precautions, word had gotten out. Jesus was seen one evening helping the youngsters bring in the sheep. On Sabbath morning, the streets were filled with people hastening to the synagogue. By the time Hannah and Timna got there, the steps were crowded.

Hannah had started early, stopping for the other grandmother in her quarters behind the shop. As usual, the stately, slow-moving older woman wasn't ready. Yet a kind of impatient peace was upon Hannah, as she darted to help Timna, who was poking around trying to find a shawl for her shining white head. "Here, use mine. Let me tie it for you." Hannah's fingers shook as she fastened the knot under the placid face that seemed so ancient, though it was actually only a few years older than her own, and less wrinkled and time-scarred. "We had better go, there will be a crowd."

"They will make room for us," Timna said, with her benign little smile.

"Yes, surely. Oh, if only Joachim could have lived long enough to witness this day."

"Or my Jacob. Or Joseph, his father."

Jacob? Well, perhaps, Hannah thought, although the poor man had never even seen his grandson. "Yes, Joseph," she acknowledged. "It would be a proud day for all our men."

People did indeed make way for the two grandmothers struggling to ascend the worn stone steps—Hannah pausing to catch her breath, Timna supporting her heavy body with an effort on her stick. Hannah's bare head was high; her little deep-set eyes darted around, bright with pride and a touch of defiance. Though most of them greeted her warmly, it seemed to her a few halted their conversations almost too quickly. Were some of them laughing, arguing among themselves? No, no, she must not imagine things. Everything would be all right now; today everything would be resolved, justified, all the old scores settled.

She could hardly wait to join Mary in the balcony, stand beside her gazing down on the ultimate triumph. She hoped Cora and Deborah were here—oh, yes, there they were, waving and beckoning. And seeing Cora's big, assured, dominating, yet warmly effusive face, and Deborah beaming beside her (looking gaunt, however, and so much older than Mary), the two of them moving aside so generously to make room at the railing, Hannah's heart melted. Mary was right. It was selfish and foolish of her to harbor those ancient resentments so long. It hurt too much, it spoiled things; she should be ashamed.

A wave of love smote her, an anguish of tenderness for them, and for the people on the steps, pushing to get inside to hear Jesus. Many of them were strangers, people who seldom set foot in a synagogue. Whatever their motives—to scoff or to marvel, even hoping for miracles, some of them (she'd noticed a few cripples)—never mind, it didn't matter; they'd soon understand. And her whole precious family, who had rallied to welcome Jesus home, to defend and support him now . . .

The familiar scratching and crooning of the pigeons on the roof . . . the acrid smell of the lamps fluttering in their ruby globes, like frightened little hearts beating . . . the music beginning, and the men below—oh, the men in their bright Sabbath robes, standing so solemn and yet expectant below. Her own heart was stabbed fiercely afresh as she thought of Elizabeth, whose son would never again stride forth in Temple or synagogue. . . . And Joachim . . . *Oh, Joachim!* she silently cried. *Look down, wherever you are—let your spirit look down on your grandson in his glory. You may even see him perform miracles here today.*

Why not? All her life she had dismissed such claims as preposterous nonsense. But so blind was her passion for her own that more and more Hannah had come to believe that nothing was impossible for them. Certainly not for Jesus. His very existence was a miracle. Jesus could do anything. Jesus performed healings in the synagogues, it was said, even on the Sabbath—one reason he was criticized by the authorities. Well, let them criticize him here, if they dared! And a sudden wild conviction came upon her, a concept so staggering that she felt faint. He would heal Elizabeth of her suffering, if she were here. He could touch the eyes of his own uncle, poor Esau, and make him see again. Perhaps even *Joachim,* she mused, half in terror, even *Joseph!* though both had lain long in the tomb. Why not? He *had* raised the dead.

Hannah had gone white; she was shaking so, Mary reached out, alarmed, and drew her back from the rail. "Mother, are you all right?" she whispered. "You had better sit down."

"No. No, not yet." For the services were already proceeding; she could hear the psalms being finished, then the rhythmic monotones of the Shema. The leader of the synagogue was speaking, the same big, thickset, black-bearded rabbi who had taught Jesus in school.

"Today we are honored to have with us a guest," he announced, "though it is hard to speak of him as a guest, since he was raised here among us—Jesus, the son of Mary and Joseph, and once my student in the synagogue school. It is my privilege to call him forward to read to us today from the book of the prophet Isaiah. And to speak to us, if he so desires, as he has spoken to those gathered in synagogues throughout all Galilee."

Heads craned; there was a little rumbling stir of anticipation. The women in the gallery pressed forward, so anxious to see him that Hannah was glad for Mary's protecting arm. How could Mary, his own mother, be so calm? a tiny tower of strength supporting her, as if they two stood alone in a pending storm. But no, not alone; Hannah felt her sister-in-law's huge silken bosom against her, smelled Deborah's tart-sweet perfume; and just behind her felt the hand of her second daughter, Salome, on her shoulder; was aware of Judith there too, all three of her daughters with their daughters, and her sons' wives with their children, all loyal, expectant, proud; and her eyes filled and her heart nearly burst with thanksgiving.

And now they saw Jesus, moving forward with his long graceful stride that was so like Joseph's, giving only a fleeting glance upward, as they had secretly hoped, his jaw slightly jutted, his beautiful face intense. To Hannah's disappointment, he was not wearing the pure white robe and fringed mantle that had been described to her as his usual garb for preaching, but rather a simple ordinary blue Sabbath cloak, no brighter and even less fine than the garments worn by most of the men.

Even so, he was like a prince compared to them. There was a radiance about him, as if the sun streaming through a window had focused all its light upon him, so that he stood for an instant in a golden pool there on the platform, waiting to take the book from the rabbi's hands. To his grandmother's eager eyes, there was even a nimbus around his head.

The gaze of the two men held. Both were deeply moved. "This is a proud moment, my son," the leader rumbled, handing over the heavy scroll.

Jesus opened it to the place. A hush fell as he studied the words. Then, in a clear ringing voice, he began to read: " 'The Spirit of the Lord is upon me, because he has anointed me to preach good tidings to the poor. He has sent me to proclaim release to the captives, and recovering of sight to the blind. To set at liberty those who are oppressed, to proclaim the acceptable year of the Lord.' "

Jesus paused, considering. Then, with an air of finality, he rolled up the scroll and handed it to the rabbi; gravely he sat down.

For an instant the people were startled; then, with a rustling of garments, a scraping of benches, they too were seated. All eyes were fixed upon him, waiting: expectant and puzzled, for he only sat for a time with his face in his hands. Surely he was going to speak, Hannah thought frantically. He needn't, of course, but it would be folly not to—here to his own people, in his own synagogue. Mary had said Nazareth wasn't important, but it was—oh, it was. These people would be insulted if he didn't; they would never believe the wonders they had heard of him.

At last he lifted his head, faced them directly, clear-eyed and confident as his voice rang out: "Today this scripture has been fulfilled in your hearing!"

There was a moment of shocked silence. People looked at each other, bewildered, trying to take this in. What did he mean? What was he trying to tell them? What was he about to proclaim? A few sat back, arms folded, intrigued, bemused; others were leaning forward in an attitude of hope and anticipation.

Smiling now, Jesus met the challenge in their questioning faces. Gracefully, eloquently, in his voice that was like music, he told them, "I am indeed one sent by the Father of us all, to lead you into the paths of righteousness and truth. To show you the true meaning of the laws that have been perverted and corrupted so long. For this I was sent into the world: to comfort the poor and lonely and heavy-laden, and those who grieve. To free those who are captives, not only to Caesar but to sin. To help the hurting, to heal the sick, in body or in spirit."

He spoke to them as he had spoken to the multitudes on the hillsides beside the sea. Of love and forgiveness and mercy, of giving up earthly possessions for the greater riches of the heavenly kingdom. A kingdom that can be realized right now on earth, if God's children are willing to love each other as themselves, share with each other, and "do unto others only as you would have them do unto you." He had been sent to cure not only blind and crippled bodies but, far more important, blind and crippled souls. To show them the way to eternal life.

And at first the congregation listened, most of them charmed and awed, as the multitudes had been. It was so beautiful Hannah wanted to weep. At last Nazareth had its chance to hear him, and their response so far was plain: They were proud of him. Drawing a deep breath of relief, she squeezed Mary's hand.

But suddenly, to their dismay, a man got to his feet, a kind of lazy uncurling of his angular body. Mary and Ann, her oldest daughter, exchanged startled glances. They were striving to recall him, this scornful, vaguely familiar pockmarked face. Oh, yes, Ruben, an older boy, who had sometimes swaggered along, bullying Jesus on his way home from school, tormenting his first little dog, Jubal.

"Where did you learn all this, my friend? I remember you from synagogue school. But I don't remember you ever went on to study things like this in Jerusalem." People were craning their necks, most of them shocked and irritated at the interruption; but a few were grinning and nodding their approval. "Aren't you a carpenter's son? Didn't you and your brothers cut trees once from my father's land? I guess you're a pretty good carpenter, and not too bad a shepherd— at least you spent plenty of time on the farm—but where did you learn all this? What gives you the authority to make such claims?"

"That's right," another voice shouted. "Who are you to instruct us?" The man sprang up, short, stout, bull-necked, contemptuous. At sight of him, Hannah sickened and covered her eyes. The whole family gasped, and the women turned anxiously toward Salome, who sat white and still as death. For this was Abinadab, a friend of her former husband and a member of the town council; it was he who had written her bill of divorcement. Hannah reached backward, groping for her daughter's cold hand.

"Who is he to come back to Nazareth and preach?" the man demanded hotly in his gravelly voice. "I know his whole family. Look, a lot of them are here right now." His pudgy finger began to point them out. "His brothers—James and Josey and Jude. Where's Simon? Oh, yes, over there. And his mother, Mary, and his sisters." Disdainfully, he indicated the balcony. "How dare he come back to Nazareth pretending to be a prophet?" He wheeled to address Jesus in scathing tones. "You're no better than we are. Answer me—aren't these people related to you?"

Jesus' head was high. "I am very proud of my family," he said fervently.

"That's not what *I* heard: Not in front of your rich friends, I'm told. Not when they came to see you in Capernaum. They weren't good enough for you there; you pretended you didn't even have a family!"

Josey shuddered, and cringed lower in his seat, cursing himself. What ever had possessed him to confide his lingering rancor about that night to anyone, even to his own wife? Evidently she'd said something at the well, and the gossip had spread. But he was too miserable to hide. Gritting his teeth, Josey sprang to his feet. "No, no, it wasn't like that at all!" he protested angrily. "It was all a misunderstanding."

The crowd of men weren't listening. Aroused now, arguing among themselves, attacking, defending, vying to be heard. But the rough voice of Abinadab still predominated. "You may be able to fool strangers with your so-called miracles, but just try that here!" The man was shaking his fist. "I challenge you: Perform some miracles for us right now, if you dare!"

"Yes, yes, *let* him try it!" an old man shrieked from the rear. He was crippled and palsied, racked with pain. Half doubting, half in desperation, his sons had brought him today.

Jesus lifted his hand to quiet them. And in a moment, like the waves of the sea, they became calm once more. Yet he could only stand, sad and incredulous, regarding them. Hannah, waiting prayerfully, was aware that something was wrong. Did Mary sense it too? How could she sit with such absolute composure, staring at the deeply troubled face of her son?

Jesus' heart ached for them, and for all those so dear to him who had come with such high hopes today. Yet he could not, would not, use his powers merely to impress or persuade.

"I know what you are thinking," he said with great dignity. "Physician, heal yourself. If you can do all these things in cities like Capernaum, do them for us in Nazareth. But first let me say that you misjudge me if you think I claim any special glory for myself. The honor belongs to the One who sent me. The Son of Man can do nothing of his own accord; I can do nothing on my own authority."

"Second, it grieves me to remind you: No prophet is acceptable in his own country. It is written that even Elijah and Elisha, when they came back to Israel, found they were powerless to heal their own people. Though there were many widows there, Elijah could help only a foreign woman from Sidon. And though there were also many Jewish lepers, the only one Elisha could cure was Naaman, a Syrian. I'm sorry," Jesus said abruptly, "the resistance is too strong. Healing requires faith. I find little faith among you. I can do nothing here."

Pausing only to embrace the rabbi, Jesus stepped down from the platform and started up the aisle. Though many eyes followed him with affection and respect—even awe—there were also catcalls, laughter, jeering. His face was grim. He hurt deeply for this humiliation to his family. But worse were the pitiful cries of those who were crippled, blind or ill. "Please, please!" they begged plaintively, and he could only pass them by.

What happened next was so confusing the women in the balcony could only lean forward, trying to see, mystified. There seemed to be a scuffling in the back, muffled voices. Heads below were turning, a few men getting angrily to their feet. Although up front, where the rabbi was leading worshipers in the final prayers, others seemed oblivious of the commotion.

Abinadab had slipped out while Jesus was speaking, giving a curt nod to his cohorts. Mostly louts from neighboring villages, Ruben and a few others from Nazareth. Arms folded, they were waiting for Jesus, a menacing phalanx, blocking the door.

"Heretic!" Abinadab snarled. "Comparing yourself to prophets, too good for Nazareth. Son of Man, eh? Take him!"

The men pounced.

Mary realized now. Shocked and appalled, she grabbed her mother. "Come quickly. We must go."

"Go? Go where?" Hannah gasped, feeling foolish and helpless. It was all wrong, a bad dream, a ghastly mistake. Her knees jelled; she must sit down—she was overexcited and not thinking straight. If she just rested a minute or two, all this would pass.

Mary gave her a quick, frantic glance. Yes, this was best. Better that her mother stayed behind.

To Hannah's surprise, the balcony was soon cleared. She realized, with a little start, that even Timna was gone—people had helped her down the steps. Where was everybody? She must join them, make the effort. What was going on? She felt stupid, sitting here, shaking. She was needed!

Hannah rallied, alert now and vigorously alive in every nerve. Heart pounding wildly, she started off, but turned back to snatch up her shawl, which Timna had left behind in her haste. Jesus had given it to her, it flashed through Hannah's consciousness; she didn't want to lose it.

Outside, incredibly, it was still a beautiful day. The sun still shone, the trampled grass smelled sweet. People were streaming across it, or standing in pairs or horrified little groups, watching the place where someone had been thrown down upon it. It was hard to see, because of the surrounding huddle of sweaty backs. There was the blunt sound of kicking and pummeling, men panting, dark laughter.

Women were sobbing, or standing in frozen silence. "No, no, don't!" a man was muttering, though he made no move to stop it. "Let him go, he meant no harm." Others came running from the synagogue, fists clenched.

Cora and Deborah were pointing and screaming. "Jesus! It's Jesus—somebody help him. Oh, poor Mary!" Hysterically, they tried to comfort her, where she stood a little apart eyes scanning the synagogue for her sons, while tears streamed down her cheeks.

Fiercely, though still clutching the shawl, Hannah fought her way through the edge of the ugly circle. She glimpsed the blue robe, bloodied and torn from his back. Jesus was on his knees. Every time he tried to rise, a foot kicked or an arm shoved him down again.

What'll we do with him?" grinned his old tormentor, Ruben; one long, brutal foot was planted on Jesus' neck.

The circle closed in, but Hannah could hear the brief agitated discussion. Should they beat him, hang him, or throw him in prison? No, it would be more sport to drag him along the streets.

"Then what?"

"Take him up onto the hill and shove him off!"

"Which hill?"

"The highest one, you idiot. Where we can throw him onto the rocks."

Hannah felt herself shoved roughly aside from behind. "Get out of the way, Grandma," said James.

And as she stumbled, Hannah gasped; she would never forget the look of cold, stark murder on that usually sweet, peace-loving face.

Ruben floundered; he had time only to look over his shoulder before he was felled by the blow from Josey. He pitched forward, felt the hard ground, smelled bloody grass. He was vaguely aware that Jesus was being pulled to his feet by James. Two of the attackers tried to flee, but were caught by Jude and Simon and dragged back, to stand stubbornly defiant before the wrath of Mary's sons. The brothers had been tricked into a spurious debate inside, only racing to the scene when a frightened onlooker brought them word.

"You beasts—you will pay dearly for this!" Josey raged, his round face livid, his small bright eyes ablaze. "If there's any justice in Nazareth, you will be punished."

"No, Josey, stop," Jesus ordered. He stood before them half naked, bruised and dirty from the ground; his battered nose was bleeding, one eye already swollen half shut. Blood also trickled from a corner of his mouth. He brushed the blood away impatiently with the back of his hand. "Forgive them. I forgive them, and so must you. They don't realize what they have done."

"But they should be arrested! They're brutes, they deserve it—this is wrong!"

Abinadab had been watching a safe distance away. Now he stalked up, pugnacious and self-righteous. "Why are you defending this imposter?" he demanded. "Why are you interfering?"

Josey wheeled on him, breathing hard, "Because he is our *brother!*"

The men started off, not noticing Hannah in the confusion. But she ran determinedly after them, fighting not to cry. "Wait, Jesus, wait!" she called, holding out her shawl. "Put this around you!" And hearing her, her grandson halted. "You're hurt," she wailed, "you're almost naked. Just look at you, people can't see you like that!"

Jesus smiled at her as best he could, and reached out gratefully to take the shawl. His bruised hand squeezed hers for a second. And despite herself, Hannah wept.

Chapter 11

SIMON Peter started the long journey back to Caesarea Philippi in a daze.

He was aware that a light drizzle was falling, spattering the dust at his feet and cooling his hot flushed brow; that he had deliberately caught up to his brother Andrew, instead of walking with Jesus as usual, and was trying to make brisk conversation with him. But over and over, his mind was crying, "Me? To think that the Lord has spoken thus to *me*." He was torn between exultation and pain. For despite that high moment of praise and commendation, he had failed the Master in the end.

A sense of his own unworthiness overwhelmed him, together with this awed jubilation that was almost too much to be borne, let alone understood. No, he dared not even stride along beside Jesus right now—he might say something foolish again. The old secret shyness struck him, a sense of his awkwardness, his cursed ability to blunder, blurt out something stupid—ironically, often at the very moment of his deepest love. Peter's pride wrangled with his shame.

If only he could be more like James and John. Look at them now, swinging along ahead, their clouds of bright hair shining even in the mist that veiled the sinking sun. Cavorting, calling back something to the weary group trudging behind, which made them laugh. No wonder Jesus enjoyed them so, especially John. Their high spirits were a relief after the serious business of the day.

Agonizing business, so much of it—all that misery, the sick, the dying . . . the *dead*. Even the heady triumph of healing could not cancel out the heavy burden, for it only multiplied. The more people they cured, the more the ranks of sufferers swelled, an endless stream of

sufferers—leprous, epileptic, sightless, deaf, dumb, maimed, many of
them mad, screaming obscenities, possessed. Some nights they peopled the darkness; he could see their desperate faces, hear them groaning. He would jerk upright, sweating, echoing their groans. Adah
would have to shake him, sometimes even slap him, before she could
comfort him back to sleep.

Inadvertently, Peter groaned now. His back hurt and his feet were
killing him; his heart was troubled.

"Don't worry, brother," Andrew tried to cheer him. "Only a few
more miles and we'll be home."

"Home?" Peter grinned wryly and slapped him on the shoulder.
I'm afraid it's a long way back to Capernaum."

"Yes, but we'll be there, too, again in a few more days."

How could Andrew be so agreeable? Peter wondered. Actually
pleased, if surprised, at his company. His own *brother*. Peter felt guilty
about that too. That long, homely, innocent and forgiving face. So
much more likable than I am, Peter berated himself. More naturally
enthusiastic, trusting and certain of what he believed. In his easygoing
and generous way, Andrew had always had more friends. And he had
been Jesus' first disciple. Strange—it sometimes troubled Peter—that
Jesus had not chosen Andrew to be his close companion, instead of
him. Andrew never spoke of it; if it bothered him, he gave no sign.
Of course, I'm older, Peter thought. But look at James and John,
they're even younger.

And now this latest, larger recognition from the Master! Peter's
heart pounded, his throat was dry. Again that surge of astonished
rapture, mixed with remorse and dismay. An honor far more than he
deserved or had ever dared to dream of. Beyond the power of man to
imagine, let alone a dull, ordinary, silent but sometimes brash, blunt-
tongued fisherman . . . *And he had ruined it.*

Fumbling, Peter tried to open the bag that hung over his shoulder;
what little water was left might relieve his aching throat. Seeing his
dilemma, Andrew twisted the cork from his own. "Here," he offered.
"I have plenty, take mine."

Peter gulped a few swallows, splashed a little on his sweaty
arms—they were itching from many insect bites. The light shower had
stopped, the mist was clearing, the sun was an orange disk about to
sink into a blue cleft of the mountain; he was anxious to be on. Yet

he stood a moment, one foot planted on a rock, wishing he dared blurt out his feelings to his brother. Confess his own stupidity, ask Andrew's advice. But no, it might be embarrassing. Andrew, like the other apostles, had heard Jesus bestow that tremendous honor on him. A pronouncement that had staggered all of them. As for his own failure . . . Peter cringed. Andrew had always been so proud of him, why risk disillusioning him now?

No, this would have to wait for Adah.

He had missed her sorely these past few days. The prospect of seeing her soon, holding her big body against his, cheered him as he plodded on. Adah had stayed behind with several of the other women, to rest and to wash some clothes. His heart reached out to her, stirred by the grudging, surprised admiration he often felt. That his wife—any of them—would be sturdy and loyal enough to make this long trek up into these Gentile highlands. A rough journey, they'd been warned, but no, the women would come—at least a few of those still faithful to the cause: Magdalene, Joanna, even the twins' mother, Salome, when she could.

Most of the women had gotten discouraged; defeated not so much by the hardships as by the hostility they encountered. The pointing fingers, jeers, sometimes outright abuse. "Why don't you go home where you belong?" men shouted, and sometimes their wives—shocked and often very angry at the spectacle. The very idea—women traveling about openly with men! And treated almost as equals, or so it seemed. One by one those first women had fallen away, humiliated. Or frightened. (Like a lot of once enthusiastic disciples after what had happened to Jesus in Nazareth; news of that near calamity had spread.) Scared off by the constant threats. For it was no secret that spies were everywhere, Temple agents forever on their trail, even way up here in alien territory, Caesarea Philippi, where there weren't many Jews, but mostly Greek and Roman pagans.

No, it wasn't an easy life for the women. And much as they helped, especially at the healings—holding crying children, reassuring relatives, comforting people, encouraging them to wait patiently for their turn—there were drawbacks. With women along, there were far fewer invitations into homes. To welcome a famous holy man and his coterie was one thing, but female companions? Unheard of! Other women discussed this in dismay or alarm, gossiping, some defending, others attacking. And some a little envious, wondering if they would have the nerve.

Oh, dear brave gentle Adah and her friends, never retorting, always smiling back, practicing everything Jesus taught them about turning the other cheek, returning evil only with good.

Peter remembered how one day Adah had been denounced by a screaming young mother with toddlers at her skirts and a baby on her shoulder; its tiny mouth was malformed, in a head piteously large. Adah had turned toward her, almost bursting with compassion. "Bless you," she had cried, reaching out her arms. "Oh, you poor darling, let me hold him." And when the mother drew back, indignant, Adah had counseled, "Bring him to the meadow in the morning." To her surprise, the mother was there, and gave the child over to Adah's cradling and crooning. And Jesus held him too, talking softly to him and stroking the silken head. And he cupped the little face in his hand and lightly kissed the cleft lip. And lo, the child became beautiful and whole before their eyes.

Adah wept for joy as she handed him back. But even then this mother and her still disapproving husband turned their backs and walked away, without a thank you either for Jesus or for Adah. Let alone an invitation, though the travelers had no place to stay—they had slept in the field the night before.

Forgive, forgive, forgive, Jesus kept saying. It didn't matter. The very word meant to give without expectation of repayment, or even gratitude. Hold nothing against the one to whom you have given. And Adah never did. She had prayed for that couple every day, and their precious little boy. She hoped to return to their village sometime, that she might look them up, and take the child a toy. And the other children too, of course; they must not be left out.

He was with her at last, in their small room in the two-family house Adah had found for them on the outskirts of the city. But Adah had been so overjoyed to see him—hurling herself against him in a way that amused him, for it always reminded him of the way Jesus' dog Benjy acted whenever his master returned—and their lovemaking so unexpected (even before the simple supper she had waiting), so ardent and humanly satisfying, that Peter could only lie for a time, exhausted and drowsing. Reluctant to disturb this overwhelming physical peace.

Beyond the wall he could hear youngsters scuffling, a father's reprimand. Nearer, dishes rattled, Adah was humming; there was the smell of the food she was reheating over a few coals still smoking in the brazier. Peter drifted off. . . . He was lying again on a grassy hillside, he heard voices murmuring, arguing, the swift bright gurgling of a stream rushing from a nearby cave . . . cold water splashing on his face. "Come, my darling—" His wife was bending over him, a wet cloth in her hand, a basin at her feet. "You must wash now, and eat."

Peter roused, startled, with a sudden sense of anxiety and distress. Where was he? What were they doing here? He stared at her blankly, looked miserably around. He felt bewildered and unworthy, and yes, alarmed. These poor surroundings; his own crude humanness. Was the strain of this rigorous, impassioned life they had chosen getting to be too much for him? Might he be losing his mind? Now all that he longed so urgently to pour out to her filled him with apprehension. Be careful, be very sure.

Adah could feel his agitation. She was not a clever women, but she was astute; years of living with Peter had taught her to wait out his silences and his occasional storms. He loved her, and he had to confide in someone. Eventually he would speak. But later that night when she could feel his great body trembling beside her, she could wait no longer. "What is it?" she asked tenderly, rising up on one elbow. "Tell me."

Yes, he must try. But how could he phrase it? His mind groped back: He could see the crowds dispersing, some of them jubilant, entranced, others frowning, arguing, suspicious, but whether friend or adversary, asking almost the same questions: Who was this man who traveled the length of the land, healing and feeding the masses, and proclaiming the kingdom? Prophet or madman? Charlatan, magician, heretic, pretender to the throne? Magician or messiah—another of the long line of self-appointed saviors, albeit with more incredible powers? Whence did his powers come? From the nameless One in heaven, or demons that squirmed up from the bowels of the earth?

This Nazarene, this wandering Galilean—traveling into Phoenicia and Syria, as far north as Tyre and Sidon, and south, far south into Judea, even Jerusalem, the very camp of his greatest enemies, those in charge of the Temple—hounded, harassed, challenged, threatened with arrest, but always escaping, triumphant . . . Could Herod's fears be right? This must be the murdered John, resurrected! Or maybe Elijah, Jeremiah, one of the prophets . . .

"We were resting," Peter began. "We had paused to drink from a stream that pours out of a small cave near the Jordan. A cave where they say the pagans sometimes worship their nature god, Pan." He remembered the sylvan glade, the smell of moss and water, and the vines that spilled down from the trees. And the feeling of wonder in his own heart at a God who could create so much beauty, whatever his name.

"We were talking about this," he went on. "The fertility rites the Canaanites perform. Right there, where we were. And how confused people are about religion. How we know, you and I know, all Israelites know, there is only one true God. Yet these Greeks and Romans—how they laugh at us and scorn us and think we're crazy. And we ourselves, our own differences, how confused Jews are about Jesus. You know how the crowds are, you've heard them yourself."

"Over and over," Adah agreed.

He held her a little closer, still struggling to express it. "Jesus stood only a few feet away. He knew what we were talking about, he always did, we could speak freely. He was washing his hands in the stream, but then he came to join us, stood there, wiping them on his tunic. But his face was very serious as he asked, 'And who do men say that I, the Son of Man, am?" Peter hesitated, remembering their own confusion before the unexpected question.

"What did you tell him?"

"Well, various people spoke up. Judas was one, I remember. It was hard to explain. That people were wondering if he might be one of the prophets come back to life, even John the Baptist. What else could we tell Jesus? It was all we could think to say."

"And then?"

"Then he asked us another question. One that was a lot more important—that was plain. 'But who do *you* say that I am?' " Peter was breathing hard. It was a moment before he could go on.

"Tell me," Adah urged. "Tell me what was said."

"I spoke up then. I blurted it out, I couldn't help it. 'You are the Christ!' I told him. 'The Son of the living God!' And he came to me at once—I'll never forget the look in his eyes—he strode to me and put his hands on my shoulders and called me blessed, Adah!" Peter's voice was humble, marveling. "And he said, 'Flesh and blood has not revealed this to you, but my Father who is in heaven.' And he called me by my name. *Peter . . . the rock . . .* Never have I heard him say it quite like that, in those tones. And he said that on my confession he would build his kingdom."

"The words you had just spoken?"

"Yes. And there is more. Jesus said—I swear it—that he was giving me the keys to the kingdom of heaven, and my authority would prevail, both in heaven and on the earth."

Adah gasped. Carefully, she disengaged her big warm body from his. She rose and began to plod about the room. A finger of moonlight poked through the single slot of window; two red coals still glowed, like watchful eyes. They hissed as she threw a cup of water on them. She felt dazed and somehow . . . appalled. How could this be? What did it all mean? Wealth, power, fame? For big rough Peter and herself? Ridiculous! Yet for one blinding instant she was dazzled. Then alarmed. Like Peter himself, she wondered if perhaps her husband needed rest. The constant traveling, the insecurity, never knowing where they would eat or sleep. The feverish adulation—even that was a strain, but worse were the attacks. The false stories about Jesus, reflecting on all of them: that he was a wine bibber, glutton, lawbreaker; that he consorted with known sinners, had them in his company—a tax collector, a former prostitute. The narrow escapes from actual bodily harm, or arrest. And the incessant parade of the sick and afflicted, hobbling, led, carried, some of them even crawling, all of them crying for help, or pleading with their pitiful eyes.

Was Peter himself getting ill? He had felt feverish to her caressing hands. Waking, his eyes were strange. Had he misunderstood, or even imagined this incredible thing he had told her?

And now, as Adah went back to him, she realized that her husband was weeping. Silently, tearlessly, but with those great dry shuddering sobs that convulsed his whole body and tore the heart from her breast. Only once had she known him to cry thus—when the body of their stillborn son had been placed in his arms to hold before they must take it away.

"Peter—oh, my dearest, what is it? What is wrong?"

"I failed him," Peter choked, when he could speak. "In the end, I failed him. Surely now he realizes I don't deserve such an honor."

"Why? In heaven's name, *why*? I don't understand."

"It was only because I love him so much. I couldn't stand it—for after that Jesus began telling us things he says we must be ready for. Little by little every day, things he had never spoken about before. That the time is coming when the chief priests and scribes and elders will succeed. That he must go up to Jerusalem and suffer, that he will be arrested and tried—and killed."

"No!" Adah protested. "Oh—*no!*"

"I couldn't stand it, Adah—even though he also told us we must not be afraid, that he would rise up again in three days. I walked away from the circle and wept as I am weeping now. . . . And that night I couldn't sleep. I rose and went to him where he was lying under the stars with his cloak across his face. He lay so still—like a corpse. It was like that stormy night on the lake, as if he might be already dead. I was terrified, beside myself. I pulled the cloak from across his face and shook him, bidding him wake up. 'God forbid, Lord!' I told him in my desperation. 'You, who are truly the Messiah, need not let this come upon you. Or upon us, who love you so?' "

"You did right," Adah said fiercely. "You acted out of love."

"Jesus *turned* on me!" The words seemed torn from his tongue. Groaning, Peter threshed about, beat the pallet with his fist. "He told me to get away from him! He said I was a hindrance to him, not on the side of God but of man."

"You are no hindrance, you are his rock. Jesus depends on you," Adah defended. "You have served him utterly, asking nothing for yourself."

"But what he said was true: I was speaking as a man. I was thinking of myself—and you."

"You *are* a man, how else could you speak?"

"But if this *is* God's plan—"

"Are you mad?" Adah cried. "Or is God? Would he not rescue his own *son*? The Messiah that he himself has sent to us?"

Absently, frantically, Adah began to rebraid her tumbled hair. "And even if this were not so, what can be right or just about the condemnation and death of an innocent man? This healer that we have followed, given up everything for—this good, generous, decent rabbi who denounces hypocrisy and cheating and bloodshed, and teaches that God is love. Don't tell me he is also so weak he will let sin triumph, and they will nail him to the cross of a common criminal in the end!"

Helplessly, Peter held out his arms to her, and his wife went into them. "There is much that I don't understand," he said, as she nestled close. He was quiet now, no longer writhing in self-torment. "I only know that there is no turning back. Yes, even though there be a cross ahead . . . And other crosses too, Adah," he said after a minute. "Our own crosses to carry. That, too, he told us: 'You must deny yourself and be willing to take up your cross if you would follow me.' "

"Aren't we already doing that?" Adah asked bluntly.

"Yes, in many ways." Peter gave her an appreciative squeeze. "But it could get worse," he warned. "If need be, we must be willing to die for him." At her shudder, he held her closer. "But oh, Adah, Jesus also promised that whoever loses his life for him will find it again. He said that he would return personally with his angels, and repay us for all that we have done."

She was too stunned to answer. But telling her had relieved him. With a sigh, Peter turned away from her, and burying his great head in his massive arms, slept. Adah lay rigid, staring into the darkness until dawn. . . .

Peter was resigned and cheerful the rest of the week. Then, after the Sabbath, he bade Adah wait with Magdalene: Jesus had asked him and the twins to go up into the mountains with him. "We may climb Mount Hermon. The peak is not far, but we'll probably be gone all day. You may want to go into the marketplace."

Adah kissed him. Never mind that she had no money to spend. It was enough to see him so happy again, so proud to be restored to Jesus' company and confidence. It was a bright blue jewel of a day, yet she insisted Peter carry a cloak. "It's always winter on Mount Hermon, you will need it. Yes, and boots." She looked at his big callused feet in their broken sandals. How many miles had they already trudged; why couldn't he rest one more day? Yet it was important to be ready whenever the Master wanted him.

She hurried back into the small crowded room and began rummaging among their few bundles, hoping by some miracle she had packed the boots. She had to return with only a pair of leggings, which he stubbornly refused. But Peter was grinning as he turned to wave at her and Andrew. His brother had come running up at the last minute to wish him well. Andrew, too, was beaming, though there was a trace of something wistful in his eyes.

"Do you need anything?" he asked Adah solicitously when the others had disappeared. "There are some colorful bazaars in the city. Have you visited them?"

"Yes, with Magdalene several times," Adah laughed. "She has the money to spend."

"I have a little," he offered. "Not much, but it might help."

"No, no, no, I'm happy just to look. Most of all I'm thankful to see Simon Peter himself again."

"Yes, he was very upset; I couldn't understand it." Andrew stood rubbing his long jaw, pondering. His high forehead glistened. "Peter never explains himself to me. It had something to do with the Master, that I could tell. For all his bluster—you know this, you're his wife— Peter can be easily hurt, he's really very shy."

Adah squeezed his hand. "Andrew, we've both lived with that a long time."

"I think secretly he feels unworthy. Peter never seeks favors. But once they are bestowed!"

"Yes, then he's both humble and very proud. And so are we!" Adah cried. Suddenly they hugged each other there in the sun. Over Andrew's shoulder she could see Magdalene coming, looking so beautiful her heart brightened. It might be a good day, after all, to visit the bazaars.

Up and up they climbed, Peter, James and John, rejoicing, seeing no one except for a few shepherds in the foothills, grazing their sheep. No preaching and healing today, no crowds to be kept at bay, no stink of rotting flesh and running sores or sights of human misery, no sounds of wailing and pleading or the horrible hiss that demons sometimes make, spewing from a tortured mouth. All was clear, clean, still, the rocks glittering like diamonds in the sun and snowlight, the very trees and shrubs as crisp as if cut from embroidered silk, before they fell away. Their leaves and thorns and sparkling branches cast shadows on the frosty ground, for in these heights it was winter always.

The air was like chilled wine, to be drunk in glorious drafts, making the head light, then even lighter the higher they ascended. They drank it deeply into their lungs, free and young and a trifle giddy, as at a joyous banquet. Peter was soon panting, though beaming as he tried to keep up with the twins. James and John were leaping about like gazelles, pausing to bombard each other with snowballs, then scooping up more snow with which to challenge him. Peter ducked, and with flailing hands warned them away.

Jesus was already far ahead. Though he had invited them to go with him, after his first cordial greeting he had set off, with a pace they could not match. At first, looking up, they could see his long legs leaping rocks, or striding along as if on a special mission, his white garments blowing. Then he disappeared.

Halfway to the broad white cone, Peter paused to wrap his cloak around him, thankful that Adah had insisted he bring it. Too bad she couldn't find the boots; he wished he hadn't resisted even the leggings. His sandals were already soaked, his ankles turning blue. He saw that James and John had stopped pelting each other with snowballs and were donning their cloaks too.

"Master, wait, we must rest!" Peter bellowed, shielding his eyes to the glare. His voice was loud from years of trying to outshout the sea; it boomed back at him now in repeating echoes. "Master . . . wait . . . ! Master . . . wait . . . !" But Jesus was too far above them to be seen.

"Do you suppose he's going straight on to the summit?" James, too, was searching the white expanse. "It's a long way and we're tired already, and cold." He hoisted himself nimbly onto a rock and began to massage his wet feet. John joined him and they sat discussing it, puzzled but accepting. Their delicate, fine-boned faces were untroubled, if a little surprised. "There is something on his mind," they agreed. "Jesus has said almost nothing; he hasn't even looked back."

"Jesus knows we will follow him and find him—wherever he is," Peter said. All three were gazing upward toward the truncated cone, divided into three peaks. "It will probably be the highest summit," they decided.

Meanwhile, catching their breath, they gazed in wonder at the magnificent panorama spread before them in every direction below. West, the valleys and hills of Lebanon, green-striped but bronzing with summer; the cities of Tyre and Sidon, looking like fragile doll villages that might topple right into the blue Mediterranean. South soared Mount Tabor, Mount Hattin and the whole overflowing range of violet-blue mountains that encircled the shining harp-shaped mirror they knew so well. Today they remarked the lake's brilliance and a sight they had never seen before: as if one shoulder of the Silver Woman wore a glistening white mantle, which could very well be a reflection of the very slopes from which they watched.

Refreshed, they climbed on, and soon were relieved to discover the slightly drifted tracks of the one they were following. It was hard going now, the snow deeper, the air even more thin. James and John no longer pranced about like schoolboys, but plowed forward, hoods pulled up over their bright heads, bent into the wind. Peter labored behind them, unable to keep up. The hood of his cloak was blown away from his scarlet face; he was puffing, eyes wet, nose running, his heart hammering fiercely in his chest. Yet a wonderful excitement claimed him, a kind of blind senseless joy at being here in this dazzling place on such a day.

Everything glistened and sparkled with an intensity he had never seen before, even on the water. And it flashed through his mind, in a humble marveling, how his life had changed. From a dull, stolid fisherman, not even very religious, routinely muttering his prayers, seldom even attending the synagogue—to this! The very dangers of following Jesus, the terrible possibilities, had added a reckless color and sense of purpose to his life. And to be so close to him—*one of the chosen three.* Selected to be with Jesus whenever the occasion seemed important. A sudden awareness of that honor struck him afresh.

What was so important about climbing a mountain? Peter couldn't imagine. Only that he was committed, his heart nearly bursting with love. If it were the Master's will, he would drop dead for him right now, in the snow; or he would hurl himself from the mountain's highest crest. . . .

At last, breathing hard, light-headed, nearly exhausted but filled with anticipation, they reached the place where Jesus must surely be, and stood blinking and looking about for a moment, their eyes at first half blinded with the sun and snow. Gradually their vision cleared; they saw that it was a broad and level spot, surprisingly covered with green grass, for the sun poured down upon it like a golden funnel.

Overhead the sky seemed close enough to touch, a pure cloudless blue. It was at first very still. The wind was not blowing here.

And now they realized they had been led to sacred ground, and even then were witnessing something profound. For at last their eyes began to focus on the one they sought.

And they knew him and knew him not, for he was standing in radiance at the center of the circle, his white garments shimmering beyond even the radiance of the sunlit snow. Jesus' head was thrown back as if in prayer, his countenance utterly changed—effulgent, transfigured. And awe and terror smote them, so that James and John covered their eyes for an instant, and stifled the cries in their throats.

Then they saw, to their further astonishment, that two men were with him. Whence they came and how they got there, the apostles could not fathom. Their eyes sought confirmation from each other, to make sure they were not dreaming. For now, in the stillness, they could hear the men speaking in low tones. And Jesus turned to the strangers and answered them, though it was impossible to hear what was being said. What were they discussing? Could it be perhaps what Jesus was to accomplish in the time he had left? For suddenly they realized—with a shock of recognition it came to Peter, James and John—these two figures were not of this world.

"Moses! Elijah!" Peter tried to moisten his dry lips. Silently he whispered their names. The prophets had returned. Surely with a message straight from heaven.

Peter swayed, he had to fight for control. He must stand fast, he must not faint. He dared not fall prostrate either in awe or in terror, as James and John had done. Why should any miracle overcome him now? After all the miracles he had witnessed! Had he not helped Jesus steady the man climbing down from his bier on his way to the grave? Stood beside Jesus when with a word and a touch of his hand, he drew life back into a little girl? . . . He needs me, he has made that clear. He has a reason for allowing me to be here with him now. I was the first to acknowledge him as the Christ. He has promised me the keys to heaven!

Oh, to prolong this moment, fix it in time forever, mark it with his zeal! Staggered before the vision, light-headed from the climb, yet he was gripped by sublime conviction, given the courage to step forward. He heard his own voice saying, "Jesus, Master, we are here!

We have followed you through the snows to be with you. Now I know why: we must build three tabernacles. Only say the word and we will find materials—one for you, one for Moses and one for Elijah!"

But even as he spoke, Peter realized, to his dismay, that a bright cloud was coasting over the face of the sun, casting a shadow upon the strangers, so that he could see them less clearly. They were dissolving, vanishing before his eyes. And as Peter stood frozen, bewildered, a voice came from the cloud. Peter could hear it distinctly, the same voice his brother Andrew must have heard when Jesus came up out of his baptism in the Jordan. Speaking in tones both reassuring and yet astounding.

"This is my beloved son, with whom I am well pleased. Hear him."

It was too much. Now Peter, too, hurled himself prostrate upon the ground.

In a moment he felt Jesus' hand, warm and firm on his shoulder. "Come, Peter, rise, don't be afraid." One by one Jesus bent over them, touching each in turn. And looking up in awe and wonder, they were relieved to find themselves staring at the same dear familiar face. Jesus was smiling, their friend unchanged. The dazzling white raiment was once more a simple homespun tunic, and over it he had thrown his own heavy but somewhat shabby cloak; Magdalene or someone had actually mended it in places. "Come now, we will rest a little while, then we must start back."

Unsteadily, they got to their feet. They heard no other voices. The place where he had stood was vacant. The sun still shone brightly on the grass.

"Moses and Elijah have gone," Jesus said simply, as they looked around. "Though they were here. You saw them. It is one reason I wanted you with me. That your faith in the Son of Man might be confirmed. But only to strengthen you for what is to come."

Adah waited wearily for Peter that evening.

She had not enjoyed the bazaars with Magdalene, after all. Her mind had been preoccupied with Peter all day, filled with a vague unease. He had not seemed well that recent night, and it was a long hard climb in the cold. Jesus would not let anything happen to him, of course. And Peter had been so pleased. And yet . . . She could only pray that he wouldn't do or say anything for which he would come home blaming himself.

She was also tired from lack of sleep. And too heavy to find pleasure in all that walking, just to look at things she didn't want or need. It was hard enough just lugging her big body from town to town, following the men. And why examine baskets and jugs and knickknacks they could not carry with them, or use during their brief stay in other people's homes? Even the lacy shawls, the embroidered vests and girdles and dresses, the jewelry and perfumes, failed to entice her as they did the other women. They seldom had; even as a girl she had sense enough to realize such adornments only called attention to her size—her overgrown body and plain, big-boned face.

Once her father had actually brought her a little scarf. . . . red and gold stripes, like a pretty little snake—fascinating; she had dared to touch it, even tried clumsily to tie it about her lanky hair. Laughter! How ludicrous she must have looked. His only present, though she found a half shekel once under her pallet. Who else could have hidden it there? She feared to spend it, and feared to show it to her mother. . . . Always so little money, even after she married Peter. She had learned to be thrifty, even when Peter's hauls were good; she had put it away, saving for just such a day as this, and a good thing too. Every penny must count. It troubled Adah that Magdalene, in her gratefulness, her fervent loyalty and love, wanted to buy things for her and Peter.

Magdalene's money could be better spent. *Was* better spent, for most of it went into the common purse for food and lodging for all of them. But there was an air of richness and plenitude about Magdalene, a generosity that spilled over on gifts for others. Oddly, it did not bother Adah how the money had been earned; there was in Adah a bawdy streak of humor. With a kind of indignant, wry amusement, she remembered the near stoning by those self-righteous men. Had they dreamed, those who squandered money on such favors, that one day it might be used for such a noble purpose?

"Find something," Magdalene had urged today. "Just something to remember our visit to Caesarea Philippi, for we start home tomorrow."

To please her, Adah had fingered a few trinkets—beads, spices, dishes—and chosen a little bracelet made of shells. It jingled on her plump wrist now as she lighted the lamp. The shells were a luminous pink inside, and they glistened in its light. Beyond the wall she could hear the other family shouting and arguing as they got ready for the evening meal. Such rowdy children; she would be glad to leave. She tried to take comfort in the bracelet, to rejoice in it, a symbol of celebration and escape. But she was still anxious about Peter. And she knew, when he walked in, that again he had undergone some shattering experience.

His big ruddy face was pale and shaken; he looked dazed, groping about for a place to put his wet cloak. Wordlessly, she took it from him and then knelt with the basin she had waiting, to wash his feet. They were swollen and blue; she massaged them vigorously and dried them for him.

When would he speak? Not until after prayers and supper. Later. How much later? He was bursting with it, that was plain. It was hard for him to keep a secret; he suffered. He had to confide in someone. He loved her. He would have to confide in her.

Peter only pretended to eat. At last, giving his wife an embarrassed, apologetic look, he pushed his plate away. Adah took it without comment, pausing only to kiss the place where the hair was beginning to thin on his bushy head. Humming as usual, she began to scrape the food into a small bowl. It must not be wasted; she would save it for the family next door. They seemed to be quite poor.

She could feel Peter staring at her, in torment, biting his thick cracked lips. Her humming stopped. She came to his rescue. "What is it?" she asked, over her shoulder. "You may as well tell me."

Adah waited. Patiently. The sounds beyond the wall were quieting; she could hear only the baby crying now, and the bang of a pot. Her heart was beating hard. She wanted to bang a pot herself.

"Nothing I can share, even with you," he finally said. "Do not ask me more."

"Very well." She went on with her task, began wiping the table.

He got up, clumsily, moving out of her way. "I cannot tell you," he insisted. "No, no, I cannot speak of it. It is . . . something you could not comprehend.

Adah threw down the cloth. "Are you so tongue-tied or am I so stupid that I could not comprehend whatever it is that is troubling my own husband?"

"Forgive me!" Peter passed a trembling hand over his eyes. "I saw a thing today that I *dare* not speak of," he cried. "No, no, do not tempt me. We were charged to tell no one, for it is beyond mortal comprehension—not just yours, but mine as well, though I saw it with my own eyes!" He had been charging about the room; now he sat down again, in misery, his hairy fists clenched, yet there was an expression of wonder on his face. "Oh, Adah, bear with me. . . ." He groped, almost piteously, for her hand. "It was so beautiful—terrible and beautiful at the same time. This . . . vision that we saw, James and John and I. One day I will describe it to you. But not until I am free to. I cannot, not until—" Peter choked. A tear darted suddenly down his cheek.

Adah was gripping his shoulders from behind. Gently she reached over to wipe it away. "Until what, my beloved?"

"Until . . . Jesus has risen, as he promised. For what we witnessed today confirms what I was trying to tell you before. Jesus *is* the Messiah—this I know, even more surely than in the moment I confessed him. He is the Messiah, who must suffer and die for us. Oh, I have hoped and prayed so desperately that it need not happen, no matter what he said. And today my hopes were raised to heaven. But I was wrong—Jesus made that clear. He will have no tabernacle on earth, only a tomb. He *will* live again!" Peter whispered passionately. His eyes were wet but shining. "But he has pledged us to silence until that time. As we came down from the mountain, he made this command: We must tell no one of the vision we have seen today until the Son of Man is raised from the dead."

Chapter 12

"JESUS . . . my son. Tinoki, tinoki—my little one!" Mary heard herself crooning an endearment she hadn't used in years. "Wake up. You are home—it is all right!"

He sat up, in a cold sweat, a boy again smelling breakfast, afraid he had overslept—he would be late for school! But no, he had been fleeing through a great city, a tangle of dark streets. . . . His pursuers were waving crutches, armed with stones, some brandishing whips, others marching ponderously along consulting their scrolls. . . . The ill and the dying were reaching out to clutch him before he escaped, some of them shouting hosannas, others sneering. . . . *There he is! Take him!*. . . . He was about to be caught, dragged before the Sanhedrin. . . .

"Hush now, my darling." He felt his mother's hand, cool on his wet brow. "You were crying out. Go back to sleep now; you are so tired."

She began to pull the covers about his shoulders, but he restrained her. "No, it's time I got up and gave a better answer to my brothers. How long have I slept?"

"Around the clock, I'm afraid. They left for the festival yesterday." Mary hesitated. "At least Josey and Simon and their families. I'm not sure about Jude. James isn't going—his wife is ill again."

Jesus nodded wretchedly, and plunged his face into his hands. Two of his brothers had arrived in Capernaum a few days before on a pretext of business, but actually to persuade him to come home once more. Simon and Josey were waiting for him one night on his stoop. They were here, they admitted, at their mother's imploring. She was

⟨ 153 ⟩

very uneasy about him—his health, his rest; she often had nightmares that he was in deep trouble, even danger.

Jesus had grinned faintly. "Would I be any safer in Nazareth?"

"You will be as long as we're there!" Josey blustered. He flexed his burly arm, and so did Simon. Suddenly they were all laughing and embracing each other, fighting playfully, as they had as boys.

This was true, Jesus thought in a rush of grateful affection. They had not hesitated in that time of near disaster. Despite all that had happened—the embarrassment and failure of his visit, the outright public rejection—his family still missed him, wanted the best for him, stood ready to defend him.

"And why waste any more time here?" Simon glanced around the barren room, finding it hard to hide his distaste. His once cowlicky red hair was now subdued, his beard trimmed and curled in the Persian fashion. He had married a slightly older woman, a widow of refinement and means. At her persuasion he was limiting his carpentry to making cabinets for the better homes. He'd had no idea his supposedly successful brother lived so poorly. "You've been around Galilee long enough," he advised flatly. "You'll never get anywhere out in the provinces. These people already know what you can do," he condescended. "Besides, they're not important."

No, wait—Jesus had quite a number of important followers here too, Josey had hastily tried to correct. Lawyers, judges, doctors . . . "You weren't with us, so you didn't see them. But Simon's right," he assured Jesus. "The really important people are in Judea. You have disciples there too. Why hide yourself out here? Go to Jerusalem if you want to become well known."

"Come with us," Simon said—it was both an invitation and a challenge. "We're going to the feast soon. If you can really do these things, show them to the world."

Jesus had turned from the cupboard, where he was crumbling food for Ben. "Have you forgotten what happened the last time I went to a feast in Jerusalem? The Feast of Weeks. Or maybe you didn't hear. I nearly got myself killed."

They regarded him uncomfortably. "Of course we heard," said Josey. "Everything you do comes back to us."

Simon's mouth tightened. "And reflects on us."

"And if you *did* perform this miracle on the Sabbath?" Josey protested, sounding doubtful. "You *know* that's considered against the Law."

"God does not close the pool at Bethesda on the Sabbath," Jesus said quietly. "Or prevent the sun from shining, or babies from being born. The man was suffering; he had been ill for years. He'd been lying by the pool for days. He was on the point of death."

"But did you have to encourage him to take up his bed and carry it though the streets?" Simon reminded, sounding judicial. "That, too, is an outright affront to the Law."

"What would you have had him do with it? Leave it behind? He needed it."

"Well, it was foolish. No wonder the authorities were after you. Sometimes it seems you're deliberately out to provoke them."

It was useless. They didn't understand. And whatever their motives—to bait or to encourage—they didn't actually believe. More vehemently than he meant to, Jesus put down the bowl for his dog.

"I will call attention to these tyrannies whenever I can. People must be freed from this stupid enslavement to the Sabbath simply because the priests say so. It is *not* sinning to take care of normal human needs. No, no, that's a terrible corruption of God's commandment. The Sabbath was made for man, not man for the Sabbath!"

The other two shook their heads, despairing. They had not meant their mission to go like this. But now that they were into it, there seemed no turning back. Jesus had done worse than that, they'd heard—that's what really upset the Sanhedrin. "The man actually believed you'd forgiven his sins—or so he told the Jews," Josey plunged on, incredulous. His color was high. "It's said you stood on the Temple steps claiming you had this power and authority, straight from the Father. That the Father loves you and wants you to be honored with him—that he has shared all knowledge with you because you are— you refer to yourself as—" Josey choked, unable to say the words.

Coolly, almost objectively, Simon took over. "As God's own son. That you promised eternal life to all those who believe in you. This is preposterous. Personally, I refuse to accept such rumors. You are not mad, and I refuse to think you're a heretic. Making yourself equal to God! You would never say such a thing. Forgive us—we're your brothers and we love you," he insisted. "But you must be more careful."

"You have your answer," Jesus said abruptly. "Go to the feast

.yourselves." He was very tired and deeply discouraged. It had not been a good time for them to appear. "Frankly, I can't see why you would even suggest that I go back again to 'prove what I can do,' as you say. I would only embarrass you and stir up more trouble before my time has come. You have all the time in the world—I don't."

"Then you're not coming?"

"To the Feast of Tabernacles—no, I don't think so. But since our mother is worried—yes, for her sake, of course I'll come home for a little while."

Now, with Mary sitting there beside his bed, Jesus was infinitely glad to be home. He had roused up in his concern. He lay back again, eyes closed for a moment, one arm flung over his curly head. When he opened them, she was gazing steadily at him.

"Tell me," Mary said. "It may help to confide in me. Things are not going well?"

Jesus nodded, ran a hand distractedly through his hair. "I'm tired and disappointed, Mother—you did right to send for me. I'm getting frustrated—yes, and angry with the people who refuse to understand. My work is faltering, even in Galilee, where it began."

"But the multitudes that follow you! We heard—we thought . . . we saw them ourselves that night in Capernaum. Though we have worried—"

"That scene at the house of Zebedee was deceptive. Don't judge me by the numbers that have flocked to hear me, but by those who actually want the kind of kingdom I have come to establish. People are not repenting; they're not willing to change their lives and make the sacrifices I demand. All they want is food and miracles for themselves. It's what I was afraid of when the power first came upon me. The wonderful joy of healing, relieving human suffering, helping people in need: how I looked forward to it, though I sensed the danger even then—that that's all they would really want of me in the end."

Mary had never seen her son like this; sad and yet with a new fierceness. "They won't believe the kingdom of heaven is within them, it *can* be enjoyed right now, here on earth, by following what I teach about doing the will of God. No, no, they want a messiah who will solve all their problems for them, heal them, feed them. An earthly king who will overthrow Rome and make them all healthy, happy and rich! And when this doesn't happen, they fall away, many of them.

Many of my first, most enthusiastic followers are gone. Disillusioned, or scared away by all the false stories and threats. The Sanhedrin has sent agents all over the country warning people to stay away from me. That I'm an impostor, saying and doing things that could get them in serious trouble."

"*You?* Oh, my darling, you of all people!"

"True, for everyone who's afraid to come or drops away there are always others, but mainly looking for miracles, what they can *get.* And even where we have done great good, my apostles and I, we have been rejected. Lately my men have come back from some of their journeys appalled at the treatment they received. Chorazin, Bethsaida, Tyre and Sidon. Even Capernaum! I fear for those cities," he said grimly. "I have upbraided them, even cursed them aloud for their unbelief."

Jesus got up suddenly and began to dress. Mary followed him to the chest, where he was impatiently searching. "Let me help. Is this what you are looking for?" She handed him his tunic, gazed at him a moment, eyes large and questioning. "I cannot believe what I am hearing. Not from you."

"I am not perfect, Mother."

"But you are . . . the son of *God!*"

"Only the Father is perfect. Yes, the Father and I are one. But I have been sent to earth to live as a man, feel as a man. I am a human being too," he pleaded, on a note of despair. "You know that. I eat, I sleep, I get tired, I get indignant—righteously indignant, I hope—when things go wrong. I lose patience with my apostles because they sometimes seem so blind or heedless, either not listening to what I say or unable or unwilling to understand."

Mary continued to gaze at him, bewildered and protesting. Why? she wondered—even as on that tragic day when she had sent for Jesus, sure that he would save his desperately injured father. But he had only knelt by that beautiful broken body and wept. "You have been given special powers," she whispered, her face intense. "*Can you not change all that?*"

"No," Jesus said. "The Father did not send me to earth with magical powers to change the hearts of people. I cannot turn them into instant perfect beings. He gave me only the power to heal their bodies, if they believe in me, and to speak the truth to them." He paused, gazing out the window. "God could, if he had willed it, have *had* his perfect kingdom on earth long ago. The multitudes marching in step, saying, 'Yes, Father, no, Father,' at his command. But that's not how he wants his children to change! They must first love him— enough to believe in the one he has sent. It must be their free will to love and obey the Father, and their own choice to change. If they refuse, they will perish in their own sins. They will never eat the bread of eternal life that I have been sent to offer them."

Jesus was calmer now. He sat down on the couch to put on his sandals. "Even their healings," he continued, "must be with their own knowledge and consent. It is why, as you know, I have not healed your own brother, Uncle Esau. He does not wish it! We discussed it, I offered; but after some thought, he is unwilling. He has walked in the darkness too long; he would have to learn his way all over again in a world of sight. He is afraid. . . . And the wife of James—though we have never discussed it, I know that she scoffs at the very thought; she does not believe. But she also saw her mother die in childbirth, and she is terrified at the prospect. It is why she miscarries so often— she is secretly afraid."

Jesus stood up; he felt better, as if a number of things were resolved. "And when people are healed, physically or mentally, they must do their part. They cannot return to their old ways of sinning or self-abuse, which may have caused their misery—at least in part, though there are many exceptions. People must assume responsibility for their own lives. I will help them, the Father will help them, if they sincerely pray and do their best. But neither the Father nor I can walk for them or eat or sleep or love or refrain from sinning *for* them. This they must do for themselves."

Jesus held out his arms, and his mother went into them. They stood hugging each other there, with the bright morning sun streaming in. Outside, birds were singing; donkeys brayed and clattered on the cobbles; they could hear people hurrying by on their way to join a caravan, many of them carrying jugs of wine or oil. The Feast of Tabernacles was a popular one. *The* Feast, most country people called it, to celebrate the last grape and olive harvest. Most would spend the week in one of the charming forests of booths and tents which sprang up all over Jerusalem and surrounding neighborhoods at this season—

reminders of the time when Jews were wanderers on the desert before they reached the Promised Land.

"Oh, Mother, I remember happier days, when our whole family would go to the Feast. And all the places where we camped. I can still smell those olive boughs."

"And the grapes," Mary said wistfully. "How your little brothers would throw them at each other!" She laughed. "And the time Elizabeth and John came down from their big house to join us. But it was so crowded I seem to remember they left before morning."

"No, that was John and I, after you thought we were asleep. We slipped out, hoping to find another procession—"

He could feel his mother trembling, suddenly fighting tears.

"John . . . " she moaned softly. "Oh, Elizabeth, *Elizabeth!*"

Jesus held her tighter. "I will go to see her; I'll do what I can for her."

Mary drew back, blinking. "But you're not *going?*"

Jesus nodded. "I've decided I must. Simon and Josey are right about some things. I can accomplish little more in Galilee. I'm living like a fugitive, always one step ahead of a posse of Pharisees. It's time I faced them."

Mary wiped her eyes, leading the way to the kitchen. "Your brothers are confused about you," she tried to explain. "They didn't mean to upset you; they just want to be proud of you. If you can do these works, they reason, you should be doing them in Jerusalem, where it matters—but in accordance with the Law. They really hoped to persuade you of this, and also to restrain you, if possible, from saying . . . well, dangerous things. It actually seemed to them that such an appearance might stop some of the stories that have worried them."

"They don't know what they're asking. They don't really believe."

"No, perhaps not. It's . . . hard for them. They love you and would like to, but please understand they are sincere. They honestly hoped your behavior this time might result in more success, and help to quiet your critics."

Jesus sighed deeply and shook his head. "They are right about one thing. I must be willing to act where I will be seen. If the world is to see this light, it must be shown in high places. . . . Not that that won't cause trouble," he added.

"But you *will* be careful?" she pleaded.

"I'll try not to embarrass my brothers. I'll go in private this time. If possible, I'll keep still. But if I am moved in the Spirit to speak later, I cannot promise not to. I can do no less than my cousin. John wouldn't compromise, no matter how many people he offended."

Mary's eyes flashed, bright with pain. "And what a price he paid!"

"Yes." Jesus went to where she was setting out bread for his breakfast, and held her close again. "The price of truth comes high, Mother—we both know that. I'm not afraid for myself; my only concern is you. Oh, if only I could spare you!"

One afternoon, near the end of the feast, Lazarus heard Jesus for the first time.

"Wait, listen," said his older friend Nicodemus, as they were about to make their way through the usual crowd gathered around the Temple steps. "This is someone I want you to hear."

Lazarus hesitated. His black eyes, always alert, interested, were faintly bemused. "A Galilean?" He had caught only a few words, enough to notice the accent. "He speaks like a Galilean."

"He is," said Nicodemus calmly. "But a strange one. Different. Listen to what he is saying."

"But he's attacking the Pharisees," Lazarus exclaimed after a moment. "That's *you*." He regarded his tall patrician companion in astonishment, standing so calmly by, robed arms folded, a little smile playing on his long lips. "Calling you hypocrites, nothing but whited sepulchers!"

"Well, aren't we?" The older man's eyes twinkled—keen, kindly, wise. "As a Sadducee, I'd think you'd agree."

"Agreed!" said Lazarus, slapping his shoulder. They both laughed.

"There's hypocrisy and corruption on both sides of the Sanhedrin. But listen" Nicodemus cocked his silver head. "Look at his face and listen: He has lots more to say."

"Do not tremble before the judgment of those in high places," Jesus was telling the people. "Seek only the approval of the Father, who loves you and wants the best for you. Do not venerate the scribes and Pharisees—no, nor the Sadducees; they are all of one breed, strutting about the synagogues and streets in their fine clothes, their phylacteries prominent on their foreheads. They pray loudly in public, where they will be heard, and hide their sins in the darkness, where they will not be seen. They demand the highest seats at the banquet tables, where like the priests they devour the meat of the poor. Do not honor these men, I say, honor only the Father, and the Son who has been sent to you to warn you of the judgment to come."

Lazarus' black brows had shot up, but he was listening intently, chin propped on his hand.

To mingled shouts of "Hosanna!" and some baiting and heckling, the voice of Jesus continued to ring out: "They impose on you taxes and burdens they refuse to bear themselves. And what do they do in return? Nothing, save hound and seek to punish anyone who seems to break a single rule about the Sabbath, or what is clean or unclean. You men in the marketplace, I tell you solemnly no food that a farmer brings you to sell is clean or unclean, no matter how it's raised. You women preparing your families' meals—don't be afraid of what you can serve or how it is cooked. My Father in heaven has created all food for the nourishment of the body. Nothing that goes in by way of the mouth can corrupt it, but what comes out of the mouth. For what comes out of the mouth proceeds from the heart—evil thoughts, murder, adultery, fornication, theft, false witness, slander. These are what defile a man.

"Listen to me, hear me, believe what I say, for these are not my words but those of my Father who sent me."

Lazarus gave a little start. Frowning, he looked at Nicodemus. His friend, whom he loved and admired, was taking this in as if transfixed.

"Does he speak here often?" Lazarus asked in low tones.

"No, he's usually out in the provinces. But he's generally here every day at festival time."

"But where does he get his eloquence? He sounds so . . . learned. I can't quite place the school where he must have studied. Hillel . . . Gamaliel . . . Eleazar . . . ?"

"I don't know," said Nicodemus. "One of the academies in Galilee, maybe, but I doubt it—his parents were poor; they had six children. But he's obviously a scholar; nobody questions his learning. It doesn't matter," he said with conviction. "Jesus has a higher source."

"Even so, by whose authority is he here?"

"He refuses to say. The priests and elders are always sending somebody to question him, to try to arrest him for supposed lack of credentials, but he's too smart for them. Last time they almost got him, until I interfered. I'm surprised you haven't heard."

"I'm a busy man. I don't come here often myself."

Nicodemus laughed softly. "You don't know what you're missing! So far they haven't succeeded," he went on. "The people won't have it, most of them. Especially the poor. Look at them—"

The two poised, well-dressed men turned to survey the crowd: Jews from all over the known world swarmed through the magnificent Temple gates at festival time. Jews from Babylon, Persia, Greece, Abyssinia, the west, the desert. Rich and poor, in elegance and rags, a riot of multicolored costumes. Wrapped in sheets or sheepskins, even lion skins, they came, or wearing fine linens and woolens and silks, brilliantly dyed. But here on the north portico steps it was sackcloth and the worn, faded garments of the poor that prevailed. Here they gathered—grizzled earth people from the country, the wretched who dwelled in the walls and hovels of the lower city, the destitute from all over the land. Their gaunt, life-scarred faces were lifted, some of them mouths open, like starving birds frantic to gulp and savor every crumb of hope and promise from his table.

Had he not said, was he not saying: "Come unto me, all you who labor and are heavy-laden? . . . Ask and you will receive, knock and the door will be opened. . . . Eat of this bread that I offer you, drink of this water—believe in me and you will never be hungry or thirsty again!"

"Yes, yes, hosanna!" their glad shouts interrupted. Or they nodded and nudged each other, murmuring, "The prophet has come at last. This is the Christ, this is the One, and the authorities must know it." Though some were more reticent, some impatient for miracles, while a few detractors cupped their mouths to call out the ancient taunt, "Nazarene, Nazarene! Can anything good come out of Nazareth?"

"Leave him alone," demanded not only the poor but others who wanted to hear him. "Can't you see he's a wonderful man? He may even be the Messiah."

"He can't be! We know where he comes from."

Jesus motioned toward them, smiling faintly, unperturbed. "Of course you know where I come from," he sang out proudly. "You know where I was born and raised. But sad to say, you don't know the One who sent me to you with these truths. I do know him, for I come directly from him. For the sake of your own souls, believe in me as the scripture has said, and live!"

Lazarus was frowning. He had an insatiable curiosity and he never made snap judgments; he gave every speaker, whatever his station, complete, patient attention. His own response would be crisp, fast, incisive, but even in disagreement, pleasant. "The man is making some powerful claims. But I'm afraid they're right—he can't be the Messiah. Everybody knows the true Messiah is to come out of Bethlehem."

"He does," said Nicodemus. "Jesus was born there."

"How do you know?"

Nicodemus took his arm. "It's too noisy; we can't talk here. Come—there's a bench over there, beside the wall."

Lazarus glanced uneasily over his shoulder. "Will he be all right?" His own sense of decorum made him embarrassed for the man. Such brilliance and fervor and beauty, even in outrage. Those haunting eyes. That such a man should expose himself before the crass mob! Let alone the Temple police, who stood about, arms folded, uneasy, knowing their duty was to find some cause to seize him.

"Don't worry, they won't touch him," said Nicodemus. "His miracles, you know. I think some of them are a little bit afraid of him."

They walked across the grass and sat down on the marble bench. The sun was almost blinding on the Temple's lavish gates and golden roof, setting everything afire. The bench was cool and it was quieter here, though people continued to stream by, many heading for their homes or inns or caravans, as the feast was almost over.

"You sound as if you believe this man," Lazarus challenged, his alert interested eyes fixed on his friend. "Why?"

For a moment Nicodemus stared down at the grass between his knees. Then he lifted his long thoughtful face. "I have been following his career for years. Ever since he was twelve years old. The first time I ever heard him was in the Temple. He was waiting for his parents— they had become separated. He was questioning the men gathered there, and giving them answers as well."

"At twelve?"

"Yes. It was so remarkable I stopped to listen. Joseph of Arimathea was there too—you may know him, a scribe, a very learned man.

He was questioning the boy intensely that day, and we both were astonished at his answers. We both saw great promise in him. We had no idea, of course, of this!" Nicodemus gestured in the direction of the crowd. Jesus was still speaking. "At that time I asked him myself about his birthplace, which he said was Bethlehem—which seemed impossible, of course, in view of the slaughter there that year. Later I tracked this down, and found his facts were right. Later, much later, I sought Jesus out, just to be sure. It was right after he started his ministry—about three years ago."

Nicodemus turned away suddenly, visibly shaken, his lean throat working. "I went to him in secret one night. Even then he was preaching much as he does today, warning of disaster even to the Temple unless we changed our ways, especially there. As a member of the Sanhedrin, I didn't dare to be seen with him in public, I'm almost ashamed to say. Now I have more courage; they all know where I stand. Joseph of Arimathea, too, is now bold enough to defend him. But then, with all that first trouble between Herod and John the Baptist . . . Jesus is John's cousin, you know, or was. Poor John, a radical to the end. A lot of people were being careful about Jesus too—at least I thought I had to be.

"Anyway, that night . . . Where was I? Oh, yes, Jesus told me things I'd never heard before. That a man must be born again, both by water and the Spirit, else he cannot enter the kingdom of God. I can hear him yet. His words were so beautiful they burned themselves into my heart: 'The wind blows where it wills, and you hear the sound of it, but you do not know whence it comes or whither it goes; so it is with everyone who is born of the Spirit.' When I asked him how this could be, he was surprised at my ignorance, that as a teacher of Israel I did not know this already and understand it. We talked most of the night, I remember. It was the most important night of my life. He shared with me the great secret he is only now declaring to the world. Jesus is the promised One. He is God's only son, sent into the world not to condemn it but to save it. He is the light of the world, and he offers eternal life to all who believe in him." Nicodemus paused, deeply moved. "I have followed him ever since. He has become like a son to me."

Lazarus sprang up suddenly. "Take me to him," he said briskly. "I, too, would know this man,"

"Of course. But then I must be on my way. It's getting late."

Lazarus' heart was pounding as they went back across the grass. The baiting and cries of praise had stopped. The crowd was dispersing, although a few people still surrounded Jesus, trying to draw him into argument, or hoping for miracles. Three young men who seemed to be his aides had appeared and were attempting to dissuade them. Only a few police officers lingered, sweaty and tired, anxious to be off but keeping a watchful eye for any disturbance.

Jesus looked over their heads, his face brightening at sight of Nicodemus.

"This is my friend Lazarus, of Bethany," Nicodemus said, when they had embraced. "We often do business together."

The eyes of Jesus and Lazarus met. There was instant recognition between them, as there had been between Jesus and Simon Peter. A sudden overwhelming sense of their mutual destiny.

"Come home with me," Lazarus heard himself blurting. His voice, usually so crisp and clear, was thick with excitement. "Come for supper. I have two sisters who will be happy to meet you. Come stay with us!"

Jesus hesitated. "How I'd love to," he said, "but I have some men with me." He indicated Peter, Andrew and Judas, who had sought him out at the festival. "I cannot leave my friends."

"I would know them too!" Lazarus cried. "Bid them come with us, all of them." He moved toward them on his long quick step, robes billowing, holding out his hands. It had been years since he had felt so happy about anything.

Chapter 13

*L*AZARUS and his sisters lived in a handsome house set high on a hill in Bethany, a village of mostly small flat-topped dwellings scattered around the shoulder of the Mount of Olives. Though only two miles from Jerusalem, it was quiet here and restful. In many ways it reminded Jesus and his men of the villages and countryside of Galilee, for the groves of Lazarus stretched to the horizon; and within the walls of that gracious house they were to find a second home.

Although surprised to see them that first night, the sisters were overjoyed. Lazarus kept too much to himself, they thought. It was exciting to have him troop in with these vigorous strangers. Martha, the elder, was especially thrilled. Cooking was her passion; she always prepared far more than the three of them could consume. In her precise, caring way, she planned it so: extra portions for the birds, dogs and other creatures that came to her door, and even more left to take to the poor. Her brother indulged her in this; he was a generous man, with large holdings. And he sensed, sometimes with a twinge of guilt, that such appeased her secret maternal need.

The three clung to each other. They had been orphaned while Lazarus was still at his studies in Jerusalem, and his sisters were much younger. He had given up everything to care for them, and for the family properties. Lazarus was of medium height, attractively sharp-featured, with fine bones. He walked with a rather long step for a man his size, as if in a hurry to get where he was going. Though he was now only forty years old, his thick hair was snow white. Its black had begun to frost at the death of his young wife in childbirth, and whitened completely, almost overnight, when their child also died—a little girl of five.

Mary and Martha had put aside their own dreams to rush to the baby's mothering—it was itself a weak little thing. Lazarus had married late, feeling uncomfortable about it, for he had not yet succeeded in finding anyone quite good enough for his sisters. He felt responsible for them; he could not give them up to anyone who could not provide well for them—and he had come to depend on them. Every suitor who showed interest he discouraged, until the whole parade of young men around Bethany had disappeared.

Mary and Martha, at first busy caring for the pleasant but sickly young wife, then for the child, had not resented this too much. Mary, the younger, prettier and more lively, did sometimes weep as she cradled her pillow, fantasizing a husband's arms around her, his babe in her belly. Martha was more shy and dignified. Though she sometimes complained to Mary, she was in some ways relieved. They felt safe with Lazarus. He had become both father and husband to them, his child their own.

The shock of that terrible loss only drew the three closer together. They had worshiped the bright little thing. The house, however luxuriant, was empty and silent without her. They were bereft, at first bewildered, realizing that again they had only each other. Now more than ever the sisters began to live for their brother who had plunged feverishly back into business to assuage his grief.

Dispensing with servants, they hurled their energies into keeping the house, like themselves, exquisite, charming, meticulously clean. Everything glistened and shone—the cedar walls, the marble floors, the beautiful silver and glass. Sometimes Martha's hands ached and swelled from the eternal scrubbing and polishing. Then she would slip into Mary's room and choose a fragrant unguent to rub into them, from the array of bottles on Mary's dressing table.

Mary helped cook and clean too, but mostly at Martha's direction. Mary had a more ardent, creative nature. She loved to dance and sing; or she would sit dreamily brushing her long wavy chestnut hair, enjoying the way it flashed and crackled. She delighted in walking barefoot on the velvety Persian rugs, with their jewel-bright colors. She had found and bargained for most of them in the bazaars. She had even designed and had a craftsman make some of the furniture, and the lovely alabaster lamps. But she was happiest planting and tending the flowers that were such a glory in the garden; and bringing armloads into the house, which she would spend hours arranging—often to Martha's irritation. At times they argued, as women will, though they had outgrown the subtle rivalry that had troubled them as girls.

Martha was a tall, quiet, sweet-faced woman, quite striking with her milk-white skin and her now silvering black hair, always so precisely parted in the middle. Her big dark gentle eyes were rather wistful. She had a way of keeping her head low, then lifting it suddenly to gaze with a searching intensity into the speaker's face, as if seeking something she never found. Her laugh, when it came, was tentative, restrained. She had few friends and little social life, for she was aware of her status as an unmarried woman. But she was very graceful and composed. Even in the marketplace, where other women battered their way, or stood laughing and talking, she dealt quickly and coolly with the seller, then glided on, people making way before her dignity and seeming assurance.

Unlike Mary, who enjoyed such forays, she could hardly wait to get home to the place she loved best, her kitchen. Lazarus had humored her by building on an extra room where she could have her own indoor oven with its shelves for bread and its ever-turning spit. It was her haven. She worked and rested there as with a lover, giving to it her finest creative energies. No one could prepare a joint of kid more delicious, or sweetmeats as delicate. Even her vegetables were tempting, with wines and sauces of her own invention; her bread, more crisp than that of most women, was yet soft to the tongue.

Her oven's warmth was a comfort to the cold despair that sometimes racked Martha in secret. She would pull back her skirts and warm her long slim legs before it, admiring them with the dark silken growths of hair.

Now into this quiet and private place new inspiration had burst. Life once more began to pour through the spacious house. The women, and in some ways Lazarus too, began to live for the festivals, when Jesus was sure to join them. Though there were days between— and this filled them with constant hope and expectation—when he might come anyway: sometimes alone, more often bringing several of his apostles. Shy burly fishermen, most of them, but all of them fascinating, for they brought an aura of adventure and travel with them. How many places they had been! Capernaum, Tyre and Sidon, the great northern mountains, Caesarea Philippi, the Sea of Galilee. And with *him!*

Though Martha lived in the very shadow of a great city, her own world was small and circumscribed. She had never been anywhere except to Hebron and Jericho, and a few times, the nearby Dead Sea—such a desolate place, smelling of salt and sulfur: like her own existence, desolate and barren in the seemingly endless periods between Jesus' visits. Then—ah, then—birds sang and the house teemed with life.

Martha visualized the multitudes that followed Jesus, praising him, shouting hosannas. She tried to imagine the miracles, and failed. They were simply beyond her comprehension: feeding thousands, raising the dead. Such reports made her uncomfortable, for they removed him too far from the glorious miracles they had witnessed here. It was enough that Jesus had cast out the demon of grief from her brother, and poured a heady new wine of life and emotion through all of them. The *Messiah?* The phrase eluded her; like his miracles, it was not really important. Martha knew only that she lived fully and sweetly in his presence. That Jesus had enemies, critics who spoke out against him in the synagogues and the Sanhedrin—even some who wanted to destroy him—appalled her, filled her with such personal pain and fright she refused to countenance it. No, no, it could not be—not that wonderful man who could bring such joy!

Sometimes all twelve of Jesus' band would be gathered around her long table (fourteen, counting Lazarus and Jesus). Rugged, enthusiastic men—how they ate! How they laughed and argued sometimes, how their rich male voices rang out in the songs and prayers. The sisters, serving, scarcely could believe their good fortune: to see Lazarus so filled with life and happiness again. Eating heartily once more, involved in fervent discussion of spiritual things. The voices sometimes continued far into the night, after the sisters had cleared up and Martha spread out the dish towels to dry.

Martha would lie awake, smiling to remember the men's compliments, fulfilled at having pleased them. But growing uneasy, realizing that Mary had not said good night but was probably still with them, sitting on a cushion, eyes wide in that eager way she had of drinking in every word. Even participating! It was a letdown after such a beautiful evening; Martha felt disappointed and somehow betrayed. She would toss and turn, or lie alert, listening for Mary's voice mingling with the others, or later her footsteps stealing softly to bed. Martha would stare at the ceiling, one hand over her mouth to stifle her own bewildering storm of emotions: loving and resenting her sister; torn between admiration, envy, even a kind of pride in Mary, and all the while hurting and disapproving.

Martha had tried to reason with her, in vain. "It just isn't— seemly," she groped. "An unmarried girl alone with men."

"Martha, Martha, these are our guests!" Mary gazed at her, astonished. "And they are men of *God*. Besides, our brother is there." Laughing, she flung her arms around Martha and gave her a fond little shake. "Can you imagine *Lazarus* approving anything that might be even slightly unseemly for either of us?"

"No." Reluctantly Martha laughed too, still troubled but ashamed of her misgivings. "Forgive me."

"You are missing so much," Mary urged. "Why don't you join us?"

"I'm too tired," Martha protested. "I couldn't! Oh, no, I just— couldn't." She wished she hadn't said anything. She hated being the scolding sister. If only she could be free and open, like Mary. Not so bound up in herself. If only she could be more relaxed around men, not afraid to show the love that was sometimes bursting like some forbidden joy in her heart. Why did her hands tremble so in the presence of Jesus, her throat get so dry?

She would never forget that first night Lazarus had brought Jesus home. Their first sight of him—the sudden assault of his beauty and goodness when he smiled at them, his eyes, his whole being radiating love. The rapture that held them frozen for a moment before such a guest. Obviously a prophet or a prince. Yet Mary had known at once what to do. While Martha was still fumbling around, trying to find enough vessels for the washing, Mary had rushed to her room and brought forth her most precious oil to anoint Jesus' feet. She had unpinned her own flowing hair and was drying them with it when Martha returned. Martha had been stricken to see it, feeling remiss, but also a little shocked. Though this was a not uncommon tribute for some women to pay a very special guest, it seemed to Martha somehow—well—brazen. It had made her uncomfortable the few times she had witnessed it in other homes. Martha shrank before such a fervent display. She could not imagine herself doing such a thing. Nor, for that matter, Mary—until that night.

Martha never mentioned it, nor did Mary, but both of them often thought of it, examining its significance in their hearts.

Toward the end of fall, the two worked joyously, preparing for Hanukkah, the Feast of Dedication. Together they polished all the lamps and filled them with fragrant oil. For this was also known as the Feast of Lights, to celebrate the victory of Judas Maccabaeus and his reconsecration of the Temple after it was defiled by Antiochus Epiphanes and his pagans. A time when golden candelabra blazed in the Temple and people danced in the brightly lighted streets. Every home must shine. Lazarus carried lamps outside to hang from the trees and bloom up and down the steps. This year, though it was fairly warm—a few roses still bloomed in Mary's garden—an early snow was falling, adding to the sparkle. And Jesus was coming! Again and again that final day, Mary dropped what she was doing to run hopefully to the doorway and peer out.

He had promised—stopping as he always did on his way to Jerusalem—he would join them here as soon as the festivities were over. But as the day wore on, waiting became harder to bear, for both of them. It was growing dark, the snow was falling faster, and the wind blowing harder.

Even Lazarus looked worried when he came in, though he tried to keep his fears from his sisters. Had there been trouble again in Jerusalem? He hadn't been in the city all day, but surely, if anything had happened to Jesus, he'd have heard of it.

Despite the controversy Jesus provoked, it was hard to believe he could come to serious harm. Jesus was too clever to be entrapped; his answers were always not only quick and wise but profound. As a Sadducee, Lazarus himself had debated with Jesus several times; the man was impossible to refute. Pondering, Lazarus felt better. No, this was truly a man of God, and more. More even than a prophet. Perhaps even the Messiah that had been promised so long! Surely Jesus was beyond the mere scheming treacheries of men. Surely he had God's protection.

"Now don't fret," Lazarus encouraged briskly. His black eyes sparkled with anticipation. "Just keep the food hot. Jesus will be here soon."

"Jesus!"
"Nicodemus!"
In wonder, the two men stood for a second there on Solomon's Porch, where each had taken shelter from the unexpected snow. Then with shouts of joy, they embraced, drew back a little and stood gazing at each other, hands still on each other's shoulders.

"I was looking for you," the older man exclaimed. "But the last place I expected to find you was here in the Temple. Not after what happened this afternoon." His lean distinguished face was both relieved and dismayed. "Word reached me at my bank; I left as soon as I could. Oh, Jesus, my son, thank heaven you are all right! Is it true they were about to stone you?"

"A few. They didn't succeed. Some of the crowd were unruly, not many." Jesus looked serious but unperturbed. "It was not hard to dissuade them—the rest wanted to hear what I had to say."

"But I do worry," cried Nicodemus. He wiped his wet brow with his sleeve. Their garments were blowing. The snow that glittered and wheeled on the lighted steps was drifting in here too. They moved with one accord to the deeper shelter of the arcade. "Things seem to be getting worse every time you come to a feast. The Sanhedrin out to get you—and now this!

"The Sanhedrin hasn't succeeded either," Jesus reminded him. "Thank you for your help, Nicodemus," he said, gratefully. "But as a Pharisee in good standing, you can't go on defending me."

Nicodemus shook his head. "I have to speak out, just as you do. Yes, Caiaphas is furious—and he will do what he pleases, no matter what anybody says. But the high priest isn't the only one, or the Sanhedrin either. For every Jew that loves you there are a hundred who would kill you—look at what happened today! Why do you keep returning to Jerusalem," he begged, "knowing the hostility here? Much as I love you and long to see you, it frightens me, for one day they will succeed. I had hoped you were still safely preaching somewhere in Galilee."

"This is my city too, it is sacred to me."
"Very well, yes, come if you must." Nicodemus sighed and

pressed his arm. "But where are your bodyguards?" He looked anxiously around. "Are they not with you this time?"

"The twelve are not my bodyguards," Jesus corrected, "but my apostles. They have more important things to do."

"What could be more important than protecting you?"

"Healing, teaching, carrying on my work for me."

"Well, whoever they are, they should be with you!"

"I don't ask them to go everywhere with me," Jesus told him. "Especially to Jerusalem right now. It might provoke an uprising. There's no use in subjecting them to unnecessary risks—some of them have families." He was shivering, hugging himself in his threadbare cloak, stamping his feet to keep warm—they were almost naked, Nicodemus noticed. But his face was cheerful.

Nicodemus winced, hurting for him, and feeling frustrated. This tall, handsome prince of a man was so fair and fascinating he turned heads even when he walked unrecognized in the streets; yet clad so humbly, usually in simple white homespun, with some kind of nondescript cloak when needed. Clean, pleasant, yes—it became him—but scarcely the kind of attire to attract the attention and approbation of people whose opinions counted. The members of the Sanhedrin were the aristocracy; they dressed well, lived in fine homes. How could Nicodemus expect to convince them they should listen to the remarkable things this young teacher was saying? That his claims, however incredible they might sound, were true and they should pay him serious heed?

They dismissed the very idea. Who was such a one to attack them, let alone lead them into the kingdom? Ludicrous. They were men of substance. The last thing most of them wanted was a messiah, upsetting the system. But if and when the true One ever came, he would surely be at least their equal, not some poor peasant without even a decent pair of boots.

Concerned, but with a kind of pitying impatience, Nicodemus glanced again at Jesus' feet. He had tried to press money on him, urging him to buy a fine wardrobe, but Jesus had only laughed. "No, Nicodemus. Give your money to the poor, as I command. How can I ask others to sacrifice worldly possessions unless I'm willing to do so myself?"

Now Nicodemus sighed, but his keen, kindly eyes shone with

eagerness and affection. "Come home with me," he invited. "We will celebrate your safety this last night of the feast. Joseph of Arimathea will be there too—he's another defender of yours, you know; he wants to see you. I will rest better if I know you are fed and out of the cold."

Jesus smiled, "I will be well fed," he reassured him, "thanks to you. I've promised Lazarus and his sisters to spend the night with them."

"Good, that makes me happy. A fine man, Lazarus. I'm so glad you're friends. The kind you should be cultivating," he added. "But it's cold and still snowing." Nicodemus indicated the swirling veils that nearly obscured the street. "Let me at least send my servants with a litter to carry you to Bethany."

"No, though I appreciate your offer. I could never ask other men to bear me on their shoulders."

"A carriage, then?" Nicodemus persisted. "I want to be sure you get there safely."

Jesus shook his head. "That won't be necessary." They embraced in parting, and stood holding each other a moment. "Dear Nicodemus, you worry about me needlessly. Though I love you for it, I would spare you. I must accomplish my mission. No harm can come to me until my work on earth is finished."

Nicodemus drew back, his gentle face working. "And then?" he whispered.

"I cannot tell you," Jesus said gravely. "Only that you must not worry. There is nothing that you or anyone can do to prevent it."

It was dark by the time Jesus reached the house of Lazarus. He could see its lights beckoning brightly from every window, and make out the figure of Mary peering from the doorway as he climbed the final steps.

"He's here, he's here!" Mary called out joyfully. "He's coming up the steps!"

Lazarus appeared behind her, and came leaping down through the snow to meet him, arms outstretched. "You're late. We've been worried. Peace be with you!"

The women embraced him, exclaiming, brushing at the snow that covered him, smiling to behold him. He was here, safely here, their friend, their darling, almost a member of the family, and more, a famous guest. People talked of Jesus wherever you went; a thrill of wonder pierced them that he had chosen their home as his refuge.

And tonight—although they also enjoyed his comrades—they had him all to themselves.

Martha stepped back for a moment, breathing deeply to steady herself. Silently, then, she took his wet cloak and carried it outside that she might shake the snow from it. The night was white and still, with a new moon shining. The wind had quieted suddenly and the snow seemed to be resting; only a few flakes still coasted down, feeling delicate and cool on her flushed cheeks. Vigorously Martha shook the heavy wrap. Heart pounding, she held its precious weight against her breast a moment before carrying it back inside. Moving in her graceful, gliding way, Martha hung the cloak over a chair before the hot glowing brazier to dry.

The others were already in animated conversation. Jesus had been explaining why he was late, and Lazarus was questioning him further. Evidently there had been some trouble in Jerusalem. Martha was torn; she was anxious to hear more—and would later—but supper could not wait.

Smiling nervously, she excused herself and hastened to her kitchen. Fragments of conversation trailed her: "But why, why? When they can see for themselves all the marvelous works you are doing." "It's not what I do, but what I say. They accuse me of heresy, even treason." Martha gasped. How *could* they? There seemed to be some mysterious plot to silence him. It couldn't succeed, of course, but the very thought was chilling. The awful threat to Jesus—and to them.

But she must pay attention to what she was doing. Protecting her hands with her apron, Martha lifted the meat on its spit. But it was heavy; she nearly dropped it, trying to slide it onto the platter. And it was much too done she despaired—falling apart. The vegetables would have to be reheated, their sauces added. Where were the olives and cheeses? Oh, yes, Mary had attended to them—she hoped.

Martha checked the long low table, so pretty in the lamplight with its linen cloth. Mary had put flowers in an ornate glass in the center— a nice touch, but they crowded things. Martha's long hands were trembling as she placed them firmly on a chest. Where was Mary? Still talking with the men, of course. Oh, well, no matter; really now, be honest—you'd rather do it yourself. Mary gets underfoot. Martha gave a fond if exasperated little laugh. And oh, the secret joy of preparing food for Jesus!

Martha worked as fast as she could. The coals were sputtering and smoking from the grease. She was beginning to feel hot and sweaty. Her black hair, parted so precisely and combed so carefully for him, in a new way atop her narrow head, was coming down; she could feel strands of it on her neck and her perspiring brow. And now look, she had spilled the sauce! She felt it splash hot on one thigh, and saw to her horror the brown stain on her dress: her best white embroidered dress, worn only on special occasions.

No, no, she could not manage alone; it was all too much. Mary *should* be out here helping! Listen to her: Mary's lilting voice could be heard above those of the men, sweet and fervent, unrestrained. Martha stiffened, taut with listening, the way she lay sometimes at night. Feeling lonely and somehow betrayed. Forgotten, unimportant—Martha pushed back her hair and glanced bleakly around her kitchen—and yes, suddenly, cruelly old. Resentment rose within her, a devouring pain. No, now stop this, don't spoil things! But it hurt, it hurt, became bitterness, a fury of emotions she could not control. She scrubbed futilely at her skirt a minute, then threw down the wet cloth. This was intolerable. Mouth tight, eyes flashing, Martha glided back into the common room to confront them.

The sight of the three so deep in conversation held her speechless for a minute. The room was bathed in the soft glow of lamplight; there was the sound of coals ticking in the copper brazier, and a sense of the whispering snow outside. Jesus half reclined on a low couch as he spoke; Lazarus was perched on a nearby chair, leaning forward, clasping his knees, an expression of intense listening on his keen, sharp-featured face. Martha saw with a little stab that someone had removed the bouquet of flowers from the chest where she had just put them; they were now on a small table beside Jesus.

Mary, of course; for her sister was seated on a silken cushion, her small chin cupped in one hand, the other holding a rose; while her beautiful hair spilled over her shoulders. In this light it was almost the same shining copper color as the brazier, glittering and flaming. Again that little stab of pain, then deeper, sharper, fiercer. Martha blinked rapidly, for now she realized, with a kind of blind hopeless sense of futility, that while she was toiling in the kitchen Mary had once again performed for Jesus that lovely, womanly, but somehow so abandoned rite to honor him.

"Forgive me, Lord," Martha broke in—she could restrain herself no longer—"but it's growing late, and the meal not yet served. I really need Mary to help me."

Mary looked up, her radiant eyes contrite. "In a minute," she pleaded eagerly. "This is so important. I want to hear what Jesus is saying about eternal life." She turned back to him. "Life is so wonderful, I want to live forever! But I have always heard from the Sadducees, men like my brother"—she smiled at Lazarus—"that there is no resurrection, life ends for everyone at the grave. But you say the Father does not want us to perish, He will raise us up if we follow your commandments. You have already told us many things, tell us more. What can we do to inherit eternal life?"

"Not my commandments," Jesus reaffirmed quietly, "but God's. My teaching is not mine, but that of him who sent me. To enjoy eternal life, simply begin with the greatest of all commandments: You shall love the Lord your God with all your heart, and with all your soul and with all your strength, and with all your mind. And the second, which is like unto it: You shall love your neighbor as yourself."

"What about your *sister?*" Martha exploded, to her own astonishment. Her voice shook with indignation; her whole body was trembling. She stiffened herself against it, her fists locked tight at her sides. "If my sister really loved me, she would be in the kitchen helping prepare your supper! Lord, don't you *care* that she has left me to do all the work alone?"

There was a moment of shocked silence. A branch scraped against the window; they were aware of the snow and the rosy clucking of the coals. "Martha . . . *Martha!*" Jesus exclaimed in sad surprise, getting to his feet. He stood above her, his dark eyes filled with affection and concern. "Dear Martha," he remonstrated gently, "you are troubled about too many things. Men and women don't live by bread alone, we also must have food for the spirit." He held both her hands and squeezed them to comfort her, but his voice was positive. "What Mary has chosen is the better thing."

"*Better?*" Martha gasped. Her face, flushed from the kitchen, had gone white at his reproof. Her teeth bit fiercely into her lower lip to still its trembling.

"Yes," Jesus went on, "for it's not what we eat that is important, but what we do to nourish the spirit. Mary took the sponge from Lazarus to bathe my feet, and she let down her hair that she might dry them. She went into her garden to pick its last late flowers to place beside me. But the greatest tribute of all she has always paid me, and that has been simply to sit and listen to my words."

Martha burst into tears. They stared at her incredulous as she stood weeping, hugging herself yet trying to hide her head in her arms; pathetic and terrible with her straggling hair and her racking sobs. They were stricken; they had never seen her like this—not Martha, always so poised and preoccupied, seemingly devoid of emotion save for her bubbling pots and recipes.

Suddenly Martha threw back her head and faced Jesus, with the tears still running down her cheeks. "I love you, Master!" she wailed brokenly. "Take me with you. I will give up everything for you, everything—my sister Mary, even my beloved brother—only do not scold me, do not speak so to me, not when I have worked so hard to please you!"

Jesus was gazing at her, deeply troubled. "Martha, forgive me," he said kindly. "You know I would never want to hurt you." He held out his arms to console her, but she wrenched away.

"Those flowers!" Martha accused. Her eyes were blazing with a resentment Mary and Lazarus realized must have been smoldering for years. "Is their fragrance sweeter than the aroma of the meat I have cooked for you? Is that bouquet more beautiful than the table I have set? It should be, for Mary spent half the day arranging it while I slaved in the kitchen. Look at these hands," she demanded, and spread them before him. "See that blister? It came from a burn as I was trying to make the oven burn hotter. See that scar?" She panted. "I cut myself while preparing the roast—and there are others, Master, all for you. No, no, my hands are not smooth and white like Mary's, and you will find no rings upon them. Why? Because you have urged us to sell whatever we can and give to the poor. See, I *do* listen to you. Even as I work, I hear more than you think. I have sold my jewelry, what little I had, and given to the poor. For you!"

"Martha, Martha," Jesus was murmuring over and over as she wailed, beside herself. "Dear, dear friend . . ." He caught one of her frantically gesturing hands, which were indeed touchingly work-scarred, and held it affectionately, but with great firmness, to quiet her. He pressed it against his breast. "My heart is full of love for you— all of you; full almost to bursting because of the beauty and comfort of this home. It is my refuge, it nourishes my body and my soul. But it grieves me to think my coming here should cause you so much work, and arouse such conflict and pain within you."

Martha straightened suddenly, went whiter still with fear. What if he did not come again? What if her outburst should drive him away? She could not bear it. With a long moaning shudder, she drew back. Still gasping her breath, she accepted a handkerchief from Mary and began to dry her eyes.

"Oh, oh, oh," she whispered, "I am so ashamed!"

"You are very tired," Jesus said with compassion. "I understand, because I am very tired myself. Come, let us eat the wonderful meal you have prepared, then you must take your rest."

"Yes." Lazarus spoke up quickly. "It will restore us. We will laugh and sing and pray as always. Then—it's late—all of us must get a good night's rest."

Mary had put her arms around her sister, tender and solicitous, murmuring to her, anxious to make amends. "I will do all the serving," she insisted. "You are not to do anything; you must sit down and be served with the men."

"No, no." Martha finished blowing her nose. "I wouldn't think of it. The flowers are—beautiful," she choked. "You did right to place them beside him. Now let us put them back on the table." She realized she might be incoherent, for she was still shaking, poking futilely at the dissarray of her hair: still appalled at her own behavior yet curiously at peace, as if she had been delivered from demons that had tormented her far too long. But most of all, delivered of something glorious—her love for Jesus. She had carried it in secret, but now she had borne it for him like a child, given it over to him to be received. She did not ask his love in return, only that he accept what she had delivered in such travail.

She must say the words again, she felt so happy and so free. Mary had hurried to the kitchen; and, to spare Martha, Lazarus too had left the room. She was alone with Jesus. She turned to him now, smiling, composed, direct. "I do love you," she informed him simply. Her eyes glistened with the innocent candor of her feelings. "I would follow you to the ends of the earth if you asked me."

"Dear Martha," Jesus said, and covered his eyes. His heart bled. For he remembered those same words cried out in such desperation by a peasant girl on the hillside with her sheep. The one woman whom God in his infinite grace and wisdom had given him to love. He remembered that pure bright rapture that was never to be fulfilled; he remembered the terrible pain of parting. And he thanked God for it: that the Father had created his son to be human—man as well as Son of Man, sent to earth to live as a man, tempted as a man is tempted, and so to experience that most important, beautiful, yet agonizing of all human experiences, human love.

Jesus knew what Martha was feeling. He could share her suffering.

Martha rushed on bravely. "You have told us there are sometimes women with you in Galilee. Peter's wife and others. I would be one of them. Take me with you, let me serve you!"

Jesus was shaking his head, though his face shone with gratitude. "Martha, Martha, you are needed *here*," he told her warmly. "Your brother and sister need you; and *I* need you too, right where you are. This house would not be the same without you. What would I do without your wonderful food that is always waiting for me? Or the kind thoughtful things you do to make me welcome?" Smiling, Jesus took both her work-scarred hands and kissed them. "These dear hands are already serving me. They have made this house my home, Martha, and it is a house of love."

Martha managed a faint smile too, though her eyes were wet. Nodding, she drew a deep sigh and returned the pressure of his clasp. A part of her was disappointed, but she was also weak with relief. She felt safe, and cleansed, and free. She had told him. Risked everything to make her statement and confirm it; but now she was safe, she need not leave. She could stay on in her own little world, warm and secure, awaiting his coming. She had made this a house of love for him, he had said so. Whenever she was lonely, she would think of his words and be comforted.

Later, when the sisters had gone to bed, Lazarus and Jesus went outdoors to gaze down upon the city, glittering under its rare mantle of snow. The storm had ceased, the air turned warm once more, and now only a delicate furring still covered the ground. But on all the square rooftops below them the snow had spread its white linen as with a thousand tablecloths. The bare trees and shrubs that clung to the Mount of Olives were like guests in ermine coming to the banquet; and when the wind stirred, dancers in gossamer veils drifted up and down the countless tiers of steps.

It was very quiet. The slender new moon cradled a star. Lights were bright in all the little houses. In the distance, beyond its great dark walls, they could see the massive towers and domes of Jerusalem, almost all of them aglow. In the center, the golden crown of the Temple shone, its spires now delicate as wands against the soft blue-silver sky.

Brushing snow from the wall, Lazarus hoisted himself upon it. He sat there a moment, gazing out over the lovely scene, but his black brows were frowning. "Jesus, I brought you out here to talk, lest Martha hear us," he said. "I hope her outburst didn't offend you. She meant nothing by it. Martha works very hard to please others, but she also works to please herself. Nothing makes her happier than preparing for your visits. It would break her heart if you found her words reason not to come again."

"And mine," Jesus echoed quickly. He pulled himself up beside Lazarus. A few steps down the hill, in their terraced garden, Mary's last late-blooming roses lifted their bright heads above the snow. "Few men are as dear to me as you are, Lazarus. Even my own brothers."

Lazarus regarded him, still frowning. "Your brothers don't support you, do they? I have never seen them with you."

"My brothers support me in their own way; they would fight to the death for me. But they are not yet ready to believe in me."

"Can't your mother persuade them? She knows who you are: she gave you life. I do wish I could know her. I have heard her beautiful story from Nicodemus."

"It's been very difficult for her. And my brothers too. I can't blame them; some things are simply beyond their comprehension."

"Tell me more about your mother."

"She is . . . wonderful," Jesus said helplessly, with a little laugh. "She saddles up the donkey herself sometimes and comes riding out to find me. Often stays a few days helping the women who attend to us in the country. Not here, usually," he added. "Jerusalem is too far for most of them to come, and we don't need them so much here."

"How many women?"

"Five or six. Sometimes more, sometimes less—they come and go." Jesus named the most dependable, and described some of their adventures. "It's a hard life on the road. Few women could stand it— certainly not Martha, I'm afraid. I hope she realizes that's why I brushed aside her offer. I was not rejecting her."

"That's really what I wanted to discuss," said Lazarus. He sounded concerned and a trifle embarrassed. "She really does love you—how much I had no idea. I would never have believed she could speak so to any man! But I assure you she meant only the purest kind of love."

"I know that," Jesus said, "and I am honored. Love is so precious, any declaration of love should be honored and cherished, for it is a precious thing."

"But many women must love you," Lazarus reasoned, in honest admiration. "How can they help it? Mary does too. I can see it in her eyes—and in the eyes of women everywhere you go." Lazarus pondered, frowning, chin in hand. "Forgive me, Rabbi, but as a Jew who has always kept the Law, why haven't you taken a wife and had children, as the Law commands? Don't you believe in God's first commandment, to be fruitful and multiply?"

Jesus shivered. It was growing cold. He was suddenly greatly burdened; his humanity coursed through him, unleashing a pain and longing he had thought he would never feel again. He wanted to confide in Lazarus, to speak of it at last, for never had he felt closer to any man. But he knew he could not, dared not, for once the name of Tamara crossed his lips he would be undone.

He smiled faintly. "Lazarus, your question is natural, especially since a rabbi is supposed to set a good example. I'll answer with the words from the old rabbinic parable of the unmarried rabbi who was challenged by his students about this very obligation: 'I can only say that my soul is enamored of the Torah, and the world can be populated by others.' " Jesus paused. "Seriously, there is nothing I would like better, were I just a normal man. But my mission is such that it cannot include a home and family. It would not be fair to them—or to the purpose for which I came. Meanwhile, God is love. If anyone loves me, man or woman, let us rejoice, for it is not to my glory but to his."

They sat silent for a moment, gazing down on the panorama of rooftops and the sparkling city beyond. "Never have I seen Jerusalem more beautiful," said Lazarus. "Or the Temple so radiant. It seems to shine with a special light."

Jesus nodded. But when he replied, his voice was both ironic and sorrowing. "Let it shine on as long as it can," he said. "For the time is coming when it will be plunged into darkness with the rest of the city; when nothing will be left of the Temple, not one stone. See all those buildings?" he continued, with a broad sweep of his hand, as Lazarus gasped. "The Antonia Fortress, the citadels and towers, Herod's palace there against the sky—that fox, he will no longer have a place for his lechery and murders, for it, too, will be gone, razed to the ground!"

"But not the Temple!" Lazarus protested.

"Yes, the very Temple. Every corridor and colonnade, every marble step, every lavish gate, all its rich adornments, its silver and gold and precious gems—all, all will be thrown down, destroyed utterly; nothing will be left standing, not so much as a single stone."

"But why?" demanded Lazarus. "In the name of the One we worship there, whose own presence dwells in the Holy Sanctum, why would he let such a thing happen? Why would he not protect it?"

"The Temple must fall," said Jesus. "The Temple is destroying itself. It will fall by the weight of its own corruption. And the City of David with it."

"But I thought you loved Jerusalem and the Temple!"

"I would lay down my life for them," said Jesus. "That is why I grieve for them, because they will not listen to my warnings. This beautiful scene that you and I are enjoying now, Lazarus—it is doomed. It will vanish, and there is nothing I can do to save it."

Lazarus stared at him, astounded. "When will this be?" he asked. He was a practical man, a man of action. "If this is true, then I must be ready. I must protect my sisters—we must be prepared to flee!"

Jesus was shaking his head; he made a little gesture of restraint. "I didn't mean to frighten you, or even to warn you. Only to confide in you what I know will be. But when—even I don't know."

"What can we do?" Lazarus persisted, still alarmed.

"Don't worry; go on living as you have. Enjoy life, love your sisters, keep the commandments, feed the poor, comfort the sick and those in prison, welcome the stranger as you have welcomed me. For in doing all these things you will be doing them for me. Live so that when that hour comes, you will have nothing to fear. If you truly believe in me, I promise you will be spared."

The snow was falling again, the wind rising. Brushing at their garments, they went back into the house. Only two lamps burned now, casting shadows.

"Where will you be?" Lazarus asked anxiously.

Jesus stood thoughtful, arms folded, gazing into the dying coals. Finally he raised his eyes. "I don't know that either," he said. "Only that the time is growing short before I must leave you."

"Well, wherever you go, be careful," Lazarus pleaded. "Though we will miss you, stay out of Jerusalem until things are quieter." Their eyes held; they were bound by a sense of love and foreboding. "Nothing must happen to you," he cried softly. "We love you so much, all three of us. We couldn't bear it!"

"Or to you," said Jesus fervently. He reached out to press his friend's hand. "Take care of yourself, dear Lazarus, for I have loved few people as I love you."

Chapter 14

*T*HE courier had hoped to find Jesus in Jericho.

Jesus would surely be there, the frantic sisters had told him, for that had been their friend's destination when last they had seen him. True, that was some weeks ago; he and his men might have moved on, but seek him first in Jericho.

"But find him, only find him as fast as you can. Give him this message: Our brother is ill. The one whom he loves so much is gravely ill. He must come!"

The boy was already breathless from climbing the hill to this great house in such urgency at night. The house was warm and enticing, despite its atmosphere of crisis. He sensed the beauty of a bedroom where one light burned, and the charm of a pretty woman sitting by a bed, holding a man's hand. She came to the door with the tears streaming down her cheeks. "Tell him we need him!"

The older sister handed him a small parcel, already efficiently prepared, containing a letter of instructions, some money in case he needed it, and a little food. Her pleasant face was still distraught, but now she seemed composed. "You may get hungry," she said kindly. "Eat when you can." She mentioned the names of several people in Jericho who might know Jesus' whereabouts.

The boy listened carefully, feeling his responsibility to these gracious women in their fine house which he had often admired from a distance. He assured them he would stop for nothing. Yes, it was a rough journey through the mountains, but he knew shortcuts; he had run it a number of times in just a few hours. He realized he wanted their admiration almost as much as he wanted to reassure them. He was a poor boy, proud of his running, lean and strapping, with a tough-sweet smile and determined eyes, nimble as a cat. He had won every race he entered, beaten even a few Greeks and Romans.

Tucking the parcel in his girdle, he set off, his long legs streaking along alleys and through rocky fields until he reached the highway, then pacing himself as he climbed and descended through the starry night. The skies were brilliant, with a strong moon rising; he had the eyes of a jackal, and no fear of falling. He was pleased and excited. To be entrusted with a message for the famous healer! He might even be lucky enough to accompany Jesus back. Though it would be nice to linger in Jericho, the luxurious winter capital of Herod and his son, a playground of the wealthy. It was warm there, like summer compared to Jerusalem. He thought of them, sunning themselves under the palm trees or wallowing in the Roman baths while other people froze or starved. . . . The youth, whose name was Caleb, entertained himself with fantasies of such a life, as well as speculations about the controversial prophet. Jesus was a poor man himself, people said, who hobnobbed with both the rabble and the rich.

By the time Caleb reached the outskirts of Jericho, he realized it had been folly to take off at such an hour and run so fast, whatever the emergency. The city, known for its merriment far into the night, was still sleeping; only a few scattered lights burned among the hills and in occasional windows. The strange palm-lined streets were dark and silent, though the skies were beginning to gray. Caleb was panting; his side had begun to hurt. He could accomplish nothing until morning. He walked along slowly, and looked about for a place to rest. To his surprise, he could hear a fountain spilling its frail music from a leafy copse nearby. Exhausted, he flung himself down on the grass. He would eat the food the woman Martha had given him, and cheer himself by listening to the clashing of palm fronds and the sweet liquid sounds of the fountain until daybreak. . . .

The next thing Caleb knew, someone was shaking him, hands were cuffing his bewildered face. "Wake up, give an account of yourself!" A boot kicked him into consciousness; he could feel the metal of a Roman breastplate as a soldier yanked him to his feet.

"Where am I?" Caleb muttered stupidly, blinking. To his dismay, the sky was rosy overhead; light glinted on the solder's helmet. He could hear roosters crowing and the rattle of carts on a nearby street.

"You're on palace grounds, you idiot!" the soldier barked. He was a ruddy-faced, thick-lipped youth, not much older than Caleb. "What are you doing here?"

"I'm a runner from Bethany, with an important message to deliver. I got lost and fell asleep."

"Then your message must be for Herod?" The tall young soldier was scowling, eyeing him suspiciously.

"No. Oh, no," Caleb corrected hastily. "I'm seeking a man named Jesus. The healer and prophet from Galilee."

"*Jesus?*" The young guard gasped, then threw back his head and howled in disbelief. "Well, you won't find him here!" He looked over his shoulder, and lowering his voice, grinned wryly. "At least I hope not, or he may find his head on a plate for breakfast." The guard continued to stare at him as Caleb laughed uncomfortably. "Are you one of that rebel's followers? If so, you found a strange place to sleep."

"No, I'm simply a courier," Caleb pleaded, heart hammering. "Sent to tell him one of his friends is very ill, it's urgent that he return at once to Bethany. Here, I have a letter to prove it." Desperately Caleb fumbled in his girdle for the parcel; to his horror, it was not there. Then he spied it, fallen where he had opened it under the tree. But even as he retrieved it and produced the letter, he wondered if he dared show it to anyone associated with the king. Caleb himself had not read it; he made it a point of honor not to do such things. Yet now it occurred to him—what if it contained some word that might offend the monster? And had or hadn't the woman named Martha also given him a list of people he might contact in Jericho?

Cursing himself for a fool, he watched the soldier unroll the scroll and scan it briefly. To his relief, the guard handed it back without asking to see anything more. "Sorry I had to be so rough." He stood, hands on his hips, imposing in his uniform, but no longer sinister. "I had to make sure." Again that cynical grin as he glanced in the direction of the dazzling complex of buildings on the hill above them.

Their eyes met, with an unspoken disgust. They were aware of the palace stirring, servants coming and going, wagons of foodstuffs arriving, the clang of great iron gates opening; several soldiers on white horses thundered down the winding road that led to the street. Guard and messenger felt, as one, its aura of luxury and licentiousness. Even some of the Romans who served Herod were shamed by the vileness and cruelty he represented.

"Have you any idea where I might look for Jesus? I was told he might be staying with friends in Jericho." Caleb felt he could trust the young guard now. He had already lost too much time; he must have some clues and be on his way. "Perhaps you know where some of them live."

"If I knew I wouldn't dare tell you, and I don't advise you to go asking for them. Word travels. It could put them under suspicion, and you too. This Jesus also has a lot of enemies." The ruddy young guard pushed back his helmet, obviously concerned. "I can tell you this much: He was here, he and his band—what're they called—apostles? I understand they left a week or so ago. I suggest you move on, up north along the Jordan, somewhere in the vicinity where—" He halted, hating to say the name. "Where that other one that was preaching and baptizing got into so much trouble," he said grimly.

"John the Baptist?" Caleb blurted. "Surely they can't be baptizing this time of year. The water up there must still be muddy and cold."

This struck the young Roman funny. He suddenly threw back his head and laughed. "But I hear this one's a miracle worker. If so, maybe he's warming the water!"

Caleb laughed too. They stood grinning at each other a moment, discussing his mission and wishing each other well, before he dusted himself off and hurried on.

At first the brisk morning air revived him, along with a few remaining mouthfuls of Martha's bread, which he munched as he loped through the waking city. Those nice women, concerned for his comfort even in their alarm. He must reach the healer as soon as possible and bring him back in time to help their brother. If only Jesus had been in Jericho! The sooner the return to Bethany was started the better.

It was still some distance to the river. Caleb realized he must pace himself if he was to last the day; he was very tired, but he dared not pause to rest lest he fall asleep.

By asking questions of fellow travelers, he learned that Jesus had been staying in a small town also named Bethany—Bethany beyond the Jordan—but was holding services on the river to the north. Doggedly the boy trudged on, turning north when he finally reached the river. The water roared by, gray and swollen after the winter rains;

it looked uninviting even though it shone silver in the noon sun. These last miles were hardest of all, plowing through thickets and over rocks, along paths that were often spongy, for the river had overflowed its banks in places; he must detour, circle its serpentine course. But his spirits lifted as he realized that soon, surely within the hour, he would find the famous Jesus; actually see him and have the honor of delivering in person a message that, however grave, he must have in order to hasten at once to the aid of his friends.

Finally, in midafternoon, Caleb could hear voices above the sound of the water. And clambering over the last rock, pushing aside the branches, he came upon a clearing where many people were gathered. He rested, breathing hard, and awed by the scene: Below them, two men stood in the river. They were baptizing, he realized. Men and women were coming up out of the water, being dried and embraced by others, rejoicing. The crowd was singing and praising God. Some were laughing, some weeping. An air of great joy prevailed. And it came to him that Jesus was somewhere among them, and that many miracles of healing had occurred here today.

Even the water! he realized, with a shock. Here it was no longer turbulent, gray and forbidding, but blue and sparkling in the sun, sweet and clean. The soldier's jest, at which both had laughed so heartily, was no longer funny.

Shaken, almost overcome with excitement and anticipation, Caleb made his way across the grass. People waylaid him to proclaim their healings. "I can see, I can see!" an old man shouted. "You, boy—you with the torn shirt—are you my grandson come to lead me home? No, no, my grandson would never look so muddy and worn, though it's a miracle to see anyone after so long. You are beautiful, lad, the whole world is beautiful! I can find my own way home."

Many were weeping with joy as they pointed to the white-robed man a little way up the hill. Caleb breathed a prayer of thanks. He was almost weeping himself. He didn't think he could have waited much longer to deliver his message; it was all he could do to stand.

Jesus had sensed his coming. All day he had known.

He turned away from Peter, Judas and several others with whom he was conferring and watched the young figure hurrying to him up the slope. He held out his arms to catch the panting boy when he stumbled. "He has come a long way," Jesus told them in a voice of quiet authority. "He is very weary. Give him something to eat."

To Caleb's amazement, he felt himself cradled against a strong hard breast. The body was warm and tough and real; he could even hear the great heart beating. And when he looked up, he saw not the face of a god, as he had somehow imagined, but a face that was very human—the kindest, most beautiful and tender face he had ever seen. With an effort Caleb pulled away; it seemed to him, incredibly, that he had slept a long sweet sleep, from which he wished never to waken.

"No, Master," he protested, "there is no time to think of me! I have an important message for you, from two sisters in Bethany. Their brother is ill. They have sent me to tell you that the one whom you love is very ill."

Jesus gave a little start; though this, too, he had known. His eyes filled with tears. But his face remained strangely inscrutable. To Caleb's surprise, he did not reply.

"Here, I bear a letter for you." Puzzled, Caleb fumbled in his girdle. "Perhaps you will realize, when you read it—"

To his dismay, Jesus only nodded, took the scroll woodenly and walked slowly away with it, across the hill.

The other men crowded anxiously around the courier, asking questions. Lazarus was their friend too—how bad was he? Jesus would want to leave at once; they would hire donkeys in the village, better yet horses, if they could be found—with horses, Jesus could reach him before midnight. One of them would ride with him, the others could follow on foot. . . . Troubled, they looked to where Jesus stood alone with his letter, gazing into the distance.

He returned at last, sober and thoughtful. Finally he spoke, and they were astonished at his words.

"When you have eaten and rested," Jesus told Caleb, "go back to Bethany with this message. Tell Martha and Mary that though I long to be with them to comfort them, I cannot just yet. I will come later. Meanwhile, they are not to worry about their brother, Lazarus."

There was stunned silence. "But they wouldn't have sent for you if it weren't serious!" Peter blurted. "We must go at once. You, Master, at least. Please go, while there is still time to save him!"

The boy was dumbfounded. To have run so far, made such an effort, for *this*? He couldn't believe it. "Rabbi, forgive me," he pleaded, "but I, too, must speak. The women were distraught; they're convinced their brother is dying." His voice broke. "I don't think I could *face* them without some hope that you will arrive without delay!"

Jesus listened to him gravely. He turned then and stood for a time with his eyes closed, the scroll pressed against his lips. Finally he drew a deep painful breath; throwing back his shoulders, he faced them. His words had a ring of conviction they could not comprehend. "Tell Martha and Mary to trust me," he told the boy. "For this sickness is not unto death, but unto the glory of God. Assure them it has a meaning that one day will be revealed." Firmly, to encourage him, Jesus squeezed the boy's arm. "Tell the women their brother Lazarus, whom we love, will come to no harm because of it."

Caleb backed away, too shocked to reply. In his bewilderment he stared bleakly for an instant at the people—all these happy people still proclaiming their miracles!—and his mouth went bitter with disillusionment and doubt. Poor ignorant fools, how soon would they find out they, too, had been deluded? If the man could really perform such wonders, wouldn't he fly at once to help someone he loved? So this was the famous healer!

Caleb was too angry and hurt to accept food in this place, or even rest. With a little sob, he fled. And his anger gave him strength. He plunged back to Jericho, where he spent some of the women's money on wine and a night at the inn. He did not even climb the steps to the home of Lazarus until the following day. And when at last, cringing with guilt, he approached that imposing house set high on the Mount of Olives, and saw the face of the woman at the door, he knew it didn't matter anyway.

Lazarus was dead.

Jesus moved, those next few days, through such pain as he had not known since the death of his cousin John. Telling his apostles to wait for him in the village, he paced the banks of the river alone, praying about Lazarus, and haunted by memories of John. John's fierce-bright face beaming upon him that day of his baptism, John's voice shouting the message: "Behold the Lamb of God, for he is standing among you even now!" Despite his anguish, Jesus smiled. There was something faintly comical about John, presenting him to the masses like some prize fish: the Christ, the long-predicted catch! John, the defiant, his ministry so quickly over . . . and mine, begun on these same banks that spring day, drawing to its close . . .

The pain of the young courier's disappointment hung heavy on his spirit, as well as the dissension among the apostles, who were mystified at this seemingly useless delay. He knew they were debating it among themselves, some of them very upset.

Peter had been appalled. "Lazarus, of all people!" he groaned in his bewilderment that first night. "I can't understand it. If he refuses Lazarus, what about us? What if it was me or my wife? What if it was one of us?"

He had flung himself down on the floor of the inn beside the twins and mumbled about it with them until the rest growled for silence. James was all for action. Jesus himself had sent them on healing missions; why couldn't they set out? John was less sure. It would be foolish to go without Jesus' approval, and what if something happened to them? That would only make things worse for everyone.

In the morning the others joined in, puzzled and torn, but apprehensive. Most of them sided with Judas, who finally took charge; in his coolly superior way, Judas was able to convince them. "Don't question the Master," he ordered impatiently. "Jesus knows what's best for us. It isn't safe for any of us to go back to Jerusalem yet. Remember what happens every time he goes there. They're out to get him. Not only the Sanhedrin, that's bad enough, but now even some of the people. They tried to stone him the last time! He could have been killed, and us too, if we'd been along."

"But Lazarus is his friend!"

"Lazarus is in no danger," Judas stated flatly. "Didn't you hear what Jesus told that courier? No, Jesus wasn't abandoning Lazarus; it hurts him not to go to his aid. But we are his friends too; he realizes it's more important right now to protect us."

And it seemed to Jesus poignant that, of them all, only Judas should suspect even faintly what he was enduring.

His greatest anguish was for Martha and Mary. The scene of Lazarus' death was vivid before him. He had longed with every impulse to run forward to meet the boy, take his hand even before he could speak, and rush back to Bethany with him to comfort the sisters in their grief and put an end to their suffering, as he had done for so many others.

Yet he was powerless to move—at that moment, or now. He must not, he could not. There was a reason for this delay, a purpose beyond anything the Father had yet designed for him to accomplish. This, his last, greatest miracle, must await the Father's bidding.

Finally, early on the morning of the third day, Jesus roused his apostles. The time had come. He had been alone by the river the night long, praying. Now he knew what he must do.

He stood regarding them, these big rough men sprawled about like logs on the floor of the inn, but also somehow like children. His heart ached for them. "Wake up, little flock," he said whimsically, and went about shaking them. "Wash, say your prayers, have a bite and let's be off. For we are going back to Bethany."

They sat up, yawning and rubbing their eyes, scowling, confused. It was almost daylight; roosters were crowing. They could smell the bread from the ovens in the courtyard below. To their surprise, Jesus seemed brisk and cheerful, though they knew he had spent another night pacing the river, in meditation. He had bathed and refreshed himself, he told them, by taking a long cold swim.

Puzzled, they scrambled to their feet, stretched mightily, and began shaking out the cloaks that had been rolled under their heads for pillows, or wrapped about their bodies to keep warm. They had been restless; it was a relief to be in action, but why had the Lord changed his mind? Mumbling in surprise, groping about for belts and sandals, they exchanged questioning glances, and looked reluctantly to Judas for guidance. He was obviously taken aback, the small white scar on his olive face twitching.

"But, Master, can it be safe yet?" Judas protested, for all of them. In a smooth, swift gesture that somehow bespoke his wounded pride, he whipped his girdle about him. "Why should we go back where the Jews might seek our lives again?"

"There are twelve hours in the day to worry about such things," Jesus said, for all to hear. His smile was reassuring. "But if a man walk in the light he needn't be afraid. I am the light; you can walk safely with me."

Thomas looked up from lacing his sandals. "But why go now?" he asked anxiously. "Is Lazarus worse?"

"I am concerned for Lazarus," Jesus acknowledged after a minute. He beckoned them all to draw nearer, and now his eyes and his voice were serious. "If any of you are afraid, then stay," he told them. "Although I urge you not to. For your own sakes, I want you to be with me. But whatever you do, I must go now to be with our friend and his sisters."

They set off shortly, bypassing the longer, heavily traveled Jericho highway, and cutting across the barren rocky hills of the wilderness. All day they walked, murmuring among themselves, but mostly in silence, for the road was narrow and winding, snaking up and down, through ravines, along the rim of canyons and above deep wadis. A pall of dread was upon them, and the landscape did little to cheer them; this was a desolate place, lonely and deserted, with few signs of life except for the coneys that scurried among the jagged rocks, the vultures hovering overhead, and here and there wild goats rambling. Now and then one of the creatures would come to a halt and stare at them curiously from a boulder.

Jesus led the way, striding alone some distance ahead, much as he had on the day when Peter, James and John had climbed the mountain with him. They spoke of it privately, marveling and speculating; feeling that again some very important experience could be impending.

Judas looked grim. Twice he marched impatiently forward, determined to catch up with Jesus and draw information from him. Each time he fell back, his olive face flushed with defeat. With his usual cheerful arrogance, he simply threw up his hands for the benefit of the others. But they could not forget his warnings. Judas was right, they knew from experience. They had been assaulted before, quizzed, threatened. The spies and Temple agents were assigned to watch not only Jesus but anyone associated with him. It would be midafternoon or later before they reached the suburbs of Jerusalem. The streets would be swarming. Pray heaven they would not be recognized and waylaid, by either friends or enemies. If they were recognized, anything could happen.

Their path had finally merged with the dusty highway. For the past hour they had been plodding up its last steep hill, along with other travelers. Most were on foot or riding donkeys; some were mounted on camels, or leading the graceful, heavily laden beasts, whose bells chimed accompaniment to the rattle of hooves and wagon wheels, and the voices which were growing more excited as people approached the crest of the hill that overlooked Jerusalem. All were anxious to get where they were going, and paid no attention to them. Halfway to the summit was a crossroads, one road leading directly southwest to Bethany. Jesus had halted and was waiting for the others there.

Before joining him, Judas insisted the men take counsel. "Something's wrong," he said, scowling. "I can feel it—something's going to happen." He was biting a knuckle, shaking his head. "As you know, I've caught up to Jesus several times today, but I could get nothing from him; he simply told me to be patient." Judas shrugged, in his half-charming, half-cynical way. "Maybe somebody else . . . You, Peter, you're his favorite—why don't you speak to him, find out what you can before we go further?"

Peter nodded. He, too, had been growing troubled. He didn't want to do this, but somebody had to. Telling the others to rest beside the road, he trudged doggedly ahead.

Jesus was sitting on a rock, chin in hand, gazing toward Jerusalem. Dimly in the distance, through the haze, a scattering of rooftops could be seen.

Peter crouched beside him. "Master, we will soon reach the Mount of Olives," he said bluntly. "Some of us are getting anxious. Please tell us what we may expect to find there."

Jesus started up out of his reverie, and gazed at him, nodding. The apostles must be told. They had waited long enough; they must be prepared for what lay ahead. But the words of death were too brutal to hear just yet. How could he make the truth easier for them? "Bring the men to me," he said after a moment. "I will try to explain."

Peter trudged back, beckoning to the others to gather around him. Again they conferred earnestly for a few moments. And watching them, Jesus was touched. How dear they were to him, these men who had given up so much to follow him, risked everything—families, homes, friends; even their livelihoods. Frightened? Yes, often. And confused and upset, but no matter—in the end he could depend on them: They were obedient and loyal; they were his children. Now, as the twelve came toward him, heads lifted, he saw the expectancy in their eyes, and sensed a renewal of their absolute and somehow innocent dedication. And for a moment he turned away, he could not face them.

Andrew spoke first, his long homely countenance solicitous. "Lord, are we in danger, that you look so concerned? Or is it that you are troubled about Lazarus?"

Before Jesus could answer, Thomas broke in. "Please don't be concerned for us," he said fervently. "We have been discussing this among ourselves, and we are agreed—should any harm come to you, we are prepared to die for you!"

Jesus straightened and rose, holding out his arms to embrace them. "My dear little flock," he assured them, "we are in no danger. You, all of you whom I love, will reach the Mount of Olives with me safely."

"And Lazarus? Then your heart is no longer troubled about our friend?"

Jesus drew a long, painful breath. He must tell them before they reached the village; the whole place would be in mourning. But again the words seemed too cruel; he would put them off as long as he could. "Lazarus has fallen asleep," he said gently. "I feel he has slept enough. I am going to waken him."

He spoke out of compassion for them; he had not anticipated their misunderstanding. "Then Lazarus is recovering!" Peter exploded. In his joy he flung his arms around Jesus, and began shouting the good news for all to hear. "Jesus says Lazarus will be all right, he's only sleeping!" The others, too, were jubilant, and they began to embrace each other in their relief.

"No," Jesus interrupted sternly. The truth could be postponed no longer. "I was only trying to spare you. Now I must tell you plainly: *Lazarus is dead.*"

The apostles gasped and stared at him, too shocked and disappointed to respond. Finally Peter spoke, and his voice was plaintive. "Master, why did you let this *happen*? We thought . . . when you did not heed the messenger . . . Why did you mislead us?" he pleaded.

"It was already too late," Jesus told them. "Lazarus died before the messenger could reach us. And for your sakes I am glad I was not there." He drew a hand across his stricken face. "Nonetheless, let us go to him."

Martha roused from her stupor and stared at the neighbor in disbelief. She was trembling. Four days of moaning and fasting had left her weak. It was hard to hear above the fresh burst of wails and shrieking outside—the last shift of mourners had arrived—and the house still hummed with the voices of people here to console them. For days it had swarmed with friends coming and going, speaking in low tones, crouching beside the sisters, begging them to eat a little something, or drink a little wine.

"Martha, didn't you hear me? He's on his way! One of the mourners just told me. That man Jesus—the famous rabbi!"

Martha jolted to awareness. A hot wave of life licked through her as she staggered to her feet. She could feel the plump motherly arms around her—a woman named Dinah, who was usually the first at a house of death, and the last to leave. Martha's heart beat wildly; never had she felt such blind exultation, heightened by the chill of her very outrage. She stared dazedly into the woman's fat, kindly, excited face. "Where is he?" she heard herself mumbling. "How do you know?"

"One of the musicians saw him. He was seen on the back road, the one that bypasses the village. He must be coming here!"

Dumbly Martha pushed past her. She would go to him. She must see him first. What she would say to him she didn't know, only it must not be here in her brother's house, among all these strangers— the confusion, the hideous noise, and the helpless, hopeless sound of Mary's sobbing. Mary had been sobbing in that same soft, incessant way almost from the moment they had known Lazarus would not live. . . . Where did such tears come from? Martha marveled abstractedly. She herself, to her dismay and embarrassment, could bring no moisture to her own dry, burning eyes. There was only this searing anguish in her breast and throat, this agony of burning.

Martha went groping into her kitchen, once such a pride and place of comfort. Yet it meant nothing anymore; how could she ever cook here again? It was as a tomb, this place Lazarus had provided; she was sickened by its odors. Yet here she could dip water from a jar and bathe her lacerated face. Her hands shook; she spilled the water and hadn't the strength to wipe it up. She dropped the comb she was trying to drag through the matted hair straggling about her shoulders, its black now gray with the ashes she had dumped upon it. She brushed at it frantically, then glided swiftly into her chamber to pin it up. Jesus must not see her looking like this, but what more could she do? She could not bear to look in the mirror.

Even so, she would go to him; let her sister stay behind if she wanted. In her chamber, Mary still sobbed, huddled in a corner, while two friends crouched beside her. The three looked up astonished as Martha appeared, hurling her best cloak around her: a brightly colored one, covering her garment of sackcloth.

"Jesus is coming," she announced bitterly. "I'm going forth to meet him."

Mary lifted her grief-ravaged face. Her voice was desolate. "Tell him not to hurry," she choked, though without recrimination. "Tell him he is too late."

Martha plunged blindly down the hill, past the people who were still arriving—would they never stop coming? All of Bethany had already come to pay their respects to Lazarus, and half of Jerusalem, it seemed. Martha had no idea he'd had so many friends. They looked at her in amazement in her bright-rose cloak, so incongruous with her mourning, saw the expression of dry, spent misery on her face, and made way for her. Poor Martha; they recognized the symptoms of grief hysteria. She had always been a strange one, living only for her brother. But why was she leaving her guests? A few paused to watch uneasily as she swerved and disappeared down the little-used road, wondering if they should follow.

It was a beautiful day, Martha noticed absently; spring seemed to have stolen over the hills during these last black days. Lilies were vivid little flags among the rocks that glistened in the sun. There was a pink haze over the orchards; the olive trees were greening. But how could there ever be life or spring for her again? *And it needn't have been taken from her.* Her teeth were bared, her fists clenched. She was still weak and giddy from fasting and the few swallows of wine well-meaning visitors had forced upon her. Her head raced with all the things she would say.

But when she finally saw Jesus approaching alone under the trees—for he had told the others to wait behind a little way—the words vanished. Martha halted, trembling. She no longer felt the love-rage burning, only this cold white emptiness. She could not speak at first, she could only stare at him bleakly.

"You could have saved him," she said at last, in a voice of dry despondency. "If you had stayed with us a little longer . . . if you had even come when we *sent* for you. Lord, if you had been here, my brother would not have died!" She flung a hand over her grimacing mouth. And at last, in a releasing flood, the hot tears fell. "He was all we *had*!"

"I know, I know." Jesus reached out his arms to her and enfolded her, like a child. He drew her down beside him on a rough oak log that lay beside the path, and held her against him, patting her shoulders, which were shaking so violently in their bright wrap. He stroked her silvering hair, where some of the ashes still clung. "I loved him too," he told her, the muscles in his throat working. "Do you think I would have let any harm come to him had it been within my power to prevent it?"

"But God himself has given you special powers," she cried fiercely. "You are a prophet, a healer, some people say the Messiah. Even now," she pleaded, as the tears ran down her cheeks, "I'm sure that even now God would give you whatever you ask!" In her desperation she had pulled away from him and was searching his face.

"Don't grieve, Martha," Jesus said. "Please don't grieve. I promise you that your brother will rise again."

"Yes, yes, I know that," she moaned. "I know that he will rise again at the last day, in the resurrection. But *now* . . . what of *now*?"

Yes, *now*. What of now? . . . Jesus stared past her into the distance, sorrowing as he remembered: His grandfather Joachim lying on the threshing floor. His father, Joseph, crushed. And John, poor John . . . Father, dear Father, what of now?

At last Jesus turned to Martha, and cupping her face in his hands, looked deep into her eyes. "*I* am the resurrection and the life," he stated gravely. "Anyone who believes in me shall never die. Do you believe this, Martha?"

Martha bit her dry cracked lips. "Yes, Lord," she cried softly. "I believe you are the Christ, the one sent to save the world." It was a joy to confess this, as it had been a relief and joy to confess her love. "You are the Son of God!"

"Go, then, and tell Mary. Go as quickly as you can and bring Mary back to me."

Heads turned as Martha rushed into the house. A little huddle of men broke up, relieved. People had been worring about her, trying not to let Mary know. Martha had not looked well, and it was growing late. Soon they would have to return to their homes, but how could they leave Mary without being sure her sister was safe?

"Praise heaven!" exclaimed Absalom, a rugged, gentle bull of a man who had served Lazarus for years. "We were about to send a party out to search for you."

"Forgive me, but I must speak to Mary." In her gracious but determined manner, Martha pushed past them into her sister's chamber, her face white and fixed.

Martha knelt beside the still-weeping figure, and with an effort, Mary stopped crying. She was exhausted, drowned in her own tears. She pressed a fist fiercely against her lips, lifted her swollen face. "What is it?"

"The teacher is here!" Martha whispered. "I have seen him; he is asking for you."

Mary got quickly to her feet, wiping her eyes. "Where is he? Take me to him."

To the surprise of everyone, the sisters reappeared together. Speaking to no one, only clinging to each other, they left the house— Mary still bowed with grief, Martha supporting her. And watching them, the heart of Absalom broke afresh. He had known the family since their childhood, taught Lazarus his trade, and prayed that such fine girls would find good husbands. When the young wife died, he had built her bier and helped carry her to the cave; the little daughter too, when she was five. And now his shoulders still ached with the weight of this final burden. Absalom was himself bereft, and he was torn at sight of the sisters.

"Each day they go to the tomb to weep," he muttered. "Later they will have to manage, but today they should not make this sad journey alone. Let us follow. . . ."

Jesus stood waiting for the women.

His apostles had arrived, feeling they had lingered long enough at the bottom of the hill, as he had bade them. Now they meandered uncertainly about this small clearing beside the path. Faintly from the hilltop they could hear the sounds of mourning, the musicians' dirge, the echoes of wailing. They were uneasy, awkward before the situation, filled with dread, but troubled by this further delay. Why didn't Jesus take them at once to be with Mary and Martha, and comfort them as best they could? But Jesus only stood waiting, apart from them, one foot planted on a rock, his white garments blowing in the soft wind that had risen.

He was gazing in the direction of Jerusalem once more, his hands locked together, his face grim. What he was thinking they didn't know, nor what he was confronting. They only knew that he was suffering.

At last they saw the sisters coming down the path, trailed by a number of others. It was hard to recognize Mary and Martha without their brother—the three had always seemed as one; hard to believe these were the same charming women who had so often made them welcome—these two with their faces cruelly lacerated, their eyes red and swollen.

And seeing them too, Jesus straightened, and went to meet them. With a glad little cry, Mary broke free from Martha and came running toward him, hands outstretched. "Lord, dearest Lord!" she wept, as she fell at his feet and kissed them. "If only you had been with us, our brother need not have died."

And her words unmanned him. For though they were the same words Martha had uttered, there was in them no rebuke. Jesus could conceal his own agony no longer. His eyes filled as he drew Mary to her feet. He looked about at those who had followed—all these people, all this grief! They, too, loved Lazarus; or they had loved others that were torn from their arms, and in comforting Mary and Martha the memory of their own grief overwhelmed them. So that all mankind was one in this endless torture of loving and parting, and it must be comforted. It must be shown that death can be overcome.

His spirit groaned; he was deeply troubled. And looking about at those who had followed, he asked, "Where have you laid him?"

Absalom stepped forward, the family friend. "Come and see."

And covering his face with his hands as they walked to the tomb, Jesus wept.

The cave was back up the hill a little way, behind a thicket of trees. A tangle of vines spilled over its entrance, though some of them had been torn back to make way for the huge gray disk that blocked its entrance. Each day someone swept the rocky earth before it, but dry leaves and twigs still drifted about. Sparrows dipped and twittered among the trees. The people had fallen silent. In the stillness they could hear the little birds, the rustling branches, and a sound of small animal feet scurrying somewhere. The enormous granite rock glittered in the light that was filtering through the leaves.

Jesus lifted his eyes and his arms to heaven, and groaning again in his spirit, he prayed. Then, turning to the big man Absalom and his apostle Peter, who stood closest, he ordered, "Roll away the stone!"

Martha gasped and clutched his arm. Her face had gone white with horror as well as hope. "Lord, by this time my brother's body will be decaying," she whispered. "There will be an odor, for he has been dead four days."

Jesus looked at her steadily. "Didn't I say to you that if you believed, you would see the glory of God?"

He turned again to the men. Though they had stepped forward, they hesitated, hearts pounding, regarding the great stone. It was a heavy granite wheel, of the kind used for pressing olives. Once more Jesus ordered sternly, "Take away the stone!"

Breathing hard, the men put their shoulders to the wheel, pushing, pushing, feeling its stubborn weight against their bodies, and the grit of it against their sweating palms. When it did not budge, Andrew and Philip leapt forward to help, and little by little the stone began to move, and finally to roll. A bat whipped out of the cold dark opening; they could hear the chirping of swallows that nested inside this place of death, and the sound of water dripping.

And raising his arms and his eyes once more to heaven, Jesus prayed. "Father, thank you that you have heard me. Forgive me for my purely human fears, for I know that you always hear me, as you will hear me now. All that I have said and done is because of these people, that they may witness your power over death itself, and so believe it is you who sent me."

He strode forth then to the very door of the cave and looked in, stooping, for it was low, bracing himself against the sides. He stood for a long moment, gazing at the shelf where the body of Lazarus lay. Behind him he could feel the shocked and frightened people watching, feel their doubts, their hopes, their awed and terrible anticipation. And summoning all his power, Jesus felt his own body shuddering as he called out in a loud voice: *"Lazarus, come forth!"*

The words echoed in the chill rock walls of the cave. . . . The people could hear them. . . . Could Lazarus hear them? . . . Father in heaven, let Lazarus hear them. Waken Lazarus, let him rise up as I have promised, that they may believe.

And with a thrill of joy Jesus felt his power rush from him again, pouring through the body of his friend; he felt the stilled heart stirring. With a sob, Jesus went to him, crouching because the ceiling was so low; and ripping aside the linen strips, he took the hand of Lazarus, that Lazarus might feel his warmth through the binding of his grave clothes.

"You are awake now, Lazarus," he said gently. "Don't be afraid, I am here beside you. Come with me."

Then, leading his friend by the hand, and stepping out of the doorway before him, Jesus brought him forth, that the people might see him. Still wrapped in his burial windings but whole, and about him no odor or evidence of decay.

Weeping and smiling, Jesus embraced him, and pulled the napkin from his bewildered face. Jesus kissed him. He reached out then to Mary and Martha, who stood frozen, eyes wide, fists pressing back their own cries of wonder and joy, not yet quite daring to believe.

"Behold. Your brother, who was dead, lives again! Unbind him and let him go."

Chapter 15

"*N*OW tell me again," said the high priest, leaning forward on the gilded chair, and shifting his weight to ease the burning in his rectum. "What is this preposterous thing?"

A cushion would help, but Caiaphas didn't want to make himself look foolish by groping around for one. He was a man of small stature, and very defensive about it: an abrupt, sour-mouthed little man, who felt secretly inadequate for his high office, and suspicious that others looked down on him for the way he had acquired it—from his father-in-law, the powerful, conniving Annas. Part of Caiaphas shrank in self-contempt, another part drank in the honor with a fierce delight: the wealth, the pomp and ceremony. Yes, and the awe and reverence it was his right to command, for was not the high priest considered the living incarnation of the sacred Law?

But oh, the problems. His head ached after another restless, fretful night. The hot pitchforks in his rear never ceased their tormenting. Such scant sleep as had finally come was peopled with demons. And when he rose he felt bilious—probably all that wine he had drunk in his desperation for some relief. His own wry sense of humor did not ignore the irony: that he, head of the priestly class, bound by the rules of ritual cleanliness, anointed with the holy oil, as once the kings had been, should suffer these embarrassing afflictions of the flesh. Nonetheless, it was all he could do to perform the opening ceremonies at the Temple. He had hastened to his couch in his richly appointed quarters off the council chamber, hoping for a little rest. . . . And now this!

"Come, come," he snapped, "don't stand there gawking at me like a scared fool. What is it?" The man's name was Gideon; he was a very tall, kindly but imposing doctor of the Law, a member of the Sanhedrin for years. Caiaphas had always felt inferior to him.

"I'm sorry to bring you this message, but I feel I must. Though you'll hear about it soon enough, I'm afraid." Gideon hesitated. "It's about that man Jesus," he said, as the high priest groaned. "He has just raised a man from the dead."

"Oh, no!" Caiaphas groaned again, and made a gesture of contempt and dismissal. "Not another one. Why bother me with these tales? These rumors—people will believe anything!"

"But the others, those we have heard of, were off somewhere in the provinces," Gideon reminded him soberly, "Capernaum, Nain. This is nearby, right here, not even a Sabbath day's journey—"

Caiaphas gave a little start, visibly upset. *"Where?"*

"Bethany. The whole town is feasting and celebrating, for they know the man well. He is there now among them, joining the celebration. Yet some of the people tell me they helped place him in the tomb! Four days he was in the crypt, they claim."

Caiaphas covered his mouth, fearing he might be violently sick. "I don't believe it. People go mad, no matter where they live." He sat, small, spare and rigid, scowling at the man, struggling for control. "How do you know this?" he demanded.

"I have just come from Bethany," Gideon acknowledged uneasily. Something about him made the priest grip the arms of his chair. "I saw Lazarus myself. He was there, alive and well, walking about!"

"Lazarus!" Caiaphas choked. "Are you trying to tell me this was *Lazarus?*" He sat stupefied for a second. "The fool, the fool," he muttered, half to himself. "One of the most astute men in the city—or so we thought. A fine man, good Sadducee," he sneered, "until he was taken in by that charlatan! Tell me," the priest asked angrily, "do you know what really happened? Did you witness this so-called miracle?"

"No. Not exactly. I had done business with Lazarus; his groves furnished most of the olives for my press. Other transactions. I knew him, knew the family. I was simply going to his home to pay my respects. But when I reached the house I found it empty. The mourners had all gone to the burial cave. Then I heard them returning." He swallowed. "But to my astonishment, they were not weeping, but laughing and singing, rejoicing and praising God, for Lazarus was there among them!"

Gideon had maintained his dignity throughout. Now he began to pale, and his voice trembled. He felt suddenly faint. His eyes roved questioningly to another chair, and with a weak gesture the priest indicated he might sit down. "Sir, I *saw* him," he said, "still in his burial wrappings. His hands and his feet had been freed from their bindings, and the napkin taken from his face, but as he came toward us, walking between his two sisters, there was no doubt—at least not then—that he had indeed been in the grave."

Caiaphas had sprung up and was stalking about, beating his small jeweled fists together. He, too, felt faint. "Did he stink?" he heard himself asking crudely.

"No. There were no signs of decay. He seemed a little dazed, he looked astonished, but there were no signs of decay."

"A trick!" the priest spat, outraged. "Obviously a trick. Or Lazarus is demon-possessed. He's become one of that fraud's chief supporters. Entertains Jesus in his home, he and his sisters—even that band of rabble that travel with him. They've gotten Lazarus so confused he'll do anything for Jesus; give them money—anything. It's a trick."

"Yes, perhaps," Gideon said doubtfully, and wiped his brow. "But the Jews don't think so. The story is spreading, people are excited, even many who weren't sure before, or were actually against him. Jesus will be more popular than ever, I'm afraid."

"And you?" The priest's sarcastic eyes narrowed, bored into him. "What do you think?"

Gideon pondered, detesting the man but reluctant to offend him. The whole thing seemed more incredible by the minute. He was forced to remember: There had been a few skeptics even among the jubilant crowd; he had heard their private whisperings: jealousy, envy, doubt, or a desire to curry favor? Whatever, he knew there were some who would rush to report this to the authorities. "I don't know," he said honestly. "I only know I'm a loyal member of the Sanhedrin. I feel it my duty to prepare you before you hear it from someone else. There's no telling what may happen."

Caiaphas wheeled suddenly, pointing a finger. "Let me tell you what is *going to happen*," he exploded, "the next time that pretender shows his face in Jerusalem! We're going to put him away for good. There'll be no more preaching at the Temple, no more chicanery of healings, no more disturbances during the festivals. Even John the Baptist never caused us such trouble as this!" Breathing hard, careful of the *emerods*, Caiaphas eased himself back into the chair. A few cushions had spilled from his couch onto the floor. In desperation he grabbed one and stuffed it under his bottom, never mind how he looked. "We've been too lenient. It's a disgrace the soldiers haven't arrested him and dragged him in before! They've disobeyed orders; they'll be severely punished, along with the impostor." He paused, relaxing on the soft, silken comfort of the pillow, regaining his composure. His receding chin lifted; he sat drumming the arm of his chair, planning. He spoke crisply now.

"I'll call a meeting of the council for tomorrow. Get word to Nicodemus," he ordered, "Simon of Cyrene, Joseph of Arimathea, any others you can. I'll send out messengers, of course, and take care of informing the priests serving here. Oh, yes, and have signal fires lit so nobody will have an excuse that he didn't know. We must have a good turnout—this thing has gone far enough!"

It was a relief finally to take action. He was suddenly grateful to Gideon for bringing him this awful news, and said so, curtly. Though he seldom rose in the presence of taller men, and when he did never looked up, Caiaphas not only got to his feet, he embraced his visitor and kissed him. Then, turning his back abruptly, he began summoning servants, acolytes, couriers, and finally the litter bearers to carry him home. It was getting late, he was exhausted, and the itching and burning were almost intolerable. It was all he could do to keep from clawing himself. . . . He could hardly wait to get home to his wife and her cooling salve.

Caiaphas felt better about himself as the litter bearers carried him toward his palace. He sank back, sighing, buoyed up by his performance, and cheered by the prospect of the almost certain triumph to come. It also pleased him to know that eyes lifted in awed fascination as the conveyance passed along the busy streets. Shopkeepers halted as they took down their awnings and gathered up their wares to bring inside; mothers with children held them up to watch. Recognizing from the liveried guards, the curtains with their golden fringe, the proud insignia set with rubies, that the most important person in Israel was passing—the very high priest!

Like an ark it bore him, a precious vessel, sacred and unseen. Sometimes Caiaphas was tempted to part the silken folds and bow to the people, as an emperor would. Or as Annas often had, for his father-in-law was a vain old peacock who'd behaved as he pleased: grown fat on the priesthood, sucking the treasuries dry during the seven years he had reigned, then clinging to the post like a leech for himself and his five sons. Yet even after he was deposed by Tiberius for his treacheries, Annas' power over the people had not waned. They still loved him and acclaimed him, trusted him to make decisions for them as he had so long.

Caiaphas could not help a grudging admiration for the sly old villain, who socialized boldly with the Romans, entertained them royally, and worked hand in glove with them to keep the peace. Which meant mainly preserving the good life for the upper classes while appeasing the common herd. For instance, there was the way he'd handled the uproar when the new prefect Pilate insulted Israel by displaying the Roman eagle, images of Caesar and other emblems on the citadel. It was no secret, at least around the Temple, that after a showy public confrontation, which included leading an outraged delegation all the way to Caesarea to protest, Annas quietly bribed Pilate to take them down. (The prefect bought his first big estate in Sicily shortly thereafter, and built a handsome villa on the shores of Pompeii for his wife.) Well, the old scoundrel could afford it, and his cunning only won him more adulation from his stupid worshipers.

Caiaphas stiffened with disdain. He refused to look out. His dignity as well as his common sense forbade it. Why risk the resentment, even contempt, he might see on those faces? (Now stop this! Jews revered the office he represented. Why did he always imagine rejection?) No, better to remain hidden; the last thing he needed was for them to catch their sanctified high priest grimacing with pain from the jolting and bumping.

These idiots on whose shoulders he perched! Crossing the bridge that led to the upper city, they nearly dropped him when a team of runaway horses clattered by, whinnying wildly. He could have been killed! Caiaphas clutched the straps in terror. And why were they taking the long, steep route that led up so many steps, tipping him back even further on his tortured bottom? Worse, leading him through the massive bronze gates (he could hear them clanking as they opened) and across the vast courtyards of his father-in-law's palace! Though the word was a misnomer, for the complex of severe but shining marble buildings housed not only the priestly family but bodyguards, servants, officers and clerks—a domain that rivaled Herod's. Caiaphas boiled with humiliation. Was there some conspiracy to parade him past like the helpless captive they would always consider him?

Here, though hunching back to hide himself, Caiaphas could not resist parting the swaying curtains slightly and peering out. A gush of moist, sweet air filled his nostrils. There was the musical lilt and splashing of many fountains, sparkling in the light that rained down from the lamps in hundreds of windows, though it was not yet dark. The swimming pools lay full and glistening. Early roses were already a mass of pink, giving off their perfume, other flowers beginning to bloom. Years ago Annas had arranged to have water piped directly from the Temple to his gardens; and while he was at it, the blood from the sacrifices was piped in too, to fertilize the soil. The result was a flourishing paradise, not only of native plants and flowers, but of rare oriental shrubs and trees—gardens to surpass any in Jerusalem.

Yes, the old man had done all right for himself. Again that rush of grudging admiration, half envy, half dismay. And the wily old schemer didn't think he was finished yet. After years of ruling the country himself, then through his sons, he planned to keep right on through his daughter's husband. . . . Caiaphas bridled, remembering the night he had been summoned to the house they were passing now—the biggest one, with the Corinthian columns—and informed that he, a mere Levite, little better than a servant in the Temple, would henceforth conduct himself with special care, for there were certain matters pending that could very well result in his being appointed high priest!

Caiaphas had been staggered, almost overcome. The sheer effrontery of the man, his skill at manipulation! Although he shouldn't have been surprised; his wife had been hinting at this for years. Each of her brothers had loathed the job, and eventually wanted out. All of them had been educated in Alexandria or Rome, where they were athletes who participated in the games and became friends of the gladiators. All were pagans at heart. Even here in Jerusalem they openly attended the Circus Maximus and the theaters. The complicated rituals of the Temple bored them, and they sickened of the bloody mess of preparing and offering animals for sacrifice. There were offices almost as lucrative and a lot less taxing, which were the exclusive property of the high priest, to be distributed among his family. Each son finally persuaded him: The eldest was now in command of the treasury. One had charge of the breeding and selling of the ritually perfect doves, which every woman must sacrifice for her purification after giving birth to a child. Others raked in rents and generous profits from the money changers, the stock dealers and the merchants who sold a vast array of goods to the worshipers. Theirs, too, the business of providing everything needed for simply running the enormous complex of the Temple: the curtains and linens and priestly vestments, the incense and herbs and oil used for the ceremonies, the food, the furnishings, the wine—every item considered holy, since it must first pass through the sacred hands of the high priest or his clan.

Eventually running out of sons, Annas had nobody left but a son-in-law to keep this vast source of wealth in the family, let alone the high honor. But that was all right with the old man. Maybe even better. Caiaphas could picture him rubbing his big hands in anticipation. Annas was an ebullient, hawk-nosed, curly-bearded lion of a man, who towered over Caiaphas in everything—height, voice, looks, personality, self-assurance. This one, Annas was undoubtedly sneering, would be easy to manage.

Resentful, cowering inside, Caiaphas had accepted the offer when it came. His wife, Priscilla, had persuaded him. "You can do it. You must. He can't live forever, and remember—we, too, have sons to think of."

She was right. Caiaphas adapted quickly to life in his own palace—which was only a little less splendid than this one—in the pomp and prestige of the Temple. It amused him sometimes to see how people deferred to him, bowed down before him when he appeared before them in the grandeur of his huge jeweled turban, the gems on his breastplate flashing. He enjoyed donning that heavy and rather ridiculous headpiece which made him look so much taller, and strutting about in his costume of scarlet and blue, decorated with pomegranates, his waist girded with a sash of spun gold, the bells on his broad, winglike sleeves tinkling. A commanding figure.

To his own surprise (he had never been challenged before), he promptly mastered the intricate ceremonies, which he executed with a grace, skill and vague disdain which surpassed the art of even his predecessors. The shadow of Annas still hung over him; Caiaphas knew he was being watched, influenced, maneuvered; yet within him (almost from the time he first donned that turban) was born a stubborn determination not only to outlive his father-in-law but to cling to this office even more tenaciously than he had.

Meanwhile, he would somehow prove to Annas—yes, to all Israel—that he was worthy of such attention, he, too, had the power and authority to lead them. Well, now the opportunity was at hand. He regretted he hadn't asserted himself sooner in the matter of Jesus. Three years now of fret and worry. Caiaphas realized he had seemed inept, his attempts to put a stop to the nuisance mere scoldings and hand wringings. His own soldiers, probably sensing his vacillation, wouldn't obey him. Instead of arresting the man, they only came slinking back, saying he was doing no harm. A few, Caiaphas learned to his shock and embarrassment, had actually been mesmerized by the impostor, believing him to *be* the long-promised king and deliverer!

But no, wait now—don't blame yourself. Caiaphas gritted his teeth, threshed about miserably in his curtained cage. Most of this frustrating delay was the old man's fault. Pooh-poohing the threat, advising patience, caution. Time and again they'd discussed it—although you didn't *discuss* anything with Annas, you *listened* to his lengthy, often eloquent, rambling discourses and pronouncements. Stretched like a beautifully groomed, amiable lion on his golden couch, he would roar a welcome—half rising to clap you on the shoulder, at the same time shoving you down into a chair while he paid you a false compliment—and proceed to belittle the issue.

The last time was not much better than the others:

"Now, now, calm down, we're doing all we can. The man is being followed, observed, investigated. So far he poses no threat, not compared to some of the self-appointed messiahs I've dealt with. So he comes from Galilee, which seems to breed the Zealots, and yes, sometimes one of them has to be stopped, put to death if he gets out of hand. But only as a last resort. When you've been around as long as I have, you'll realize the best thing to do with most of them is to ignore them. Get worked up about every crazy prophet and messiah that comes along and you won't have time for your own wife, let alone the Temple!"

"But this one—"

"Yes, this one—from what I hear, he's different, preaches peace, turning the other cheek, forgiving the enemy. Not a bad idea, really. Let the people listen, it won't hurt them; they have to believe in something, don't they? They love that dream—that old myth of their messiah is what keeps them happy. The worst thing you can do is take it away from them; attack the one who's promising them the sky and you're in trouble. No, no, don't touch their current messiah; you just make him more of a hero. Leave him alone and they get tired of him, or disgusted with him and turn on him themselves. Didn't I hear that some of the people tried to stone this Jesus the last time he came for a festival? Too bad they didn't succeed, but that's not up to us. In time, if there's evidence he's really blaspheming, saying things that could disturb the faith, threaten to overthrow the system, get Rome on our backs—"

"He claims to be the Messiah of God," Caiaphas managed to break in, tightly.

"They all do; he's just crazy like the rest of them. Now if—"

"He also attacks the scribes and Pharisees," Caiaphas persisted.

"Good—they deserve it. They're all hypocrites—well, most of them, pretending to be so righteous while they steal you blind. Actually believing in a God that personally looks after them and when they die will usher them into heaven! No common sense, none of them, not like us Sadducees—we know better. Now if—"

"He's said he will tear down the Temple!" Caiaphas almost yelped in his frustration.

Annas reared up slightly, pursing his moist pink lips. For a time he lay contemplating, playing with his carefully brushed and oiled double-pointed beard. "Mad, utterly mad," he muttered, nodding. Then wearily he sat up, stretched, yawned audibly and got to his feet, signaling with a sly grin that the interview was at an end. "Trust me, I'll look into this further. Meanwhile, don't be so serious. You're working too hard, you look a little peaked." To Caiaphas' outrage, the old man stooped slightly, so that the hated beard brushed his own newly balding head. "Tell my daughter to give you a potion. You're nervous as a cat, you're actually shaking."

A big hand grabbed Caiaphas' shoulder, steered him amiably but firmly to the door. There, to his own astonishment, Caiaphas halted, stared at Annas a second, and heard himself asking an incredible question: "You don't believe in the Messiah?"

"What?" The old man stood open-mouthed. "Which messiah? This one?"

"The Messiah. The prophecies, the . . . predictions," Caiaphas quavered. He was indeed shaking now. "You know—the Anointed One. You spoke of it as a myth to give people something to look forward to—"

Annas threw back his bushy head and roared with laughter. "My dear son," he condescended, "every so-called prophecy is a sentence or two plucked from the psalms or uttered a long time ago by a man who frothed at the mouth. Strung together, they form a lifeline we Jews have been taught to hang on to through every imprisonment and persecution. That someday we'll have our own king, a magical personage sent down from heaven to free us from whatever ruler we happen to be under—right now it's the Romans—solve all our problems, make us not only free but probably happy and rich."

"This rabbi Jesus is telling the poor that very thing right now: The kingdom of heaven is at hand. He's telling the rich to sell what they have and give it to them, the poor—"

"Ridiculous, outrageous—the very idea!"

"And you don't believe any of it," Caiaphas repeated. For some reason, it was important to him to be sure. "It's all a lie, or just a story. There will never be a deliverer, a true Messiah."

"Now wait, don't put words in my mouth. I said no such thing. In time, yes, it's possible, sometime in the future. But not in our lifetime, not now, not here in Jerusalem, that's sure. Why, it would change everything, turn things upside down. Give our money to the poor and let them run things? A fine mess we'd be in! Drive out the Romans? Most of us have never been better off. Old Herod built our Temple for us, bless his black murdering soul. Look at it—even Rome itself doesn't have a building so magnificent. And so long as the Herods and their Roman friends stay out of it, we have no quarrel. No, we've prospered under the Romans; barring a few massacres when hotheads drove them too far, they've treated us well. I'm not saying the real Messiah won't come sometime, if things get worse. But the worst thing that could happen, at least for us, would be for him to appear right now."

"Forgive me, Sir, but if—if it were possible that this man is—could actually *be*—the One . . . ?"

"It is not only impossible, we could not have it! Possible or impossible, we cannot have it. Whoever he is, he must be—" Annas caught himself. "If there is any likelihood at all, if there is the slightest possibility—well, you're right, he will have to be stopped."

"Then you agree—the man is a threat."

Annas had thrown up his hands, sick of the whole business. "You've badgered me into it. Have it your own way. But be careful, don't be in any hurry, leave any final decisions to me."

Caiaphas braced himself, remembering.

At least the old man had caved in. But there would be no more waffling or waiting for approval. This business about Lazarus had to be dealt with right now. True or untrue, it was *his* crisis, a chance to prove what he could do. Unfortunately, they couldn't capture the disturber immediately—no telling where Jesus was now—but he'd never miss the Passover. And maybe a good thing, impatient as Caiaphas was for action. What better time to demonstrate his own authority than to strike when all eyes would be on him?

Caiaphas slept better that night; his wife had prepared both a soothing salve and a sleeping potion. And when he strutted into the Hall of Hewn Stones the next day, it cheered him to see that despite the late notice, the place was swarming, the huge vaulted chamber echoing to the sounds of many voices. Both parties were generously represented, not only Sadducees and Pharisees, but many priests and scribes and elders. Almost the entire seventy-one members were there already. For the astounding news about Lazarus had indeed reached them. And though all of them were incredulous, and some of them uncertain, most of them were deeply concerned, if not alarmed.

They were debating it among themselves even before Caiaphas arrived to mount the marble steps in his robes of office, and reign above them from his gilded throne, a sour but mighty man in his majestic turban, hearing them out before he rose to address them.

What were they going to do about this Jesus?

Out in the provinces, though many had fallen away, others were still following by the thousands—through Galilee and beyond, north, south, east and west, Capernaum, Tyre and Sidon, Caesarea Philippi, and all along the Jordan. That was bad enough, but to have this threat rising up right here on their very doorstep, deep into Judea, the very Temple! Three years it had been coming on. They'd been warned— why hadn't they faced it before? And now, right here in Jerusalem— if he wasn't stopped, many more would believe his claims. To have a well-known man like Lazarus openly walking these streets after being in the tomb four days! True or false, people are so eager to believe.

What can we do about a prophet people think can raise the dead? Kill him? . . . Wait now, let's be fair. A rebel, yes, but a devout Jew, a rabbi preaching regularly in the synagogues as well as in the fields, worshiping at the Temple, seeming to know every letter of the Law. Impossible to trap him; some of us have tried. He only turns the questions back on us. Yet he scoffs at many of the laws, eats forbidden food, doesn't always wash before meals, heals on the Sabbath. . . .

Heals. That was the word that aroused and excited them most. Shouting and waving their arms, the members of the council clamored to be heard.

What are we gong to do about Jesus? He's giving the people miracles. And the people want miracles, no matter what else he says and does. "Heal my leprosy, make my blind child see, feed my family!" (Why not, if he really fed the multitudes?) "Bring back my father, my wife, open all the graves, raise the dead!" Where will all this lead? If we let him alone, especially after this Lazarus thing, the whole nation could soon believe in him. The people will want to crown him king! Do you think the Romans would stand by and let this happen? What about Caesar, Herod, Pilate, Tiberius? They'd make short work of us. We wouldn't *be* a nation anymore!

What are we going to do about Jesus? Who attacks everything this body stands for. Calls us hypocrites, liars, whited sepulchres, thieves—worse things than even John the Baptist did. Who's insulted this sacred Temple, claiming it's too filthy to survive, he himself will tear it down. You priests, do you want the altars empty, the fires to go out? No more animals to be brought for the sacrifice—and your food? No more meat to be carried home?

What are we going to do about Jesus? We'd better think now, all of us. Our very livelihoods could be at stake. How many of us deal with the Temple? Buy and sell for it, change the money necessary for the offerings, invest its funds in properties, are merchants for all the goods it uses—getting a fair price, let's remember, thanks to our revered high priest and his sons. Scarcely a one of us here but would be affected. Why, the economy of the whole country could be overturned! What if there were no more tithes pouring in from the farmers, a tenth of everything they raised or earned? No more tithes and offerings even from the laborers and fishermen? Even those peasants out in the provinces would be affected. No telling what this man has promised them, along with the kingdom of heaven. A kingdom he's claimed can be theirs right here on earth! No wonder they're following this Nazarene!

Half the day the impassioned arguments continued. Most of the time Caiaphas merely sat listening, although stamping the floor with his gem-studded scepter now and then so that some speaker might be heard. He also squirmed and shifted wretchedly, for the salve's effect had worn off. The itching and burning raged afresh; he felt as if he were being stung by a swarm of bees. And a wild thought struck him, an idea so incongruous Caiaphas managed a wry grin. This miracle worker they were debating evidently healed far more serious afflictions; maybe if he arranged to see Jesus privately . . . !

Caiaphas finally lifted his jeweled hand. Feeling majestic, even tall, in his turban, he scowled them to silence. "Enough! The will of this body seems obvious. You consider Jesus of Nazareth a threat to the people of Israel. It is therefore decreed that he be brought to trial before he can do further harm."

"But what is his crime?" Nicodemus shouted. He had been trying to ask the question for hours. Now he strode determinedly forward to confront the high priest himself. "Is healing a crime? Is raising a man from the dead? Lazarus is my friend. If bringing such a man back to life is a crime, then let it be, for the world is better by one good man!"

Joseph of Arimathea had also lumbered to his feet. "True!" he thundered in his thick breathy voice. "Jesus is a holy man. We condemn him at our peril."

"He is a blasphemer," Caiaphas yelled. "Making people believe he is the Christ, inciting the poor to riot." Furiously he stamped the floor again. "You know nothing at all," he sneered. "Either of you. You're both fools for defending him so long, and any who agree with you are fools. Innocent of these charges or not, he must be put to death. Isn't it better that one man should die than that all the nation perish? If Jesus cares so much for the people, let him give his life for the people!"

Caiaphas could bear no more. In his anger he threw his scepter down and stalked from the chamber. He did not realize, departing, that his words, like those of the prophets, would echo down the ages.

Chapter 16

*T*IME was running out, Jesus realized. Calvary drawing nearer. The weight of his own cross had been constant on his shoulders for months, its shadow hovering, growing darker, dogging his every step. And no matter what direction he took, all roads led back to that inevitable hill.

It was not to escape this that he had fled with his apostles after the raising of Lazarus, but only to avoid the frenzied excitement of the crowds. "Go quickly," Lazarus himself had urged that very night, white and shaken as he was. "Once word of this spreads you will be besieged, you will have no peace."

Jesus nodded. He had already chosen Ephraim, a forested area in the mountains, with a few scattered stone houses. They would rest there and pray. And he must prepare his men; there was still so much they didn't understand. "Tell no one." He held his friend almost fiercely in a brief farewell. "We will be back a few days before the Passover."

He began rounding up the apostles, who had joined in the celebration. "No, no, we must leave," he warned. "Hurry, don't linger, even to say goodbye."

Once again he must deal the blow he dreaded. Again he must face their shock and disappointment. "Why, Master, why?" He didn't blame them. His heart ached for them. To have arrived here so weary, worried and confused—until the relief and jubilation of what happened at the tomb! Now was the time to rejoice with the others. People were swarming around them, embracing them, bombarding them with questions; the food and wine would soon be served. They had earned the right to stay, not to flee back into the night like thieves.

"It's for your own safety," he had to tell them. "Scatter, hide your faces lest we be recognized and questioned. Take the back roads to Ephraim. We will meet there tomorrow."

The place was so small and so far into the desert that nobody knew or cared. Here the exhausted apostles slept, or sat trying to listen to what Jesus was teaching. But their minds were still preoccupied with the miracle of Lazarus, jubilant over his return, confident now of coming triumphs. The Passover was coming; surely some wonderful thing would happen. In spite of—even because of—what Jesus had done! Those who had wives would send word by special messenger: Come, come join us! They had been away from home a long time.

Jesus, too, wrote a letter, one night of terrible loneliness, long after the others slept. Concern for his mother was an agony almost equal to the specter of the cross. Spare her, keep her safe, don't let her have to suffer this with me. Yet he knew she would come, she must come; that, too, was written. . . .

And the apostles. There was no way, of course, to spare them. He had already tried to warn them, attempted to prepare them, but it was evident they were not ready. It seemed heartless to trouble them just yet. Let them rejoice a little longer. Soon, very soon, he would make it clear. On the way back to Jerusalem, he would make sure they understood. It would happen at Passover. And they must be strong. They had been chosen for this because they were strong, tough men, used to hardships, and loyal. They must be brave enough to face the ordeal.

And they would have to carry on.

Lazarus returned from his first day in Jerusalem with the news. "Oh, Lazarus, what is it?" Martha cried, seeing his ashen face as he walked in. "Are you ill?" A horrible fear smote her. He looked almost as he had on the night they had lost him. And it flashed through her mind that the excitement of the past few days had been too much for him.

People coming day and night. Begging to see him, visiting the tomb, many bringing flowers. Stopping him on the street when he ventured out. Touching him—Lazarus, who had always been such a private person. People mad with curiosity, asking for the story over and over. Jesus, this remarkable Jesus, when was he returning? When could they see him too? Would he stay with them during the Passover, would he be speaking at the Temple?

And now . . . Lazarus' sisters had begged him not to go back to his office in the city; they had worried all day. That could be even worse for him, and *they could not stand it*. None of them could endure again what they had just been through.

Mary, too, rushed in, guided her brother to a chair and quickly poured him a glass of wine. Lazarus downed it and sat for a moment composing himself. "You were right," he acknowledged crisply, when he could speak. "It was foolish for me to go back so soon. What happened to me is the talk of the city. I was besieged, I accomplished nothing."

"Then you must never go back. Stay here with us!"

"No, no, don't worry about me," Lazarus interrupted impatiently. "That's not the reason I'm so shaken. It's . . . Jesus." Lazarus plunged his face into his hands for a moment. When he looked up, his alert black eyes were stricken. "My sisters, we must realize—this marvelous thing he has done for us has *not* helped his cause. It has only made things worse for him."

They were staring at him, incredulous. "But it proves that he is all he claims," Mary protested. "This miracle. You are living proof! Witnesses can attest to it; I've heard followers are already multiplying because of it."

"And he is the *Messiah*," Martha cried, in soft, indignant wonder. "The authorities would be fools not to recognize that now. The people believe it, the people will demand it." Her voice rose, shaking. "They dare not persecute him further—not the Messiah!"

Lazarus smiled cynically. "That's exactly what they're afraid of. Not just any messiah—*the* Messiah. It's the last thing they want," he tried to explain. Politically and financially it would spell ruin. Lazarus went on to relate all he had heard. "This time the high priest means business. Jesus is in real danger if he returns for the Passover."

"But he would never miss the Passover!"

"Pray God he will this time," Lazarus said. "Pray heaven he'll stay on in Ephraim until this blows over. Or go back to Galilee— anywhere but Jerusalem." Lazarus covered his eyes; he could restrain his tears no longer. His narrow shoulders shook. "I feel so *responsible*," he said. "If only he had not come back to Bethany. Truly, I would rather have stayed in the tomb!"

. "No, Lazarus, no, you must never blame yourself!" Falling on their knees, they embraced him and tried to comfort him. "Jesus would not have it so. It would only hurt him."

They talked it over more quietly when prayers had been said and they were at their evening meal. "We must do what we can to protect him," Lazarus said. "As you say, Jesus would never miss the Passover. And he will probably stay here, at least a few days, as he always does." Lazarus studied the bread he was about to dip, trying to conceal his concern. He didn't want to worry them needlessly. "But after we've seen him, I think we should go to Jericho for a while. We could rest there, it would be good for all of us."

The women gasped. "But what about the Passover?"

"I think it would be wiser if I didn't appear at the feast myself this year."

His sisters were dumbfounded. The room had grown cold. Martha was dimly aware that she should add fresh coals to the brazier. "Then you're afraid *your* life, too, may be in danger?"

"On, no, no, no," Lazarus protested. "Only that my presence could be"—he hesitated—"an embarrassment for Jesus," he said carefully. "I'm not afraid for myself, only for him. And of course for you," he added, "in case anything *should* happen to either of us. You've both been through enough." Suddenly Lazarus straightened and began to eat. His tone was once more crisp, decisive, even cheerful.

"But come now, what am I saying? Let's not borrow trouble. Where is our faith?" he chided. "I am here, alive and well, your brother who was dead! Forgive me for worrying you." His sharp face brightened. "If Jesus can perform such a miracle, he can perform others. Let's worry no more, let's look forward to his return with all the joy we ever did—and more. . . . Martha—" Lazarus turned to her, smiling. "Begin preparing now. We'll feed Jesus and those hungry men as we never have before. And this time we won't let them slip off the way they did the last time. We'll see that they stay long enough to enjoy the victory with us."

Martha moved silently about the table, serving. Yes, oh, yes, she was thinking—to see Jesus again! There had been only one flaw in that incredibly joyful night of her brother's resurrection: in the very midst of the mad celebration, Jesus had slipped away without giving her a chance to thank him. Without even saying goodbye.

Now once more they waited, with an anticipation that had only grown more intense.

Each morning Martha awoke with a sense of excitement and urgency, for this would surely be the day. Before nightfall he would come, he would come, leaping up the steps, arms outstretched, his great dark eyes shining with their special light, and even now a loving smile upon his full, sweet lips. Nothing had changed, she told herself, over the chill ghost fears in her breast; matters had only moved forward at a swifter, more significant pace.

Jesus' hour would soon be at hand. And he would be tested, severely tested. Yet he would triumph, as he had triumphed at the tomb.

She was a very direct person, despite her air of remoteness and dignity. She believed in him. Jesus would be, quite plainly and without foolish reasoning, their king. And she would serve him. Asking nothing more for herself than to love him, she would do his bidding: manage his servants, see that his robes were immaculate, that nothing went amiss in his kitchens—she would do the cooking herself.

Thus Martha lay dreaming on her pillow long after Mary slept. And at sunrise, careful not to wake her sister, she sprang out of bed. She could hardly wait to begin. It was as if she were serving him already—in fact, she *was* serving him. Whether Mary helped or not didn't matter; let her do as she wished. This was something Martha was determined to do for him: the fires started early, the bread baked, the roasts turning on the spits by midafternoon, the sweetmeats waiting. Every inch of the house scrubbed and shining, fresh oil in every lamp, fresh flowers in every container. And the food in the cupboards sufficient to feed a court. Never mind that most of it had to be thrown to the dogs or taken to the poor. Tomorrow she would start over.

She worked with a calm certainty that neither Lazarus nor Mary could understand. Their eyes followed her with tender concern, and at times they tried to restrain her. Impatiently Martha shooed them away. "Passover is almost here—we must be ready!"

Ten days. Nine . . . eight. Next week! . . . Oh, dear Lord, was it possible he might not come, after all?

And then, late one afternoon when the whole household was weary and discouraged with waiting, and Martha herself had lain down to rest, he was there. "Martha, Martha, come on, wake up!" Lazarus was bending over her, his small brisk face radiant. "Jesus is asking for you. They are all just arrived from Ephraim—Peter, James and John, Judas—the lot of them. They're swarming all over the garden, hungry as lions. Mary is already attending to the basins and towels. But the meal . . . Come appease them, you're the only one who knows what to do about the meal."

Martha sprang up, for a moment frantic. To be caught napping! Her sandals—she must scramble around for them under the couch. The robe in which she had dozed was wrinkled; she must change as fast as she could to the lovely new one that hung waiting. Her hair had slipped from its pins. She must . . . not . . . hurry, Martha warned herself. "Bid them welcome for me," she said, determined to be calm. "I will come as soon as I can."

At last, breathing hard, but smoothly combed and looking gracious and composed in her silken dress, Martha went forth to greet him. Jesus was here at last, and she knew that was all that mattered.

"Martha, dear Martha," Jesus cried softly as he kissed her. "We could smell the fragrance of your roasting lamb all the way up the hill. You must have known we were coming."

There was something different about him; Martha didn't know quite what. He seemed stronger, graver, and somehow gently and yet tragically wiser, however prosaic his words.

"We have prepared for you every day," she told him proudly, with a tight little smile, though her eyes were wet. "We knew you were coming, and yet we knew it not. We have been afraid for your safety. Lazarus tried to warn us: This time you might not come at all."

"Of course I was coming. Do you think I would actually miss the Passover, or not try to see you once more?"

"But you left so quickly last time—without even saying goodbye. You performed a great miracle for us, you gave us back our brother, and we could not even thank you."

"Martha, you have already thanked me beyond any need of words. And this time, although again we can't stay long, I assure you we will say goodbye." Half whimsically, crooking a finger, Jesus wiped a knuckle across each teary eye.

Martha clung to him a minute, smiling and sniffling a little, like a comforted child. She excused herself then, and glided into the kitchen, her spirits soaring. It had not been in vain, all these days of preparation. Only a rehearsal, all of it a rehearsal for this perfect reunion meal. Never, it seemed to her, had she chosen so fine a roast or timed its cooking so well. Its savory odor filled the house; it would be done within the hour. The vegetables too, if she got to them right away. The sauces would be even better for having stood since morning.

She saw that Mary had not been idle, bless her heart. The best gold-rimmed plates and goblets were already lined up, waiting to be carried to the long table Lazarus had set up, no doubt at Mary's insistence, in the garden. Despite the extra work it caused, Mary loved to eat outside. And Mary was right. There was more room in the garden. And the sun was setting, the air was cool and sweet. By the time the men had finished washing and praying and were gathered around the table, the first stars would be coming out, the lights beginning to sparkle in Jerusalem and across the Kidron Valley.

"And the Paschal moon is rising earlier each night," Martha added, as she complimented Mary. "We may not even need torches."

Mary, usually so voluble and animated, only nodded. She seemed strangely subdued tonight, thoughtful and preoccupied. She dropped things. A handful of linen napkins had to be discarded; thank goodness there were more in the hamper. Then a whole basket of bread slipped from her fingers. "Never mind, we have lots more," Martha said kindly. (She still winced to remember the time she had so foolishly exploded before Jesus; he had been right to reprimand her.) "But you seem so nervous. Are you tired? Would you rather go visit with our guests? If so, you don't need to serve, I can manage."

"No, no, I will help you."

At last the men were seated. Lazarus had led the prayers and was pouring the wine. From beyond the open kitchen doorway Martha could hear the clinking glasses, the rise and fall of their voices as she dished up the food.

"How serious they sound," she remarked. "Not laughing and talking and arguing the way they always do, have you noticed?" To her surprise, there was no answer. She turned, expecting to hand a steaming bowl to Mary.

Martha looked around in vain. . . . After she promised! A flash of the old impatience smote Martha; followed by the sting of her own remembered shame. No, no, it was not important. Had she not worked so desperately for just this hour? Her dream come true. Jesus, the beloved, once more sitting at her table, with Lazarus, her brother. For an instant the miracle was overwhelming; she was shaken by it, moved as never before. How could she have a single angry thought at such an hour?

Head high, feeling the object of some special privilege, Martha carried the heavy smoking joint of meat into the garden and set it down before her brother to be carved. She was aware of Jesus watching her from the opposite side of the table. Lifting her eyes to acknowledge his presence as guest of honor, she smiled. Jesus smiled back. The others smiled, too, and praised her as she moved gracefully among them, serving.

There was the smell of moist damp woods and ferns, of mint and hyssop and marjoram from the garden, along with the savory odor of the meal. Night had fallen swiftly. The first stars were shining, like tiny jewels in the fingers of the trees. Lazarus had lighted the torches, which sent out little streamers of flame and drew shadows across the faces at the table. The brief sunset had left one russet banner burning above the valley, and in the distance the lights of the city could be seen. The moon was still hidden behind the mountains but rising, sending its silvery glow before it, casting a soft, almost ethereal light over everything.

How beautiful it was! Martha paused, drinking in the scene. Her only regret was that Mary was missing it. Martha looked toward the house, mystified. She would go look for her as soon as she had a minute. Why in the world? This wasn't like Mary, always so sociable, especially around Jesus and his men; their very presence seemed to nourish her bright spirits. It was hard to believe that she would disappear now, of all times. This was the first time all of them could be together, like the family they seemed, to celebrate their miraculous reunion with Lazarus.

And certainly Mary, who had grieved so wildly for her brother, ought to be here now, rejoicing. In fact, helping *them* rejoice more fervently, Martha thought, distressed . . . For again it came to Martha as she hovered, or moved back and forth to the kitchen, that the supper table, usually so lively with talk and songs and laughter, was tonight strangely silent. Something was wrong. Not with her food—no, they complimented it lavishly; and certainly not with the setting—the moon was visible now, round and beaming, pouring out its brilliance. Yet instead of the happy sounds she had expected, the men were only conversing in low tones.

Well, of course, they were tired, she must realize. And yes . . . worried. Martha halted, gripping her tray. For now suddenly it rose up in her and smote her, the thing she had stubbornly refused to think about all week. The awful possibility Lazarus had warned about when he came home that day from Jerusalem. Now she must face it: These men must be very careful of what they did and said. Not only Jesus, but even Lazarus . . . all of them.

This Passover would be like no other. All the people would *not* be proclaiming Jesus, wanting to see and touch him, like those who had sought him here so eagerly ever since the miracle of her brother. There were other people who feared and hated him—some enough to kill him.

And these men seated with him: Andrew, Peter, Thomas, Judas, the twins . . . In dismay, Martha's eyes followed them around the table: Philip, Matthew, Bartholomew, Thaddeus, Simon, and the younger James . . . grieving for them, fearing for them, protesting the dread fate they, too, might well be facing.

No wonder Mary had fled. Martha's heart went out to her sister. Despite Mary's sparkling manner, she sensed things more quickly, responded more deeply, found pain harder to bear. I must go to her and comfort her as soon as I can, Martha thought. Mary isn't strong.

But Martha was strong. She would not give way; she would do all she could for these poor men. Right now she must not stand here brooding. The sweet was waiting; she must clear away the crumbs and bones. The apostles made room for her as she moved among them with her tray, gathering up the scraps. They were her friends, her sweethearts, her children, and she rejoiced to serve them even as she grieved. As for Jesus, their leader and her Lord . . . he had moved his cushion back from the table and was leaning on one elbow, half reclining.

Martha lingered over him with special solicitude. Was he comfortable? Could she bring him anything more? But even as he lifted

his face and smiled to thank her, he gave a little start and she sensed
his awareness of another. For Jesus had glanced, in pleasant surprise,
toward the door. And turning, Martha saw her sister, looking like an
angel, standing there in its light.

Mary had changed. She no longer wore her simple dress of the
kitchen but was clad in softest shimmering white, bound at the waist
with cords of gold. Gold flashed between her breasts, where she had
pinned a shining crescent; other golden crescents swayed and glistened from her ears. Her long wavy chestnut hair was swept over one
shoulder; it, too, seemed brushed with gold in the light, and in it
bloomed one pure white rose.

Cupped carefully in her hands she held the family's most priceless
and cherished object, an alabaster jar. It had been their mother's and
their grandmothers' before them, brought all the way from Egypt during the Exodus, it was believed. In it, to be used sparingly on special
occasions, was kept the precious perfumed oil, nard.

So unexpected was Mary's appearance, so beautiful and startling,
the men caught their breaths and shifted about as one. There was
sudden silence; even the desultory conversations at the table stopped.
In the hush they could hear the rhythmic singsong of night things
chirping, the hiss of the torches, the rustling of the leaves. All eyes
were fixed on Mary. The moonlight pouring down enhanced the gold,
and the shimmering whiteness of her dress.

She seemed effulgent in the moonlight as she crossed the tiles on
golden sandals, the dress seeming to float about her as she moved.
She wore an expression both diffident and determined, a look both of
rapture and ineffable sorrow, her gaze fixed on the vessel in her hands.
She looked like a princess or a priestess about to perform some
sacred rite.

Oblivious to anyone but Jesus, Mary knelt before him. Removing
the stopper from the jar, she poured the fragrant oil into her hands,
and began to anoint his feet. Gently, adoringly, she massaged them,
these tough strong feet that had walked so many miles to comfort and
cure others—the soles, the heels, the instep, the toes, pausing only to
replenish the oil.

The apostles watched, respectful and deeply moved, except for
Judas, who sat nearest. Judas had stiffened and was averting his eyes.

But now, when Mary seemed to have finished, Judas leaned forward, frowning slightly, and offered her a napkin with which to dry them. Mary shook her head. Taking her own hair in her hands, she kissed it, and spilling her hair across the feet of Jesus, Mary began to dry them with it.

Calmly and slowly then, she rose and poured the rest of the oil onto the head of Jesus. The powerful fragrance of nard filled the garden. . . . Jesus could feel its wetness against his scalp and trickling down his beard; he felt the warmth and tenderness of her fingers, stroking it in. Jesus closed his eyes and clenched his heart against the pain of leaving them. He loved them so much, and they loved him, they had given up so much for him—how they would suffer at his going. Yet he was comforted by these ministrations. Mary knew, as some women always know, how much a man needs the touch of a woman's hands before he must go off to his agony alone.

The vase was empty now, every drop gone. Mary replaced the stopper and lifted the lovely container up a minute, glistening in the light. The men, who had sat in humble wonderment, were stirred. They had seen many things during their travels: People running frenziedly after Jesus, beseeching him, pommeling him, pulling at him, trying to touch his garments. People who wept and kissed him after their healings, others who walked away without even thanking him, like those lepers on the road yesterday. On several occasions they had seen women pay the master this same beautiful tribute. But never before had the act been so significant, so enraptured, never had they been so moved.

Judas, however, sat stiff with disapproval and dismay. Demonstrations like Mary's had always made him acutely uncomfortable. He loathed such emotional displays. And the waste! He gazed around, trying to maintain his cool composure, inwardly seething. It was hard to conceal his disgust—grown men acting like this. The fools! Am I the only one who sees how ridiculous this is? how inconsistent with everything Jesus teaches about giving to the poor? Judas ought to know; he was the treasurer for their travels, a job he shared with Matthew.

Judas carried the purse, while Matthew, the experienced tax collector, kept the records. Money was always scarce, and so many beggars followed them, whining and pleading, calling them cruel to refuse. Holy men weren't supposed to refuse. Judas didn't give a hang about the beggars, or those generally stinking poor who came to be healed. Let them pay for their healings. Yet it irked him to be mocked for being cheap. He loved money, and he didn't mind spending it— on himself or on other people, for their enjoyment. But he hated waste. And that stuff was expensive. Worth three hundred dinars at least!

Yes, Lazarus could afford it. Lazarus was rich, he could afford to solve all their money problems. And after what Jesus had done for him, there ought to be a handsome reward. But this *waste*. To see a small fortune dumped like this . . . in a few minutes. When that oil could have been sold and the money given to them!

This was too much. Judas had to vent his indignation on someone. He sprang up and with a jerk of his head beckoned imperiously to Matthew, sure that his astute, hardheaded partner would agree with him. But again Judas was rebuffed. Even Matthew was wiping his eyes like some of the others. And seeing Judas' expression, Matthew only scowled, shook his head and turned abruptly away.

Judas flinched. But his lean jaw tightened, his eyes were scornful. . . . Well, then, the sister.

Though Mary was the one he usually flirted with and flattered, Judas had always felt a secret affinity with Martha. The quiet one, the practical one who got things done. He doubted seriously if Martha approved of this sentimental scene in the garden. He had not missed her little cry at sight of Mary, or how white and still she looked, standing by with her scraps after serving the meal. Waiting until it was finished, then turning to walk slowly back toward the kitchen.

She was almost at the doorway now.

"Martha!" Judas called, and ran up the slope to confide in her, perhaps to console her. "May I speak with you?" His tone was intimate; the white scar near his mouth quivered. He would have held the door for her, even taken the tray, but she only stared at him, startled, blocking the way. "It's about Mary," he blurted, to his eternal regret. "I just want you to know—I admire your restraint. You would never do such a thing. . . . And about that expensive ointment—" he said, troubled but solicitous. "You must be very upset."

Martha was too astounded to reply. She could only turn on him, appalled. As if she had suddenly seen a snake. Then, head high, she carried her pitiful burden into the house.

Shaken, Martha stood a moment, trying to find a place to set down the tray. She could hear the dogs whining and yapping outside the window—pariahs that had the habit of slinking down from the woods each night, drawn by the food she threw out. She must feed them; they had come to expect it. But where to put things? All this clutter . . . Nudging a place on the table, she began to scrape the crusts and bones. Distractedly she opened the window and flung them out. Then she turned back, running a cold hand across her brow. Dirty dishes and bowls were everywhere. If only she hadn't worked in such haste . . . If only Mary—But no, no. Martha caught herself. It wasn't Mary, it was that *man*.

Judas! Martha shuddered, felt almost ill.

Contemptible. She had never liked him—the only apostle she felt uneasy about. He was too charming, too flattering, trailing Mary about, complimenting her, greedily admiring their furnishings. A handsome sycophant, especially around Lazarus, who didn't trust him, wondered sometimes why Jesus had even chosen him, let alone given him the purse strings. . . . Yet somehow pathetic too. That curious little white scar quivering. He had looked . . . pitiful at the door. Who and what had hurt him to make him so? Even in her outrage and revulsion, something in Martha ached for the child he must have been.

But no—the white-hot anger flared again. How dared he criticize Mary? It wasn't his business what she did with the family's rare perfume. How *dared* he try to spoil things? Martha halted, trembling, trying to sort out her chaos of emotions. Yes, at first she had been stricken. Mary's sudden appearance, so unutterably beautiful in the moonlight . . . That old wound! Martha felt as if it had been torn wide and she was bleeding, shamefully bleeding, though nobody noticed; she wanted to hide from her own ignominious suffering, become invisible, simply vanish and leave them staring forever at the vision of Mary, like an angel descended from heaven, all white and gold.

Then, quite as suddenly, the miracle of love and pride came flooding, so overwhelming she must brace herself, stand frozen, watching in awed amazement, lest she be swept away. And as Mary came toward them on her golden sandals, so carefully carrying the precious oil for Jesus' anointing, Mary's rapture became Martha's too. Jesus was all that mattered—to comfort him, thank him, demonstrate to him and to his apostles how much their master was adored.

Never had Martha felt such a tumult of joy and loving admiration. She begrudged her sister nothing. Mary had done something more beautiful than Martha could imagine, let alone perform. (If only she could!) Nothing anyone said could spoil it, certainly not a man like Judas.

Martha's anger at him was subsiding. That poor man, so . . . ignoble and yet somehow so poignant with his quivering scar. Jesus preached forgiveness and compassion. . . . Even so, she must compose herself before returning to the garden with her sweets. Martha managed to smile faintly as she moved about the kitchen. At least she could serve Jesus' favorite cakes. Flaky triangles stuffed with dates and almonds, dipped in wine and honey before she baked them. She had originated the recipe and used it only for him. A humble tribute, but her own—the best she could do.

She was aware, as she piled the cakes on a silver platter, that the atmosphere in the garden had changed. The hushed silence was over, the aura of companionship and communion evidently broken. She could hear the men talking now, but to her surprise, they did not sound united. Martha halted, puzzled. The voices were rising, the way they did sometimes in argument. They were having some urgent discussion, and she sensed Jesus' consternation. It seemed incredible that there would be dissension among them about anything this night. Unless, it flashed through her mind, Judas had stirred them up.

Well, perhaps her cakes would calm them.

Curious, Martha hastened down the slope. The moon was overhead now, giving everything a radiance and clarity seldom seen by day. Every twig and leaf and flower was etched in silver; the shadows of the fig trees traced a lacy pattern on the luminous white cloth, and flickered across the troubled faces of the men. Some of them still sat, heads low, as if embarrassed. Others had gotten to their feet.

Peter, John and Andrew were standing closest to Jesus, in obvious support of all that he was saying.

"*Stop this*," Martha heard Jesus order quietly. He had risen and stood towering over everyone, one arm around Mary. "Leave Mary alone. There will be no more talk about selling things to feed the poor. The poor you will always have with you. But you will not always have me." Jesus paused. Slowly, searchingly, his eyes moved among them, lingering on Judas. Judas stood a little apart, arms folded, head back, coolly defensive if not quite defiant. When Jesus spoke again, his voice was more sad than stern.

"Have you forgotten so soon what I have told you? That we are going up to Jerusalem, where I will be betrayed. I will be given over to the authorities. I will be killed and carried to the tomb. Mary knows this," he said, gripping her hand, "Even though I haven't told her. Women like Mary know such things, and in their love prepare the living for that hour. What Mary has done tonight is a beautiful thing. She will be remembered for this wherever you preach the gospel. In pouring this ointment upon my body, she has prepared me for my burial."

Martha caught her breath, stifled the cry in her throat. Then the thing she had feared most was true! Before, she could not face it, could not accept it. *But now that he had spoken . . .*

Dazed, Martha went to the table and set down her tray. Nothing else mattered. She was grateful for Mary's tribute. She could only pray that Jesus would be comforted by her little cakes.

Chapter 17

$\mathcal{A}$ FEW weeks before Passover that year, Hannah hobbled down the long hill that led into Nazareth.

She was shriveled now and bent, for her bones had shrunk. She was tiny and gnarled, like an old tree stunted and broken by many storms, but still fiercely putting forth a few leaves, a little fruit. She had resolved that not another Passover would go by without doing something about the robe.

For years she had dreamed about it: ever since that spring when Jesus was twelve and they had all gone to Jerusalem for his presentation at the Temple. It would haunt her forever, the sight of her grandson, surely the most beautiful and gifted boy to kneel before the priest, not as well dressed as the others. (Mary had cut down a robe of Joseph's for him; it was a little too big for him, and somewhat faded.) One day she would make or buy him a beautiful robe. She had meant to do so long before this, but there had been other children and grandchildren, many duties, little money, and she had simply kept putting it off. But she had never forgotten.

At first she had thought she would make it herself. She would bleach and comb the choicest wool from the finest sheep. She would spin the threads and weave it on her loom. She would shape it and cut it and sew its edges, being careful that it would flow softly about him, a robe without seams. She would embroider it lovingly, as his cousin John's robe had been embroidered; wonderful patterns of fruits and flowers worked themselves out in her head. But the longer she put it off, the harder it was to begin. And as the years passed, Hannah realized she would have to buy it, after all. She was never quite sure of herself anymore as she sat at the loom. Her bony knees ached so, her feet were unsteady on the treadle, the threads tangled. Her daughters-in-law would rush to the rescue, not meaning to sound harsh but scolding that it wasn't necessary now, there was plenty of cloth about the place, how much did she need—and what for?

At last she knew she could wait no longer. She had been having ominous dreams. She could not remember their content, only that a feeling of anxiety and urgency lingered. "Do it now!" something seemed to be telling her. Her days were numbered; unexpected things happened. If Jesus was ever to have the garment he deserved, she'd better get at it. She would take the bag of coins she'd been saving for years to Reb Levi, Cleo's father. His shop was still the best in Nazareth; he could have it made for her. If she had enough . . .

It pleased her to discover the bag was heavier than she thought. She had to rest several times just lugging it into town; and when she finally hobbled into Levi's store, she set it down to ease her aching shoulder.

"Hannah!" cried her old friend and adversary. "What a pleasure to see you. How long has it been—months, years? You don't get into town often enough for me to recognize you anymore. Shame on you!" Levi wagged a playful finger, but he was eyeing her with sad dismay. She had once been so lively and pert, bouncing around, her voice tart but always clear, never creaking. How Hannah had aged! But there was still the familiar spunk about her, an amusing spark in her deep-set eyes. "What can I do for you?" he asked.

"I have come to see about a robe," Hannah said. Bending, careful of one hip, she lifted the bag with both hands and set it smartly on the counter. "For my eldest grandson. The son of Joseph and Mary," she could not resist adding.

"Oh, yes. That one." Reb Levi said, cooling. Hannah could almost feel him wince. He was a proud man; would he never get over the fact that his handsome if reckless son had been rejected as not good enough for her daughter?

But that was all so long ago, Hannah fretted. How could it still matter, since Cleophas himself had remained so close to the family? Held Mary's children on his knees, become like a father to them, especially Jesus, after Joseph was gone. . . . Poor Joseph—Hannah bit her lips and blinked rapidly—who had not lived to see this day. While

Cleophas . . . somehow it seemed to her that Cleo had won out in the end. Certainly Cleo himself had never held a grudge.

Hannah was impatient with Levi, but sorry she had irked him. Nonetheless, she held her ground. "Yes, *that* one. Jesus. I would like to see some material. He will be going up for the Passover, preaching at the Temple before many people. I want him to have the best."

Levi bowed courteously and with an air of proud authority led the way past the perfumes, jewelry, rugs and other fine objects, to where the fabrics were displayed. But Hannah was surprised to notice his shuffling gait. His hair and beard, once so black and curly like his son's, were gray now, and thin, almost scraggly. And he had been such a strong man; she remembered how he'd gone storming out of the synagogue the day Mary and Joseph's banns were read. What a giant! It hurt her to see him now—puffing as he struggled with the heavy bolts of cloth, trying to pull one or two onto the counter. An anxious young clerk rushed up to help him, much as her daughters-in-law rushed to her aid at the tangled loom. And she thought sadly, *How he has aged.*

Levi impatiently thrust the clerk aside, and began shuffling the fabrics around, slamming one down, holding a length between his arms, discarding it suddenly, almost as Hannah reached out to touch it. A subtle combat seemed to be going on between them, yet he seemed genuinely to be trying to please her. . . . Such a dazzling array: silks, velvets, brocades, linens, purest white woolens, striped fabrics of every kind. Hannah was bewildered, jealous of their beauty, wanting them all. Her fingers shook as she felt them, stroked them.

"Oh, my! They're all so beautiful. It's—I'm not sure. I just want him to have the best."

"Of course, that's what we will try to find for such a personage as your grandson," said Levi, kindly patronizing. "I've heard so much about him; he is certainly the talk of Galilee."

"And Judea! People flock to hear him wherever he goes. Jerusalem—they say the crowds in Jerusalem will be greater than ever at Passover this year because he'll be there." Hannah caught herself, heart pounding, ashamed of bragging so. She stared at Levi, suddenly concerned. His voice had always been furry, but never harsh, breathy, rasping. Several times he'd paused to cough, shielding his thick lips with a big yet somehow dainty hand. "Levi," she asked sharply, "have you seen a doctor about that cough? It doesn't sound good to me. Perhaps if I made a poultice—"

"No, Hannah." He shook his head.

"I wish Jesus was here. He helps people, you know. Heals them, cures the sick—lepers, even. Many people can attest to it."

Levi recovered from his fit of coughing, regained his dignity. "So I've heard. But he isn't here, is he?"

They went back to the business of the cloth. "Look at this piece," the merchant said. And oh, but it was beautiful—of purest white linen, and delicately embroidered with rose and blue and golden threads. The most elegant thing she had ever seen. She touched it longingly. "Oh—oh! It must be very dear. I want him to have a really fine robe," she reasoned, troubled.

"Then he shall have one! Choose this, Hannah; you'll never regret it. What are his measurements?"

"But the cost. Will I have enough coins?" she pleaded.

"Never mind," Levi said grandly. "We are old friends." He threw up his hands in a genial wave, settling it. "You will have enough for both the fabric and the tailor. Only tell me Jesus' measurements and how you wish this robe to be made."

His very generosity, so unexpected after their subtle clashing, unnerved her. Hannah didn't know how to thank him. "He's a tall man, you've seen him yourself with Cleophas—very handsome and broad and strong," she said, confused. "Just make it a fine robe, all in one piece, a robe without seams."

To Hannah's pleased surprise, Levi accompanied her to the door. He was limping slightly; she could hear the rattle in his chest. He had no grandsons, not one, and she had so many. Her heart went out to him. "And it must be done in time for the Passover," she reminded. "All eyes will be upon him."

"You have come to the right place. It will be finished long before. Someone will take the robe to Jesus?" asked Levi. "One of your other grandsons, perhaps?"

"Well, I thought maybe Cleo"—it occurred to Hannah suddenly— "since he, too, will be going." An unhappy thought had struck her, the story of the Biblical Joseph and his coat of many colors. How his brothers had been so jealous they had actually sold him into Egypt as a slave. No, for shame—Mary's other sons were not like that; why, they had fought to protect Jesus from the mob outside the synagogue! Still, Hannah felt uneasy and somewhat embarrassed. "And should you see anyone else in the family, please don't tell them about this," she said anxiously. "Let it be our secret. I want it to be a surprise. The secret will be safer with Cleo."

"Whatever you wish," said Levi, smiling to himself. Evidently, having many sons and grandsons was not an unmixed blessing.

Cleophas rode up in time to see Hannah departing. She did not hear his greeting; she was getting a little deaf.

His father still stood in the doorway, faintly smiling. Levi explained the encounter, and with a gesture of tender amusement, picked up the bag of coins. "I didn't tell Hannah, of course—it would hurt her pride—but this won't even cover the fabric."

Cleophas nodded, looking serious. "Spare no expense," he said. "Add a sash with a golden buckle. I myself will make up the difference. Whatever it takes, make it the finest robe we have ever made. Jesus is my friend—more than a friend, he's like a son. I want Mary's son to have the best."

Shortly before the Passover, Mary was on her knees preparing the soil in her flower garden when Ann came hastening down the path. Her plain, usually calm sweet face was excited. "Mother, there is a young man asking for you. A courier, come all the way from Bethel, he says. It must be a letter from Jesus!"

Mary gave a little cry and flung down her trowel. Gathering up her skirts, she ran past her daughter to the house.

She is like a girl, Ann thought, following. A girl who lives for word from the beloved. A pity Jesus' letters were so rare. The family often discussed it among themselves. Was it not for this, the story went, their mother had learned to read? The boys joked about it wryly, proud if a bit embarrassed at having a mother who could bring the excitement of a messenger to their door.

For Mary's sake they were pleased whenever a letter arrived, but they were also secretly humiliated and a little hurt. Her other sons had no cause to write to her, living right here underfoot in Nazareth, hewing trees, building houses, making a decent living for their families. They did not journey to far, exciting places, making speeches, attracting crowds, doing wild and dangerous things. They teased her about the letters sometimes, joking to hide their feelings.

Mary found the house swarming. Ann and Leah had brought their children; they wanted to go shopping, Mary was to mind the little ones. Josey and Simon had come up from the shop with the young messenger, who said his name was Caleb. The boy's eyes drank in the sight of Mary. "Are you Mary, the mother of a man called Jesus?" he asked eagerly.

"Yes, I am his mother," Mary said with the old fear. "Is he all right?"

"I'm sure of it, although I did not see him this time. The letter was given to me in Bethel by one of his followers, a man named Andrew. It was written a few days before, I believe, while your son was resting elsewhere—Ephraim, his friend told me."

Trembling, Mary accepted the small roll he pulled from a tube around his neck. The children were racing noisily about. She was aware of her family hovering, curious and surprised. She could not bear to open it in front of all of them.

"You have had a long journey." She smiled, trying to regain her composure. "You must wash and rest with us awhile." Asking her daughters to prepare the basins and food, Mary hurried back into the garden.

She sat for a moment rejoicing, holding the scroll against her breast. A letter from Jesus! Never mind that in the past three years there had been only four: one written from the house of Peter in Capernaum; one composed on a rocking boat on the Sea of Galilee; one written on a hillside beyond Caesarea Philippi; one from Jerusalem— the house of someone named Nicodemus. She knew them by heart, she had read them over and over; they were her treasures.

Now she unrolled the parchment, though her hands were shaking so it was hard to make out the words. Jesus was in Ephraim, he said, a small town near Jerusalem, where he'd taken his apostles for instructions before returning to the city. He was aware—the knowledge had come to him strongly—that she planned to come to the Passover Feast. He begged her not to. Though he loved her dearly and longed to see her, Jerusalem was very unsettled right now. There were rumors of danger. He would spare her what might happen. But if she insisted on coming (as, knowing her nature, he feared she would), she must go to the house of Lazarus in Bethany. "It is a big house, high on the second ridge of the Mount of Olives. Ask in the village. Lazarus is well known—anyone can direct you." Lazarus and his sisters would make her welcome, along with whoever came with her. Either Jesus would be there himself or they would know where he could be found. . . .

Mary read the words again, torn between joy and distress. Finally she rose and went back up the path into the house. The messenger was preparing to leave. Though they were politely urging him to spend the night, he wanted to start back as soon as possible. "Do you wish to send a message to your son in return?" he asked.

Mary wavered. "There is no time to write a reply," she said quietly, glancing over her shoulder at the family as she led him to the door. She waited until the two of them were alone on the steps. "Tell Jesus that I will heed his words and pray for guidance. If it is the will of the Father that I be with him at this Passover Feast, I will come."

Something in the boy's eyes clutched her heart. Caleb stood hesitant. His voice was awed as he said, "Not long ago I had the honor of carrying a message to your son. Even though I found him, I'm afraid—I'm sorry to confess—I did not recognize him then. But now that I do, I want you to know—I am doubly honored. It is a privilege to meet and carry a message to him from the mother of my Lord!"

Mary's eyes filled. Smiling, she reached out and pressed his hand. "Thank you," she whispered. "God go with you."

There had been a murmur of voices behind her. The room fell quickly silent as Mary returned. They had been talking about her, Mary realized, speculating about the letter. They regarded her now with frank curiosity and concern. Reluctantly, Mary parted with the scroll, handing it to James. They were her family, she loved them, this involved them all. "Read this, if you wish," she said.

Wordlessly, each son studied it and passed it on, even to the girls—whom Mary herself had taught to read.

James spoke first. "Jesus is right," he said, his sensitive face troubled. "It would be unthinkable for you to make this journey now. Or for any woman." He indicated his pregnant wife. "It could be dangerous, with so much unrest."

"Yes, Mother," Ann protested anxiously. "Why now? Why would

you even consider it now, when you haven't made the trip since our father died?"

"Jesus needs me," Mary said. "I know he needs me. I want to be with him."

"*Jesus* needs you?" Josey burst out sarcastically. "What about *us*? Don't we need you? What if something should happen to you?" He snatched the scroll from Leah, who was pondering it, and tapped it with an angry finger. "This unrest our brother speaks of—why doesn't he mention that he's known to be the cause of it? I didn't want to bring this up again—I didn't want to worry you, Mother—but there have been stories that the Sanhedrin won't put up with him much longer. There's trouble every time; I shudder to think what might happen if he shows up at the Passover. I don't think any of us should go. Dangerous for our mother? It could be dangerous for all of us!"

"But we men at least are obliged to go," James reminded. "It's the Law."

"Is the Law more sacred than our lives?" Josey demanded. "Or the life of Jesus himself? Yes, it could come to that," he said, as they gasped. "He could be in mortal danger. We'll have to talk this over with Simon and Jude, but I think they'll agree. Instead of going ourselves, we should try to find our brother, as we have before, and stop *him* from going." Impatiently he scanned the scroll once more. "What is that town he writes from?"

"Ephraim," Mary said quietly. "Didn't you hear what the courier said? But he was to be there only a few more days. Jesus may be already on his way to Jerusalem."

The morning after this squabble, Mary carried her letter to the roof. She had scarcely slept all night. She must come up here where the curds were drying and a breeze was blowing from the hills, and try to decide what she must do.

Benjy, who scarcely ever left her now, was drowsing at her feet. The dog was getting old. It wasn't fair to take him on such long journeys anymore. "I'll feel better if he's with you," Jesus had said before he left the last time. "He can protect you, Mother, and he'll be company for you."

"I'm quite safe"—Mary had laughed—"and I have plenty of company. But you know I love the dog, and he will be a comfort to me, with you so far away."

At first Ben refused to stay behind. Waking to find his master gone, he had run frantically down the road in pursuit. Cleo had ridden after him, caught him and carried him home before him on his saddle. After a few days of the animal's grieving and refusing to eat, Mary, with the help of Cleophas, managed to get some food into him. Ben clung to both of them now, scorning all others, for he knew they, too, belonged to Jesus.

Now suddenly the dog lifted his head and, barking joyously, bounded down the steps. Cleo! Mary thought gratefully. Ben always seemed to sense his presence. She went to the parapet and called down to him where he knelt, hugging the dog and playfully roughing his fur. Cleophas looked up and came quickly, Ben at his heels. Despite his usual bright debonair manner, Mary saw that something was troubling him too—though at first he spoke only about the robe. The garment was finished, Cleo told her; he had personally overseen the project, even ridden up to Capernaum himself to see about a finer silk for the girdle. He was sure Hannah would be very pleased.

"As your mother requested, I have said nothing to anyone about it except you. I will take it to her tonight for her approval."

"I'm sure she'll love it. It must be beautiful."

"But I want you to see it, too, before it's delivered to Jesus. Perhaps you could meet me there? Then, if you both agree, I will take it with me when I leave for Jerusalem tomorrow."

"Tomorrow?" Mary stared at him, bewildered. "But the caravan doesn't leave for the festival for several days."

"I have important business to attend to," Cleophas claimed. "I don't want to wait for the caravan. Can you tell me where I might find Jesus? I understand you had a letter from him yesterday—the courier stopped in the shop, asking directions."

"Yes, I was just waiting to show it to you. I need your advice about what I should do." Gratefully Mary drew the scroll from her bosom. "Oh, Cleo, I'm so glad you've come. I've been beside myself with worry. My sons don't understand." She tried to tell him about it as he read the message. "The girls, yes—Ann and Leah came and sat with me last night while their brothers were arguing. My daughters know how I feel; they, too, believe in Jesus and would stand by him if they could. Ann even offered to go to Jerusalem with me, if that was my decision. I can't let her, of course—she has her own family to think of. But the boys are saying terrible things, at least Josey, Jude and Simon. They don't think any of us should go to the Passover, certainly not me!"

Cleophas rose from the bench, his face grave as he handed her the scroll. It was a moment before he replied. "For once your sons are right," he said soberly. "No, Mary, you must not go." He began to pace the roof, the dog padding faithfully beside him. "If I were your husband I would forbid it. But since I'm not"—Cleo gave a little groan and drew a fist across his brow—"I can only beg you. Jerusalem is not a safe place these days. Please don't risk it."

"But Jesus needs me! I know it, I feel it." Mary was staring blindly into the distance, clutching the letter to her breast. "No matter what anybody says, I want to be there. Something tells me I have to be with him."

Despairing, Cleophas crouched beside her and took the parchment from her, that he might read it again. And his heart sickened, for the words only reinforced the rumors that had been flying, and the news he had heard from a Roman before leaving the shop a few moments ago. The Sanhedrin in Jerusalem had met; lesser sandhedrins throughout the land were being warned: The presence of Jesus at the Passover was considered a threat; they feared an uprising. Firm orders had gone out for Jesus' arrest.

Cleophas shuddered; his blood ran cold. If this succeeded, if they actually brought him in, it was not unlikely he could be put to death. But how could he tell Mary this?

"Jesus loves you so much," Cleo said carefully, "he wants to spare you. And so do I. I pray you will change your mind." He rose and stood considering, deeply troubled. But if he dissuaded her and this terrible thing happened—would she ever forgive him, or herself? Did anyone have the right to keep a mother away from her son at such a time? He drew a long, painful breath. "But if you insist," he said at last, "if you are convinced you *must* go, then I want to be with you."

Cleo sat down beside her and gripped her small white hand. His voice was not quite steady. "And if anything should happen to Jesus . . . heaven forbid, but if anything should *happen*," he muttered thickly, "let me take care of you."

To his distress, Mary drew quickly back, small, proud, unyielding. "My sons will take care of me," she informed him.

"But you tell me they are not even going to the feast this year," Cleo protested. "Mary, this is serious. When Josey and James—any of them—would actually disobey the Law rather than take the chance—"

"James may go," Mary claimed hopefully. James would do anything for Jesus, he would go in a minute, but his wife was begging him not to. Not that Mary blamed her; the girl was so young, and expecting another child. "I remember that terrible week Joseph went up to the Passover without me, because of the babies. I had a dreadful premonition. It was the most agonizing time I'd ever spent, waiting for him to return. And when I saw him, his face bruised and bloodied. . . ! The Romans had ridden them down where they worshiped, right in the Temple. It was a miracle any of them escaped!"

"I remember," said Cleophas. "I was there."

Patiently he sat listening, his square jaw set, as she rushed on. He kept stroking the dog, who now lay still on the floor beside him, eyes blissful, half closed. It hurt, it hurt, to hear these frequent reminiscences of Joseph, yet curiously his heart always quickened. He had developed a strange hunger for them; though it was another man Mary dwelled on, that man had been his friend, the brother he'd never had. Mary's words brought Joseph back. . . . Still, it was he, Cleo, who was near to her now, feeling her warmth, smelling her delicate perfume, seeing the rise and fall of her bosom. Close enough to love, futilely or not.

Meanwhile, his mind coped with the problem. "Mary, listen." Cleophas sprang up suddenly. "Never mind the others. If you are determined to go, I will take you. You can go with me tomorrow."

Mary was startled. "No, No, impossible. I can go with the caravan. I will be quite safe with the caravan."

"There is no time to wait for the caravan. And a caravan is too slow—all those people and mules and donkeys, all that baggage. I may as well tell you: The quicker we get there the better."

Mary was staring at him, alarmed in a way she had not let herself be before. "Cleophas, what is it?" she whispered. "Is there something you haven't told me?"

"Yes," he acknowledged miserably. "It's one reason I came. I would like to spare you, but you will hear it soon enough. By now your family has probably heard it. The rumors are true—the Sanhedrin has put out warrants for Jesus' arrest.''

Mary paled. She gazed at him bleakly for a moment, and a small cry escaped her, a pitiful, almost mute whine, like an animal that has been struck or badly wounded. Cleo couldn't stand it. "Mary, don't," he begged. "Please don't." Fiercely Mary pressed her hand against her mouth to stop the sounds. But her hands groped blindly about. Cleo reached down and held her until her violent shaking stopped. "Hush now, hush, hush, it's all right," he muttered.

Yes, she must think, she must not give way to this. She must keep control, she must plan. Mary made a feeble gesture. "Then you're right—we must not lose any time. I will pack tonight. I will . . . Let me think—which donkey? The best one is lame; the other one—I believe Jude needs it for hauling some timbers tomorrow.''

"Never mind donkeys," Cleo said. "We don't need donkeys, I will have horses.''

"But I have never *ridden* a horse," Mary cried. "Cleo, I'm afraid.''

"It will be a gentle horse, and I will ride beside you. Mary," he said sternly, seeing that she was pale, "if you are to go with me, as I now believe you should, you must be willing to do as I ask.''

"But horses!" Mary gasped. "Only Romans ride horses, horses are pagan, no decent Jewish woman—''

"What about a decent Jewish man?" he broke in.

"Yes," she acknowledged, "some, a few like you. But you have always been a law unto yourself.''

"Mary, you are the mother of Jesus, who has already broken many traditions. Would you be unwilling to break one more if it meant reaching him in time? Possibly even to help him?''

"All right, yes, anything—forgive me. But, Cleophas, another thing," Mary said nervously, suddenly remembering. "We cannot travel alone together. It would not be seemly!''

It was exactly what he needed. That Mary, in her innocence, should consider such a matter now. Cleophas threw back his head and laughed. "I assure you, Mary, your honor will be quite safe." He wiped his eyes and, bending down to her again, took her hand and kissed her fingertips. "But you are right. I would have no word said against you. Fortunately, this can easily be resolved, I think. Only yesterday in Capernaum I learned that several of the women who traveled with the apostles were preparing to leave for Jerusalem. Peter's wife told me. It's possible we may overtake them."

"Then it *is* serious," Mary said, dazed as the truth bore in. "Otherwise they would not go so far, or start so soon."

"Yes, Mary, there's no use denying it. But one thing more: The woman called Magdalene—I spoke with her at Peter's house. She is coming to Nazareth tonight. She wanted to see you before going on. She will be riding a donkey, I suppose, but I will have a horse ready for her too. If things work out as I hope, the three of us can ride together."

They left the next morning, shortly after daybreak.

Roosters were crowing, birds beginning to sing. The dove-gray sky was gradually brightening, the air was crisp and cold. Benjy circled the horses, sniffing their strangeness, barking furiously and bounding away when one of them kicked. Ann darted out of the house to hold him back while Cleophas lifted her mother into the saddle. Mary's face was white with fear. She struggled, groping for the slippery leather reins, which Cleophas placed firmly in her hands. He tucked her skirts about her attentively, like a husband, and accepted the blanket that Leah brought him. This, too, he tucked efficiently about Mary's legs— where she sat sidewise, obviously afraid of falling.

He tipped back his head and smiled at her reassuringly.

The woman Magdalene was already seated on a big black horse, quite composed. And though the beast stamped its hooves and tossed its magnificent head, she only leaned forward to pat its sleek neck. Obviously she had been many places, done many things. Her full-lipped oval face was very beautiful beneath its sheltering hood. Her dark eyes smiled at Mary's daughters, who stood watching the preparations with a mixture of anxiety and excitement. They had left their own families to see their mother off. They were determined to stand by her—what's more, to make her guest feel welcome.

Mary's announcement the day before had rocked the family. That she would decide to leave so suddenly, with Cleo! Her sons, at least, were shocked. Cleophas must be mad to suggest such a thing, or their mother herself must be ill. And to leave on horseback, of all things, with a woman like Magdalene. Bad enough that a woman with such a past had become a prominent follower of Jesus. Whether she was reformed or not, it still didn't look right. It was embarrassing to have her show up in Nazareth right now, like a friend of their mother's. Mary herself had misgivings at first. Oh, no, not Magdalene, she had thought; not when her decision to go at all was sure to cause such consternation. And her own feelings about Magdalene troubled her. Several times, when there was no one to go with her, Mary had ridden off, against the wishes of her sons, to find the place where Jesus was preaching. "Mary, Mother Mary!" Magdalene always cried, running to greet her.

Curiously, Mary had not wanted to be called Mother by this beautiful woman who obviously hungered to draw close to her, to love her, and through her learn more about her son. For as they worked together around the house or camp, or walked together along the road, Magdalene begged her to share memories of Jesus, from the beginning: what he had been like as a little boy, his friends and family, his schooling, when the great knowledge of his mission had come upon him . . . Mary was torn. Her heart went out to this motherless woman, yet something within her resisted. She did not want to serve up these morsels of his life to any woman. The old unreasonable fears rose up in her, the anxiety even then lest his course be diverted or affected in any way by human love. He had already endured such torment and triumphed over it; he had enough to contend with, let him be spared anything more.

But now nothing mattered except getting to Jesus. If this was the only way, so be it. Let her put aside her own foolish feelings, the family might as well be horrified by one more thing. . . . And when Mary actually saw Magdalene the night before—her sweetness, her beauty, like an angel in her simple dark blue wrap, with her soft hair shining—every reservation vanished. They fell into each other's arms, weeping. And later they went together to Hannah's house, where Cleophas was waiting to show them the robe.

Nor had Hannah withdrawn from Magdalene, as Mary had feared, but only held her close, and wept with them. "If only I could go with you!" she cried, as if this strange trip they were undertaking was but a cause for celebration. "Did you ever see a more beautiful robe?" she gloated, spreading it out before them. Jesus would be so surprised. They must tell her all about it when they returned—how it fit him, how it became him, how many people admired it, what they said. "If only I could be there" she cried, "see for myself!"

"You will see," Cleophas said kindly, glancing at Mary. "The next time Jesus comes back to Nazareth, he will model it for you."

"Well, let us hope, but at my age—" Only then did Hannah begin to tremble, her sunken eyes dim. "I wish Joachim had lived to see his triumph!"

Thank heaven Hannah hadn't heard yet. If only there were some way to keep the truth from her, they agreed, walking back to Mary's house, where Magdalene would spend the night. Even there a pleasant surprise was waiting. During their absence, Ann and Leah, those dear girls, had slipped into Jesus' room to put fresh rushes on the floor, fresh linens on the bed. A small charcoal fire was burning; there were flowers on the chest.

And now this morning, at the last minute, James, Jude and Simon came hurrying up. Partly to inspect the horses, and perhaps to make a final effort to dissuade her. Their opposition had nothing to do with Magdalene, Mary realized; their only concern was her safety. "Be careful," they pleaded, though they trusted Cleo (he had taught all of them to ride). . . . "Don't worry," he assured them. "She'll do fine. We'll avoid Samaria—if I were riding alone I'd chance it, but not with your mother. We'll take the Jordan mountain route."

It seemed to Mary that her sons were almost envious: they might even change their minds about the festival. Jude said suddenly, "Mother, wait and I'll run to get my things. If there's still time, I'll come with you. I could ride behind you!"

Mary shook her head. Curiously, she did not want him; she had a sense of freedom and escape, to have asserted herself like this and be riding off with outsiders.

James gave her a small package containing a present for Jesus. "Tell him I'm not sure—I will come if I can. Tell him I love him."

They set off at last, Mary still stiff and frightened in the saddle. But when she turned gingerly to look back, she was touched by their still-anxious faces as they waved. She had misjudged her children: Whatever they did was because of love.

Cleophas rode close beside Mary the first few miles, talking in a cheery, soothing singsong both to her and to the horse. "Easy now, steady, that's right, gently, gently, there's a good girl, steady now, we're going down a hill, we're going to cross a stream, it's all right, let go, you're as safe as in your own bed." At times he reached over to pat her or the white mare, whose head reached forward continually in rhythm with its flowing muscles. At times he threw back his big head and sang, comical songs Mary had never heard before. Magdalene, trotting a little way in front, slowed down, turned her face and smiled.

Gradually Mary's tensions eased. She stopped grasping the saddle horn in terror every time the creature lurched; she let the reins slacken as Cleophas suggested. Above her misery, the sick and trembling anxiety about what lay ahead, she could not ignore the beauty and wonder of the world. She dared to look around and try to enjoy the bright morning. From this living, moving perch, how different the world seemed! She had always been so small, she was seldom eye level with people; now she could look down on the heads a little below them on the village streets. And to be eye level with the flowering trees—how sweet the fragrance of almond and persimmon blossoms—or to duck under them, with their dew-wet branches across your face . . .

They rode across the boggy Plain of Esdraelon, still wet and puddled with the last of the winter rains, soft and green under the plodding hooves, surrounded by the mountains. Cleophas told them they would cross the lower slopes of the Gilboas. The view would be beautiful from there, and they could bypass the pagan city of Scythopolis, once known as Beth Shean, where most people stayed, and be that much nearer their destination by nightfall. He knew of an inn much farther along the road.

The highland forests were bursting with saffron and purple crocuses, the hills a riot of narcissus in a hundred hues. At times they pulled up and rested, gazing out across the green velvet plains and valleys. And Mary's spirits rose, the terrible fear was quieted. She even managed to laugh a little at some of Cleo's jokes and songs. Magdalene sang too—what a rich, throaty voice she had, and her laughter rang out at times like birdsong. Mary sensed they were being deliberately cheerful for her sake; trying to divert her. When they stopped at a well, Magdalene insisted on drawing the water and bringing it to Mary, even sponging its coolness on her face and hands. Cleo went off into the roadside grasses and came back flushed and proud as a boy, with his arms full of flowers. Mary plunged her face into their bright colors, drinking in their sweetness, and rode for a time with them tucked in her girdle, one of them in her hair, for the day was now warm enough for them to throw back their hoods.

How foolish are most of our fears, Mary told herself. How needlessly we suffer over things that may not happen. She remembered her terror of the horse, which so quickly became her friend, its powerful rhythms carrying her swiftly, safely to Jesus. Her apprehensions about Magdalene; the problems with her sons. Even her worries about Hannah's disapproval. Yet her mother hadn't blinked an eye, at either Magdalene or the journey, and had only been excited about her robe. Mary smiled. Dear Mother, going to all that trouble. It was comforting to think of the lovely garment secure in the saddlebag beside her. . . . They would soon see Jesus! They would find him safe and well, and he would wear the robe proudly there at the Passover, perhaps even in some glorious unspecified triumph, as Hannah so hopefully predicted.

Thus Mary mused, to the rhythmic beat of the hooves, while the beautiful countryside seemed to flow about them. By late afternoon, however, anxiety and discouragement began to claim her.

They had encountered few people on the shortcut Cleophas had chosen to avoid Scythopolis. It was finally necessary to take the highway, however; and when they reined up and gazed down upon it, they were astonished to discover it crowded as far as the eye could see. The sound of many hooves came up to them, the clang of bells and the jingle of harnesses, mingling with the voices. An entire camel caravan was passing, the beasts bulging with goods to be sold at the festival. There seemed to be no women and children among those who followed, for these were merchants getting an early start. Businessmen from Syria, Babylonian dealers clad in heavy silks and turbans, some on foot but most mounted or carried in litters. Slaves were pulling carts, or bent double with the enormous bundles on their backs.

There was no choice but to ride down among them and pass as quickly as possible. Before descending, both women hastily donned their veils. The air on the Gilboan slopes had been cool and sweet; here the heat smote them like a sudden merciless fist. There was the sour-sweet stench of animals and sweaty human bodies, of garlic and dung and a spicy, oaty fragrance that came from the baggage. The din after the silence was defeaning—hooves clattering on the pavement, bells ringing, donkeys braying, the shouts and laughter of the men, gesticulating to one another or, in surprise, toward them: two veiled but obviously beautiful women riding horses! Wives or concubines, no doubt, of the powerful-looking black-haired man who expertly guided them through and around the maelstrom.

The heat, the stench, the noise . . . Mary was reminded of those last desperate hours when she and Joseph had first struggled to reach Bethlehem. Her horse shied when a camel bared its teeth and emitted its hideous shriek as she passed. She was so startled she was almost jerked from her perch. Cleophas was instantly beside her, but Mary was frightened.

Her flowers had long since wilted. Her back ached from the unaccustomed position in the saddle; her hips were sore. She felt hot, dirty and very tired; and then—as they rode on, far ahead of the other travelers, and the sun lowered—chilled, stiff with cold. Pulling her cloak about her, Mary huddled deeper, praying that they would reach the inn before dark, as Cleo promised. "Be patient," he urged, seeing their discomfort. "Only a few more miles." The two women exchanged commiserating glances. Mary saw that Magdalene, though younger, must be as tired as she was.

And when at last they reached the inn, it was little better than a square stone wall, moss-grown and decrepit, with an open enclosure for the animals, and a wooden loggia to shelter the people. A few travelers were already wearily climbing its steps, to hurl down their bundles and unroll their cloaks on the floor. There was, however, a small whitewashed building where the manager lived with his family. Cleophas tied the horses, and bidding them wait, strode confidently to the back of the house, where several ovens were smoking. Watching, Mary was again reminded of that night when Joseph had hurried into the inn, frantically seeking a place for her to bear her child. Magdalene reached over to press her hand. "Don't worry," she said. "Cleophas is a good man. He will take care of us."

She was right. He came back presently, grinning. The family kept several small rooms for people with gold in their pockets. He knew them well; he had stayed here often. "There will be water brought to us," he said, lifting the women down. "And food for our supper."

Mary had not realized how weak and trembling her legs were

until she tried to stand. Cleo had to support her for a minute. Magdalene stumbled too. And later, as they were bathing, Mary noticed that Magdalene's feet and ankles were badly swollen. "Oh, my poor girl," she cried, "you must soak them in the basin for a while. Here, let me add more water. And I have some herbs that may help, if I can find them."

Over Magdalene's protests, Mary searched her bags until she discovered the tiny packet and shook its spicy contents into the water. "Our feet have dangled all day," she said. "Tomorrow we must remember to dismount and walk about more often."

"Oh, Mother Mary, no," Magdalene kept objecting as Mary knelt beside her with towels and oil. She reached out a restraining hand. "I'm younger, I should be waiting on you."

"Nonsense. You are like my—" Mary could not bring herself to say "daughter." "You are my friend. And my son's friend," she added.

"We both love him," Magdalene said simply. But her eyes were pleading. There was an instant of awkwardness between them as Mary went on drying her feet and massaging them with oil.

"Yes," Mary said finally, rising. "We both love him. And together—surely together we can help him."

The room was small and spare, smelling of mice and the rather acrid oil in the lamp that flickered in its niche. They could smell a bonfire burning somewhere; its wood smoke drifted through the slit of window. The servant girl who brought them their supper suggested they eat outside; a low table had been set on the stones. They would be warmed by the coals still glowing in the ovens, and able to hear the singing of some Bedouins gathered around their campfire on the hill.

Cleophas was already there, seated on a cushion with his lute. He had washed himself and anointed his hair and beard, and donned clean garments. The women, too, had changed. They all felt refreshed, drinking the fig wine from Jericho which the manager saved for special guests, and devouring the excellent bread and meat. Mary had thought she was too tired to eat; she hadn't realized she was so hungry. The thing that had driven them so hard all day wasn't mentioned; they tried not to think of it. It was almost like a party. And after the final prayers were said, they lingered under the stars, listening to the music of the shepherds, while Cleo softly strummed his lute.

But when Mary lay on her pallet next to Magdalene's, her torment began. Every bone and muscle ached, hooves pounded in her ears and began to stamp across her back and belly. She clutched herself and whimpered, as she had when her labor first began, lurching along beside Joseph on the donkey, fighting their way through the crowds on the highway, desperately trying to reach Bethlehem. In her misery Mary cried out. Startled, Magdalene rose up on her own pallet and reached over to comfort her.

"Mary, dear Mary, what is it? Why, you're trembling, you're cold. Here, let me wrap you in my cloak—it's heavier and it's really very cold in here." Grateful to serve her, Magdalene tucked the cloak around her, and brought another blanket for her feet. "There now, that's better. You were dreaming. Now you can sleep again. . . .

But as she turned away, Mary reached out to grip her hand, still moaning. "Tell me," Magdalene pleaded, "what is it? Please tell me, Mother Mary!"

"I'm—in—labor!" Mary gasped. "No, no, I'm not mad—but I feel it. I hurt, I hurt—I cannot bear it. It's—with me—as it was the night he was born. That day Joseph and I were trying to get to Bethlehem in time. We were both afraid—I was so afraid. I'd never had a child, my mother was far away, and the stable—you know he was born in a stable? Thank God Joseph found room in that stable, but it was so cold at first—and it hurt, it hurts!"

Panting, Mary threshed about, the tears streaming down her face. Gently Magdalene bent to wipe them away.

"It was warm by the time he came. There was this terrible pain— I nearly went mad, I couldn't bear it—but then I heard him crying and he was in my arms, my precious baby! There was ecstasy then: I have never known such joy. But this time, now, I am in agony—about to lose my baby!"

"Hush, hush," Magdalene whispered, stroking her hair. "We will find him, he will be all right." She sat for a time holding Mary's hand, her own throat aching. And finally Mary quieted.

"Forgive me," Mary said at last. "This journey today has brought it all back so vividly. I'll be all right now. Forgive me for keeping you awake, but it has helped to talk about it."

"I am honored that you told me."

"There were shepherds that night too," Mary went on presently. "They gave us some soup. I will never forget—they, too, had built a roaring fire near the door. Hot barley soup, how good it tasted. And there were other shepherds; we could hear them singing. And before the night was over some of them came to see us, shy and careful, not wanting to wake him but anxious to see him, bearing gifts. Such rude but loving gifts. Let me think—what were they? A comb of honey, as I recall, or no, maybe it was a sack of figs. Some rabbit skins, a sheepskin rug—I have it yet." Mary laughed softly. "One boy carried a newborn lamb."

She was no longer trembling or in pain. Her memories were balm; she wanted to comfort herself with them, and to comfort Magdalene, for these were the things she had hungered so long to hear. Mary's last reservations were gone. She told about the strange dark Oriental princes who came riding up one day, resplendent on their camels, bearing richer gifts. She touched on the flight into Egypt, and spoke of Jesus' boyhood, his first trip to Jerusalem, the time they thought they'd lost him.

Only once or twice did Magdalene ask questions. "And did he know who he was from the beginning, even as a child?"

"Oh, yes, I'm sure of it. I saw it in his eyes, in many things he said and did, even as a little boy—his first day of school. Yes, he had to know, at least in one layer of his being. But you must understand, he was a perfectly normal child—very gifted, yes, but otherwise not different from his brothers. His destiny became more clear to him as he grew older. We didn't speak of it in the family, but it was clear to him and to us, his parents. Nothing must be allowed to interfere with it, nothing. Whatever the cost—to him or to any of us. God himself would not allow it, I realized that. Yet as his mother, I, too, bore a sacred trust. I felt I must help him, as any woman would help her son: I must strengthen him if he weakened, I must—" Mary's voice broke off. "That is why, if I have seemed at times aloof—"

An owl hooted. Animals stamped in nearby stalls. There was the acrid smell of the dying fire.

"You have never seemed anything but the precious mother of Jesus," said Magdalene. Her voice was grave and sweet. "And there is something I must tell you, if you aren't too tired to listen. It is why—

the main reason why I was so anxious to see you before I left for Jerusalem. Your son saved my life. Saved me from almost certain death . . . By stoning," she added as Mary gasped. "I am not a pure woman, Mary—at least I was not then."

"I have never judged you, Magdalene. Who am I to judge?"

"You are God's own chosen one. You are the mother of my Lord." With a final squeeze of Mary's hand, Magdalene went back to her own pallet. "I was possessed of demons, many demons," she said. "Jesus delivered me from them. Once they were out of me—once I was free of them, my soul was free. I could love with a purity of spirit few women know. My past—my very past," she whispered desperately, flinging one hand across her brow, "added to my freedom. Only someone who has been bound as I was can know the release from this bondage."

"Are you speaking of bondage to the flesh?"

"Yes." Magdalene turned suddenly, to prop herself upon one elbow. "You know, you must surely realize, your son is beautiful. Could the very Son of God be less than beautiful? Many women have loved him—how could they help it? For they see not only the beauty of God that shines from him, but the unutterable beauty of his face and body. And this is natural, isn't it, for didn't God make us so? But please believe what I tell you, for I share it not out of vanity but only in the hope you will understand—"

She couldn't go on for a minute. Mary waited puzzled, heart pounding. Then Magdalene continued. "Unlike you, his blessed mother, I have no special honor from God. And yet, and yet—I feel that I, too, have been chosen to love Jesus in a special way. A way that will protect him. Because I was freed—he himself freed me from all bondage to the flesh—I can serve and tend him. Yes, I love him, but it is not simply as a man but as the living essence of God. I worship him. I would gladly die for him."

Mary had been lying still, very still. Now she rose up and held out her arms to the woman who sat head high, her profile beautiful in the moonlight, but with tears running down her cheeks.

"Dear Magdalene," she whispered, "we mustn't cry. Neither of us must cry anymore. We must trust God to protect him. Sleep now, for it is late. Sleep now . . . my daughter."

"Yes, we are both so tired." They held each other tightly for a moment, then drew apart, drying their eyes. Magdalene crept back to her own pallet. "Listen," she called out then, softly into the darkness. "Cleo has been snoring for some time."

The sounds, so male and steady, were both comical and reassuring. Laughing in relief, and still clasping hands between their beds, the women closed their eyes. . . .

Mary slept, and dreamed. She was a young mother back in Nazareth again, and Jesus was coming home with something in his arms, a poor battered little pup. She could hear it whining and scratching at the door—but no, it was simply whimpering as Joseph and the children tried to set its broken leg . . . except the dog wasn't their first one, Jubal, but the cruelly beaten, half-starved bigger one later—Benjamin, Benjy, Ben— who tagged Jesus to school, helped him herd the sheep, trotted along on his missions, no matter how far. . . . He had wandered back to Nazareth, was barking and scratching, demanding entrance. . . .

Mary awoke with a start. There was a commotion in the courtyard: a sound of barking. Angry voices. "Get away, you pariah dog! I'll teach you to come bothering guests!"

More barking, yelping, more voices, one of them familiar. "Wait! Don't drag him away! I know this dog—he's ours, he belongs to us; he must have followed us here. Here, Ben . . . here, Ben . . ."

Mary sprang up, incredulous. Huddled in her cloak, she ran to the door in time to see Cleo scoop Ben up bodily, holding and rocking him like an overgrown child, trying to still his trembling. Gently scolding him, Cleo turned and saw Mary. "Go back to sleep, Mary. I'll take him inside and tend to him. But first, if you have some of your herbs and salves with you—his feet are bleeding. He also needs food and water."

"Of course!" she cried. 'I'll help you!"

Magdalene roused too. The three of them worked over him, as Mary's family had done in her dream. Meanwhile, they pondered what to do. To leave Ben here was unthinkable; he would only be abused or chased away, and it was plain he could walk no further. "We will simply have to take him along," Cleophas decreed, stroking the now blissfully sleeping head. "He will have to ride with me, up front on the saddle."

And thus it was that the little party set off the next morning, carrying Jesus' dog with them to Jerusalem.

Chapter 18

*T*HE highway on the road from Jericho was already alive with travelers. It was too early for much shouting and singing, and the climb up through this final ridge of limestone mountains was steep. But the people were cheerful, and laughed to see the dog, nose high, riding before Cleophas on the saddle like a king. A few Roman legionaries rode among them, superior on their horses, in their glistening plumed helmets. They also smiled to see the dog, and some of them saluted.

"They think we're Romans too." Cleo grinned, as the crowds made way.

Even so, it was slow going. The roads between the soaring honey-colored cliffs, and above the rocky gorges, were narrow. In places they could move forward only in single file. At this rate, Cleophas feared, it would be late afternoon before they reached Jerusalem. The sun was high in the sky, and they were only halfway to their destination.

Finally, at a place where the highway widened, he maneuvered his mount up beside one of the soldiers to consult him. The man listened thoughtfully, nodding, then beckoned them to follow. They trotted along beside the now swarming road a little distance, then, with a rattle of stones, the puffing horses went plowing up to a wooded ridge, where the young soldier pointed toward the south. Even from here they could see the undulating green hills known generally as the Mount of Olives. They needn't ride clear into Jerusalem to reach Bethany, he told them. Follow this path; it was a shortcut that would lead them almost to the very door of the man they sought.

"Then you know Lazarus?" Cleo exclaimed.

"Lazarus? The one people think was raised from the dead? Everybody knows him, or claims to. At least, they've heard of him and are trying to see him. *Dying* to see him, I might say, if you don't mind the joke." The soldier laughed doubtfully, pushed back his heavy helmet and mopped his pimpled face.

The horses were leaning forward, munching at the welcome grass. Cleo studied him. "Then you don't believe this miracle?"

The youth shrugged, glancing at the women. "Who knows? You Jews seem to believe in miracles—for I see you are Jews," he said, with a little nod of respect. "I only know you aren't the first ones I've directed to his house." He bent to pat the neck of his sweating horse. "But you may not find Lazarus there," he warned. "He may have fled."

"Why?" Cleo asked.

"It's rumored your priests would prefer him dead!"

Mary spoke up. "And the one called Jesus?" she inquired calmly, though her heart pounded sick in her breast. "The one who is said to have performed this miracle?"

"He's the one they're really after, of course. We've been warned this could be the biggest Passover ever. More Jews than ever will be coming just because of him. Although they're taking bets all over Jerusalem whether he'll even show up this year. Anyway, Pilate's taking no chances. See all those soldiers?" The youth turned in his saddle to indicate a fresh group that was overtaking the pilgrims ahead of them on the road below. "Contingents have been called up from all over Judah to keep order, in case of an uprising."

Cleophas was scowling. "Then it's that serious?"

"Yes, if the Jews really believe they've finally gotten their Messiah."

"They have," Mary heard herself say proudly. Suddenly, to her own astonishment, she was pulling the horse around to bring her face to face with the young man. "He is my son."

The youth flushed scarlet. "Forgive me," he apologized. "I didn't mean to be rude. But if this be true, then I feel sorry for you, Madam. I will pray to my own gods to protect you . . . and your son!"

Slapping the reins, he rode off without waiting for them to thank him. But below he halted before joining the procession, turned anxiously in his saddle and, looking up in wonder, gave them one final salute.

The path sloped downward for several miles, then gently upward through groves of olive trees, the first they had seen all morning. It was cooler here, though sun filtered through the silvery leaves. At times they had to duck between the branches, all beaded with the tiny budding olives. They dismounted and walked the remaining distance, which was surprisingly short. They soon reached the hilltop and were standing in the dooryard of the handsome white house that could only be the one Jesus had described in his letter.

Martha and Mary were carrying bundles across the stone terrace and piling them against the wall. They paused, shielding their eyes in their confusion, surprised at the sight of horses and the dog. Then, with glad little cries, both women came swiftly toward them, calling over their shoulders, "Lazarus, Lazarus, they're here! Jesus' mother is here!"

Their brother appeared from the house and strode eagerly out to greet the visitors, embracing them, joining in the introductions and questionings. He read their anxious faces at a glance. "If only you had gotten here sooner," he said. "Jesus left only a few hours ago, he and his men."

"Oh, no!" Mary moaned softly.

"We urged them to stay longer," Martha said. "They arrived only last night, and we had so little time with them."

"I'm surprised you didn't encounter them on their way to Jerusalem," Lazarus said.

"We came by a back way," Cleophas explained. "It saved us several hours."

"Yes, there are a number of shortcuts. They went directly down the mountain toward Bethphage."

"Then if we hurry, perhaps we can overtake them. Were they on foot?" Cleo asked. Lazarus nodded.

"Oh, no, please don't go just yet," Martha was pleading. "Rest here, at least a little while. We long to know you. Jesus has told us so much about you! Please," she appealed to Mary. "Come inside. We have so much food; let us serve you."

"And there's so much to tell you about your son," her sister broke in, radiant. "What he has done for us! Our brother—" she marveled. "Lazarus wouldn't even *be* here if it weren't for Jesus."

"You must forgive us. We are very grateful," Mary said, "but we are so anxious to see him."

Yes, of course, they understood. Though it grieved the family, they agreed there was no time to waste. "But you must at least have a drink of cold water," they insisted, "and some of Martha's cakes." Both sisters hastened into the house to get them. The dog must have some too. Half apologetically, his presence had been explained. "Ben followed us; we had no choice but to bring him."

The dog had sprung down from his perch and was sniffing around the bundles. Cleo whistled him back.

Martha knelt to feed him—these last of the sweets she had baked for his master. Her hands trembled. The dog's nose was cold to her touch; she petted him gently, feeling his silken hairs under her fingers, and gazed into the yellow, forever hungry eyes. Any creature so faithful . . . I loved him too, she thought. I, too, would have followed him anywhere.

"You must come back," Lazarus was urging, as they remounted. "To our regret, we won't be here. We are going to Jericho for a while, but you are welcome to stay in our home. All of you," he said cordially, smiling at Magdalene and Cleophas. "It would be an honor."

Mary gazed at him, this attractive, vigorous, keen-eyed man her son had restored to life. Before he could continue, she asked quietly, "Are you leaving because of Jesus?"

Lazarus hesitated. "Yes," he acknowledged. "Your son and I talked it over. He agrees it would be best, not only for him but for us. You, however, will be quite safe here. We will leave the key under that large urn near the door."

"You're very kind," said Mary, "but we have other arrangements—my aunt doesn't live far. But about Jesus—will he be coming here again?"

"I hope so, but I'm not sure."

Despite the name Bethphage, which meant "city of unripe figs," the groves of Bethphage bore richly, and their fruit was very sweet. The place was also known as the village of many donkeys, for on the adjacent farms, hundreds of these gentle beasts of burden were bred. Some families had as many as ten or twenty, kept in the fields or tied to their doors, waiting to be sold or rented for trips into Jerusalem or up through the rugged mountains. Here, too, caravans often paused to feed and rest their own animals, or to trade them for fresh ones before moving on.

Unlike the sleepy surrounding villages, there was usually activity and sometimes excitement on its streets. And today the air of excitement was heightened; Mary, Cleophas and Magdalene felt it the minute they rode through the ancient stone gates. People were pointing, gesticulating. A little knot had gathered around an old man, who was waving his arms and crying out loudly from the doorway of his shop.

"My donkeys, my donkeys!" he was shouting. "They have taken my donkeys!"

Curious, Cleo rode as close to the huddle as he dared. The man was quite bald, but he had a long white beard, which nearly covered his chest. Lifting his arms to heaven, in his full-sleeved striped cloak, he was beating his breast and crying, "A mare and her colt that I had tied to my doorstep only this morning!"

"Who did?" Cleo asked, bending down. He was puzzled and somehow concerned.

"Two men, who were sent by the holy man. Two strapping young princes, sons of the king!"

"What holy man? What king?"

"The one called Jesus. The one who's been performing miracles all over the land. Healing the sick, even lepers, they say, even bringing back the dead! Our own neighbor Lazarus—we all know him well, don't we?" he asked of the crowd that was pressing nearer, growing, clamoring assent. "I wasn't at the burial, worse luck, but my friend here helped carry him to the cave—"

"It's true, it's true!" the friend shouted. "And now, I tell you, Lazarus is alive!"

The old man began to wail and sway; he was sobbing—whether from ecstasy or anguish was hard to tell. "And now this Jesus, the Messiah, sent two men here to claim my donkeys!"

"The Messiah? Are you sure?" Cleophas motioned to the women to ride closer.

"Yes, only such a one could have known their perfection!" The owner's eyes, still streaming, were also shining. He wiped his nose with the back of his hand. "The two men—let me see—what were their names?" He turned to consult his grandson, who was bouncing with eagerness to be of aid. "Oh, yes, Andrew and Philip. They came directly to my beasts, saying the master had sent for them. And oh, what understanding, what compassion! For he said the colt must come along with its mother, for the little one was not yet weaned."

Cleophas was frowning. "Then you're not troubled at the loss of your beasts?"

"*Troubled?*" the old man shrieked in amazement. "I am honored! Never have I known such an honor. That a holy man, let alone the Messiah, should ask that I provide the ass on which he might ride in triumph into Jerusalem!"

"Tell me—how long ago did they leave?"

The old man quieted, and looked about at his audience for a moment, confused. "Half an hour, maybe more; I can't be sure."

"They are just down the road." A woman holding a child spoke up excitedly. "I saw them myself, the man and a group of his followers. People are cutting branches and laying them in his path. They are spreading their garments before him, like carpets on which our friend's donkeys may walk."

"I just came from there too," said another man, running up. "I'm going back to join the procession as soon as I can."

"Have they started for Jerusalem yet?"

"No; there's a lot of singing and shouting of hosannas, but they seem to be waiting for someone."

Cleo drew a long, grateful breath. "Come," he said to the women, as he maneuvered his horse about.

To his surprise, Mary slid down from her perch. Now that they had found him, it did not seem right to greet Jesus on horseback. Her son was so tall; she had looked up to him ever since he was twelve years old, and she would look up to him now.

"Since it seems to be so close," she told them, "I will walk."

"Oh, Mary, no!" Magdalene pleaded. Her own fears for Jesus, her desperate desire to see him again—these she had suppressed throughout the journey, for his mother's sake. She had kept silent, never intruded. But now, when they had come so far and hurried so to find him, she could keep silent no longer. "Please. Let's get there as quickly as possible, lest we miss him!"

"He will wait," Mary said confidently, for she knew this in her heart. "Didn't the man say they were looking for someone?"

"Magdalene's right, Mary," Cleo reasoned, anxiously. "Why keep them waiting longer?"

"Because I don't think it fitting," Mary said. "I would like to leave the beast here. These people are to be trusted. Perhaps we could leave all the horses with them. I'm sure our possessions would be safe."

"But the gifts you are bringing Jesus," Magdalene reminded. "The robe—" She caught her breath in sudden recognition. "Wouldn't this be the very occasion his grandmother predicted?"

Mary nodded. "Yes, I have thought of that. I will carry the robe. If Cleophas will be so kind as to untie the bundle and hand it down."

Cleo had already leapt from the saddle. He raised his arms to help Magdalene descend. It was hard to control his impatience, but anything to humor Mary. "Then we will all walk. We will leave our two horses, but lead yours with its baggage. But we must hurry to get on our way before it's too late."

Two dark-skinned youths who had been hovering, frankly listening, sprang forward, quick as monkeys, to catch the reins Cleo tossed them. They were both grandsons of the old man whose donkeys had been chosen, they claimed, pointing to the shop. The horses would be tied to the very posts. The boys would guard them with their lives until the owners' return. "Do so and you will be paid well," Cleophas promised. . . . No, no, no, it would be an honor, for they knew that these people were somehow related to the holy man.

Whinnying, with a fine jangling of harness and clopping of hooves, the mounts were led away by the nervous but exuberant boys. They were bursting with pride; all eyes were upon them, admiring their boldness and the beauty of the steeds. A host of other boys chased after them, dancing around, keeping a safe distance, but a few were begging a turn at holding the reins. Horses were a rare charge in this village of the donkeys.

Cleophas pondered the situation as he led Mary's horse behind him into the countryside. It was nearly midafternoon. The trees, which grew thick and luxuriant beside the dusty road, cast deeper shadows. They must hurry. Faintly, from around the first bend, they could hear sounds of singing and shouting. Jerusalem wasn't far, just across the Kidron Valley, but if this was indeed to be a triumphal procession into the crowded city, it couldn't be delayed much longer.

If only Mary hadn't insisted on walking. Yet she was right, he realized. There was something unnatural about seeing any woman, especially a Jewish woman, on a horse. A horse was a symbol of authority and power. And for them to have come prancing through this crowd on horseback, while Jesus rode an ass—! Cleo shuddered. No, no, it would have been a terrible blunder. . . .

If only they *got* there in time. He was growing more agitated by the minute. If only Jesus hadn't already ridden off on one of those donkeys he seemed to have commandeered. Cleo was frowning, troubled at the prospect of the coming scene. . . . True, all the prophets had ridden donkeys. And once, long ago, the kings—even King David. But things were different now. In these modern times, kings were carried on litters, or appeared before their subjects astride a magnificent steed. . . . Then what about the famous prophecy of Zechariah?

The words came to him suddenly, shaking him: "Behold, your king comes unto you; he is just and having salvation, lowly and *riding upon an ass, and upon a colt, the foal of an ass."*

Cleo's throat was dry; he didn't know what to think. . . . That frenzied crowd in Bethphage, the ones overtaking them now—all were calling Jesus not only king but Messiah! Even that old man who'd provided the donkeys . . . Could it be the donkeys—the very sight of the donkeys that convinced them? Was this a visual fulfillment of the prophecy they knew so well, believed in so passionately, and had waited for so long? . . . Cleo set his teeth against the pride and concern in his breast. He didn't know, he didn't know; he knew only the pain of loving Jesus as his own son.

People were appearing on the road from all directions now, ahead and behind them, running or astride their own trotting donkeys. Many were already carrying branches, others paused to scramble up the banks to wrench pine or olive branches from the trees, or boughs of the fragrant white blossoming myrtle. Others feverishly picked flowers growing along the roadside. There was the smell of bruised grass and flowers along with the tang of the new-cut branches and the acrid odor of the dusty road.

Some of the people who had seen them in the village looked in surprise at these plodding strangers, who carried no tribute. Two boys raced by on their donkeys, madly waving shaggy palm leaves, and calling, "Don't you want to see the king?" A little way ahead, however, they halted, consulted, and trotted back, to try and share them with Mary and Magdalene. "We have plenty, from Jericho," they explained. "They say he's the Messiah! You should have something to wave."

"Thank you, but we have gifts for him behind the saddle," Mary told them, smiling.

"Then you'd better get there," the boys advised, gesturing. Ahead of them the people were indeed disappearing; they were among the last ones, along with a few hastening stragglers.

"The robe!" Mary remembered as the boys galloped off. She appealed to Cleophas. "Right now, before we arrive, shouldn't we get it down and have it ready for him?"

Cleophas groaned inwardly. Again she was right. There would be no time later; and on this occasion, if ever, Jesus must have his new robe. He reached up quickly to bring the heavy bundle down. But even as Mary's trembling fingers undid the straps and brought the garment forth, Cleo suddenly groaned aloud. The distant barking of a dog reminded him—for the first time he missed Ben.

"Benjy! Where is Benjamin?" Stricken, they all froze and looked about. He must have jumped down when they stopped in Bethphage; in all the commotion they hadn't noticed. But they dared not even consider going back for him. "If he found us before, he will find us again," Cleophas tried to reassure the women. "Or he will wait for us there with the horses."

Mary was shaking out the beautiful garment. Magdalene helped her smooth it and hold it higher, that it might not touch the ground. Both caught their breaths, relieved. Though Mary had taken it out each night and hung it over a chair, they were afraid it might be wrinkled. But the lovely fabric was smooth as cream to their fingers, its delicate filigree of blue and rose and silver glistening in the afternoon sun. Together they folded it carefully for Mary to hold in her arms, against her breast like a child.

Cleophas, too, was pleased and proud. But there was no time to waste. "Do you need anything else?" he asked, on a note of urgency. "If not, I'll put this back." He began to fasten the bag, which was heavy with Mary's things and other gifts.

They had proceeded a few paces when Magdalene cried out, "Wait, wait, the girdle—we forgot the girdle!" And he must pull the bag down once more, for the women to rummage through it for the splendid blue satin sash Cleo himself had chosen, with its semi-precious stones. Jesus would never wear real gems, Cleo knew, yet it was a stunning adornment, and it thrilled him to see it now. Magdalene would carry it.

The shady road sloped down between the green hills. They hurried along, hearts pounding from the pace, but glad to hear the music and shouting still rising, even louder from the hollow below, where a throng of excited people swarmed about, clutching their palms, or boughs from the flowering trees. They were laughing and singing, elated, waving to each other, or throwing down their flowers and clapping their hands in rhythm to the music and the psalms. There was the shrill, sweet sound of pipes and flutes, the clashing and flashing of cymbals. On the sunny pasture hillside a circle of girls had clasped hands and were skipping about in a spontaneous little dance; small boys were turning somersaults or rolling ecstatically on the grass. Other people perched patiently on rocks, or the embankment beside a sparkling stream.

On the road, at the center of this welter of color and commotion, they glimpsed two white donkeys, a mother and her colt. Both were draped in scarlet shawls, and as they watched, a woman scurried forth to fasten wild roses to their bridles. Two others, a man and a woman, ran down the road a little way ahead to spread garments in their path. The apostles seemed to be milling about, anxious to start, but the three couldn't see Jesus at first, for he was surrounded.

Then the crowds parted, and they caught a glimpse of Jesus, kneeling. And they knew that Ben had found him, for they heard the dog barking, and coming closer, they saw that Jesus was hugging him, while Ben frantically tried to lick his face. Jesus stood up then, laughing and crying as Benjy lunged at him joyfully again and again.

The dog spied them then and came galloping to meet them. Jesus followed, tears still wet on his cheeks as he made his way to them through the excited people, who were dazzled anew at sight of the horse Cleo was leading. Murmuring endearments, Jesus kissed and held each one, while the dog waited, tail wagging in triumph.

"I knew you were coming," Jesus said with emotion. "It's late; we must go, but I couldn't bear to leave without first seeing you."

Several of his followers also hastened up to greet them: Peter, James and John, eager to begin the triumphal procession, but happy to see them, and full of questions. Where would they stay? Had they encountered Adah or Salome on the way? It had been some time since

Peter had heard from his wife, but he felt sure she and some of the other women were coming. Yes, Magdalene told them, the women might already be in Jerusalem.

The conversation was interrupted by Judas, who rushed up on his long, officious stride. "Master, we dare not wait any longer," he warned. "The people are getting impatient. We must not let their enthusiasm wane."

"That's right," said Peter. He mopped his big ruddy face, proud but concerned. "Word has gone on ahead, they say people are lining up for miles." The din of voices increased even as he spoke. "We must start soon if we aren't to disappoint them."

Mary stood hugging the robe. "Yes, you mustn't keep them waiting," she said to Jesus, eyes shining. "But you can't go without this! It's a gift from your grandmother," she explained, unfolding it, with the help of Magdalene, who again sprang forward to keep it from brushing the ground. "Hannah had it made for you—the best she could order from Cleo and his father. She says to tell you she would have made it herself, but her fingers are too stiff to sew now."

"On, no!" Jesus protested, with a little moan. "She can't afford it—she shouldn't have done such a thing."

"Thank Cleo," Mary said, glancing toward him gratefully. "He knows how much such things matter to Hannah. And she's right!" Mary thrust the robe upon Jesus, wanting to weep at the one he was wearing. It was not only old and threadbare, but soiled where the dog had jumped on him. "You can't ride into Jerusalem looking like that. Put this on," Mary ordered her son. "Hurry! Now—right now; never mind the audience. Take off that old thing," she insisted, "and give it to me. Cleo will hold the new one."

She reached out to help him, and there before his men and his frenzied admirers, who were laughing and shouting with delight, Jesus obeyed. He unfastened his old familiar garment and handed it to her, while swiftly, expertly, Cleophas wrapped the splendid new one around him.

Magdalene, watching, caught her breath. The robe became him; never had she seen him so beautiful—his sun-dark cheeks so pink, his eyes so bright, his lips so red. At the last minute she remembered the girdle, and stepped forward to present it to him, and he fastened it around his waist, its gems dazzling in the sun.

"If only your grandmother could see you," she said, her rich voice throbbing. "She is so proud of you. We were there, your mother and I, when she first saw the robe. It is a garment fit for a king!"

"Our king, our king, let us follow our king!" the people were shouting with renewed enthusiasm. "Hosannas to our king!"

Judas, who had witnessed the whole performance, grasped Cleophas by the arm and drew him aside. He had noticed the horse, now tied to a tree by the roadside, cropping grass. He also recognized Cleophas as the wealthy family friend he'd heard about. "My name is Judas, son of Simon Iscariot," he introduced himself, and kissed Cleophas on both cheeks as an equal. "Forgive my haste, but I must speak to you. Surely you must feel as I do—" Lowering his voice, Judas jerked his head toward the sleepily waiting donkeys. "A man like Jesus can scarcely command much respect in Jerusalem if he rides in on the back of a common ass."

"Our king, our king!" The chant was growing louder.

"These people don't mind," Judas patronized, rushing on. "They're common people. But I do, and I'm sure you do. Jesus needs the attention of a better class of people if he's to succeed."

Cleo drew back, trying to conceal his distaste for this presumptuous man. "What are you trying to tell me?"

"Jesus is dressed like a king, he should make his entrance like a king, riding a fine steed like yours."

Cleophas gave a brusque laugh. The sheer effrontery! "You seem to have forgotten the prophecy every schoolboy knows: When the Messiah comes, he will *choose* to ride to victory on the back of an ass!"

Judas' face darkened. The words stung. He could feel his scar twitching in his embarrassment. "I still think I'm right," he declared, as coolly as possible. But his anger was evident as he stalked off.

Andrew and Philip were already leading the donkeys up to Jesus, who stood in conversation with his mother and Magdalene. "Don't try to follow," Jesus was telling them. "I can see you are very tired. Go back to Bethany and rest."

"I want to go on to Ein Karem," Mary told him. "I'm anxious to be with Elizabeth."

"Yes, go there, she needs you," Jesus said. "I will come to see you there."

"And you?"

"We will stay in Bethany most nights. It's the best place for my men. Don't worry; I will be with you every moment I can."

As he spoke he was stroking the nose of the colt. It was uneasy, for it had never been ridden, and the dog sniffing around added to its nervousness. Hooves rattled the stones as the colt shied, striving to nuzzle its mother. With his hands and his voice Jesus gentled them both. "Hush now, be still; there is nothing to fear," he murmured. "You must go now, Ben." He knelt to hug the hot, quivering body once more. "No, no, you can't come with us. Go to Mary."

Mary's eyes were shining. She was holding the collar of the whimpering, straining dog. "You must start," she told Jesus. "We have already detained you too long. You will ride before the people in glory, as the prophet Zechariah proclaimed. Don't worry about us. We will wait for you in Ein Karem."

"Hosanna, hosanna!" The shouts grew louder as the donkeys began to move. For seeing him thus, attired in radiance, with the gems like a rainbow at his waist, the people intensified their fervor. "Hail to the son of David, praise him! Blessed be the one who comes in the name of the Lord!"

Mothers held up their little ones to behold him. Some ran forward to kiss his sandals or the hem of his sparkling white robe. Frantic to demonstrate their loyalty and love, they waved their branches and pelted him with flowers. For was this not the man said to be the Messiah? Here on their very roads!

He could multiply fish and fruit and bread, it was claimed. There was a story he had even walked on water. Those who traveled with him, and many who had witnessed this at the Temple, vowed he could heal every manner of sickness, even leprosy and blindness. Above all, just up the hill in Bethany, he had brought a man back from the dead! Nothing was impossible to him. . . . They were laughing and crying. God had sent him to them at last—the one who could drive out the accursed Romans, solve all their problems, become their king!

Ben was panting, frantic to follow, his eyes beseeching. Mary had to kneel down and lock her arms around his neck to hold him. She could smell his hot breath, and the tang of the horse, which was tied again and munching the fragrant grass. Butterflies dipped about, circling like dancers. The sky was very blue, with a few white clouds drifting. And as the crowds moved farther away, she could hear the birds singing in the trees, as if to take up the cheering.

She was aware of Cleophas and Magdalene behind her. Cleo put a hand on her shoulder. Magdalene was shielding her eyes, still waving, in case Jesus should turn. Mary freed a hand to wave too. She knew he couldn't see them, of course; there were too many people, still singing and shouting and playing their pipes, the sounds growing fainter.

The dog had started to bark again; he didn't stop barking until the procession was out of sight.

Chapter 19

"SEE how they love him!" Mary cried softly, as the sounds of the cheering died away. "All those people—and there must be thousands more in Jerusalem. I wish now we'd followed."

"That would have been difficult," said Magdalene gently, "with the horses and the dog."

"And you're so tired," Cleo said, patting the beast which they insisted Mary ride back to Bethphage. He exchanged concerned glances with Magdalene. They could see Mary was exhausted, fatigued as much from emotion as from the hours in the saddle: the soldier's warning this morning, the fear of missing Jesus, even the thrill of finding him, there in all the commotion and frenzy of his admirers. Cleo held out his arms to Mary. "Come, let me lift you up. And when we get to the village, perhaps we should try to find rooms for the night."

"On, no, please," Mary protested. "Ein Karem isn't much farther—it's in the valley only a few miles down the road. I'm anxious to see Elizabeth. She must be so worried; I want to put her mind at rest."

Again Magdalene and Cleo regarded each other, troubled. But they said nothing, trudging along beside her, with the hosannas still echoing in their heads. Not until Cleo had reclaimed their horses from the boys (reluctant to part with their charges, but ecstatic at his reward) and the two were riding together a little way ahead did he mutter his apprehensions.

"I'm worried about Mary. I hope she's right, but I fear the consequences of all this. I don't think this ride will accomplish what she dreams."

Magdalene nodded. "It can't," she moaned softly. "If only it could. Like his mother, I'm so proud of Jesus. But the priests won't like it. And I know how cruel those priests can be."

"Do you think I should warn Mary?"

"Not just yet. She's wise and brave. She'll soon realize. Let her be happy as long as she can."

Mary felt their solicitude. It was in their faces as they waited for her to catch up with them, in their voices asking directions. The road wound down into the beautiful terraced valley that cradled the village of Ein Karem. Its name meant "spring of the vineyard," Mary remembered, for a spring bubbled at its entrance, and the surrounding hills were rich in grapes and olive groves.

"Straight ahead," Mary told them, still wearing her bright fixed smile as they drew near. "Then the left fork in the road and halfway up the hill . . . See—that beautiful pink stone house with the many steps leading to it. And all those beautiful flowers. My aunt loves flowers!" She was speaking excitedly, trying to sort out her emotions. For the hope, the desperate hope, had begun to wane. In its place was only this blind frantic joy at the prospect of seeing Elizabeth again. As it had been when she was only a girl, newly and mysteriously pregnant, fleeing to her aunt . . . as it had been when their sons were twelve years old . . . as it had been so many times since—at least until the death of Joseph . . . so it was now. Everything would be all right once she was safely with Elizabeth. No harm would come to Jesus—not yet, not yet! And perhaps even, dear God, never.

"We will have to leave the horses at the bottom, by the spring. There is a cave there, and sometimes a stableboy."

That wouldn't be necessary, Cleo said; he would take them with him. "I'm going on into the city as soon as we know you're safe." He had friends to stay with there, and business to attend to.

"But you'll come back?"

"Yes. I'll keep you both informed."

Magdalene thought it best to go on too. She wanted to join Salome and the other women. "I know where they're staying; they will be expecting me. And, Mary, you and your aunt will want to be alone."

"Come with me, at least to meet her," Mary pleaded, catching Magdalene's hand. For suddenly she realized she was not prepared to face Elizabeth, after all: Have I forgotten my aunt's own agony, such a little while ago? What will I say to her? How dare I come to her, either to rejoice about my son or to share my terrible fears for him? How can I expect her to comfort and guide me, after what she has gone through?

Even as Mary hesitated, a woman rose up from the flowers, and shielding her puzzled eyes for a minute, came slowly down to them. "Elizabeth!" Mary cried out, shocked. For the aunt, whose step had once been so brisk but graceful, came gingerly, feeling her way. Pain had cruelly carved the tall, rich, almost sensuous body, whittling it until it was now almost the size of her sister Hannah's. The hair, once so black and stunning with its silver stripes, was still abundant but had turned snow-white. There was only a hint of her dimples in the sunken cheeks. Those great expressive eyes sparkled now at sight of Mary, but they, too, were deeply sunken.

It was almost like greeting a strange, somewhat prettier Hannah. And when Mary held her aunt's thin, trembling body, Elizabeth clutched her as if never to let go.

They clung to each other wordlessly for a second, making no sound. Then, with her old composure, Elizabeth drew back, smiled, and stretched out her hands to greet the others.

Mary forced a smile as she and Elizabeth walked through the big empty house. Like her aunt, it had changed. There was an unfamiliar spareness about it, Mary realized, startled. Their feet echoed on the cold marble of the once richly carpeted floors. Things seemed to be missing. Where was that beautiful chest that had always stood by the entrance? The first thing she always noticed and admired—that chest with the huge branched golden candlesticks on it. Where were the mirrors, the delicate chairs and silken couches?

Soft draperies still blew at the tall arched windows, and the vases still held flowers, but the sense of opulence was gone. It was as if the winds of grief and terror had assaulted even Elizabeth's home, wrenching it, peeling away its very flesh as it had hers, stripping it down to the bone.

Elizabeth's head was back, her throat arched; she, too, was trying to smile, but her fingers bit into Mary's arm, and her voice, which was still rich and sweet, shook. "I promised myself, 'I will *not* break down before Mary,' " she scolded lightly. " 'I know she will come again, and when she does I will be brave.' "

"That's just what I was telling myself all the way here!" Mary cried. "I will not weep, I will not weep, I will not burden my precious aunt—"

"I knew you would come when you could. Especially now, at this Passover, for you must have heard what is happening here in Jerusalem." They had reached the rooftop and stood by the rough stone parapet, leaning on it as they so often had, looking toward the city. "But I wondered what I could say or do to help you." Elizabeth turned to Mary, bewildered.

"But I'm the one who should be comforting *you!*" Mary cried out in anguish, throwing her arms around her. "Forgive me for waiting so long. I wanted to rush to you the minute we heard about John."

For a minute they held each other in a fierce desperation, while tears ran down their cheeks. Then, blinking rapidly, Elizabeth wiped her eyes and drew away. "That would have been a mistake," she said, in her old pleasantly decisive way. "Come, let us sit down. We must talk. And we must be honest with each other. It would be foolish and false to pretend, I see that now. Only in being honest can we draw courage from each other."

"You were always my source of hope and courage. Today, coming here, though I resolved not to burden you, I was also selfish, I could think of little else."

"It's good that you didn't come before," Elizabeth went on. "Your first duty was to your own son."

"That's what Cleo insisted," Mary explained anxiously. "And so did Jesus' brothers. They thought we must try to find him and bring him home."

"They were right. His life, too, was in danger." Elizabeth halted, one hand pressed to her mouth. Yet she must say it. "As—oh, Mary, I don't mean to frighten you, but . . . it may well be now."

"I have to face that," Mary said calmly. "It's why I came. Why I dropped everything to get here, rode day and night, actually rode a horse!" She managed a wry little laugh. "Me, a decent Jewish woman. And I must tell you, my backside is very sore." It was good to hear Elizabeth laugh too, softly, throatily, in the old way. And as Mary spoke, her own spirits rose.

"But now, today—we just *saw* him, Elizabeth! And oh, but he is beautiful, and he's not afraid. The crowds are acclaiming him; they were gathered all along the road from Bethphage. People there have heard of his miracles—Lazarus, whom he raised from the dead, was a *neighbor*. They're following Jesus into Jerusalem." Mary could see and hear it all again, the ecstatic singing and shouting, the branches waving, and she could not refrain from trying to describe the scene.

"He was wearing a fine robe, Elizabeth, that Hannah had sent for him. I insisted that he wear it for her sake, and oh, he looked like a king! If only his grandmother could have been there to see it." Mary gestured toward the west, where the sun was setting; all the golden spires of the Temple were ablaze. "Even now the procession may have reached the Temple."

She stopped at the look of doubt and growing alarm on Elizabeth's face.

"Oh, Mary, I fear the authorities will not like that."

"But surely now they will have to recognize him for what he is. Surely God is with him and will let no harm come to him."

"Dear little Mary, pray heaven you are right."

"Oh, I know, it may seem cruel, heartless of me to be filled with hope and joy, after your own terrible loss."

"No, Mary, please. Don't forget—Jesus is my nephew, and your son. I love him—I love him as I loved John." Elizabeth swallowed; she was silent for a moment. "True, my heart has been torn from my breast. But nothing could give me more comfort than for this to happen. It would make my life worthwhile, for that is what John proclaimed!"

"*It must be,*" Mary said fiercely. "Nothing must happen to him. *Not yet, not yet!*" she implored. "I know it won't be easy, I know there will be a price, I will never forget what that old man said in the Temple, and what you yourself have suffered—the very sword through the heart. When the time comes, if it must come, I am prepared to pay the price. But first—please, dear God in heaven, I keep praying, let him have this!" She knew she was incoherent; she began to sob, all pretense of courage gone. "I came to help him. To see what I could possibly do to *help* him. Before it is too late!"

"Yes, of course," Elizabeth said gently. "We must think what can be done."

"It . . . perhaps it's a mad idea. But if we could get someone in the Temple to speak up for him. I have a friend there, a very old friend, although I haven't seen him for years. A priest who once loved me. But even better, it has come to me that you . . . You are so respected, you know so many people in the Temple—in the whole Sanhedrin," Mary pleaded. "As the widow of Zacharias, could you not get someone of influence to speak for Jesus to the high priest?"

Elizabeth was gazing at her in dismay, slowly shaking her head. "Oh, Mary, you know I would do anything for Jesus. You know I would give my very life for him." Stricken, she reached out to grip Mary's hand. "But I have no influence anymore, and very few friends. I am the mother of John the Baptist," she reminded, bitterly. "Don't you think I tried everything under heaven to save my son? Forgive me, Mary, I don't mean to sound harsh. But a widow has little status, even the widow of a high priest. And when her son has flouted many things the Temple stands for, offended the scribes and Pharisees, and even worse, Herod—! No, Mary, if they would not listen to me then, I'm sure I could find no one who would listen to me now." Elizabeth rose and paced about, walking almost as powerfully and gracefully as she once had, for this angry memory had strengthened her.

"And it would not be best for Jesus," she said. "It would only remind them that he is John's cousin. That would not look well for Jesus, Mary, knowing that he is kin to the man who was"—Elizabeth gave a quick little intake of breath—"whom Herod . . ." She was staring into the distance, one hand to her throat, as if to strangle the words. Finally she managed, through tight lips: "knowing what happened to John."

Mary was shaken. "I shouldn't have asked you," she whispered. "I should have known. But I am grasping at straws."

"No, no, no, don't blame yourself. I, too, was desperate; I would have tried anything. As you must," she encouraged. "This friend you spoke of, this priest. How well does he know Jesus?"

"They have met only a few times. But Abner was always kind and good. And he was also a friend of Joseph's. I believe he would do anything he could for us."

"Then don't let me dissuade you. Or depress you, Mary, with my talk of John. His fate need not be the fate of Jesus. The prophets didn't always agree, as you and I decided long ago. And John, who was himself a prophet, never prophesied anything but honor and glory for his cousin. Take heart from that! Miracles can happen. Jesus himself performs them all the time. Let us take heart from each other. Let us cling to each other and cry when we must, sharing all that we hope and fear. But rejoicing, too, that God chose us to be the mothers of such sons!"

It would soon be dark; the air was growing chill. A pleasant smell of food drifted out to them, almost obliterating the ever-present odor of meat smoke and offal from Jerusalem, where the first lights were coming on. Shivering, Elizabeth got to her feet, contrite.

A servant had appeared to summon them to supper: a very old lady, toothless and bewhiskered, who remembered Mary from long ago, and wept. "The mistress has been so lonely," she confided brokenly before hobbling off to her pots. "She has lived only for the sight of you again."

"Let me help you," Mary offered, for it was plain there was no one else about.

"No, I will," Elizabeth said. "Dinah and I usually work together, but tonight I quite forgot."

Mary gazed about, bewildered. "What happened to the others?"

"They fled."

A charcoal fire was glowing in the brazier, taking the chill from the almost empty room. One lone but beautiful lamp hung from the ceiling, illuminating the white linen cloth on the table, which was small, but set with a few pieces of fine china and silver. Elizabeth herself got up from time to time to serve the food or pour the wine.

"The servants were terrified after what happened to John," she explained. "Not that I blame them. I lay awake many nights myself, fearing that Herod's henchmen might murder us all in our beds."

"Oh, my dear Elizabeth," Mary gasped. "That too?"

"Dinah is the only one left. Perhaps it's just as well. I have no money to pay them."

"But you are the widow of a high priest!"

"That meant nothing in the end. Nothing. My son—our son—was executed for offending the king. I am old and in disgrace. You may wonder about the bareness of this house." Elizabeth made a brave, half-merry gesture and laughed. "Why I no longer wear any bracelets or rings. I have sold everything. It doesn't matter, I no longer care—

I don't think I ever did. It was mainly because of Zacharias, or so I tell myself. John disapproved; he thought it unfair that we lived in such comfort at the expense of the people, and he was right."

"But you were also working to serve the people," Mary protested. "My uncle worked very hard, and so did you."

"We could have lived more simply," Elizabeth said. "The people work hard too, and few of them live as we did. No, Mary, John was right—as Jesus is right. It is hard for those who live in luxury to enter the kingdom of heaven. I have sold all I could, not only to exist but to give to the poor. I will die soon, and when I do I want to be sure I join Zacharias and John in the world to come."

They had finished. Together they cleared the table, and washed the dishes as quietly as possible, so as not to wake the old woman, who had fallen asleep in her chair. Her mouth was open, she was snoring. Gently Elizabeth roused her and led her off to bed. "You must come too," she told Mary over her shoulder. "I have never seen you look so tired. Your old room is ready; I have changed nothing there."

It was indeed the same: That familiar round copper mirror. The oriental carpets, the graceful Greek chest. The same soft bed with the short, curved golden legs . . . Mary stood in the doorway for a moment, almost dreading to enter. She walked slowly in then. Aching with memories, she sat dazedly for a time on the bed. Here she had slept as a girl far from home—the first time she'd ever been away from her mother. And here, every time she and Joseph came to the festivals, she had slept in the arms of her husband. She had not thought she would ever rest in this room again. Not without him.

Mary stroked the coverlet. Material things, she thought, protesting. How was it that these lifeless objects should survive, mute, bland, exactly as before, long after life all about them has changed? Yet people—warm living people whom you love—only die and vanish?

Joachim. Zacharias. Joseph. John . . .

But not Jesus! Mary bit down hard on her lips. Oh, Joseph, our son still lives. The son God sent us both to raise. I will save him, she vowed. But oh, if only you were here to help me!

Elizabeth came in to blow out the light and tuck her in. Her aunt's hair was so white in the moonlight, her hands, smoothing the covers, were so thin. Mary's heart was flooded with love and tenderness. How lonely she is, Mary realized; she doesn't want to leave.

Mary reached out her arms. "It would please me if you would sit with me a little while," she said, smiling. "The way you did when I first came to you, remember? Weary as I am, my head is spinning with a thousand things."

"Are you sure? Oh, Mary, it would mean so much to me, for I, too, find it hard to fall asleep." Elizabeth sat down beside her, and held her hand. For a long time she didn't speak. An owl was hooting outside the window. The fragrance of roses drifted up from her garden. Faintly in the distance they could hear the sound of camel bells, as a late caravan moved slowly toward the city gates.

Elizabeth sighed deeply. "Night after night I lie awake, praying for sleep and yet dreading it too, lest I dream."

"Would you like to tell me more?" Mary asked carefully. "I have longed to know more about John. But I've been afraid to ask, lest it hurt you to speak of it."

"No, I want to, I need to!" Elizabeth assured her. "I have had no one I could talk to about what happened. And nobody knew John better than you and Jesus—you have a right to know. But it doesn't seem fair. I don't want to upset you."

"We are both grown women," Mary said quietly. "I am not a child to be disturbed by anything we can share. As you have said, we must be honest. We have come too far to hide our feelings."

"Then it will relieve me to tell you." Elizabeth drew another deep breath and tipped back her head; for a moment there in the moonlight, she seemed once more the strong, beautiful woman she had been. "But bear with me, for it is a long story. . . ."

"John was imprisoned, as you know, in Herod's palace at Machaerus, which is on the eastern shore of the Dead Sea. John's disciples got word to me, almost at once.

"I nearly went crazy, thinking what I might do to secure his release. I appealed to everyone I knew, people of any influence—I even went to the high priest. That was a mistake: Caiaphas is so afraid to make decisions, afraid of his father-in-law's disapproval, afraid most of all of Herod—of anything that might offend Rome. But he did send me on to Annas, who still has a lot of power: a ruthless but amiable man; I've known him for years. I pleaded with him, Mary, asking him to remember his friendship with Zacharias. He only laughed and scolded me for raising such a renegade son. John's continuing attacks, and his growing popularity with the Jews, were making Rome uneasy. They wanted him silenced. Even before he was foolish enough to denounce Herod for his morals, they wanted John stopped."

"John was a prophet," Mary said. "He was fearless, as fearless as Samuel or Ezekiel, or any of the prophets sent to warn the people!"

"Yes, John refused to bridle his tongue. He would strike out against evil wherever he found it," Elizabeth went on. "When I saw that my pleas were futile, I began again, asking only that I be given permission to see my son. That did not seem too much to ask, and I thought surely it would be granted. Herod, I had heard, was not really vindictive, at least not as much as his wife. Some of John's disciples were allowed to visit him, and they brought me word: They said the king came to see John every few days, half afraid of him, they believed, half intrigued by all that John was saying. Herod is terribly afraid of death: He seemed to want to prove that he is not really evil or in danger of eternal punishment. He wanted John to reassure him.

"To my dismay, even that permission was refused. It was for my own sake, I was warned. It would not be safe for me to visit John in prison—the mother of a man that defiant. For John would not recant, and Herod was losing patience. Besides, it would be a long, arduous journey. It's really not far, not nearly as far as you have come, but on a tortuous road through the wilderness to the Dead Sea. I am not an experienced traveler, Mary. As I have told your mother, I don't see how anyone, especially women our age, can come all those miles to the festivals. I don't have the stamina, perhaps because I never had to. Anyway, the very thought of setting out for Machaerus made me shudder. Even so, I must try. With or without permission, I would go to my son.

"I had a premonition of disaster, dreams so horrible I would not want to describe them to you. I could not eat or sleep. I knew I had to go to him and tell him how much I loved him, no matter what he said or did. And so it was secretly arranged. Two Temple guards, young men who had served with John at the Temple when they were boys, agreed to help me. They were on friendly terms with some of the soldiers at the palace. They would go with me. They would arrange to have a donkey for me to ride. We would leave at night. I would be veiled. Mary, I have never been so frightened in my life. You think of me as strong—I am not. I had never been put to the test before, and I was terrified.

"We dared not follow the highway, which is used by caravans to deliver goods to the palace; we would have to cut across country, which was shorter but through some of the worst terrain. Never have I been in such mountains; it was like a nightmare, with only torches to light our way. Two of John's disciples were to meet us en route and lead us in, under cover of darkness. But we got lost. By morning we had barely reached the Dead Sea—that evil-smelling place—and there were still miles to go. Back north to circle the water, then far south and east again.

"We were exhausted, and the donkey was lame. We were cold from the night in that desert wilderness, then burned by the sun. But the worst was over, I thought, for we had paused in a village, to eat and rent another donkey. And I still had the gifts I had brought for John—a bundle of warm clothing, for I had heard the cell where they kept him was damp and cold. And some food. Do you remember those spice cakes he and Jesus used to devour like wolves? How we used to scold them? I brought as many as I could carry. And some cheese and fruit." Elizabeth laughed shortly, and her eyes were bright.

"Go on," Mary urged gently, though she was apprehensive.

"I felt so much better after we had eaten a little and set off again. It could not be much farther, I thought. Not much longer until I saw John at last. I forgot to tell you I had also brought a change of clothes for myself. These disciples who were helping had led me to believe they could hide me a few days, either in their homes or perhaps even in the palace itself. Oh, but my heart was pounding! I had fantastic plans. Once there, a miracle could happen. I might even ask for an audience with Herod! Why not?"

"That does not sound like a woman afraid."

"No. No, by then my worst fears had dissipated; I was actually encouraged. I remembered the miracles of deliverance God had performed. I thought of Daniel in the lion's den. And the three men who were cast into the furnace, but the fires did not burn—Shadrach, Meshach and Abednego, delivered by the angel! I began to chant their names—such musical names. I actually began to sing. More practically,

I remembered the things John's followers had told me about the king. That Herod admired John in some ways. And that he was susceptible to women. I know it sounds mad at my age, but in my desperation it even occurred to me that if necessary I might try my charms upon the king!"

Elizabeth emitted an ironic little laugh. "I had not changed then as much as I have now."

"You are still beautiful," Mary murmured. "You will always be the most beautiful woman I have ever seen."

"This was the state I was in as the day waned. Any moment now we would encounter the men who had volunteered to guide us to the place where we would wait for darkness to fall. The sun was already low in the sky; soon it would be setting. But where were they? We dared not go much farther. We could already see the palace towers above the trees—although it is less a palace than a fortress, not beautiful at all, but ugly!"

Elizabeth swallowed. "Ugly!" she said again. It was a moment before she could go on. "By then all of us were concerned. We decided to go into a thicket beside the road to rest and wait for them. I was very thirsty, I remember, for my anxiety had returned. My tongue clove to the roof of my mouth, I could scarcely speak. But I kept thinking I did not want to drink more water, because there was no place to relieve myself. And fear, such fear as I was beginning to feel, increases the need to relieve myself. Thus we waited until after the stars came out.

"His friends, John's young friends, tried to cheer me, but I could hear them conferring. And they took turns watching beside the road. We could often hear footsteps or hooves approaching, but it always proved to be strangers, or Romans. They urged me to try to sleep; one of them put the bundle of clothes I had brought for John beneath my head. By then I was ill with fatigue and fear and exhaustion. I slept. . . . I don't know how long."

Elizabeth got up and walked unsteadily to the window. She stood there a moment, bracing herself as she looked out.

"I finally awoke—someone was shaking me. It was John's friend Noah. And I will never forget his face. 'They are here,' he told me. 'Stephen is speaking with them now.' 'Where have they been?' I gasped. They had ridden out early that morning to find us, he told me; the disciples had been searching for us all day. 'Why did they come so early?' I asked, witlessly, scarcely awake. 'And how did they miss us?' 'They wanted to reach us before we came farther,' he said. We had taken the wrong turn.

"He lifted me up and supported me, for I could hardly stand. And when I did, the back of my dress was wet—cold and clammy, for I could not contain myself, I had had an accident as I slept. I pulled away, appalled, for how could I go into the palace like that? And seeing my shame, he threw his coat quickly around me and said, 'Come, Elizabeth, they have something they must tell you.' And I knew . . . even as I stumbled with them through the bushes—" Elizabeth's voice suddenly broke; she clutched her throat. . . . *"Something had happened to John!"*

Mary sprang out of bed and ran to her, holding her, murmuring softly while the sobs racked her aunt's tiny frame, violently, as if to tear it apart.

"Forgive me, please forgive me," Elizabeth choked at last, weak and spent. "I thought I had wept myself dry, that there were no more tears to be shed. Yet to have you here at last—oh, Mary, you will never know what a help this has been!"

"I am glad you told me," Mary said. "I had to know." She kissed her aunt's wet cheek, lovingly smoothed her hair. "Would you like to sleep beside me? Would that be a comfort to you?"

Elizabeth straightened, wiping her eyes. "Later, perhaps. It may keep the dreams away. But first, I would like to be alone a little while, on the roof."

Elizabeth left quickly. She did not trust herself. For there was more, even more. She paced the roof, torn between relief at her unburdening and the fear that she might already have said too much. Yes, they had promised to be honest. But what happened next was too terrible to tell anyone; certainly she could not be so cruel as to inflict it on Mary, especially now.

Elizabeth could not remember how she had finally reached the fortress palace, only that it was morning, chill gray morning, and the gates were wide open. Nobody stopped her when she walked in to beg for the body of John.

"I have no right to release it," said the chief of the guards. A number of soldiers surrounded her, looking shocked. It was plain they thought her mad—her hair had fallen down, the frenzy in her eyes. "Only Herod can do that."

"Then take me to him!"

"The king is ill. He is still in bed. He is in no state to see anyone."

"Then I will wait."

"You must get out of here!" they warned.

"Herod won't see anyone," the captain muttered. "He's as horrified as you are. He doesn't want to be reminded of what happened—he'll punish anyone who does."

"Give me my son's body that I may give him a decent burial!" Elizabeth screamed. She was suddenly faint; the men's faces were looming and receding. She tottered toward some steps, thinking to sit down. A soldier caught her. When she came to, it was in a dank and dismal place, smelling of vomit and urine. The prison, she realized, struggling to sit up. Chains rattled, a rat scurried up the stone wall, there was blood on the floor.

One of the soldiers was crouching beside her, rubbing her hands. "Lady, please—you must leave! We carried you here for fear Herod would find you. Now you must go. I will show you the way."

"Tell me where he is," she moaned. "I must see John. I must see my son once more!"

The young guard paled. "Lady, believe me, this is better. It would have been a sight no mother could stand."

"Why?" she asked. "What do you mean?" For she did not as yet know the manner of his murder.

As they spoke, there was a thunder of boots on the iron staircase above them; voices echoed in the cavernous stone walls. Early as it was, some of the soldiers had been drinking. Some of them leaned on the railing, grinning. "Besides, it is not here," one of them bellowed down. "It has been disposed of."

"How?" she begged, scrambling to her feet. "Where is he? Tell me where my son is, that I may at least pray at his grave."

"There is no grave," she was told. Her son's head had been hurled into the Dead Sea, his torso fed to the dogs. . . .

This was not true. Some of John's disciples had already been summoned by Herod to get the body out of the palace. They had taken it reverently away and placed it in a tomb. But Elizabeth learned this only weeks later, after John's friends had found her, in a state of collapse, and brought her home. She had no recollection of being carried from the prison or of the journey back. But the hideous specters would haunt her forever. And she dared not share them with Mary, lest both of them be destroyed.

Chapter 20

*I*T was no use. Judas couldn't sleep.

It seemed to him madness that Jesus had decided they must spend their nights in Bethany, in the very house where it wasn't safe for Lazarus anymore. How could the other men lie snoring? They were so exposed here! So easy to find, if the authorities decided to strike, and a wonder they hadn't before, after that terrible scene in the Temple. Lazarus and his sisters had fled even before it happened; they were taking no chances. Oh, no, leave it to Jesus and the apostles, if they're willing to risk it; never mind what happens to *them*.

Evidently Jesus didn't want his own mother here in case of trouble. Or she had refused. At least, she was staying with some relative in Ein Karem. Mary's aunt, the mother of John the Baptist, Peter had told him, although that was hard for Judas to believe. A terrible omen! Judas shuddered. A man whose head had been served up on a bloody platter. It was foolish for Jesus to go there, as he did every night to see Mary. Now was no time to call attention to his kinship with that tragic predecessor.

The moon was too bright. It poured through the window as if from a great white pitcher, creating weird shadows that pranced upon the ceiling from the tossing trees. It seemed to him that he must stay awake, on guard. Branches cracked, there was a rustling of leaves in the garden. A water pot went crashing—had somebody knocked it over? Were those footsteps he heard? A rattle of swords approaching? Any moment there might be a pounding at the door.

No, now, rest; it was only the wind and the trees and those pariah dogs that slunk down from the hills every night, to bark at the kitchen windows until somebody threw them some food or drove them off.

But they always came back to prowl around, sniffing and rattling things, seeking garbage. Even in his fitful sleep, they stalked him—demons sent to heighten his fear and misery. Judas cringed.

Wasn't it enough that he must stay in this place? Must he suffer that torment too? He would get up and try to chase them away if he dared. But he had been terrified of dogs ever since a starving cur had attacked him in childhood, knocking him down. He had been barely four years old, yet he could still feel that horrible impact, see those snarling jaws tearing a piece of meat from his hand, and as he screamed, feel them sinking into his own flesh.

Judas stroked the ridged white line where the fangs had left their mark. His stepfather had rescued him from the dog and bludgeoned it to death—the only act of protection and love he could remember from the man. . . . His own father, Simon Iscariot, had died before Judas was old enough to know him, but Judas would always claim him instead of Obadiah, who had raised him. His mother's husband did not really like him, and resented the hours he had to spend training Judas in the scriptures; which Judas learned with a lightning speed and an intelligence that annoyed his stepfather, whose own sons were rather stupid.

To comfort himself, Judas had started stealing things, almost from the time he could reach the food on his stepbrothers' plates. Then it was their possessions. The more beatings he received, the deeper and more fierce was his obsessive need, and the cleverer he became—deft and quick-fingered in the marketplace, cunning at hiding or devouring his loot: sweetmeats and hot, crusty pies from the trays of peddlers; coins from merchants and sometimes the rattling cups of the beggars. A wild thrill possessed him, enhanced by the very terror of being caught. Later came self-detestation, which did not, however, diminish his cynical but precious sense of triumph. He often stole things he did not even want, and tried to buy back his self-respect by giving them away.

He wanted desperately to be admired, thanked, loved.

He was very good-looking, with his olive skin and his big, long-lashed, secretive eyes. There was something both sensuous about him and cold. Most people were attracted to him, and then repelled. He had few friends, no circle of other boys with whom to share pranks or games, no place of his own in the family. He yearned, above all else, to belong. So when Jesus, that incredible man, actually invited him into the sacred circle, Judas was staggered. At first he was nonplussed; then his fierce ego was challenged. Nothing was impossible to him, after all. Nothing!

Never had anyone spoken to him so kindly, or gazed on him with such affection. A passion of love arose in the breast of Judas, beyond anything he had ever experienced or imagined. He would not only follow this rabbi, he would crawl on his hands to follow him if necessary. In return, he expected, naively, to be equally loved. Thus it was a rude shock to discover that despite all that Judas was determined to do for Jesus—his slavish hovering and protecting and smoothly taking charge of situations—he would never be one of those closest to the master's heart.

Never like Peter, James and John . . . Especially John.

Yet, to his surprise, Jesus had honored him above the others by entrusting him with the purse. Jesus had recognized his skill with numbers, his talent for bargaining, arranging accommodations, the quick assertive efficiency about him. While the other men were dawdling, or trying to make up their minds about something, Judas got things done. Judas' pride was soothed; smiling and ordering people about helped conceal his disappointment.

The responsibility of the purse troubled him at first. Knowing his weakness, Judas had been afraid. Then he resolved no, no, he would never betray the one he loved. Ignore me though he does sometimes, preferring the others, I will rise above this jealous pain—which was in its own way bitterly exciting. He would overcome his problem, prove himself to Jesus. . . . Besides, it amused him to realize, there was so little money. Scarcely enough to tempt him. Not yet. The fortunes lay in the future. Judas' blood pounded at the prospect. For, having served the master well and honestly as treasurer now, would he not be appointed to that post when the purse was filled to bursting?

Yet as time went on, Judas began to worry and wonder. What if this kingdom was *not* of this earth, as Jesus himself kept telling them? (Though Judas doubted if any of the apostles really believed this—how could they?) Or what if their leader even—*failed*? Met with disaster, like so many others, including his own cousin John!

At times Judas berated himself for being a fool. He began to nurse his grievances, to watch for slights and disappointments. . . . And, like the whining dogs outside, they would not go away; they pawed and tore at him as he lay in his misery now.

Judas had wanted desperately to go with Jesus to the bedside of that little girl—the daughter of the ruler of the synagogue in Capernaum. With a quick perceptive flash, he, too, had known that she was dead, even before the servants came running from the house. And known what would happen: Jesus would raise her! A terrible eagerness possessed him to be there. Jesus would bring her back to life, just as he had the only son of a grieving widow in Nain. The body was being carried through the streets to his grave; moved with compassion at the mother's grief, Jesus had walked up to the bier, taken the young man's hand and bade him rise. And he sat up and the mother embraced him, for he was alive! The other apostles described it to Judas, who had missed it. The people were astounded; even the apostles were shaken—this was the first time they had seen such a thing.

All this, while Judas was off haggling with a merchant about the price of a chicken! Judas writhed at the irony; he had been buying it for Jesus. He had wanted to surprise the Master by cooking it over an open fire for him.

"Take me with you!" he invited himself eagerly this time. But though Jesus pressed his arm and spoke kindly, his answer was, "No, Judas." Instead, he went off with Peter, James and John.

The usual three.

That night, for the first time, Judas helped himself to a few coins from the purse. After that it became a habit. Never very much, not enough to be missed. Only enough to assuage his bitterness for a while, and give him a sense of independence. He didn't feel guilty, for it was justified—didn't he work harder than the rest? He had earned it. Dipping into the purse was his reward. It became as needful and heady to him as the petty thefts of his childhood. And when funds were mysteriously missing, he enjoyed the game of explaining, laughing at even Matthew's gullibility, and the pleasure of knowing that if worse came to worst and he was caught, no one would beat him. Never again would he suffer that hideous indignation. In some obscure way he felt he was getting even with Obadiah. And all the while, Judas continued to love Jesus, to adore him and yearn for his admiration, approval and affection as he had once yearned for his mother's love and the approval of his stepfather. . . .

Thank heaven the wind was dying down. Judas listened. . . . Even the dogs were finally quiet. But still he could not sleep. He got up, stepping carefully around the sprawled forms of Philip, Andrew and Thomas, and crept through the quiet house that had always seemed such a haven before. Filled with such treasures. The kind of things Judas had always coveted, and would someday have—or so he had believed.

He was aware of them even now—the Persian carpets under his bare feet, the silken cushions and draperies, the golden candlesticks gleaming in the moonlight. Yet there was no longer comfort or promise in the fine objects all around him. Not after all that had happened a few nights before. That alabaster vase! He winced to see it, cool and shimmering on its stand. Looking somehow superior, a taunting reminder of his humiliation.

Judas bridled. He still felt he'd been *right* about that ointment. But the way that sister of Lazarus had looked at him when he voiced his simple protest. The contempt in her eyes, the utter scorn. More cutting than words. Though how could anything hurt more than Jesus' lecture to him in the garden, where everyone could hear? Judas plunged on past the offensive vase and onto the terrace, where he leaned against the wall, biting his lips to keep from crying. How dared anyone, even the Master, speak to him like that?

To be scolded, after all he had done . . . to have his authority questioned . . . It hurt, it hurt, it stung!

Why, oh, why had he been fool enough to come back here with the rest of them? He could have gone somewhere else, like Peter, who was staying in the village with his wife. Jesus might have been glad to get rid of him. Well, at least he didn't have to face Martha, the hag! Too cowardly to stay in their own house, all of them. No wonder Mary and those other two felt the same way, didn't want to chance it.

The very thought of Mary, Magdalene and Cleophas aroused his antagonism. For it seemed to Judas that if they hadn't arrived when they did, the whole course of events might have gone differently.

It had something to do with the horse and the dog.

Judas could hardly bear the sight of that dog. To have it tagging Jesus almost everywhere they went had been one of his worst trials.

He had been immensely relieved when the creature was finally left behind in Nazareth. . . . But then to have it suddenly appear, just as they were about to start their procession! Not only a shock but an embarrassment—that a man like Jesus would actually kneel to embrace a dog, suffer it to lick his face! And the prospect of having it *follow* them before all those cheering people. The final humiliation—as bad, almost as bad, as having the Master mounted on a common ass, when he might have ridden a steed.

Judas was still stricken at that defeat. He had stormed off, shocked and disgruntled. Determined to complain to the other men. What an opportunity missed—and it would reflect on them. They were Jesus' chosen few, his very court, or would be when he reigned . . . *if* he reigned. Until that moment Judas had dismissed the Master's warnings that danger and even his own death lay ahead. He had simply refused to countenance such talk. It was preposterous; unfair and cruel—simply unthinkable after all they had sacrificed to follow this half-mad way of life. A life already fraught with danger—that was part of its fascination—but filled with adulation and opportunities too. Never had any of them known such dreams, or had so much attention.

Jesus had trusted him with the purse; why didn't he trust his judgment in the matter of the horse? But would it have made any difference? Judas wondered.

For the ride into Jerusalem, begun with such wild promise, had become a disaster. The crowds, shouting their frantic hosannas along the route of the Mount of Olives, were mostly from Bethany and neighboring villages, wild to see Jesus since the raising of Lazarus. By the time they reached the valley, where the party must descend and cross the dismal gorge, then climb the steep path to the city gates, many of them had dropped out. Few of them had the courage or desire to continue, for they had seen Jesus, and it was getting late . . . *thanks to the arrival of Mary and the others with the horse.*

Judas writhed. If only the procession had started sooner. If only he had never seen that wretched horse!

Again he wondered: *Or would it have made any difference?* Judas would never know; he knew only that he was bitterly disappointed. A few faithful did trudge along all the way, still singing and waving their branches. But there was no one to join them in the Hinnom Valley, that foul sewer of carrion and garbage, where nothing grew.

And although a number of enthusiastic clusters awaited their arrival in Jerusalem, there were not as many as Judas had expected.

Yes, many heads turned at the sight of the man in his glittering coat, mounted on one of two white donkeys with roses in their bridles, and followed by such a delegation. "Who is it?" they asked, shielding their eyes. "Jesus, the famous prophet Jesus," they were told. "The one who heals?" some of them gasped. "The man who has raised the dead?" "Yes, yes," the cries went up. "Jesus, the son of David, who has come to save us. Blessed be the king!"

In great excitement, more people joined the procession, or ran about spreading the word. Soon a large swarm was accompanying them, some people shouting praises, some merely curious, others wildly trying to get close enough to beg for healings. Several hundred, maybe more, Judas calculated, by the time they reached the Temple. But barely a drop in the sea of pilgrims that overflowed the city for the festival. Most of them didn't even know Jesus was there! How could they see him on the crowded streets? Moving along on a lowly ass!

But worse—and Judas cringed in anguish at the memory—was what had happened at the Temple. Instead of pausing to pray and teach the crowd that was surrounding him and growing larger every minute, awed and eager for words of wisdom, Jesus had dismounted and charged directly into the Court of the Gentiles.

Greatly distressed, Judas had followed, in time to hear him berating the money changers. "How dare you cheat these people?" Jesus was demanding. "It is written, 'My house shall be called a house of prayer,' but you have turned it into a den of thieves!" And then, to Judas' horror, he began kicking over the tables, so that coins spilled over the marble floors, clinking, rolling in all directions. People began scrambling for them, including Judas, who found himself on his knees, trying to retrieve a few bright shekels.

"Master, what are you *doing*?" he cried out, appalled, still on his knees.

Jesus wheeled upon him, eyes blazing. Never had Judas seen such an expression of outrage and disdain. "Get out of my way," he ordered. "These men are defiling the Temple!" And on he strode, into the dirty courtyard with its sheds and stalls, where birds and animals were being bought and sold for the sacrifice.

Here the stench was overpowering, and the floors filthy with the creatures' droppings. Birds screeched, cattle bawled, and there was the persistent plaintive blatting of the sheep. Before anyone could stop him, Jesus began flinging cages open, kicking down barricades, wrenching gates wide for the animals to escape. More tables went crashing, more money went flying, over the angry protests of the shocked and frightened sellers, who were frantically trying to rescue both their coins and their livestock.

Jesus was brandishing a long whip of cords—Judas had no idea where it came from. It whistled as it cut the air, and though it struck no one, the people scattered before it, as well as the beasts and doves. "Get out, get out!" he commanded, repeating the scripture. "You are robbers, all of you. My Father's house is no longer a house of prayer— you have turned it into a filthy marketplace!"

He was in the bazaar now, another thriving area, where worshipers could buy shawls, flour, incense, candles, souvenirs, hawked by eager sweating dealers. Here, too, the Master's warnings rained. Tears of sorrow and indignation were streaming down his face. Here, too, the tables and tills were overturned. . . .

He is mad, Judas thought sickly then—and now. I have been following a madman, and the authorities will be upon us; they will make us pay dearly for this madness. We, all of us, will be arrested and nailed to the cross. . . .

Attention, Judas thought in anguish. The procession had only attracted attention. Rumors were spreading like wildfire. The Messiah had come—he was already preaching at the Temple, denouncing the hypocrites there. He was threatening to tear the Temple down, some people said. Hurry, it might not be there much longer! He could work miracles—he was performing miracles every day, healing people right on the Temple steps. This could be the Passover they'd waited for so long, when the true Messiah appeared!

And though some jeered, others took it seriously. The courts were crammed with the curious, even many Gentiles, lured by the commotion. Never had Judas seen such mobs striving to reach the place where Jesus was speaking. Each morning they came early to the Temple, fighting to get near him on Solomon's Porch, where he stood— arms folded, his magnificent head thrown back—teaching and healing.

Yet there was little cause for rejoicing—only this mounting anguish of suspense. For always, shouldering their way to the front of the crowds, were not only Temple agents but priests and scribes themselves now, playing their infernal game of questions, meant only to expose him and justify the arrest already planned. By whose authority did he speak there? What about the baptism of John—was it from men or from heaven? Was it the duty of a Jew to pay taxes to the Romans? As usual, Jesus outwitted them, hurling back questions they could not answer. And the people loved it!

If only Jesus had rested on his laurels, and gone on with his parables and healings. But no, Jesus had to choose this critical time, which was already like a tinderbox, to attack the very authorities who were out to get him!

It was folly. A mistake as mad as driving the merchants and money changers from the Temple. Judas could feel the opposition growing, the net tightening. They wouldn't tolerate such insults much longer. He almost wished they would strike and get their bloody business over with. If only Jesus would flee, while there was still time. If only somebody could persuade him. Peter, John, somebody—since obviously the Master wouldn't listen to Judas. And even *they* wouldn't listen, he knew miserably, if he tried to persuade them. Yet for the sake of them all, certainly the sake of Jesus, something had to be done. . . .

Judas was very tired, he must go back to the bedroom. But as he turned, that night, Jesus came to him (though Judas could never be sure he was not dreaming) and held him and wept with him, saying, "I love you, Judas. Please don't suffer. I forgive you."

"But you are pure and I am evil. I am jealous and full of rage. Though you trusted me, I betrayed you, I steal from the purse!"

"I know," Jesus told him, gazing deep into his eyes.

"And you still forgive me?"

"Of course I forgive you. And I have come to comfort you. For I know your suffering, and I am suffering with you. I must share the pain of every man. . . ."

Judas was still on the balcony, in a cold sweat. Only a moment ago Jesus had been there beside him. Now he had vanished.

Judas began to shake. The fiends of dogs were howling again, nosing and barking and rattling the garbage. He could not sleep, he must do something to get out of this accursed place. He must stop this drama of threat and terror before it went any farther.

Jesus was mad, he knew that now. He must be saved before he did himself further harm. Judas must warn the priests: Take him now, before he destroys himself and Israel with him. Deal with him gently, take him away, hold him in custody until after the Passover, at least. Then release him, to wander the countryside as before, healing and helping people. He is a good man, confused but not really dangerous. The people love him; let him light their lives a little while before they— all of us—go down into the grave. . . .

It was chilly, here in the long marble corridor of the house of Annas, but Judas was sweating, every inch of his taut body wet. He had been waiting, it seemed, for hours. If they didn't call him soon, his garments would be drenched. He was also shivering with anxiety, and from the cold. Springing up, he strode about, hugging himself to get warm and trying to regain his composure.

His growing impatience also made him resentful. How dared those two treat him like this? What was going on behind that ornate arched door where Caiaphas, the high priest, had disappeared after a quick half-curt, half-cordial greeting, to confer with his father-in-law? Didn't they realize how important Judas was? Not just one of the lowly fishermen who constituted most of Jesus' enclave, but a brilliant man, a leader: someone who realized their concern about the Master and had volunteered, at great personal risk, to help them.

But he would have to leave. The night was growing late. If he didn't get back to Bethany soon he would be missed. Jesus had gone to see his mother; he might easily have returned by now and miss Judas. Jesus might suspect. Although how could he hope to keep this from the Master? Judas wondered wretchedly. Jesus knew everything; with his eyes of love he bore into you, reading your soul, and pitied you and loved you. *The only person who ever really loved and trusted me,* it came to Judas sickly.

A sudden revulsion swept him—followed by a quick, angry yet welcome sense of relief and reprieve. He would show those priests! The interminable delay had saved him; he would get out of here while he could.

Just then a manservant, looking aloof and condescending, stepped through the fateful doorway and beckoned to him. The gesture riled Judas. *As if I, too, were no better than a servant!* But then the man, sensing his resentment, came dutifully down the hall to him, and announced respectfully enough, "The priests will see you now."

"Oh, *will* they?" Judas could not resist retorting, to show his displeasure. How he loathed it, this sense of inner cringing, even before a slave. But to flee now, to stalk off in injured pride, would accomplish nothing. And they might have him pursued, it occurred to Judas in sudden panic. He might be arrested as an accomplice, forced to testify—instead of treated as a public-spirited citizen, to be praised . . . and paid.

Although the reward, whatever it was, meant nothing, Judas told himself. He would spend it on somebody else, or give it away; he really enjoyed being generous, proving to other people, and himself, that he was not greedy. He might even refuse payment altogether. . . . All he wanted was to be *loved*, he knew bleakly. In a curious way, it was actually love that was leading him blindly through that door to where two men waited to question him: the puzzled hurt of his love for Jesus . . . who loved him, yes—in that genuine caring way he loved all men—yet who didn't really *like* him very much.

The sting of that struck again, like a venomous snake. Goading him, giving him the courage to proceed. Not once, Judas remembered bitterly, did Jesus choose me to go with him on special occasions. No, no, it was always Peter or the twins. Never did his face light up at sight of me the way it did with them . . . or, yes, even that *dog*!

Incredibly, it was the dog that seemed to hound Judas' footsteps into the huge, sumptuous chamber, with its many lamps sparkling, and he could not kick it aside. Ben seemed to crouch there before him on the Persian carpet, panting and looking up at him with his blank yellow eyes. Judas could see Jesus dropping to his knees to hug him, as he had just before they were about to ride into Jerusalem. As he had even today when Ben came slinking around the Temple, of all places! There seemed no way to get rid of him. . . .

Annas and Caiaphas had risen from their couches and were taking Judas' measure, as he was taking theirs. In his quick, astute way, Judas sensed the subtle animosity between them, buried now by some decision they had come to. With a courteous but vaguely disdainful wave of his big hand, Annas bade him sit down to warm himself before the fire that blazed cheerfully on the marble hearth.

"Your teeth are chattering," Annas observed. "You look chilled to the bone."

Judas winced—what an impression to make. Yet he did not miss their quick exchange of glances at how otherwise attractive and seemingly confident he was.

"I am," said Judas, determined not to grovel. "It was cold in the corridor, and I was kept waiting a long time."

An angry envy filled him at the splendor all around him: paneled walls soaring up to an ornately carved ceiling; gold and silver, silk and velvet, pitchers and vases and fancy chairs and tables; flickering candles giving off an incense at once heady and revolting. He had an impression that the old man's taste was atrocious—oversplendid and fat with ugliness and pretension. (If he owned this place, it flashed absurdly through his mind, he would throw out much that was in it and transform it into something fine.) Yet Judas yearned for it, hated Annas for it, and was abject before it. Meanwhile, he could only sit there as proudly as possible in his damp and rumpled garments, head back, ready to present his offer.

"Then we will not waste more of your time," said Annas rudely yet almost joyfully. Turning, he directed Caiaphas to pour their guest a glass of wine. The old priest flung himself back down on his couch of rich brocade, and sprawled there in the Roman manner, rings flashing as he locked his hands behind his leonine head. "Now tell us, what is your relationship with this impostor from Galilee?"

Judas gulped, caught off guard, as much by the sheer ebullience of the man as by the luxury of his surroundings. Even reclining, Annas somehow overpowered them both; though twice their age, he had more energy than either Judas or Caiaphas had ever possessed. Judas was aware of his keen, challenging, vaguely cruel eyes; his thick mouth turned down at the corners even as he smiled. Annas had the ability to diminish people. Even Caiaphas, who sat now, leaning forward, at a handsome, gold-embossed ebony desk—even the haughty high priest seemed to be squirming before him; like Judas, making an effort to appear undaunted and composed. For a second Judas sympathized with Caiaphas.

"How did you get mixed up with Jesus?" The questions began to rain down on Judas from both of them. "Tell us how you, a bright man like you, first fell under his influence and served him so gullibly, it seems, so long. Did you support him from the beginning, or were you lured in later?"

Judas gasped in astonishment; he knew he must fight back. "With all due respect, sirs, it is not I who am on trial. I have come only out of loyalty to Israel to help solve this matter if I can—to give you information—"

"Yes, very well, we are grateful. So give us what we need before we take him—as you can be sure we will." Had the man preached sedition? Had he attacked the priesthood, as he attacked the members of the Sanhedrin? Was it true he had vowed to pull the Temple down with his own hands, but when he chose, he could raise it up again? "Were you present when he violated the sanctity of the Temple by driving out the money changers and freeing the animals meant for sacrifice?"

"Yes, on one occasion."

"Did you try to stop him?"

"No, it was useless. I realized then that he was mad, quite mad, and for his own sake he must be restrained. I beg you, don't be too hard on him, he is a good man, he has done much good for the people, he has done no harm—"

"Then you are here to *defend* him?"

"No, no, no—but yes, in part," Judas pleaded in agony; for this much he must do for the Master. "He has no intention of trying to overthrow the government, to drive out the Romans and take command. His kingdom is not of this world— Wait now, let me explain," Judas amended, as they both jeered in disbelief. "Yes, Jesus speaks of a kingdom here on earth, but only a heavenly kingdom. An earthly paradise that man *can* enjoy right now. One that can be achieved not by overthrowing anybody," he insisted, "but rather by repenting of our sins, forgiving each other and truly loving our neighbors as God commands. Meanwhile, as we learn to live such lives here, we are preparing to live forever in Paradise when we die." Judas mopped his brow; he could see they were restless, agitated. "I'm afraid I haven't made it very clear."

Impatiently, Annas threw up his hands. "Well—it's nonsense!" He laughed shortly. "It's hard to make nonsense clear." Sitting up, the old priest crouched on the lounge, grinning faintly, like a lion licking its chops as it regards its prey. "We'll get back to the so-called kingdom later. Speaking of nonsense—what about all that ridiculous talk of miracles? Feeding thousands of people with a couple of loaves of bread?"

"And a few dead fish," Caiaphas broke in, snickering.

Walking on the water, even raising the dead? Had Judas seen these miracles, participated in them himself? What kind of trickery or sorcery was it that made people believe such things? Sorcery, the black arts, were serious matters, forbidden by law. Even healings, however authentic, were not always from God but from witches, the devil.

"It's said that you men heal too. Is that true?"

"Some of them, yes." Judas was squirming. Even in this he had been disappointed. His words were partly defense, partly confession: "I'm afraid I never could."

Annas sneered slightly. Judas could feel his disdain. "Don't worry, it's not that important. Let's get back to sedition: *That is!* No matter how you put it, the man has a lot of people thinking he's going to be their king."

"They're wrong, it's not like that at all, as I tried to explain."

"The people don't think so. It's all over Jerusalem that Jesus rode into the city one day on an Abyssinian ass, as foretold by the prophets, and the crowds went crazy, screaming and throwing flowers and calling him king!"

"Why didn't you stop them?" Caiaphas broke in acidly.

"There were not that many," Judas said. "Actually only a few hundred by the time we reached the Temple. Jesus paid little attention to them, he made no claims whatever."

"He sounds mad indeed," Caiaphas snorted.

Annas only leaned back, fingers locked, and sat for a moment, studying his rings. "Another madman who thinks he's the Messiah," he sighed. But when he looked up, his eyes were cunning. "Tell me," he demanded softly, "have you heard him make such claims?"

Judas was writhing, the sweat beginning to pour from his body again. He wiped his brow with his sleeve. *The Father and I are one. . . . For the Father loves the son and shows him everything he does. . . . Anyone who rejects me rejects the Father. . . . I am the bread of life, I am the light, I am the way, the truth and the life; no man comes to the Father except by me.* . . . The awesome litany of these phrases he had heard so many times were chanting in his head. Judas swallowed, not daring to answer; he stared wretchedly into the fire, unable to meet their eyes.

"Tell us, you fool!" Annas roared suddenly. "You know him, you've been with him these past three years. Have you heard him? Do *you* think he is the Messiah?"

"I don't *know!*" Judas moaned.

They stared at him in silence. "Then why are you here?" the old man asked contemptuously. "Are you for or against him? Nobody asked you—you came of your own free will." He leaned forward. "You look scared. . . . Look at him!" Annas said to Caiaphas, cruelly bemused. "He is cowering." He turned back to Judas, his tone almost fatherly. "If you want to back out, you are free to leave right now Don't be afraid. We will not have someone follow you and chop off your head. Not tonight anyway!" Annas laughed uproariously, and Caiaphas, to his own disgust, politely joined in.

"No," said Annas seriously, "it was your duty to come to us." With an expansive gesture, he signaled his son-in-law to refill Judas' silver goblet with the deep red wine. "And we are grateful for your offer to lead us to him. For his own good," he added.

"When?" Judas whispered. He held the cold goblet with trembling hands and tried to sip the wine, but his mouth was so dry he could not swallow.

Caiaphas spoke up. It galled him to have Annas acting as if everything was his own idea. "Thursday night," he said.

"But that is the eve of the Paschal supper," Annas protested.

"Exactly. Take him by surprise after he has finished. We would not interfere with that," Caiaphas said piously, savoring his own wine for a second, then setting down his cup. "Put him away—at least until the city is free of all these pilgrims. Thousands—I've never seen so many, have you, Annas?" he deferred. "It can't be done publicly, a lot of them are crazy for him. . . . We differed about that," Caiaphas informed Judas. "I finally agreed. My father-in-law is right—it must be done in secret or there could be trouble."

"Where will he be?" Annas broke in eagerly. "They say he's a good son—is he likely to be with his mother? I understand she's visiting Elizabeth. Beautiful women, both of them; I've seen them a number of times, poor things. I knew Zacharias well, of course." He was shaking his head as he rambled. "I feel sorry for them—a pity to have such sons!"

"No," Judas said unsteadily. "He had promised to have the holy meal with us."

"Us?"

"His apostles," Judas admitted. "The place hasn't been chosen yet, not to my knowledge. But I'm sure it will be somewhere on the Mount of Olives, near Gethsemane." His voice shook. "Jesus loves to go into the garden there—to pray."

"Good, good." The two priests exchanged signals. Annas got to his feet, as if the whole matter was settled. "And you will let us know as soon as you can." It sounded like an order.

Judas bridled. Something stubborn and wounded held him back. He was furious with himself for having submitted to their inquisition, and now this—manipulation. No mention as yet of any reward; not even a hint of money! Not that it mattered in itself, he thought indignantly, just this brisk assumption that he was now in the palm of their hands. It was crawling through him again, that old bewildered protest: Why didn't people appreciate him? No matter what lengths he went to, why wasn't he praised and rewarded? In his folly he had surrendered himself up to be used by these selfish, scheming men.

But now, it seemed, he had no choice. "I will try," Judas said coldly, after a minute of strain. "I will report back to you."

Annas, sensing something wrong, grabbed him, pulled him up and with a kind of amiable rudeness flung his arms around him. "Good, good!" he repeated. "As soon as possible. We will expect you!"

Judas was thrown off balance, both by the action and by the tone of his words. And it struck him, during their awkward embrace, that despite Annas' power and vigor, he was in the clutches of a very old man who smelled of death and decay.

"You are a brave man to do this for the house of Israel." Annas was flattering him. "And a very handsome one—we noticed that the minute you walked in, didn't we, son?" With a lift of his shaggy eyebrows he solicited Caiaphas' cooperation. "You will never regret this," Annas continued heartily. Judas felt himself being propelled firmly toward the door. "You will be well rewarded."

At last! In sheer self-respect, Judas halted, stood rigid. "How?" he demanded.

Annas was taken aback. He looked actually hurt. "In money, of course," he said, frowning. Then he shrugged, made a grandly impatient gesture. "A good deal of money—whatever you think it's worth."

"Once we *have* him," Caiaphas reminded sharply.

"Yes," said Annas, "once we have him."

"And you will not harm him?" Judas pleaded. He felt weak, on the point of tears. "You will protect him? He will not be harmed?"

"He will be dealt with fairly, we promise you," said the old priest, shutting the door.

The two stared at each other, once Judas was gone.

"What do you think of him?" Annas asked. "Can he be trusted?"

"Nobody can ever be trusted," Caiaphas said sardonically. "Especially a traitor. It doesn't matter; he's already given us enough information to find the man without him, if we have to." He began looking around for his cloak, preparing to leave. He was exhausted. Coming here tonight was almost more than he could take. The whole ugly business—Rome on his back, Pilate, Herod. The Sanhedrin agreed something had to be done, and soon. But not, of course, without the approval of the old man.

"Get word to the council members," Annas ordered.

Caiaphas halted, groaning. "Why? I told you I have been in conference with them all day. They simply want to be done with this, most of them, get rid of him—kill him."

"Without a trial? No, we must go through the proprieties. Warn them to be ready for any emergency," Annas said wearily, striving for patience. "You may have to call them back in the dead of night. They should be prepared to come—never mind that it's a holy night, when they will want to be with their families. Make them aware that he must have a hearing, no matter when." Annas was thoughtful for a minute. "But whatever you do," he warned, "bring him to me before you make any final decisions. I want to meet this Jesus, whoever he is—judge him for myself."

Chapter 21

*O*H, no, not Cleophas, Abner thought, entering his small white cell in the priests' quarters that morning to disrobe. He stared in amazement at his uninvited guest.

"Cleo, my friend!" he exclaimed, in a voice that tried to conceal his dismay. "How did you find me? There are strict orders"—he made a little gesture of concern—"especially right now. I'm surprised they let you in."

"I bribed them."

"How like you!" Abner gave a short, dry laugh as they embraced. But he spoke without asperity. "Why have you gone to such risk just to see me?"

"Mary," Cleo said abruptly. There was no hint of his old debonair manner; his face was serious. "She is very worried about her son."

There was an awkward silence. "Poor Mary." Abner bit his long upper lip and shook his head. He was nearly bald now and his ears stuck out more than ever. He had a bulging forehead, a long pointed nose, and troubled if vaguely smiling eyes. He had always felt meek, ugly and sexless beside Cleo. Yes, and beside Joseph, who had bested both of them for Mary's hand. Though he himself had dreamed of Mary and always would, it embarrassed him even now to remember that his father had dared to challenge those formidable rivals.

The old feeling of despairing inadequacy came over Abner. But he couldn't let it stop him from shedding this smelly bloodstained garment in which he'd been serving since dawn. With deliberate boldness, trying to keep his fingers steady, he unfastened it, kicked it aside, and began to wash his gaunt but hairy body in the basin that was waiting.

"Mary has cause to worry. I wish there was something I could do for her."

"She thinks there is. We have just had a long discussion. She asked me to come."

Abner looked up, startled. "Then she's here in Jerusalem?"

"Yes. For the first time since Joseph died. She's staying with her aunt."

"Elizabeth? John's mother?" Abner frowned. "That's a mistake. It's not good to call attention to that relationship right now. And it must be hard on both of them."

"They're very close. They seem to need each other. Abner, tell me—I must know," Cleo demanded. "How far has the plot against Jesus advanced here in the Temple? Is he really in danger? If so, will you intercede for him?" As the priest hesitated: "Tell me honestly, Abner. I can judge only by rumors and the things I hear and see on the streets. What is the situation?"

"Bad. Very bad," said Abner soberly. He bent over to dry his long knobby feet. How awkward and ludicrous this was. Never mind, they had known each other since boyhood. "Jesus was warned," he said regretfully. "If only he'd stay away from Jerusalem, or be more careful. That attack on the money changers. And the things he says!"

"He speaks the truth." Cleo was hunched forward on his chair, turning a big ring round and round on his finger. "For several days now I've been listening to him, and each hour my conviction grows. More and more I realize—" Cleo's voice broke.

Abner had never dreamed this once carefree man could be so moved. "Yes," said Abner, "I agree. Jesus is right. Just as John was right." The tragedy of John hung over them, unspoken. "They're two of a kind. I saw that long ago when they were just boys in the Temple, so bright and keen, both of them. Rebels . . . John was, even then, and Jesus would be later, but both holding so much hope for the common people. Seeing through the hypocrisy and deceit that I know from personal experience. A bunch of us here *are* whited sepulchers, freshly painted for the festivals but tombs filled with rot and dust inside."

Angrily, vigorously, Abner had been drying himself as he spoke. He kicked the towel aside, as he had kicked the garment, and squatted to bring fresh clothing from a small pine chest. "Make no mistake, I'm all for Jesus. I'll never forget the first time I saw him, when he was presented at the Temple, with his father. It was his first sacrifice. For some reason, Joseph had never brought him before, which seemed to me strange. He'd never seen the lambs slaughtered, at least not in that way. I'm glad it was not my task to use the knife, or to carry up the portion to be burned, but only to bring him the body to be roasted for the evening meal. I will never forget his eyes—his beautiful, stricken eyes. He looked sick, Cleo. As if he himself had just been slain."

Abner pulled a fresh robe of simple homespun over his head, and tied it at his waist. "I have thought of that so often as I go about my foolish business. Of what use is all this burning? Over and over I hear the words of the great prophets—Amos, Samuel, Hosea, Jeremiah— that these rites mean nothing unless the heart is pure; accompanied by honest repentance, not just bribes to curry favor. Otherwise, they're an insult to our Maker. What really matters is that we keep those first commandments—to love God with all our hearts and souls and minds, and our neighbors as ourselves."

"Jesus spoke those very words only yesterday," Cleo said. "I heard him. But—forgive me, Abner, I must get back to Mary. Since you feel this way, surely I can go to her with words of hope. You will try to stop this thing. You will speak out for her son."

Abner was shoving his long feet into their sandals. A toe was caught in the thong; he bent over to try and free it. When he looked up, his face was troubled. "Cleo, Cleo," he mourned softly, "don't you suppose I have already done all I can? From the beginning. From the time word first began coming in from the provinces about his following, I have spoken out for him. This wonderful man, living so simply, never taking a penny, the way some so-called healers do. Doing nothing but good, helping so many people—why, the lepers alone! Mine was the first voice raised to protest the spying. At least, one of the first," Abner added. "There were others—Nicodemus spoke out. He's a wealthy Pharisee, as you know, he has more authority than I do. And Joseph of Arimathea, a scribe. A few others, who don't like what's going on in the Sanhedrin; people who have a lot more prestige than I do."

Abner threw up his hands. "But, Cleo, nobody listened! Certainly not to me. I'm just a lowly priest. For all the years I've served in the

Temple, I have never advanced—nor wanted to. Why should I? What inspiration has there been? My wife died years ago; I have neither wife nor children."

"Nor have I," said Cleophas.

"Didn't you marry once?"

"It was a mistake."

"But now—?" Abner caught himself. He wanted to ask about Mary, but he was apprehensive. The subject was still sensitive for both of them. He cleared his throat and started again. "I have no influence and very few friends. As you know, I was never the most sociable person in Nazareth. In fact, I've antagonized practically every chief priest since I came here—especially Caiaphas. He knows I detest him. It would be useless for me to try to interfere now. It might even make things worse."

"But something must be *done*," Cleophas said desperately. "Tell me—so far you have told me only that the situation is bad. *What is going on?*"

"I know only that there is a plot, plans have been made. I don't know the details, only that they're bound to arrest him soon."

"*When?*"

"I can't say. There is much confusion. Caiaphas seems to have been waiting for approval from his father-in-law. They hate to strike during Passover week, for fear of the crowds, but it might be their last chance. If they wait much longer, they're afraid he will get away."

Cleo's head was spinning. "But the Passover is almost here! The Pasch begins tomorrow." He was alarmed. "Then it could happen anytime? Tomorrow, or even today!"

Abner nodded, pressing his hands to his mouth. "I doubt seriously if it will be by day—again for fear of the crowds. When they take him, as I'm convinced they will, it will probably be at night."

"Why, *why?*" Cleophas groaned. "In heaven's name, why should they do such a thing to such a good man?"

"Jealousy," said Abner flatly. "The priests are his real enemies, Cleo. The others in the Sanhedrin"—his tone was disparaging—"the Pharisees and Sadducees . . . certainly they are furious at the things he says about them; they can't bear to hear the truth about themselves. But it is the priests who wield the power, and the priests are jealous. We priests have the most to lose. Once he comes—if he comes—this

Messiah, we'll be out of work. And Jesus claims to be the Messiah; not in so many words, perhaps, but it's plain in everything he says and does. And people believe it, Cleo, thousands of people. This is dangerous, I can see that; it could lead to an uprising, an attempt to overthrow Rome and proclaim him king." Abner shuddered. "It couldn't succeed, of course; it would only result in terrible bloodshed, another slaughter of the Jewish people. We might not survive as a nation."

"Surely you're not siding with the Sanhedrin!"

"No, no, no. I love Jesus. I want him to be free to go about preaching his gospel of love and healing, even denouncing the authorities, if he can get away with it—they need to be exposed. But not here in Jerusalem. And I beg you, go to him at once and urge him to leave before it's too late. I will go with you, if you think that would do any good. It is the best I can do—*all* I can do. We must warn him not to mislead the people into thinking he is the Messiah. Otherwise, he will only meet the fate of all the Zealots and false messiahs before him."

"Jesus is not a Zealot," Cleo declared fiercely, to his own surprise. "Nor a false messiah!" His teeth clenched, for this was hard. "He is the true Savior. He is the fulfillment of the Law. He wasn't sent to deliver us from Rome, but to deliver all men from our sins. Even *me*," he muttered. "So that we will be worthy to enter his kingdom—which is not of this earth, Abner, but of God."

The priest had been striding nervously about the room. Now he wheeled and stared at him, astounded. This could not be Cleophas uttering such words. Preposterous. "Come now, Cleo—you, of all people!" Abner could feel his own face grimacing, half in amusement, half in distress. "Such a Deliverer, if he ever comes, will not *be* of this world. How he will appear, or when, none of us knows. Certainly not from Nazareth, our old hometown! We laughed uncomfortably. "Not the son of someone we've known for years—much as I respect Mary and Joseph."

Cleo was torn. "I know, I know—I once said that very same thing." His heart was hammering. He could postpone this no longer. "But Jesus is not Joseph's son."

"What do you mean?" Abner gasped. There was a long moment of silence. Both were breathing hard. "Whose?" Abner demanded. And when Cleo did not answer: *"Yours?"*

Cleophas jolted, as if he had been stabbed. "Would that he were," he said gruffly.

"Then what are you trying to tell me?"

"Jesus is all he claims. He is no man's son. He has no earthly father."

"You must be out of your mind. What makes you believe such a thing? Did Joseph confide this to you?"

"No," Cleophas said loyally. "Close as we were, Joseph was proud, it was his secret. And I know that to him Jesus was as dear, as close—even closer than his own sons; for actually the two of them were very much alike. It was Mary who told me, but only long after Joseph was gone. She, too, respected her husband's pride, but she felt it important that I should know the truth. Their first son—her son, at least—was the long expected One."

"How does she know?" Abner was staggered, still trying to comprehend. "Whose son was he, then, if not Joseph's?"

"God's son, born of a virgin, as the scriptures have foretold," Cleo cried, trying to keep resentment and impatience from his tone. "Mary would never lie, you must know that. Certainly not about so sacred a thing. It was a miracle even she could not describe—or would not, even for me. But it is true, knowing Mary—it is true. She wanted me to know; I've been so close to the family, they made me one of them. And I loved the boy so much. More than ever, after Joseph died. For years he has been like my own son."

"You are lucky," Abner said unexpectedly, his eyes wistful. "To have been so close to her so long."

"Yes, very lucky. I have always loved her." They regarded each other a minute, remembering. "And so have you."

Abner nodded. "I doubt if there was a youth our age who didn't, once he saw her."

"Her father did right to give her to Joseph," Cleo acknowledged. "Joseph was the only one she ever wanted—or ever will."

"Even now?"

"Yes. I have begged her to marry me and let me take care of her. But she won't even listen, she doesn't even hear me out. All she can think of is Jesus."

"But if something should happen to him—"

"It can't—it mustn't. We must find a way to stop it!"

"Bring her to me. I will see what I can do."

"But you have said—" Cleo was puzzled. "Can you tell me what it is? I don't want to give her false hope."

"Cleo, I'm going to be honest. I long to see Mary again. I used to watch for glimpses of her in the Temple when she and Joseph came each year. But it has been so long, several years now, and she may never come to Jerusalem again."

Cleo exploded. "That's not fair to Mary!"

"No, wait, listen—it might help. I can promise nothing, of course. But I can urge her to let me go with her to find Jesus and warn him of what I know. That his life is in danger as long as he stays in Jerusalem. I will, of course, find out everything else I can. Together we may be able to persuade him; surely he will listen to his mother."

"Mary has never interfered with Jesus."

"Not even to save him? You said she was desperate."

"I don't know. I will ask her."

"Bring her to me," Abner pleaded. "She can refuse my offer— only let me present it to her. If she does refuse, I will do one more thing. I will bypass Caiaphas and go directly to Annas, his father-in-law. Again, I can promise nothing, I may not even get an audience— but Annas is unpredictable. Who knows what miracle might happen? It's only the slimmest hope, of course, but it might be enough to make him reconsider, at least postpone doing anything rash."

"Must you bring Mary into this?"

"I long to see her once more," Abner repeated. "Surely that is not too much to ask. Not here, of course, but in my quarters. I am going there now—after making some inquiries that could be of help. Take this address." Abner tore a piece of parchment from a roll in the cupboard, and scribbled. "It's in the lower city, not a very fashionable place. At the end of the alley beyond the market, and up some steps. Bring her, if possible, shortly after the sun has set."

Cleo's head was reeling. "I will try," he said.

It was almost dark when they reached the city. They could see its lights already shining as they approached.

After the quiet village, and riding through the countryside, Jerusalem was like a suddenly opened madhouse of people, lights, music, voices and braying beasts.

Roman soldiers stood guard on every corner, or rode impressively through the traffic of camels, donkeys and human beings, attempting to keep order. The shops and bazaars were open. The streets were mobbed with pilgrims. Clad in colorful costumes, Greeks and Egyptians, Africans, Sicilians, Phoenicians, mingled with Judeans, laughing and shouting, their shoes making a windlike shuffling song on the walks as they bustled along. Bonfires burned, musicians were playing, people were dancing on the Temple grounds.

Cleo reached down from his horse to grasp the halter of the burro he had brought for Mary, and guide them through the chaos. To Mary it was like a nightmare, some bizarre dream of carnival and celebration, impervious to impending disaster.

They skirted the Temple area and proceeded along alleys, and up and down tiers of steps, the animals picking their way, past caves where the poor huddled in their doorways, to a honeycomb of dwellings built upon a hillside that reared up from the paving stones. Cleo consulted his scrap of parchment, then looked up, squinting. At last he pulled the animals to a halt. "This must be the place. Wait here; I'll go up to make sure."

Presently he returned. "Yes, he's there. I will take you to him. Then I will excuse myself, and come back for you later."

"Oh, Cleo, shouldn't you stay with me?" Mary asked nervously.

"No, I honestly think it would be best for you to talk to Abner alone."

Mary's heart was pounding. She was filled with dread.

Yet when she saw Abner a strange calm came over her. She felt his innate purity and selflessness: a quality of some half-wistful, half-skeptical awareness of life, with all its troubles, that he would serve as best he could, asking nothing in return. She had sensed this as a girl—somewhat impatiently then. Now she recognized it as a balm to her troubled spirit, a place where for a few moments her emotions could be moored. She smiled and pressed his hand and sat down where he indicated, on a small couch covered with camel's hair.

Abner's quarters were small but cheerful, and tastefully furnished. A rug of orange and blue covered the entire floor. There were several footstools and chairs, a chest on which sat a pleasant array of glass jugs. At one end, shelves from floor to ceiling were filled with scrolls, their pale gold wooden spindles smooth and worn from much use.

His surroundings were as scrubbed and spare as his face, yet there was a sense of warmth and welcome, too, as he moved about, lighting a few more lamps.

Mary sat waiting, determined, but dignified and very still, only her eyes betraying the anxiety she felt. "It is good to see you, Abner," she told him when at last he sat down across from her. "You must know how much Joseph and I always appreciated the kind things you did for Jesus."

"You have blessed my home for coming. I wish I could have done more. I saw your son all too seldom."

"You know, of course, that is why I am here," Mary stated simply. "To ask you to do even more now."

"Yes," Abner assured her. "And surely you know I will do whatever I can. But I will be direct. As I told Cleo, I have little influence with the priests, but I do know of their plans. My advice is to find Jesus as quickly as possible—now, tonight. I will go with you—do you know where he is staying?"

"Yes, of course, but—"

"If necessary, I will help him escape. I doubt seriously if he'll be in any danger once he is out of the city. In time this whole thing may blow over. But now, right now, for him to stay here is simply not safe."

Mary was shaking her head. "It would be futile," she said. "Jesus would never flee, no matter what the threat. I couldn't ask him to, Abner." She spoke with quiet conviction, her hands locked across her breast. "He is a man of destiny. His actions are guided by God. But I am also his mother. I can't sit idly by and let something terrible happen to my son. Not if it can be prevented. Yet going to Jesus is not the answer; he is not the one to be persuaded. It is those who would be guilty of his blood!"

Mary paused, gripping her throat. In the silence, an awareness of the soft summer evening came upon them. Children were playing in the street below; footsteps went by in a hall, a pot crashed somewhere, a baby was crying. There was the faint fragrance of a jug of flowers on the sill, and the hot, oily odor of a family's late supper frying.

"Abner, as an old friend I ask you—yes, beg you—go to the high priest, as you told Cleo you might, and plead for Jesus. Go to Annas, to the Sanhedrin, whoever is responsible, and warn them. For their own souls' sake, they must not, dare not, take my son!"

Abner was staring at her, his thin phthisic face in torment, and she knew, as his lips twitched and he briefly closed his eyes, that Cleo was right—a ghost of the old love haunted Abner still.

"Mary, Mary," he said on a note of despair, "you know I would do anything for you. I would gladly die for you, if it would help. But it won't, I realize that now. It was mad of me to even suggest such a thing. They would not listen, the plans have gone too far."

"How do you know?" Mary gasped.

"I learned just since seeing Cleo this morning—one of Jesus' own men is bargaining to betray him."

"Who?"

"I don't know. They know I'm Jesus' friend, they tell me very little. I know only that it will be soon. Jesus' only hope is to flee."

"He can't, he won't," Mary said fiercely. "Abner, you must try!" And suddenly, incredibly, in her desperation, she heard herself saying words she had sworn never to utter. "Abner, if ever you loved me, I beg you to give me at least the hope that you will try!"

"I will try," Abner said hoarsely. "I owe you that much for coming. Forgive me for being selfish; I wanted so much to see you." He sat stiffly apart from her, arms folded, lest he be tempted to touch her hand. "Because yes, you are right: I will never get over the sweetness and the pain of loving you."

"Oh, Abner, I'm so sorry."

"No, no, don't be. Love is a beautiful thing, no matter how futile—it doesn't have to be returned." He raised his eyes and gazed at her openly now, his whole bearing honest, generous and warm. His eyes had brightened; he managed a whimsical smile. "And I'm glad your father had the good sense to give you to Joseph. You could never have loved me, or Cleo, or anyone the way you loved him. God meant you to be together. I have never seen two people so much in love. Even later, years after you were married, though I envied Joseph, I rejoiced for both of you."

"Yes," Mary said gently, returning his smile. "I could never love anyone but Joseph. Then, or now."

They rode back to Ein Karem in silence, too troubled to speak. By taking back streets, they avoided the heart of the city, but the sky was still painted with the orange glow of bonfires, and faintly the sounds of celebration could be heard. Even in the country they were aware of it, though here the Paschal moon reigned peacefully, drenching the hills and valleys with its silver light.

To their surprise, as they approached the cave and cistern at the bottom of the steps, Ben came bounding to meet them. And Jesus was waiting there, so tall and radiant in the moonlight he seemed, for an instant, a mirage. "Mother!" he cried softly. "I was about to leave." He was warm and real, reaching out to lift her down; Mary could feel her son's hard muscles beneath the white garment, and the prickling of his curly beard against her cheek.

Cleo dismounted, his face working. He was biting back tears in his relief. "We were afraid we might not see you tonight. Thank God you're all right." .

Jesus smiled. "Elizabeth has kept your supper warm," he told Mary. "Why don't you go on up? You look tired. I will help Cleo care for the beasts."

Mary clung to him, for a minute too shaken to speak. Looking up, she saw Elizabeth standing in the doorway with a lamp. "Yes," she said calmly. "I won't keep her waiting. But join me as soon as you can."

Cleo's eyes followed her small figure up the steps. How quickly Mary always moved, as if in pursuit of something both important and filled with promise . . . even now, he marveled.

"Jesus, we're worried," he said bluntly. Scowling, he took up a bucket and began lowering it into the well. "You should be protected. Where are your guards?"

"You mean my apostles? Asleep by now, I hope. They have other things to do. I don't need their protection."

"Be reasonable, Jesus. You are in terrible danger. Your mother and I have been to see Abner—"

"I know."

"He says you must leave at once. Tonight, if possible!"

"Cleo, I can't leave until my work is done."

"But Abner has found out—he told us tonight—one of your men is not to be trusted."

Jesus was petting the horse as it drank thirstily from the pail. Its neck was sleek and rippling beneath his hand. He remembered its sharp, familiar tang—like vinegar; how often he had ridden it with Cleo. He lifted his eyes to Cleo. "I realize that."

"And you know who it is?"

"Yes."

"Then get rid of him! In heaven's name, get rid of him, for he is about to turn you in."

Jesus slowly shook his head. "Judas is a tormented man," he said, with deep compassion. "He is tempted beyond his powers to resist. He cannot help his nature. I cannot turn my back on him."

"But if he is willing to betray you—!"

"It would change nothing. What good would it do for me to reject him? The authorities can take me anytime they want." Jesus had turned his attention to the donkey, which was rattling the other bucket. This time it was he who lowered the pail into the cistern; it tipped slowly on its side as the water filled it. The crank made a squealing sound as he brought it up, dripping. He poured some into another container for Ben. "Each day I have preached and healed openly before the crowds," he said, wiping his hands on his robe. "Right there in the courts of the Temple. They know where to find me. If they are bargaining with my betrayer, it is only in the hope of taking me by surprise—when they are ready."

Cleo was staring at him, incredulous. "Surely you're not going to submit to this?" he protested. "You're not going to let this *happen!*"

Jesus regarded him steadily. "I can do nothing to stop them."

"Of course you can!" Cleo bawled, unable to conceal his frustration. "You can leave Jerusalem, as Abner advised—and believe me, he knows what's going on. He seems to be the only priest who's stood up for you in the Sanhedrin. He's willing to risk everything for you now—he'll help you escape. He urged your mother to let him try to persuade you."

"And she refused."

"Yes, unfortunately—although I can see you wouldn't have listened anyway. She would never ask you to compromise. She insists it is the priests who should give in. Abner promised he would do his best—at least go to Caiaphas, even Annas."

Jesus had cupped the soft velvet nose of the horse, that it might nuzzle his hand. His face was tender. "Mother knows in her heart there is nothing she can do to save me. As Elizabeth could not save John. But it's a wonderful thing to know she tried."

Cleo could bear no more. He wheeled and, jerking on the strap, led the donkey into the cave to be tied. He was trembling, appalled, filled with a blind outrage as he thought of Mary. How could Jesus do this to them? Jesus, of all people, surely knew that to be arrested now could well mean a death as certain and brutal as that of John. . . . *And what that monstrous death had done to Elizabeth, his own death could do to Mary.*

Cleophas stood a moment, struggling to get hold of himself. When he returned, he spoke grimly. "Then you are willing to stand idly by and let this happen, regardless of the cost to others?"

"Cleo, whatever happens to me is not my will," Jesus said quietly, "but that of the Father. As I have said over and over, I can do nothing of myself. Nothing I have done on earth is of my own power. Every word I have spoken . . . those are not my words, Cleo, but only what the Father sent me to tell the people, for they lead to eternal life. Every miracle I have performed is from the Father. I am but the instrument of his power."

Jesus paused. The moon beamed down; in the depths of the dark well its shining face was reflected.

"Everything is for his glory, Cleo . . . as the final miracle will be. To make men believe in his words, and in me."

Cleo gasped. For one wild instant he misunderstood, and dared to take heart. "Then you will save yourself! Or God will save you?"

There was a charged silence between them. "No, Cleo."

Cleophas stared at him, bewildered. "You mean you are going to let them . . . *kill* you?" A sound of agony came from his throat—then anger. "But why, why, *why?*" he shouted. "In heaven's name, why should you suffer such a fate now? You are still young, we need you, the world needs you. What can be accomplished by such a pointless sacrifice?"

"It is not pointless," Jesus said quietly. "It is the only sacrifice that can really matter. It is written—the seed must be placed in the earth and die before it can rise up again and bear fruit. I am that seed, Cleo. The Son of Man must be lifted up to die. Only in this way can I draw all men to me—and to the Father. . . . It was written long ago."

"Lifted up?" Cleophas muttered fiercely. A chill smote him. "Don't put it that way," he begged. "That is the manner of the crucifixion. Only the crucified are actually *lifted up*. Common criminals—

on the cross! You can't mean that. You sometimes speak in parables; this was—surely this was only a figure of speech."

Jesus looked up. He had crouched to pet the dog, now dozing contentedly at his feet. "No, Cleo."

Cleophas paled. He stared at Jesus, aghast. "And you are not *troubled?*"

"*Troubled?*" Jesus gave a little moan.

Slowly he rose, and stood gazing at the sky. A few white clouds were drifting, like small ships among the sparkling stars. The moon baptized him in brilliance—his garments, his hair, his uplifted face. "Of course my soul is troubled! I don't want to die to this earth any more than you do, Cleo, even for a little while." Jesus' voice shook. "This beautiful night . . . " He was drinking it in. "This horse you and I rode so often across the fields . . ."

Jesus turned, and Cleo saw that his eyes were wet. "You, Cleo, so warm and alive sitting there—what a friend you are, how I love you. . . . And my apostles, my family . . . and oh, Cleo, my mother! Yes, my heart is troubled. But what can I pray?" he asked. " 'Father, save me from this hour'? 'I'm sorry, Father, but the Son of Man has fallen in love with his life on earth as a man, so change your plan, save me from what lies ahead'? No. Because it was for this hour that I was sent."

Jesus came and sat down beside Cleo on the worn stone ledge. For what seemed a long time, they were silent. Then Jesus went on.

"Cleo, I cherish every moment. But now I have to finish my mission. . . . God wants so much to spare his children the terrible burden of sin. He doesn't want them to go on butchering his creatures, or paying money to buy forgiveness for those sins!" Jesus' fists clenched; he was shaking his head. "They don't have to anymore, Cleo: I will take it all on my shoulders. By my sacrifice I can free them, I can fulfill the Law for them. I have been sent to promise eternal life to everyone who follows the words I have spoken, and believes. They will live forever in a place even more beautiful—far more beautiful than this." He gazed about at the lovely night. "A place where there is no suffering . . . You must believe that, Cleo."

Cleophas returned the pressure of Jesus' hand. "I do believe," he said gruffly. "Only this day I confessed that to Abner. Not because I wanted him to help you, but because it was on my heart. You are the

Messiah!" he cried brokenly. "Just as Mary tried to tell me long ago. But this . . . sacrifice you speak of. I still don't understand. I love you too much to accept it. I cannot accept it—" Cleo covered his face; his broad shoulders shook. "How can your *mother* accept it?"

Jesus put his arms around him to comfort him. "Because she *is* my mother," he said quietly. "Chosen out of all women on earth to give me life, and stand by me to the end. It is why I have come tonight, that we might have this time together, and I can help her face what is ahead."

"Yes, yes, yes," Cleo said thickly. Impatiently he wiped at his eyes. "You should be alone. I must go; I have kept you here too long."

"You, too, are our family," Jesus assured him warmly. "Come up with me, eat something, stay with us."

"No, I'm not hungry. It has been a long day, and I must ride back into Jerusalem. Magdalene will be waiting, and Salome—all the women who followed you and served you. They are gathered in a small house near the Sheep's Gate, and they are anxious for word of you."

Jesus smiled. "Tell them it warms my heart to know they are here. Tell them how much I love them for all they have done for me. Ask them to pray for me," he said, "but tell them not to be concerned, for the Father is with me."

Elizabeth had kept supper warm, and Mary made a pretense of eating. They were waiting on the roof when Jesus finally joined them. "I was talking with Cleophas," he said. "Forgive us for taking so long."

"No, it was very important that you did," Mary said.

Jesus sat between the women, holding their hands in his big strong ones. For a long time they sat thus, under the stars, surprised at the sudden sense of peace and tranquility that filled them. The moon was growing smaller and paler now, an opal, but the stars were fields of diamonds. The glow of distant bonfires had faded from the horizon, and most of the lights of Jerusalem had vanished; the city, weary from merriment, slept. Yet they sat on, murmuring quietly together, as Jesus spoke of all that was to come.

They were not to lose faith or grieve, he told them; what had been designed from the beginning of time was about to be fulfilled. As they already realized, they were both a part of it, chosen by the Father himself for their sweetness and goodness, their courage and their strength.

"You have already suffered much, and you will suffer more. But your reward will be very real, and greater than it is within your power to imagine. Elizabeth . . ." Taking her chin in his hands, Jesus lifted her face. "I have seen John in a vision, and you, too, will see him again."

Elizabeth caught her breath, and for a second closed her eyes. Reading her thoughts, Jesus bent to kiss them. "He is whole and beautiful, Elizabeth, even more beautiful than before. And I have seen his father with him: He and Zacharias are together in this new dimension of absolute purity and love. They love you so much, Aunt Elizabeth," he said fervently, squeezing her hand. "They are waiting for you."

Jesus turned to his mother. "And Joachim . . . and Joseph—" Jesus bit his lips; he could not go on. He could only hold her tightly against him, cradling her as she wept. . . .

Elizabeth kissed them and crept off to bed. The two sat alone together then and spoke as mother and son, of all they remembered of their life in Nazareth: his father, his grandparents, the other children, their cousins, the sheep, their dogs. "I'm so glad Benjy is with you," Mary said. "Cleo and I were both worried when he ran off again, after following us so far."

Jesus was smiling. "Yes, I'm glad he found me. Each day he shows up at the Temple and flops down to listen, as near as he can get."

"Oh, dear, the way people feel about dogs! Aren't your apostles embarrassed?"

"Only Judas," Jesus said.

They spoke again of the family. "We had good times together," Jesus said. "No man could have had a better home. God could not have chosen a better father for us. And you—" He lifted Mary's hand and pressed it to his lips. "There are no words to tell you—" He broke off, deeply moved as he remembered. "I know how hard all this has been for you. Loving all your children so much, trying to keep peace in the family . . . and the things people have said."

"It was my honor, Jesus," Mary said softly. "What mother on earth has ever been so honored?"

Again they sat for a time in silence, almost fearing to speak, knowing that time was running out.

"You must be brave," Jesus said at last. "The next days will be hard for you." He spoke of some of the things he had told Cleophas. "Spare yourself. I beg you, stay here with Elizabeth. Don't follow me. Brave and strong as you are, it is too much to ask of any woman." He hesitated. His voice, when he spoke again, was firm. "But no matter what happens, remember this: I will come back. Whatever they do, I will rise up and return again!"

Mary's hands were locked across her breast; her heart was in her eyes. "Of course you will," she said quietly. "I have always known it. For you are the Messiah sent to save the world. Nothing can destroy you, ever!" She gazed at him questioningly for a moment. "And you will stay on with us?" she pleaded.

Jesus couldn't bear it. He plunged his face into his hands. It was late, he must go; there was much to do tomorrow. He could hear Ben barking, and the clicking of the dog's nails as he came seeking them across the tiles.

Jesus lifted his eyes. "No, Mother," he had to tell her. "I will come again, but only for a little while. Only long enough to prove the truth of all I have said. Long enough to reassure those who have believed in me and worked for me." Reluctantly he got to his feet. Even this he must tell her. "My time will be short," he said. "And it must be spent with my apostles, Mother, that I may give them the courage to continue. For they will have to go on preaching and teaching and healing without me. And spreading the good news of eternal life."

"Dear son, my beloved son," Mary said brokenly, reaching out her arms. And they stood for a time holding each other, struggling not to cry.

"When will I see you again?" She held him a little away from her and searched his face. "Will you eat the Passover supper with us?"

"Oh, Mother, if only I could. To be with you and Elizabeth in this house where we shared so many celebrations when my father was alive. But my men need me. I must be with my men."

So this was it! Mary thought wildly. It had begun with his words a moment ago, the first sword piercing the heart . . . now another, swifter, sharper, deeper. . . . His apostles, instead of his mother? His *men*, when he had so few hours left on earth? . . . Then she recovered. All that was wise and courageous and loving rose up in her to hide and vanquish her terrible disappointment.

"Of course you should be with them," Mary agreed. "Those dear men, how much they have given up to follow you. This won't be easy for them either—and their sacrifice is only beginning. I am proud of them, as I am proud of you!"

"You will not be alone tomorrow night, Mother," Jesus said. "Cleo and I have already spoken of this. He has already chosen a fine lamb, which he will bring you tomorrow after the sacrifice. He will carve it for you, as my father used to do. And if it's all right with Elizabeth, I will ask the other women to join you."

Jesus kissed her again and stroked her hair. "Try not to be troubled about me, Mother. Though I am not here, I will be with you in spirit, as I always am."

Chapter 22

CLEOPHAS was doing his best to make it a festive meal.
He had risen early that morning and entered the noisy chaos
of the Temple where animals were blatting, sellers yelling and men
jostling for position to reach the tables and pay an outrageous price
for a lamb. Then, holding the struggling beast, he queued up to
present it to the priest for sacrifice. He had been hoping that by some
coincidence Abner might be the one to take it from him; but he saw
no sign of that gaunt, wry figure among the scurrying white-clad
priests.

When at last he emerged, however, carrying the still-warm bundle
of flesh, he heard someone calling his name. And looking about, he
saw two of Jesus' men waving and struggling toward him through the
crowd. At first he couldn't place them, until the homely but beaming
one reminded him. "Philip and Andrew! Sorry we can't embrace, since
I am carrying the lamb."

"I can," said Philip, whose arms were free, flinging them about
him. "*Shalom alekhem!*"

Joyfully Cleo responded. To his surprise, they seemed almost
carefree, certainly not concerned. "Where are you going?"

The two looked at each other uncertainly. Then Philip glanced
about and jerked his head. "Come, it's too noisy to talk here." Together they made their way through the courts and onto the shady
grounds. Here too people streamed past, but there was less chance of
being heard.

"We can't be too careful," Philip explained. "We aren't really worried, and yet—you never know."

"We were sent to buy the lamb for the seder," said Andrew. "We are carrying it to a place on Mount Zion," he confided, "where it will be roasted for us. The other men are there now, helping with the preparations."

"It's the home of a wealthy family who are grateful to Jesus," Philip explained. "He once restored hearing to their deaf son. They have offered us their upper room, and the use of a servant."

"Nicodemus also offered to have us," Andrew put in, "but he lives outside the city. That would have been safer, but the Master wants to eat the sacrifice with us according to the wish, whenever possible, 'Within thy gates, Jerusalem!' "

"And you must keep this location secret," Cleo stated.

They nodded, for the first time showing a trace of discomfort. "Not from you, of course—"

"Then tell me no more," Cleo interrupted quickly. "Go there in peace, and give my greetings to everyone. Tell them we will drink a toast to their health tonight at Elizabeth's. And pray for them," he added brusquely.

Cleo was puzzled. Both of them seemed so confident; they were smiling, as if even this matter of hiding their whereabouts were more one of intrigue than a genuine awareness of alarm. Don't they realize even *yet*? Cleo wondered, as they parted. Loyal as they were to Jesus— despite all the time they had spent with him, all the hardships and danger they had already endured for him—were they deaf, dumb and blind to his fate?

If Jesus told *me*, he has surely told them! But if Jesus himself had been unable to convince them, who was he, Cleo, to try now? Then too, Cleo reasoned, they might have been trying to disguise their true feelings. Putting up a cheerful front for him—as he was determined to do for Mary.

Cleo had arrived at Elizabeth's that afternoon, carrying the slain lamb. Laying it down and taking up the branch of hyssop, he solemnly dabbed a bit of its blood above the door. Then he strode into the house, shouting, "Light the oven, light the oven. The lamb has arrived!"

Kissing not only Mary and Elizabeth but the faithful old servant Dinah, he told them he would go down to his saddlebags to bring up more wine. Then he would leave the ladies to their preparations. But he would be back before the first blast of the shofar, to usher in the evening. Yes, the other guests would be with him, and he must warn them—one of them would be a surprise.

Mary gave a hopeful little cry. "Not . . . ?"

Cleo clapped his brow, cursing himself for his blunder. "No, I guess I'd better tell you. Peter's nephew will be with them, a bright little boy of six, named for his uncle. Adah would like to bring him."

Mary and Elizabeth were delighted. Yes, of course, they told him. Passover evening was a time for families to be together. These women who had all served Jesus, come so far to be near their husbands, were like sisters; it would be good to have a child among them. If there were any others, bring them. And for a little while, as they busied themselves about their tasks, their secret gnawing dread of the evening was appeased. Elizabeth spread the table with her finest cloth and lighted all the lamps; their reflections danced like fireflies on the cedar walls and ceiling.

Magdalene was the first to come swiftly up the steps; fragrant, rustling with silk, she held Mary against her warm voluptuous breast. How fragile the mother of Jesus seemed; Mary had lost weight even these past few days. Magdalene patted the suddenly shaking shoulders. "Hush, hush," she soothed in her rich, soft voice. "I have come to be with you. If you like, I will stay with you through the night."

Mary could only nod and cling to her. "Please!" she whispered. She drew away then, and groped a hand out to Salome, who stood briskly by, almost beaming. "Dear Salome, how are your sons?" Mary asked.

"James and John are wonderful!" Salome claimed with her usual half-wry enthusiasm. "They feel themselves very fortunate to be able to eat this Passover meal with your own blessed son. And to think that we, their mothers, can be together—" She stopped short then, for Elizabeth had appeared, and they remembered her tragedy with horror.

But Elizabeth, too, was bravely smiling, hands outstretched. "Welcome! Your coming to be with us is truly a gift this night. And who is this?" For just behind them, panting from the climb, was Adah, leading a little boy.

Peter's nephew was indeed bright and lively; it was a great help to have him there, racing about exploring the house, asking questions, and perched on a cushion to reach the table. And the child proved a blessing throughout the meal.

Cleophas took his place at the head of the table and went through the rites with remarkable cheer. Blessing the wine and passing it, breaking the crisp unleavened bread and setting a piece aside. Then he leaned forward, with his elbows on the table, winked, and nodded to the little boy, who had been wriggling with anticipation of this moment—he was a born attention-getter. At Cleo's signal the child piped up loud and sweet between his missing front teeth: "Why is this night different from all other nights?"

The lisp was so comical, if charming, it was hard not to laugh. Cleo was grateful: anything to divert them, to keep their thoughts from those who were absent; anything to take that haunted look from Mary's eyes even for a moment. But it was hard to control his own thoughts. Even as he told the ancient story of the escape out of Egypt, and led the singing of the psalms, his mind was in anguish. Bitter, bitter the herbs on his tongue, and the salt of the water hard to swallow.

For Mary's sake and Elizabeth's, Cleo ate heartily of the hot moist lamb, and poked the little boy's belly to insist he had room for more, but his heart was groping for words. . . . He thought of Jesus, eating this sacred meal with twelve men, who were not even his own flesh and blood. Men who had given up everything to serve him, who had already shared his hardships, and whom Jesus would not forsake. Whom he had chosen to stay with until the end. . . . Jesus, my son, my almost son—where are you this moment? what are you saying? what are you feeling? And what will be your fate—perhaps even before this night has passed?

The meal was finally over, the last cup drained, the chant of thanks, the *Hallel*, vigorously and courageously sung. They stood a little while on the moonlit roof, where Cleo did his best to make it all seem festive. He lifted the youngster up to perch on the parapet, marveling at the gold Temple shining in the distance, and the magical lights of the surrounding hills. Cleo even played his lute to entertain them, while the little boy pranced around, dancing. But Cleo's nervous anxiety was growing.

It was getting late. Far past her nephew's bedtime, Adah said.

"And we should get back to see how the other women are doing,"

Salome reminded, as they rose. Thomas' wife, Sarah, had arrived that day and was very tired, and Susanna wasn't feeling well; Mary, mother of the younger James, had volunteered to stay with them.

Hearing these and other names, Elizabeth managed to smile. "Goodness," she said to Cleo, "you have quite a harem waiting!"

"Yes, and I'd trade them all for one good wife," he quipped, his eyes on Mary.

Cleo had succeeded; insofar as possible, he had kept the evening pleasant, with no reference whatever to what was heaviest on their hearts. But now he must leave Mary behind to suffer through what might well be her son's last night on earth. And she knew it, and there was nothing more he could do to help her, but he thanked God for Magdalene.

"Thank you for staying with her," he said gruffly when he had drawn her aside, there on the steps. "Take care of Mary for me."

"Mary will be all right," Magdalene said quietly. "She has rallied; I sensed it all evening. She is prepared. But I will not leave her side unless she wants me to."

"And you?" Cleo suddenly realized Magdalene was trembling; her eyes glistened.

"We both love him," Magdalene whispered. A tear darted down her cheek. "Mary and I need each other."

Cleophas pressed her hand. "God be with you—and Elizabeth too. I am going into the city to find out what I can, but I will come back in the morning."

When Judas awoke that morning, it had been in such a state of fear and indecision he could scarcely lift himself from the pallet.

Again he had scarcely slept all night. Those damnable dogs yelping and prowling—how could the others stand it? And when he finally dozed off, toward daylight, two of them slunk into the room and flopped down beside him, to stare at him with their ugly yellow eyes.

At first he thought one of them was Ben, but then he saw that it had the face of Annas, and it seemed to be gnawing on something, a huge bag of something, and the sack broke and what spilled out seemed to be gold, a lot of gold. The other one was nuzzling up to him, breathing its foul breath on him, slobbering as its rough tongue tried to lick him, and he saw that it had the face of Caiaphas!

Judas threshed about wildly, trying to fight it off. He sat up, screaming.

"Wake up, wake up!" Andrew was shaking him. "Now, now, my friend, don't worry, it's all right—it's only a dream."

Judas winced to remember how he had clung to Andrew, whimpering like a child. "Don't leave me, please don't leave me!" And Andrew had dragged his own pallet closer and lain down beside him. Thin, long-bodied Andrew, the only one who had really tried to be his friend. Andrew was kind, he wouldn't tell the rest of them; yet it shamed Judas nonetheless. And the hideous dream haunted him, as the question had haunted him for days: The priests, the gold, the priests, the gold. *How much gold?*

At first, on waking, he was horrified that he had even gone to them. Judas shuddered. Their patronizing, their ill-concealed contempt. Bullying him with their questions, making *him* feel under suspicion. As if, instead of a very bright, astute young man concerned about his country's welfare, he was merely another gullible follower of a man accused of serious crimes. Judas had failed to convey his real importance to them; even their flattery in the end could not conceal their condescension. And they hadn't even mentioned money, it galled him to remember. Not until he himself had brought it up—and even then impatient, almost indifferent about it. That old scoundrel Annas could afford to be: He was very rich, he spent lavishly, he knew good things don't come cheap.

He had practically told Judas to name his price. He had spoken of "a good deal of money."

How much?

For two days and nights Judas had wondered. Even furious with the priests, and appalled at his own proposal, he was plagued by the question. Teased and tempted, in what had become a kind of vicious but irresistible game. How much would they be willing to pay? They will take Jesus anyway, Judas reasoned in desperation; sooner or later, it's only a matter of time. This will only hasten the process, and may save Jesus, all of us, a more terrible fate. Didn't they promise not to harm him? To hold Jesus in safe custody until he could be released? Wasn't that what I demanded?

Judas could not be sure. Over and over, incessantly, that dreadful evening played itself out in his mind, yet the details were hazy. He tried, in his regret and confusion, to suck any possible drop of hope or comfort from it. Sooner or later they would take him, and perhaps the sooner the better—it might force Jesus to make his stand. To proclaim himself the Messiah and claim the kingdom now. Here and now! The people were weary with waiting. They wanted some action, they wanted to *know*.

If he *is* the Messiah, who could resist? By his almighty power he would overcome. Nothing could stop or hurt him. Not the priests, the Romans, no one . . . But if he isn't . . . ? If Jesus, like all the others, was just mistaken, or mad . . . then, even then, wasn't it Judas' duty to turn him in?

He would be paid handsomely, and Jesus would not be harmed. Not if the priests had agreed to his terms.

And the money! It didn't matter really, not to him—but what he could do with it for his friends: Andrew and Philip, the only two he had ever felt close to. What he could do for the treasury, always so nearly empty. Do for Jesus himself! Not that Jesus would accept it, but in little ways Judas could do him favors. Judas might even—and this gave him a bitter amusement—he might even buy something for that hag Martha. Her insult still rankled; what would she say if he came bringing *her* an expensive jar of perfume? He might even tell her he was sorry for that stupid but well-meaning suggestion that her sister Mary sell the family supply. . . .

And running in and through these frantic fantasies and musings was the grim reality: I have exposed myself to the enemy. When the time comes, if I *don't* do as I promised, they will take me too. And my punishment will be severe.

These were the things that assaulted Judas when he awoke that final morning, and tormented him all day.

But *could he do it?* . . . He loved the apostles so much, he agonized. Even those who had made it clear in many ways they weren't really fond of him. They were still his comrades, the only ones he had ever had. They would consider him a traitor. They would never understand. . . .

To conceal his misery, Judas put up a bright, enthusiastic front. Cheerfully he urged the others to hasten about the various tasks assigned to them. He had long ago decided it was his duty to see that everyone did his share, and any encroachment on his own responsibilities upset him. Though he tried to hide it, he was shocked and wounded to learn that Jesus had sent Andrew and Philip to purchase the lamb. Didn't the Master realize by now that he, Judas, would get a better bargain? (But then this was a special occasion, *and the lamb must be without fault or blemish.* . . . Judas writhed. He suspects; he thinks me unworthy to choose such a lamb!)

But no, come now, Jesus knows I have other important things to do. The markets will be crowded, I must barter for the best lettuces and herbs. I must seek the best bakery for the unleavened cakes and bread. And the upper room must be scrupulously prepared. The furniture must be rearranged; Judas was not satisfied with the cloth the old servant produced for the table, or the seven-branched candlesticks—they must be polished. With a spirited bossiness, Judas set the other men at the tasks, while he personally supervised the making of the sauce for the lamb.

His own energies were feverishly high; he beamed upon them, and when several of them began to argue—Matthew and James and John, mainly about their own authority, and some of the others joined in—Judas cautioned them. This was no time for dissension, the Master wouldn't like it—Jesus would be here soon. Not that they paid much attention, not until the Master appeared in the doorway, radiant in his garment, looking like a king.

Judas was the first to break their silence, first to shout his welcome and stride toward Jesus with open arms. But during their embrace his soul was shuddering, something within him crying, *Can I do it? Heaven help me, should I do it? Can I do it?*

Chapter 23

*J*ESUS had not preached or healed that day.

All day he had rested alone in Bethany, at the house of Lazarus, praying for his mother and for Elizabeth; praying for his enemies, and praying for his men.

It was sunset when at last he climbed the curved rock steps to the upper room of the house where the twelve would be waiting. He had been there before: a long chamber with heavy oak beams and high arched ceilings, simple but graciously furnished. It was reached by these cracked but fragrant flower-bordered steps, its entrance hidden behind some potted palm trees, whose leaves were clashing musically in the breeze that blew in from the hills.

He could hear the shofar's mournful wail from the Temple, followed by the jubilant blasts of the trumpets, heralding the beginning of the most sacred night of the year. And standing there a moment, Jesus felt his heart filled to bursting with sorrow and love. For these men had become far more than his followers and his friends; they were his brothers—his children. And time was short. This would be their last supper together. Yet he still had so much to say to them. He must console them, he must give them courage, not only for all they must endure before this night was ended but for all that was to come.

And there were things he still must teach them. Above all else, it seemed to Jesus as he heard their voices through the open door, he must tell them to love one another, as he had loved them. To humble themselves and serve each other. To work together for the good of the kingdom, instead of disputing and contending over their own places in that kingdom, as some of them did. Even now. Even through the general babble of merriment and anticipation, he could hear them.

Throwing back his shoulders and smiling, Jesus walked in. He was wearing the beautiful robe his grandmother had sent him, for the first time since his triumphal ride into Jerusalem. And to their proud astonished eyes, he looked once more like a prince or a king. The noisy arguments abruptly halted; there was a shocked, half-guilty silence, followed by joyful cries of welcome. The men rushed up to embrace him, and began gesturing, proud of themselves and eager to please:

See, we have laid the white cloth on the long table ourselves, their eyes and their voices were saying. *It's a little crooked—wait, we will fix it. . . . We have brought the lamb and had it roasted in the oven. True, this good woman, a servant of the family, helped us, but most of this Passover feast we have provided, as you asked. The flat, unleavened matzot in the long basket. The wine, the sauces and the bitter herbs (these we ground ourselves). . . . Yes, some of us worked a little harder than others, but never mind: for your sake we will bury our differences and rejoice with you on this night of celebration. See how we love you, Master, we are not afraid, aren't you pleased with us?*

Jesus was. He praised them warmly and smiled at the servant. She was a tall gray wizened woman, who hovered, fascinated, for she had heard much of this man. In her excitement she had forgotten to bring out the basin of water for his washing.

"Forgive me," she apologized. "I will get it at once!"

"No, just tell me where you keep it," Jesus asked.

"Back there." She pointed to an anteroom, and before she could stop him, Jesus was striding toward it. "Wait, Master, wait!" she protested frantically, scurrying after him. "I will bring everything to you."

Jesus halted briefly. "I appreciate your kindness," he assured her. "But this is something I want to do myself."

The small room smelled of cedar and soap; on a shelf were pitchers of water, a big copper basin, towels. Jesus hung up his robe. Then, decisively, he stripped off his white tunic as well, so that he wore only the long piece of linen wound round his loins and thighs. Taking up one of the rough homespun towels, he tied it about his hips. He then filled the basin with water.

Carrying it carefully, he returned to his men.

They were cheerful now, visiting amiably as they anticipated the sacred but festive meal. At sight of him, all heads turned. They gasped.

Their eyes were fixed on him, astounded, as he bade them take their places at the table.

They had seen Jesus undressed before. They were all strong rugged males; the whole band often swam or bathed together in the Jordan or the Sea of Galilee. But it was a shock to see him thus tonight, their prince suddenly disrobed, their Master humbling himself, coming to kneel before them with a basin, like a common slave, about to wash their feet.

"No, Lord, never!" Peter barked, horrified. For Jesus came directly to him, and putting down the vessel, knelt beside him. "I can't let you do this." Peter's already ruddy face flushed scarlet, and he tried to draw away. "This is not right, I should be washing your feet instead!"

Jesus smiled. "Don't resist this, Peter." Calmly he removed the shabby sandals. And taking those big callused feet firmly in his hands, he pressed them into the water. Gently, tenderly, he bathed them, those feet that had followed him so far, and dried them with his towel. "Soon you will understand why I must do this for all of you tonight."

Jesus rose then, and proceeded up and down the long table, bathing the feet of each apostle in turn. Like a mother, he gently sponged and dried them. And thinking of the many miles all these feet were still destined to trudge without him, his heart was swollen with pity. As he finished, he gave each one an extra squeeze, as if to express his thanks, his encouragement, and secretly his goodbye.

Judas was last. He sat waiting in misery, wearing his bright fixed smile. Anxious for his turn, yet dreading it; fearing it, wanting it . . . half-hoping for some confrontation between them, open or unspoken. Lord, I really love you. Please don't hate me! . . . It seemed possible Jesus might avoid him, worm that he was. Or even just forget him, cringing here at the end of the table nearest the door. But no, when the Master finished with the rest, though he paused to wipe his hands, he did not turn away, but came to set the basin down beside him.

Heart pounding, Judas allowed Jesus to unfasten his sandals. He gazed down on the adored black curly head, torn between relief, guilty anxiety, embarrassment and pride. At least he needn't be ashamed of his sandals; he always wore good sandals, and he took excellent care of his feet. But Judas was shaking, chilled to the bone; he knew his feet would be icy to the Master's hands.

And Jesus' own soul was chilled as he felt the awful fear and nervousness of the man who sat head low, unable to meet his eyes. . . . Yet these feet, too, have followed me, Jesus thought, lifting them gently into the basin. Such beautiful feet, compared to those he had just been washing. Long and graceful, almost unscarred; he knew that Judas rubbed them with oil every night—a thought that was somehow pathetic. Jesus sponged the feet of Judas with special care, filled with a terrible pity that they must be dipped in water that was now quite dirty, and almost gone.

He remembered the bold bright beginning. With what brash confidence Judas had joined them, so proud to be trusted, so eager to please. Judas, lured by his dreams.

And for Judas it would all end tonight. These feet, these poor proud feet, would not march on with the others to undertake the most important job God had ever asked of so small a group of men. Instead, they would make one last shameful journey. Even before this meal was over . . .

Jesus lingered over them, gripped them blindly for a second. Then tenderly he dried the feet of Judas with his now damp towel.

Back in the small anteroom, Jesus threw the water out the window into the alley below. He wrung out the sodden towel. Taking a dry one from the cupboard, he wiped his own streaming body. His hands were trembling as he put on his garments. He stood at the window for a moment, breathing deeply of the sweet night air. The anguish was beginning. His contact with Judas . . . He could still feel the cold flesh of those feet between his hands, and the shape of those long graceful bones. Jesus groaned. The pain he suffered for Judas only made his own anguish more acute.

I forgive him, but he has chosen. The other men will have to know—I am about to be betrayed. But dear Father, he is already in such torment, let me deal with him as kindly as I can.

The other room, mostly in shadow before, had sprung into softly flickering light. All the lamps had been kindled; in their rosy glow the men sat murmuring together, puzzled at what had happened. But when Jesus strode toward them, once more garbed like a prince in his robe, they caught their breaths in adoration. Never had their Master seemed more beautiful to them.

John, who was to sit at his right, as usual, arranged the cushions more comfortably for him. Their eyes met in genuine affection as he sat down. Jesus gazed about the table for a moment, struggling with his own emotions. Then, lifting his hand for silence, he spoke to them:

"I have looked forward to this hour with a full heart," he said, "for I have been anxious to eat this Passover meal with you before my suffering begins." He paused, aware of their stricken faces. "You must know—this is the last time I will eat it until everything has been fulfilled in the kingdom of my Father."

Again Jesus paused, as they strove to take this in. He plunged on, determined. "Tonight I have many things to tell you. But the first is to make you understand what I have just done for you. You call me Lord and Master, and this is true. Why, then, have I knelt down and washed your feet? Because I love you," he told them simply. "The way you should love one another. Not arguing about who shall be first or last in the kingdom, but humbly, as servants, one no better than the rest. I have given you this example: You must be willing to do for one another as I have done for you."

There was a ripple of assent and self-reproach. The twins exchanged sheepish glances. Philip made a contrite little gesture to Matthew. And suddenly, on common impulse, the apostles began reaching out to grip one another's hands, joining hands around the table until the chain was complete. And seeing them thus, in his sweet and terrible humanity Jesus loved them so much it seemed he could not leave them. His eyes filled. He had to close them against this fierce assault of love.

Then, as he lifted his hands once more, his voice rang out in the blessing. The first goblet of wine was poured. And when he had given thanks, Jesus offered it to John, saying, "Take this, pass it along and share it, for I will not drink wine again until that kingdom of God has come."

Before him were the three loaves of bread. Taking the middle one from its basket, Jesus broke it in two, according to the custom, and gave one half of it to John to save for the end of the meal. And when he had thanked God for it, he broke the other half apart and began handing it out to them.

"This is my body," he told them, soberly, "which will be given for you. Eat it, and whenever you meet and break bread together, do this in memory of me."

The hands of Judas were clammy.

He had reached out with some assurance to clutch the big bony fist of Andrew, who was seated closest to him. But now, as the meal proceeded, his nervousness increased. He had broken into a cold sweat. It was hard to swallow; the dry bread stuck in his throat. He could scarcely taste the hot red *hasereth* sauce, in which they were dipping, or the savory roasted lamb. His wrists trembled as he lifted the ritual goblets of wine; their silver clicked chill against his teeth. His head swam. Was this the second or third cup they were drinking? He had lost count.

His eyes kept darting toward the door. He had chosen this place nearest the tall arched entrance which led out onto the stairs. Here—unless he lost his nerve—if he took the step he had agonized over since morning—it would be easiest to slip away unnoticed. The streets below would be dark now, and deserted except for a few Romans and other pagans. For every good Jew would be indoors with his family, singing and praying, laughing and loving, feasting—with his family.

Family. Judas thought bleakly. This is *my* family. These warm familiar bodies all around him; these dear familiar voices rising and falling—though the voices clamoring in his own head made him only dimly conscious of what they were saying . . . the only family in which he had ever felt at home. His eyes dimmed, his fists clenched.

Conflict raged within him. Here I am warm and safe. I need not leave them. *Dare* I leave them? To back out now seemed cowardice, contemptible and stupid after his bold offer. But to plunge alone into the night on such a mission, suddenly not only impossible, but—insane.

Yet if he didn't? If he failed those priests? *I promised, I promised . . . they will take Jesus anyway, and it could go worse for him. For all of us!*

Judas came to with a little start. He realized Jesus had said something that shook the others. Like a stab, one word pierced his consciousness. *Betrayed.* Jesus was talking about betrayal! Judas' cheeks flushed hot, and the scar, quivering ever since they had sat down, began its terrible twitching.

The other men were glancing at each other, appalled. Those seated nearest the Master seemed stupefied. They shifted uneasily about. "Is it I, Lord?" some of them were asking, in their shock. "Is it I?"

Judas sat upright, sure he must look guilty. His heart was hammering now as if to burst his chest. He could feel the sweat pouring down his olive face, and the uncontrollable jerking of the scar. With one hand he tried to hide it. He, too, must protest his innocence and horror.

"Lord, is it I?" he called out hoarsely.

Jesus didn't answer. It seemed for a moment that perhaps he hadn't heard. He only sat quietly, regarding the piece of bread in his hand. Then, thoughtfully, he chose a morsel of lamb from the dish, wrapped the bread around it, and dipped it into the sauce. Jesus stood up then, and coming around the table, gravely handed the food to Judas.

For a second Judas was almost ill with surprise and a sudden shamed relief. To receive this token of friendship, tonight of all nights! This special honor.

Jesus still must love him. *Jesus did not even suspect.*

Joy flooded him suddenly, and a confusion of blind indecision. But even as he accepted the food, humbly and gratefully, as custom required, Jesus bent close, and Judas saw that his eyes were tragic.

"Yes, Judas," Jesus declared. "It is you. Whatever you are going to do, do quickly."

Judas' teeth sank into the tender bit of meat; he must keep on chewing, he must not choke, he must manage to swallow. He dared not look up at the Master.

Confused, Judas groped for the bag of coins he always carried. In his nervousness he couldn't find it; it was under the table. Jesus retrieved it for him. "Thank you, Master," Judas heard himself mumbling. "You are right, I should have bought more wine, the wine is running low."

Judas rose, hastily wiping his mouth on a napkin; he must not look ludicrous. Some of the sauce had dripped onto his best striped robe—he dabbed at that too. "I will try to find some," he announced. "And on my way back I will give a few extra coins to the beggars."

Head high, striving to look jaunty and in command, Judas hastened out the door.

Peter was uneasy.

His bewildered eyes followed Judas in his unexpected departure. It seemed incredible that Jesus would send him on such an errand now, before the meal was over. Especially after the poor man had worked so hard all day, and been so unusually amiable. What was going on? What were the others discussing with such consternation?

To Peter's distress, he hadn't been sitting close enough to hear for sure. Something about betrayal . . . But there was often talk of treachery and betrayal; people couldn't be trusted, even some of those who followed them. Look how many had fallen away, even some who had been healed. Look how those friends of Lazarus, a few of them at least, could hardly wait to run to the authorities, even after witnessing that miracle at the tomb. There were spies everywhere, skeptics, traitors.

But not one of *us*. Preposterous. "Is it I? . . . Is it I?" He'd heard that much. What were they doing—playing some devilish game? But now, to see Judas leaving in such haste, his air both brazen and skulking . . . Peter was aghast at his sudden suspicion.

Turning, Peter lifted his shaggy brows to signal his dismay to John, who always sat closest to Jesus. John would know. . . . *Judas? Surely not our brother Judas?* John's face had gone white with shock and outrage. Biting his lips and blinking, John nodded in response.

No! The word exploded in Peter's head. Why hadn't Jesus stopped him? If Judas was the traitor, the man must be stopped. Peter's hand flew to his sword—something had warned him to wear it tonight. Such an atrocity must not be allowed. Please, Rabbi, let me follow Judas and hack off his head, if need be. Don't submit to this!

Often though Jesus had told them it must happen, that he would be tried before the Sanhedrin, that he would suffer and actually be killed, Peter had found it impossible to believe. Not yet, not in so short a time. Barely three years. They had left everything for him, he had promised them the kingdom. But more than all else, they loved him; Jesus had changed their lives; he could heal and change the world. Jesus could not be struck down like this, not when his work had barely begun.

Yet memories almost too painful to tolerate stifled Peter's words. He remembered his own bungling, born of love. His frantic protests, and Jesus' stern rebukes. He dared not risk it. To speak out again would only be futile, and he could not abide such a thing tonight.

Jesus had returned to his place. He was taking up the pitcher to pour the third ritual cup of wine. John removed the napkin from the remaining half-loaf of bread, put away for this moment, and handed it to him.

In like manner as before, Jesus began to break it for them. "Little children," he told them quietly, "my time has come. . . ."

No! Peter's whole body began to shake. Fiercely he tightened every muscle; he could barely sit still in his place. In his desperation, Peter looked around, even as Judas had done, lest he, too, might have to escape. He bit down hard on the fist that was pressed to his trembling mouth.

How could he bear the sight of Jesus, standing now, that look of both tragedy and triumph shining from his face? How could he bear the sweet sorrowing music of that voice? No, no, it hurt too much; he would have to cover his eyes and ears or flee.

Peter was conscious of his companions, their own faces stricken in the flickering light, but silent, controlling their grief. The servant had cleared away the supper, but hovered in the doorway, openly, hungrily listening, awed and shaken. The wine goblets still stood on the table, and the empty basket that had held the bread. Peter pushed the thing farther from him. Fixed his attention on the cup. In its cold silver a little star of light was reflected; gritting his teeth, he felt his fingers clench the slender stem.

"Drink you, all of this, for this is my blood of the new covenant, which is shed for you, for the remission of sins. . . ."

No . . . no! Peter's spirit groaned . . . had he groaned aloud? He must get hold of himself, he must listen to what Jesus was saying now.

Glory. Jesus was speaking of glory. "Soon the glory of God will surround me. God will be glorified because of all that has happened during my time on earth with you. I will be with the Father soon. . . ."

Miserably, Peter lifted his eyes. Jesus was gazing tenderly about the table, and for an instant their eyes met. "Dear, dear children," Jesus said with deep emotion, "I can be with you only a little while

longer, then I must go away. And where I am going you cannot follow. . . ."

No!

"But I am giving you a new commandment before I leave. Love
one another as I have loved you. By this strong bond of love for each
other you will show the world that you are my disciples, and what it
is like to follow me."

Peter had been beating his fists. He could not stand it any longer.
He lurched to his feet. "Lord, please tell us where you are going!" he
burst out. Tears he could not stop were running down his cheeks.
"Why can't I follow you, even now? You know I would lay down my
life for you!"

Patiently Jesus turned to him. "Will you, Peter?" he asked kindly,
though a little smile played about his mouth. "Will you die for me?"
Leaving his place at the table, Jesus came to Peter and put his arms
around him. "No, Peter, I tell you solemnly—three times tonight, even
before the cock crows in the morning, you will deny you even know
me."

Chapter 24

$\mathcal{P}$ETER would never be sure of all that happened that night. It seemed to him that he must have been in a trance from the moment Jesus began speaking. Those beautiful, promising, comforting, yet pain-laced words of prophecy, instruction and farewell. Even now, a few hours later, when at last they rose, sang one final song and went out into the night to begin their long walk to Gethsemane, the words were a confusing chant in his head:

Let not your heart be troubled, neither let it be afraid. . . . Peace I leave with you, my peace I give unto you. . . . In my Father's house are many mansions; if it were not so I would have told you. . . . I go to prepare a place for you. . . .

Fragmented, out of sequence, yet they sang and wept in his being. He would sort them out later, he would try to comprehend. Now, for now, where was Jesus going? To the garden on the Mount of Olives, yes, but where then, where then? . . . Jesus was walking alone, already some distance ahead of them on the street. Was he avoiding them, or even now hastening toward some distant destination where they could not follow?

"Your shepherd will be taken, you will all scatter like sheep," he had said. That scene at the table when they were all protesting their loyalty . . . Peter banging his fist, insisting, "Never, Master, never! I will go to prison with you, I will die beside you!"

The moon was very bright, swimming in brilliance between luminous white clouds, flooding the night. They could hear families still singing in their houses. But guards and soldiers were everywhere. At any moment someone could spring upon him; every alley was dark with threat.

"Wait, Lord, wait!" Peter wanted to cry out now. "You were wrong. Should anything happen to you, we will not scatter like sheep! Let us walk with you, protect you—the streets aren't safe."

But his feet were leaden, his heart was breaking in his breast. He was oddly comforted when Andrew persisted in making his way around the others to catch up with Jesus and walk with him, as Peter so often had. It might be his last chance. Dear Andrew, my own brother, who brought me to the Master . . .

This is my commandment: that you love one another. . . .

They had reached the steep path that led down to the ravine and on up the opposite banks of the Kidron. Peter was aware of his feet stumbling over rocks, descending, found he was groping for roots and branches to steady himself. From time to time he had to stop to choke back his emotions, try to get hold of himself. The stream, which was often a trickle, or dry as a barren woman, tonight was bubbling, flashing its skirts as it darted below them. The air was damp and cool, its usual smell of death, decay and burning refuse overpowered by the peppery sweetness of some flowering medlar trees. Peter halted, stood breathing it in.

Abide in me and I will abide in you. . . . He that abides in me and I in him will bear much fruit, but apart from me he can do nothing. . . . If they persecuted me they will persecute you. . . . I have many things to say to you, but you cannot bear them now. . . . Verily, verily I say unto you, you shall weep and lament, but your sorrow will be turned into joy. . . .

Peter realized that most of the others were passing him. He could see a few of them already below, beginning to cross the stream. They had girded up their garments and were hopping from rock to rock, pausing to dry their feet on the opposite bank. Jesus had disappeared among the shimmering olive groves, whose leaves were like silver tents, ethereal and strange on the moonlit hills.

Behold, the hour comes that you will be scattered, every man to his own, and shall leave me alone. . . .

No, no! Stricken with guilt and fear, Peter went scrambling down the bank. He seemed to be last, and he couldn't bear to be last. . . . Jesus, wait, wait—I am coming, here I am! You chose me first, remember? You called me from my nets. You performed a great miracle that very night, filling my empty boat with fish. I was the only one to walk to you across the water; you held out your hand to me and together we walked on the waves. As I trusted you then, please trust me now. I was the first to confess that you are truly the Messiah, the Son of God. You said I would be rewarded, you would give me the keys of heaven. How can you think I would ever abandon you?

Peter crossed the stream and charged up after the others, toward the garden. Around them the great shoulders of the mountains loomed, peaceful against the slate-blue moonlit sky. Behind them the lights of Jerusalem shone. In the distance they could hear the final peal of the trumpets, signaling the second watch at the Temple, and the changing of the guards. But here all was a rustling silence. The wind stirred the heavy dark heads of the cypress trees that bordered the path to Gethsemane, and the willows that drooped over its tall stone walls. There was the tang of cedar and pine and olives, mingling like a heady incense with the fragrance of the flowers that grew inside.

Peter came up, gasping with relief. The iron gates were open. Jesus was standing a little way beyond the entrance, surrounded by the others. . . . *You are my friends. I chose you and appointed you to go forth and bear fruit.* . . . It was all right, Peter thought, close to tears. They were all together; Jesus had to have faith in them. Surely he knew that whatever fate befell him, they would be with him as they had promised, to the end. I, at least! Peter resolved passionately, seeing the expression on Jesus' face—patient and kind, loving and forgiving, even now. Peter's hand flew to his sword. If necessary, he would welcome the chance to prove it.

But Jesus also looked exhausted. He had poured himself out to them utterly, Peter realized. Drained himself dry. Now he stood resting here a moment, as if almost too weary to go on. Finally he sighed deeply, and drew a hand across his perspiring brow.

"I want to go farther into the garden to pray," he told them. Jesus beckoned to Peter, James and John. "You three come with me. The rest of you stay here and watch."

Gratefully, Peter trudged on beside his Lord, their footsteps crunching on the gravel path. His heart was full. . . . *The Father himself loves you because you have loved me.* . . .

Crickets chirped in the grasses; there was the low throbbing note of a dove somewhere. They passed the big dark olive press, like a giant in the moonlight, casting its grotesque shadow. The ancient olive trees writhed in attitudes of suffering, black and silver, mimicked in shadows, sharply defined. Rocks were everywhere, glittering. And among them, in clusters and tangles, were the flowers—wild roses, hyacinths, poppies, lilies, wet with dew, giving off their delicate perfumes.

Peter yawned. Breathed deeply. It would be good to sleep here in the cool, sweet air; they had often done so. Worth the long walk from the city, and probably safer than staying in the house where they had had supper. The owner had invited them to spend the night and some of the men had hoped to, for they were all very tired. . . . And sleepy—all that food and the ritual wine.

Peter yawned again. Then he stiffened, suddenly alert, listening. . . . Those low mourning notes he heard were not those of doves disturbed; they were coming from a human throat! Peter halted, his own throat dry.

And now he realized. As Jesus walked beside him, head low, he was moaning. James and John halted abruptly too, and stared at their Master, whose face was contorted, his eyes closed. Never had any of them seen a countenance of such suffering.

"Forgive me," Jesus said, through set teeth. "But I am in great pain. My soul is in sorrow, even to the point of death." With the back of one hand he pushed the hair away from his streaming brow. "Wait for me," he said thickly. "Keep watch while I go on ahead a little way to pray."

"Wouldn't you like one of us beside you?" John asked, anxiously.

"No, no; it's enough to know you are near. Only stay here and watch."

Alarmed and concerned, they followed Jesus with their eyes as he walked on, his shoulders bowed. In a patch of moonlight beside a huge gray rock, he fell to his knees. Then, stretching his hands out upon the rock, he seemed to collapse, so that he lay half prostrate upon it.

Confused and stricken, feeling helpless, the three sat down under a sprawling tree. Its roots were knobby and coiling, like a great serpent, but it offered a place to rest. For a time they perched there, murmuring about the events of the day, conjecturing about the things Jesus had said. The night was fraught with danger, that much they knew. They must be prepared for anything. But soon the twins' heads were nodding, their voices trailed off.

"You may as well stretch out," Peter offered. "I will stand guard." With an effort, he got up, to keep himself awake, and stamped about. He tried not to look at the beloved figure not a stone's throw away, obviously in some secret agony. Yet he dared not go to Jesus, as he longed to, grasp him by the shoulder, plead, "Don't, don't, I can't bear it! Flee now while there is time. I will stay here and fend off anyone who comes for you. . . . Or let me suffer with you, die for you!"

But no, he didn't dare; that, he remembered in despair, was exactly what Jesus reprimanded him for.

Peter saw that his friends had taken his advice; they were sprawled out, huddled in their cloaks, for the night had turned chill. Their fair heads were propped on the roots, their mouths open; they were snoring steadily. Carefully, Peter eased himself down and maneuvered his big body about until his own head rested against the trunk of the tree. . . . Cicadas clattered, mosquitoes hummed, mingling with the rhythmic snores. Peter stifled a yawn and let his thoughts drift again, struggling to remember. . . .

A little while and you will see me no more, now you have sorrow but I will see you again, truly I say to you if you ask anything of the Father, because I live you will live also, the world will rejoice, if they persecuted me they will persecute you, when a woman is in travail she cries out but when her child has been delivered . . . I will not leave you comfortless, be brave, I have conquered the world . . .

Peter slapped at a mosquito droning in his ear. . . . The words, the words, a chorus, if only he could remember that last prayer for them, Jesus' last prayer . . . *Now they know that all things you have given me are from you, for the words you gave me I have given them, they believe that you did send me . . . they are not of the world even as I am not of the world . . . and the glory you have shared with me will be theirs as well. . . . Father, the hour is come, glorify your son!*

Peter came to with a start, listened, heart hammering, and drifted off again. He was fishing on a stormy sea, the wind howled and wailed, but the fish were plentiful, striving to leap into the boat, enough to sink it, but when he stooped in panic to throw them overboard he found that they were men floundering there, crying out for help, and all of them bleeding as if from hooks caught in their mouths. . . . Their blood dripped into a cup, a huge silver cup. "*Drink you, all of this, for this is my blood of the new covenant, shed for the remission of your sins."*

"No. *No!*" Peter was crying out, trying to thrust the cup away. He could hear a voice, someone imploring in agony: "Oh, God, my God, my Father in heaven, I know that you can do anything—if it is your will, take this cup from me!" Then silence . . . only the rustle of the wind in the trees. "Nonetheless, not my will, but yours. . . ."

A moth fluttered across Peter's tormented face, but it seemed to be an angel, gently floating on gossamer wings, giving him strength, saying, "I am the comforter," telling him not to be afraid. Yet when it left, his whole body was drenched with sweat.

Peter had slumped. Someone was gripping his shoulder. He jerked himself upright, blinking into Jesus' weeping face. "Oh, Peter, could you not watch for me one little hour?"

"What, what? Where am I?" Peter grabbed about stupidly for his fallen cloak. "I'm sorry, forgive me." His teeth were chattering. "I didn't mean to—"

"Yes, yes, I know," Jesus said sadly. "The spirit is willing, but the flesh is weak. Try to stay awake, Peter. I need your prayers; this is a time of great anguish for me."

How many times this happened Peter could not be sure. Only that at last he was rousing, sitting up bewildered. A storm must be brewing; he could hear a dim rumbling, see flashes of light darting in and out among the trees. Then he was staggering in terror to his feet. Jesus was bending over the startled twins. "Arise, all of you," he was ordering. "We must warn the others!"

James and John sprang up and came running. They could hear voices, branches crackling, the crunch of footsteps approaching. Peter realized now that the flash and fall of light was that of lanterns searching them out, swaying and dipping on their poles.

"Hurry," Jesus said, "for the hour is at hand. The Son of Man is about to be betrayed. And those who would take me are coming. . . . Behold, the one who betrays me is coming."

Thirty pieces of silver!

Barely a month's wages for a common laborer, Judas raged. Bewildered and indignant, he had trudged out of the palace to meet the band of Temple police and soldiers already gathering in the yard. He had tied the little bag to his girdle; he could feel it bumping against his thighs. So small to be so heavy. The chink of its meager contents mocking. A final insult from those high and mighty priests, who hadn't even bothered to see him when he came panting in.

The maid at the doorway wouldn't let him enter their chambers. They were meeting with the Pharisees and other members of the Sanhedrin, she had informed him; they couldn't be disturbed. "But they are expecting me!" he declared hotly. "I am Judas Iscariot!"

She said she would deliver the message. She was gone a long time. Once again he was forced to cool his heels while others came and went. Senators emerged and hastened along the corridors, summoning footmen and other servants for hasty conferences. Latecomers arrived, were warmly greeted and ushered in. There was an air of secrecy and stealth, of some dark adventure impending. From outside he could hear a dim roar of voices, footsteps running, and the clank of swords.

When the maid finally returned, she was carrying a little bag. The high priest had said to thank him and wish him well on tonight's mission. He was to report at once to the captain of the guards. Meanwhile, he was to have this for his efforts. The woman was actually smiling, as if in congratulation, as she handed him the bag. Seething, trying to hide his humiliation, Judas turned his back to open its strings. His fingers were trembling. But at least it would be gold—it had to be gold! He could feel the woman's frank curiosity; he was glad she could not see his expression when he looked inside. He would have flung it into her face if he dared, he would have gone storming into the session to demand his rights.

Yet he could do nothing, Judas realized sickly. It was too late, he could do nothing. Not even flee. The band he was to join were heavily armed. They could pounce upon him, question him, drag him into prison. He could be beaten—and worse. Judas' blood ran cold. Fool, fool, fool! To have trusted those priests. They had betrayed him.

Betrayed! The word made him gag, it was like vomit in his throat. But no, he assured himself desperately, this thing he had contracted to do was not betrayal but protection. To save Jesus from his own madness, if that's what it was. Or, if he was truly the Promised One, to keep him safe until his role could be established.

And the reward. The gold! Judas remembered bitterly. What he could have done for the Rabbi with the enormous reward the priests had implied—practically promised. Cheats, cheats, cheats! tossing him this measly bag of coins like a crust to a dog. And now sheer horror smote him. He could feel cold sweat breaking out, all over his body. If they had no qualms about this, they would have no qualms about what they might do to Jesus.

Judas shuddered.

Yet he had no choice now; he could neither escape nor undo the damage. They didn't need him anymore, thanks to his own stupidity. They could find Jesus easily without him. *The Garden of Gethsemane.* He himself had given them the information that first night. Fool, fool, fool! And he could not even run on ahead to warn the other apostles, restore himself in their eyes, be one of them again, willing to live or die for the Master.

He had thrown it all away; he must suffer the indignity of marching with this mob. For it would soon be a mob. Late as it was, out of side streets and alleys, even from rooftops, excited people came running, some of them armed with sticks and clubs. Dogs were barking, snapping at their heels; in Judas' overwrought state, it seemed to him that one of them was that cur that followed Jesus. He longed for a club, but he could do no more than kick at it, losing his balance.

The guard grabbed him, to steady him. "Never did like dogs," Judas muttered.

"Who are these people?" the captain of the guards snorted. "Get rid of them. We don't need an army to capture one lone prophet."

An air of exasperation prevailed as they proceeded, as quietly as possible, along the dark, deserted streets. The guards were grumbling. To be roused so late for such a trivial arrest. The whole thing made them feel foolish. They were aware of the condescension—half disgruntled, half amused—of the five or six Roman soldiers assigned to accompany them. The rabble that joined them only made it more degrading.

And Judas must lead them. Even point out the best way to reach Gethsemane, now that the river was high. The bridge was some distance downstream, he advised; it would take longer, but the bridge was safe, and the climb beyond less steep. . . . Meanwhile—Judas was thinking wildly—it would be cold in the garden tonight. And it was late, past midnight. Jesus and the apostles might have gone on to Lazarus' house to sleep.

How severely would he be blamed if the prey was not in Gethsemane? Would he be forced to tell them more, go on with them to Bethany? . . . *For thirty pieces of silver!* Judas' sense of outrage struck afresh. And his terrible regret. Never. He would tell them nothing more. Not even for gold. Let them kill him first. It would be a relief. Anything to be spared what lay ahead—facing his friends again. Seeing the face of Jesus.

There was the sound of shuffling feet, the chink and rattle of weapons; dogs barked, lucky people slept. They descended from the upper city; the Temple loomed with a mighty indifference above them, white and gold, its pillars drawing long stripes of shadow under the moon.

A low passage had been cut in the southwestern wall of the city. The men stooped through, uncomfortable, feeling their way in the darkness against the damp stone sides of the tunnel. Outside, they must clamber down a steep flight of crumbling steps. Below, beside an ancient iron gate, the keeper must be roused to open up. He was a very old man, who looked astonished at the size of the horde.

"Lock it as soon as I give the signal," the captain of the guards ordered urgently. "Don't let all that rabble through. But stay awake until we come back later. We'll have a prisoner with us."

The old man knew better than to ask questions. But it was impossible to keep back all the ruffians; some of them were even trying to climb the high gate. "Who is it?" somebody yelled. "A man called Jesus!" "What has he done?" Few of them seemed to know, or care. Although one, who threw down his stick in disgust after failing to get through, told the keeper, "He's been preaching sedition, or so they say. Healing people, or pretending to, on the Sabbath. Once, at the pool of Siloam—"

The old man gasped and rattled his keys. He'd been passing the pool himself one day when he saw a remarkable thing—a blind man weeping as he washed himself, but shouting for joy as he emerged, proclaiming he now saw clearly! The keeper would never forget the sight—nor the beautiful figure standing nearby, who seemed to be the healer. . . . That long curly hair, those great caring eyes. He hoped this would not be the prisoner they brought back tonight.

The moon had gone under a cloud. They had been warned to silence. They had not even lighted their lanterns and torches until they descended into the dark ravine. They had to be careful crossing the bridge over the swollen stream. The torches licked the air with yellow tongues and were reflected on the water.

The captain loped up from the rear, where he had been trying to quiet the ruffians; quite a number had managed to get through the gate. Fuming, he fell into step beside Judas.

"It's necessary to take him by surprise. That bunch could spoil everything." He jerked his head in disgust, motioned upward. At the top of the slope, beyond the lane, the back walls of the garden could be seen, silent and mysterious. Bats dipped; the torches hissed and gave off a rank oily smell that mingled oddly with the fragrance of the garden as they ascended and approached.

"Are you sure he's in there?"

Judas swallowed. "It is the usual place."

"Do you know where we're likely to find him?"

Judas' heart was pounding. "Yes. A clearing about halfway through the garden. A little way beyond the olive press. There's a big rock there. He . . . it's likely . . . he always prays there."

"How will we know him?"

Judas licked his dry lips. "I will greet him first. Jesus is the one I will kiss."

They walked on, entered through a small wooden door on the far side; Judas knew the garden well, for he had often come here to wander about alone, his artistic soul reveling in its flowers. But now, as the lights began to sweep back and forth among the trees, searching, searching, Judas felt suddenly so weak he could not stand. Knees buckling, he stumbled, half fell.

"Promise you will take him away safely!" he pleaded, as the officer grabbed him. "Promise he will not be harmed!"

The big captain halted, astonished. Glowering, but not unkindly, he set the informer back on his feet. "Our job is to deliver him to the Sanhedrin," he said curtly. "All in one piece," he added. "What they do to him is up to them."

The man crouched to pull aside a low-hanging limb. As he straightened, Judas felt the branch slap whiplike across his face.

The rocks, the shadows, the gnarled grotesquerie of the ancient trees, the light-silvered flashing of their leaves . . . the oil press, the barrels . . . the voices, ahead and behind . . . swords, clatter, excitement . . . a circle of familiar faces, with Jesus in the center, caught, entrapped! . . . And a strange dialogue began playing itself out, like some sweet and ghastly music in Judas' soul:

"Why do you kiss me, Judas? Would you betray me with a kiss?"

"I kiss you because I love you; I have never dared to kiss you before. This may be my only chance. You never loved me as you loved Peter and James and John."

"I love you all, I have always loved all of you."

"Not me, as you love the rest," Judas sobbed.

"It was never that I loved them more. Only that they understand more, and they will have more to accomplish for me after I am gone."

"But I was always a worm before you, you knew my nature, my weak, cringing nature underneath my swaggering front, that I stole and lied—"

"It doesn't matter now. You are forgiven, I love you, go your way in peace."

"I can't, I can't!"

The world was spinning around him, the lights, the swords, the clatter and the excitement and the mobs with their clubs. . . .

Clearly now, if softly, Judas heard his own voice saying, "Master, I did not mean it to be like this. They will treat you well, I have their assurance; don't be afraid."

Suddenly two guards stepped forward and grabbed Jesus, bending his arms behind his back. Jesus did not struggle as they bound him, only stood with dignity, his face tragic yet smiling faintly. "Why do you feel this is necessary?" he asked. "Every day I have been teaching in the Temple—you could have taken me anytime. Why have you seized me now with your swords and clubs like a common criminal?"

"Deal with him gently," Judas heard himself pleading with the assailants. "That's what the priests said, the priests have promised."

"The priests are idiots!" Peter bellowed. "Don't believe him, Lord. Break free—I will protect you!" With a sudden thrust of his huge arm, Peter's sword came down against the restraining soldier's head; blood spurted, a piece of flesh fell into Peter's other hand.

"No, Peter, no!" Jesus commanded, wrenching free of his bonds. "There must be no violence."

The victim had staggered; Jesus reached out to catch him before he fell. Jesus held him gently a moment, to quiet him, for he was young and terrified. And there, quickly and simply before them all, he took the ear from Peter, and pressed it to the bleeding head. "You were only doing your duty," Jesus told him. "The Father and I do not want you to suffer. You are healed. Your ear is restored."

Jesus turned to Peter, who looked pale and stunned. "Put away your sword," he said. "I am ready to drink the cup which the Father has given me."

No one touched him for a moment. They were too awed at first and some of them were afraid. Jesus only stood there in the moonlight, soulwracked yet majestic in his passion, his gentle head back, his eyes both fierce and sweet, shining with a love no man could understand. . . . And seeing him thus, Judas thought, *My God, my God, he is the Messiah, and I have sold him to his enemies!*

Chapter 25

$\mathcal{P}$ETER and John were wet, cold and breathless when at last they reached Jerusalem.

Unlike the other apostles, during those final moments of Jesus' arrest they had not fled. There had been a great commotion in the garden—shouts, threats, protests, the rattle of chains. They vaguely remembered the sounds of scuffling, running, branches breaking, and the scrape of feet as several apostles, in panic, scrambled over the garden walls.

Peter and John had escaped, yes, but only to hide and watch anxiously from the trees. Peter had begun to growl like an angry dog; and when he saw his Master shackled, he would have hurled himself forth once more with his sword, but John restrained him. "Hush, be quiet, do nothing! Our only hope is to follow and see where they take him."

Hearts hammering, scarcely breathing, they watched until the whole rowdy procession had disappeared through the gates. Then swiftly, crouching under branches, they threaded their way across Gethsemane until they reached a hole in the stone wall where they could squeeze through.

From this elevation they could see the arresting horde, like an ugly serpent, the glint and flash of swords and armor like scales as it coiled down the sloping roadside toward the bridge.

"They will have to use the bridge," John said. "We had better go back the way we came."

Though shorter, the route was more precarious. Once more they had to go plunging down the steep ravine, and wade across the river. The water seemed even colder and higher than before. In their haste they slipped on the rocks, and Peter badly stubbed one toe. He was hobbling as they climbed the opposite bank, but still trying to hang on to his sword.

"You shouldn't have brought that," John reprimanded. "You know what Jesus said."

Regretfully, Peter studied the weapon. "We all should have brought swords, and fought them off!" he muttered.

"No, no, that would have been a terrible thing. We all could have been killed, including Jesus. They were heavily armed. Jesus knows best—it's best to offer no resistance."

Panting, they rested there a minute, aware of the mountains, the stars, and the lights of the city rising on the hills just above them. Shrouded in moonlight and shadows when they left, now the Temple and the palaces of both high priests seemed to be ablaze, and half the city waking.

Peter was fiercely wringing out his wet cloak. His big toe throbbed, his garments felt clammy against his knees. "Well, at least you and I didn't run away!"

John was shivering; he nodded, troubled. "Frankly, I'm surprised at James. Still, we must not blame anybody. They saw there was nothing we could do. . . . And it might even make things easier for him," he said as they walked on.

"To be deserted by his own men?"

"Yes," insisted John. "Remember, we are all despised Galileans, considered hotheads; they even blame their massacres on us."

The two had reached the city walls and stood uncertainly, blinking up. It was silent here. The great walls loomed, still and peaceful, washed in moonlight, yet there was a sense of mounting urgency behind them. As if a sleeping giant were rousing, or already awake.

"Where do you think they're taking him?" Peter asked.

"Probably to Caiaphas." John gestured toward the lights. "Let's go to his palace first."

It was some distance. They walked as fast as they could. People, like moths attracted to the light, were already swarming around the courtyard when they arrived. Others came running, eager to know what was going on. A few last late members of the Sanhedrin climbed out of litters and strode through the crowd, robes billowing, and were admitted to the palace by the Roman legionaries who stood sternly, arms folded, keeping order. It had been decided that this was no job for mere Temple guards.

As quietly as possible, Peter and John merged with the crowd. Rumors and stories were flying. "They've arrested somebody, he's being tried." "No, no; the prisoner isn't even here yet. They dragged him over to Annas first, the old man wanted to look him over." "Who?" "That madman from Galilee, claims he can raise the dead, can smash the Temple with his bare hands! They've already killed all that gang that was always with him." "That's ridiculous," a more reasonable voice spoke up. "Nobody's been killed, at least not yet, and probably won't be. He's just a harmless prophet; I've heard him. They'll probably just beat him and send him home where he belongs."

Peter was shaking, more miserable as time wore on. His bruised toe, already throbbing with pain, exploding—somebody had stepped on it. His wet garments chilled his legs; he could hear his teeth chattering. The night had grown colder. He looked longingly at the charcoal fire burning in a barrel near the doorway, where several of the soldiers were warming their hands. They were beginning to yawn, more relaxed, and amiable to the people who came forward to ask questions or try to get inside.

Peter finally admitted to John, "I don't think I can stand this much longer. Maybe we should walk on to the other palace."

"I'm sorry, Peter, we'd better wait; there isn't time."

Even as John spoke, a new surge of excitement rippled through the now weary spectators. Heads turned; people who had begun to trail off halted and tried to hasten back.

"Make way, make way—let these men through!" a voice was ordering.

Peter and John watched in dismay as an officer shepherded a motley group through the crowd. Not dignitaries, as might have been expected—not senators or judges, but ordinary, even scruffy-looking individuals. The breed that lived in the lower city but hung around the courts of justice, heckling speakers in the hope of being paid to leave, or offering their testimony for hire.

False witnesses!

While just behind them surged a laughing, shouting bunch who seemed fresh from some triumph. "We got him, we got him!" the leader announced. And they recognized him as one of the gang that had appeared with the arresting party in the garden, a big rollicking lout who had wrestled briefly with one of the fleeing apostles. Now he was bright-eyed, grinning, waving his arms in self-congratulation. "He's coming, the king is coming! Take a good look at him! Drowned rat, that's what he is—we had to throw him in. The bridge was crowded, we heard the miracle worker could swim. Let's see if he can swim in fetters, I told 'em, so we threw him in!"

Shocked, intrigued, excited, people were struggling to get closer. "What happened?" somebody cried.

"He didn't perform any miracles!" the lout hooted. "We had to drag him out. No miracles tonight, he couldn't even save himself. Look at me, I'm still wet; we had to jump in and drag him to shore!"

Horror sickened Peter. And a sudden alarm. Instinctively, he shrank back lest he be noticed by those bold bragging eyes, and remembered: the one who had drawn his sword. But John had the courage to step forward.

"I take it you have just come from Annas," he asked. "What was the verdict there?"

The oaf's crude voice dropped, became almost confidential, as if he had expended all his energies. "Frankly, I wasn't inside," he admitted. "I'm not quite sure. But it must have been serious—he's been bound over for trial."

There were other sounds then—ominous, threatening: the measured tramping of soldiers approaching; and faintly but distinctly as they drew nearer, the chink and rattle of chains. Before these sounds the people had suddenly quieted; in silence they shoved and darted about, jumping to see over shoulders, straining to get a glimpse of the captive. And though there were some jeers, a few bursts of laughter, mostly there were only gasps, little bleating cries of protest and pity.

For they had bound Jesus hand and foot. Like some animal that might escape, he had been hobbled. So that, though he walked head high, his proud sweet fervent eyes straight ahead, yet his hands were tied behind his back with leather thongs, and his ankles had been chained.

And it was this that tore Peter and John apart.

His robe—that once beautiful robe—now clung to his body, wet and ripped and bloodstained, its girdle with the bright stones, missing.

There was a purple lump on his brow; one lip was bleeding. But it was those feet that destroyed them—to see those feet, once so agile and free, always swinging a little ahead of them on the road, or leaping up a mountainside—to see them inching along, awkwardly, carefully, like those of a cripple or a toddling child.

With a sob, Peter groped at his scabbard.

John's face was grim. "Go warm yourself by the fire," he said fiercely. "You're shaking all over. I'm going into the palace."

"Will they let you in?"

"They'll have to, if I insist. I'll identify myself. As a follower of their prisoner, I have a right to testify for him."

"But will you be *safe?*"

"I don't care if it's safe. I've got to know what's going on."

Desperate in his misery, Peter charged toward the warm barrel of glowing coals. A cheery circle now surrounded it. Three sleepy but grinning young Romans were flirting with a couple of maidservants who had slipped out of the palace, one of them with a bottle of wine hidden in her bosom. These Jews . . . usually so sober about their religion, except at festival time, when the streets were lively with songs and dancing. People laughed then and ran about rejoicing, pretending not to notice the uniformed legionaries brought in to prevent trouble. It was a lonely time for the alien troops, many of them mere boys. They tramped around in envious clumps, drinking to relieve their homesickness and boredom. But these Jewish girls! A welcome respite from the whole dreary business of religious confrontations, like this absurdity tonight.

To Peter's relief, they made him welcome, and remarked with some concern about his wet clothes. One of them kicked a stool closer so that he could sit nearer the fire. Another threw his own cloak about Peter's shaking shoulders, and offered him a swig of wine.

"Drink this, it will make you feel better. What happened to you? You must have been out there. What'd you do, jump off the bridge and help drag him in?"

"No!" Peter was shaking so violently he could scarcely speak. "I've never seen the man. I . . . was fishing, and fell overboard."

One of the Jewish maids was staring at him, curiously. A saucy wench of about fourteen, with jet-black hair and cunning, puzzled eyes. "Wait a minute," she said, frowning, as Peter gulped the wine. "Haven't I seen you somewhere before?" She continued to study him, then suddenly snapped her fingers. "I remember—at the Temple! You were with him on Solomon's Porch. . . . He's one of them," she informed the soldiers. "He's Galilean; I can tell by the accent—he's one of that man's disciples."

"I don't know what you're talking about!" Peter protested hotly. "Yes, I'm a Galilean fisherman, I wanted to try the river. But that's all. I'm no man's disciple!"

He was half blind with fear and fatigue. It would soon be morning, the sky was paling. He only wanted to have it over with, to get out of here. He was so tired, and his toe—he must have broken it, the pain was so intense; his whole foot was swelling. . . . To get home to Adah, find the house where the women were staying and have her hold him, warm him, comfort him. She would cut off his sandal, soak the foot in warm water, apply a salve. All he asked was to weep in her arms, fall asleep in her arms. . . .

Peter struggled to his feet. And froze.

Another servant, an older woman, was hastening down the marble steps, pausing to scan the audience. Suddenly spying him, she beckoned. Peter's heart stopped. He was aware of the staring eyes of everyone around the fire. He had no choice; he hobbled forward to meet her, if only to escape them.

"Come with me. Hurry!" she urged. "A friend of yours said to bring you inside. There may be time to testify."

"What do you mean?" Peter demanded. "Why? I have no friend inside."

"Aren't you the apostle Peter? A follower of the accused?"

"No!" Peter croaked dismally. "I am not!"

Curious bystanders drew closer, asking the same question. One man, very excited, pointed a finger. "Didn't I see you with him in the garden?"

"What garden?" Peter blustered. "I haven't been in any garden!" As he spoke, shrill and clear across the graying hills, he could hear the first cock crowing.

Peter groaned, as if a dagger had pierced his gut. For through the raucous rhythms he could hear the prophecy of Jesus . . . and his own cowardly denials.

It was too late to help anyway, Peter realized, in anguish. The trial seemed to be over. People were beginning to pour out of the building: scribes, Pharisees, judges, lawyers, priests, blinking and frowning in the chill gray light; some of them still arguing among themselves, but most of them silent, and every face grave. They were like ghosts, plodding past the fire; their faces were death's heads.

"What happened? What's the verdict?" one of the bystanders shouted.

"Blasphemy," a senator replied shortly. "Guilty. Deserving the death penalty."

The hired witnesses followed, still under heavy guard, some looking sheepish, others grinning. Last of all, the prisoner. There was a delay at the top of the steps. The heavy chains were a nuisance; two guards dropped, in obvious exasperation, as they struggled to remove them, and threw them, rattling, to the crowd. Then one of them gave Jesus a kick and a shove, which sent him staggering. With his hands lashed behind his back, he could not reach out to brace himself. He fell down the steps. Laughing and spitting at him and slapping him about, they hauled him to his feet.

It was hard for Jesus to walk completely upright. He was in pain. His face was covered with spittle, his ankles were swollen and bruised from the shackles. He was limping as he passed by the fire—almost near enough to touch.

Peter cringed, longing to throw himself at those tortured feet and beg forgiveness, yet so convulsed with self-loathing he could only pray that Jesus would not see him. He wanted to hide, or to die on the spot.

But as Jesus passed he lifted his head. And seeing Peter cowering there before the fire, he paused; for an instant their eyes met. The bleeding lips smiled faintly, and on the face of the Master was a look of such compassion and forgiveness it would haunt Peter all his life.

Weeping bitterly, Peter stood alone by the dying coals. They were sputtering, giving off an acrid odor. Nearly everybody else was gone. The maids had disappeared into the palace. The Roman soldiers stood in a huddle with their legate, who was telling them to go back to their barracks and get some sleep. Looked like they'd need it. These crazy Jews and their would-be messiahs. Easy enough for them to condemn some poor fool to death, but who had to do the dirty work? The Romans. Pilate would have to approve, of course, but unless the procurator intervened, the man would be nailed. Rotten job; took a strong stomach. Better get some sleep, and make sure there's plenty of wine. Where was that wine somebody was handing around? All gone? Well, there was more at the barracks. Better get some sleep. . . .

The sun was rising. A whole chorus of roosters were taunting Peter now. Dumbly, dully, Peter heard them as the tears ran down his hopeless face.

Thus it was that John and Cleophas found him, when they, too, came out from the palace. Cleo had arrived earlier, he said, accompanied by Abner—a priest and an old friend of the family, Cleo explained. "You may have heard Jesus speak of him. Mary and I had gone to see him, and he promised to help. He saw that I got in. We both hoped some of us would be allowed to testify."

John and Cleo tried to describe the trial to Peter as they followed what was left of the crowd down the hill. Many of the spectators, cold and weary, were trailing off to their beds. A number of others came running, aroused by the news, asking questions. Little knots of dignitaries were heading toward the Temple. There would be another gathering of the Sanhedrin there in a couple of hours. It seemed that a few of the senators, two particularly—Nicodemus and Joseph of Arimathea—had objected strenuously to the verdict and were questioning the legality of the trial. Angrily, Caiaphas had agreed that the body meet again for consultation before further action was taken. Some men were going home to get a little rest. Others were proceeding directly to the Hall of Jusice, that huge auditorium also known as the Hall of Hewn Stones, where they would debate or doze until this second meeting of the Sanhedrin was called to order.

Peter listened dazedly, grateful to have encountered the others, but too stricken to comment. Every step was torture from his crippled toe, and the agony in his breast was intolerable. From time to time he had to stop and rest, turning his head and lifting an arm to hide the tears still coursing down his cheeks.

"Peter, don't, please don't," John pleaded at last. "I can't bear to see you cry like that. It's not your fault. By the time I sent out for you the trial was almost over—all over, as far as Caiaphas was concerned. None of us got to testify for Jesus, not even Cleo or Abner."

Peter halted, his big face bitterly contorted. His nose was running like a baby's; he had to wipe it on his sleeve.

"It isn't that," he choked, struggling for control. "What hurts me so is that I denied him. Three times I denied him, just as he predicted. Pretended I didn't even *know* him. I don't deserve to live. I am no better than Judas!"

Chapter 26

CLEO did not go to Mary until midmorning. And when he arrived, it was all he could do to drag himself up those long steps. He had been awake all night, sleepless for some eternity that stretched back to a vague point he could scarcely remember. The trials, all those trials . . . incessant trials; five at least—maybe more.

Cleo tied his horse and stood for a moment, making absent gestures—efforts to straighten his beard and hair. He realized he was redeyed, unkempt. Incredible. He seemed to remember standing at a mirror in the house where Adah and the other women were waiting, and pouring water over himself. Yet it was vague now, he wasn't sure—only that the women were greatly agitated and anxious, not only about Jesus but about their men.

Yes, he had seen Peter, he told Adah—Peter would surely be there soon. And the twins—don't worry, he told their mother. Well, he had seen John, at least— encountered him at the hearing before Caiaphas, been with him most of the night, in fact. Around the Temple, the Hall of Hewn Stones. The Praetorium. Herod's palace. . . . And Jesus?

Yes, he had seen Jesus too. Sitting on a bench.

Cleo had bitten his lips, unable to go on. He could not, would not, torture them—or himself—with the scene. Jesus huddled in chains, jeered, spat upon, mocked by the soldiers as they played their favorite game, *Basileus*—the king. They had stripped him and robed him in scarlet (an old faded rag of Herod's). Blood ran down his face from a crown of thorns. (The thorn bushes were in bloom now; a few blood-drenched flowers were ludicrously entangled with the prongs— blades sharp enough to cut a finger in two. The soldiers whose jest this was had had to wear gloves of steel.) Untying one hand before dragging him away, they placed in it a reed for a scepter. And with other reeds they struck him. . . .

No, Cleo could not tell the women that. Nor Mary. No woman could stand it—he could not stand it. "Stop this!" Cleo remembered bawling, like a mad bull as he broke through the ranks. "Don't, *don't*! Please don't hurt him any more!"

For he knew this was only the beginning. The whip would be next, he was thinking wildly, the flagellums. Those whips weighted with stones and pieces of metal to tear the flesh. Wielded by men with the strongest arms. Thirty-nine lashes with the flagellums, that was usually it—no more than that by law. He'd passed the prison sometimes and heard men screaming.

"Don't beat him, promise you won't beat him," he wheedled. "Here—" He remembered fumbling for the pouch in his girdle, begging desperately, "I will pay you—see, I have money—only promise not to beat him!"

They had regarded him patiently, as if he were a little mad—as he was.

"It will be better," a sober, obviously distressed young Roman soldier tried to reassure him. "Really, they tell me it helps. Sometimes they die from the beatings, so they are spared hours on the cross. Or by then they are senseless, later they don't suffer so much."

Cleo had burst from the scene and been very sick, violently sick, unmanly and ill before the whole mob, there on the grass. When at last he turned his reeling head, his son—Mary's son—had vanished. . . .

Crucifixion. Death by crucifixion. Jesus had tried to prepare him for that one night, standing here on this very spot. "I must be lifted up . . . to draw all men to me." But nobody is ever prepared for such a brutal death. Not those who are left, at least. No, no, it isn't worth it. Jesus, son of my friend Joseph, and his Mary—my Mary—stop this. You can, you can, you must. If you are also truly the son of God, call upon your Father, call upon your merciful God himself to stop this.

It isn't worth it. Nothing is worth it!

Cleo pressed his hands against his raging head.

He was startled to realize that Magdalene had come swiftly to him, down the steps. They regarded each other a minute in silence. She was quite pale, but dry-eyed. "It's true then?" she stated.

Cleophas stiffened his jaw, struggling in vain to answer. In her quick, passionate way, Magdalene responded, embracing him, cradling his head briefly against her breast. "Come, we must go up to Mary. She is expecting you."

"Does she know?"

"Yes. All night long we have walked the roof, Mary and I, and Elizabeth, too, for a time, and prayed . . . though we knew. All night, until dawning, we saw the lights blazing, and somehow we knew. And this morning a servant who used to work here brought us the news. Mary is dressed and waiting. Both of us are ready."

Cleo had been leaning against her as they started up the steps. He straightened, halted abruptly. "Ready for what?" he gasped. He realized from her expression that the thing he had dreaded most was upon him. "Listen, you can't *be* there," he cried. "Either of you! I can't let you. He wouldn't want it. I've already seen more than I can bear. If I, a man, can bear no more . . . !"

Magdalene gazed steadily down on him from the upper step. "Then we will go without you."

Mary was sitting on a chair just inside the door. Small and white and still she sat there. Like a small white dove that has frozen in the grass, hoping not to be noticed, yet ready for flight. Though the day was turning hot, she wore a shawl about her shoulders and a scarf upon her head. Now and then as Cleo knelt beside her, a shudder convulsed her whole body; otherwise, she listened to his desperate imploring, absolutely still.

Finally Mary raised her eyes. "But he is my son," she reasoned simply. "I brought him into the world, I will stay with him to the end. I will walk beside him if they'll let me. I will hold his hand until they take him away. And when he is lifted up I will crouch at his feet and comfort him. I will caress those feet as I did when he was just a little boy. I will give him water to drink. If he wishes, I will sing to him as I used to, to put him to sleep." She was speaking in a mystical singsong, gazing at things Cleo couldn't see. But her fingers were laced in his, clinging tightly, fiercely, as if never to let go.

"Mary, you don't realize! You don't understand. It is a thing no mother could watch." Cleo paused, distraught. "You are very tired, you're not yourself. You must go to bed now, take a potion and try to sleep."

"Poor Cleo," Mary said, and laid her cool palm against his sweating brow. "It is you who must stay here and rest."

"Do you think I would leave you *now*? Mary, listen—there isn't much time, but I must tell you. I did my best for Jesus. I tried, I followed him everywhere in the hope of helping somehow. I bribed my way in, I begged them to let me speak up for him, tell them what I know. If it could have helped," he cried, "I was willing to die for him! I believe in Jesus, Mary—surely you realize that. I, too, believe that Jesus is the Messiah, the true son of God."

Mary nodded, still gripping his hand. This was important. But she wasn't surprised. Eventually those who loved her came to believe in her son. Joseph, Cleophas, Abner. Perhaps someday all her children, not just James and the girls but all of Jesus' brothers. And one day, all men—surely, someday, all men. . . .

The day was fiercely hot, the sun like a forge. The sky had a brassy hue, and the air was heavy, as if presaging a storm.

There was some confusion about getting to the city. Mary shook her head, and Cleo agreed—she could not possibly ride the horse. Cleo resorted to the two donkeys in the cave, and said he would walk beside the women. But his knees felt weak, and objects began swimming before his eyes. Leading the animals along the dusty roads, he had to keep fighting not to faint. Once he sagged; Magdalene sprang down to snatch the bridle from him.

"Please go back," he heard her throaty voice pleading. "You are in no condition—"

"No, no," he insisted, leaning against the sweaty beast for a minute, grimly bracing himself. "I will be all right. I've got to be *with* her!"

Fragments of the night's events flashed before him or drifted off as the three of them went on. Cleo remembered, or dreamed—he wasn't quite sure—that he had seen Judas in the Hall of Hewn Stones . . . the hundreds of lamps reflecting on the multicolored marble . . . the desperate face, the flash of silver . . . for some reason Judas was dashing handfuls of silver onto the floor. Such a small amount, it had occurred to Cleo, to make such a clatter . . . Judas shouting something . . . "Innocent, innocent, the man is *innocent*, do you hear? It is innocent blood you are shedding! You promised, you *promised*!" Judas sobbing as he ran from the sanctuary—of that Cleo was sure, the two had almost collided. Should I have tried to stop him?

Cleophas staggered slightly, sweat pouring from him. They were not far from Gethsemane now. Was it true that Judas had hanged himself in there? Or just another wild rumor? . . . Rumors sweeping Jerusalem this morning. Rumors last night, exciting the people who had appeared like a storm of locusts, swarming about the trials . . .

Pilate. Herod. Pilate again . . . The mobs around the Praetorium. The procurator's cold, disgusted face, eyeing the hordes on his doorstep. Hating them, knowing how much they hated him for squandering their money on this fabulous building with its fountains and baths to please his wife. There'd been a riot one year, thousands killed. . . . Loathing the job, wanting to be back with his peers in Rome: It was easy to read his face. . . . And now to be roused at the crack of dawn to settle a dispute that had nothing to do with him. A controversy between Jesus, the scribes and the priests. The government took no interest in religious matters. Why didn't they settle it themselves?

An ugly mob. Their righteous Jewish leaders refused to come inside to discuss it, lest they be soiled by Gentile contacts before their feast! Yet half of them hired by jealous priests to demand death for a harmless man. Pilate had argued and tried to reason with them in vain. "But what has the man *done?*" Finally, to appease the priests, he had taken Jesus inside with him to question him alone. Cleo had no idea what was said, knew only that Pilate returned convinced that Jesus didn't intend to overthrow Rome. "I find no fault in him. He's guilty of none of the things with which he has been accused. I will punish him and let him go. . . ."

Finally, when the people wouldn't have it, he threw up his hands, turning the whole thing over to Herod. Let Herod cope with it, Galilee was his jurisdiction, and the man was a Galilean. Let the king worry.

The palace of Herod . . . stories coming out. The old lecher was actually thrilled to see the fabled Jesus, eager for miracles: Perform some miracles! And when that didn't work, setting his soldiers on him to have a little fun . . . Jesus emerging blindfolded, wearing an old robe that stank of Herod, his sweat and his filth—about to be "crowned." Whoops of laughter, shouts of "King, the king!" Crowned then? No, maybe later—Cleo was confused. . . .

Back outside the Praetorium again. A nightmare, it couldn't be true; it seemed to Cleo he was floundering through a dream. . . . Pilate on the balcony once more, trying to reason with the wildly shouting mob—mostly tramps and prostitutes now, ruffians, thugs, scum. Somebody must have rounded them up. (Where were Jesus' friends? where were his men?) Trying to convince them without offending the priests.

Even Herod could find no crime in Jesus, Pilate told them, certainly nothing worthy of death. Enjoy yourselves with him awhile, beat him, but let him go. It was the custom to release a prisoner at festival time. Pick a man. "There is a man named Barabbas, seditionist and murderer—do you want him or Jesus? Which shall it be?"

"Barabbas! Barabbas!"

Pilate, defeated and exhausted from hours of exhorting them, called for a basin to wash his hands. "And what shall I do with your king of the Jews?"

"Crucify, crucify, crucify!" the people screamed.

And as Pilate washed his hands before them, he lifted them up for all to see: "Look, I am innocent of the blood of this righteous man. Do what you will."

Cleo stumbled. He realized the voices were coming from all around him. The heat, the shouting, the press of bodies were real. Where was he? He could no longer feel the tug of the bridle, hear the hooves on the cobbles. The stones were rough beneath his back, he seemed to have bumped his head. Someone was pouring water over his face; he gasped, sputtered, roused to see the apostle John crouched beside him. . . . Then he was lying on the grass—he could smell the grass.

"What happened? Where am I?"

"You fainted," John was saying in a voice of urgency and concern. "We carried you here. Forgive me if I leave you, I must hurry. I have tied the donkeys to that tree."

Cleo was struggling to sit up. "Where is Mary?" he cried, distraught.

"Magdalene has taken her on. . . . No, Cleo, you must lie still, you cannot come further. Your face is ashen, there is blood on your scalp where you bumped your head. Don't do this to Mary. She has enough to bear, you will only make things worse."

John hovered as Cleophas fell back, weeping bitterly, knowing

John was right. He was too weak to trust himself; the world was spinning. He had failed her, he would only add to the horror.

"I am going now to join them," John said anxiously, with great kindness. "I will go with them, Cleo. I will be with them. I will take care of her for you."

Chapter 27

*H*OW many lashes?

Two strong wrestlers were taking turns. . . . At last, panting, they paused to confer. Jesus could hear the rumble of their voices. Far short of the thirty-nine allowed, but: "Better stop now, while he can still walk." The prisoner had to be able to carry his own cross—all the way to Golgotha, beyond the city gates. He was already half gone. . . . One of them came to prod Jesus with his foot, where they had hung him against the wall for the beatings. Up all night, no rest, no water, no food, savagely beaten before they even got to him . . . time to stop. He could expire before he ever got to the hill. People were disappointed when this happened. The authorities would demand an explanation.

There was the heavy thud of their whips being thrown to the floor. Wiping their hands on their thighs, the athletes departed. Two more legionaries, much younger, came to take Jesus down. They laid him on the cold stone floor; he had collapsed in their arms. They had brought wet towels with which to sponge him off. It was less an act of mercy than of need. He might bleed to death unless they stanched the flow of blood. They must also somehow get him dressed. The two thieves, still yelling in another part of the fortress, would be paraded naked. This one was more important; their orders were to see that he was clothed.

The thick towels were quickly drenched; they had to keep wringing them out, red and dripping. The younger man's face was pale—it was the same soldier who had spoken to Cleo earlier. Seeing that his touch was careful, Jesus asked him to bathe his face as well. His nose was bashed and several teeth were broken; one eye was swollen

almost shut. During the torture, his tongue had been bitten through.
"Your . . . father," Jesus mumbled with difficulty, "the . . . centurion
. . . Capernaum?"

"He was," the youth choked. "He has gone back to Rome. But
he loves your people; he built your synagogue there." He stared at
the victim, incredulous, caught his breath. "I remember now—it must
have been you! I was about seventeen, his servant then, and deathly
ill. My master heard of you and had great faith in you. He was sure
you could heal me, though he felt unworthy to have you enter his
door. And you did. Though you never saw me, you made me well.
Because of you I am *here!*"

"You have . . . shown mercy," Jesus managed.

The youth was shaken, almost overcome. "I was his slave, but he
loved me; after you saved my life he adopted me. I owe you that too!"

They got Jesus to his feet. Covered his naked loins. But when they
would have robed him again in Herod's filthy royal castoff, Jesus struggled, and the soldiers threw it away, agreeing. The stench was too
disgusting even for them. "My own . . . robe." With his eyes he indicated his one last symbol of dignity, which someone had brought
into the dungeon. That once beautiful garment was also dirty now,
already bloodstained, and quickly soaked with fresh blood as they
pulled it over his head and about his mangled shoulders. Dazedly
Jesus remembered the jeweled girdle—when had he lost it? Maybe
somebody had found it? But they were tying a piece of frayed rope
about his waist instead. His fingers touched the place lovingly even
so, remembering the tiny grandmother who had been so proud of her
gift to him. But the pain was too great, and he could think of her no
more.

Supporting him from above and below, they led him up the narrow iron stairs, and out onto the parade grounds, where the sun beat
down, a blinding assault after the dungeon's cold black hole. Soldiers
were swarming about, gaily caparisoned, their lances flashing, but
sweating in the heat and resentful. This morning's usual brisk parade
had been canceled in favor of this grisly march to Golgotha. Their
mouths were sour with the wine they'd been drinking to fortify themselves. Their hands were rough and unsteady, trying to lash beams
onto the backs of two other victims; one was screaming and fighting
like a wild beast trying to escape, the other kept begging piteously.

Hurry, get the procession started! the commander was insisting; it was already almost noon, and a long walk ahead. These men had to be dead before sunset. Beginning of the Sabbath. Jews were very particular about their Sabbath, didn't want men still alive on their crosses after sunset, when it was unlawful either to guard them, kill them outright or cut them down.

They had shoved Jesus to his hands and knees. He felt the sudden crushing weight of the huge beam upon his lacerated shoulders, the bind of ropes and leather being lashed under his armpits and across his chest to keep it in place. It was hard to breathe. When he made feeble croaking sounds to indicate the problem, they loosened the straps a bit. Two men grabbed his arms, stretching them out as far as they could, so that his wrists could be bound tightly to the beam, cutting off the circulation to his hands.

At last, his back breaking, half crucified already, he was hauled upright, the massive *patibulum* swaying, so that he was like a great bird with wings outspread. A monstrous wounded bird, struggling to fly under the burden it carried.

The beam tipped dangerously at first, striking one of the soldiers, who jumped back, cursing. Jesus could only rock and stagger. To keep his balance, he must bend over as his bare feet fumbled slowly forward upon the burning stones, following the mounted legionaries.

Two officers on horseback were to lead the way. The frantic horses tossed their heads and whipped their tails, trying to drive away the gnats and flies. Hooves clattered on the pavement. Screeching and clanging, the gates of the Antonia Fortress swung open. Outside, a noisy crowd was waiting.

This was the last day of the Passover festival. Tired from drinking, dancing and celebrating, many people had slept late. But now most were out in force, swarming the bazaars and cafés, enjoying themselves before the Sabbath forced them back into their homes or tents or inns to rest and wait out the following holy day. News had spread, rumors were flying: The Sanhedrin had been up all night; a crucifixion might be added to the sights of Jerusalem today. Even a triple crucifixion!

While many people snatched their children and hurried off in horror, others had rushed to the fortress hoping to see the execution party emerge; more of the curious were lining the streets. . . .

Come see, come see—but be careful: One of the criminals is said to be a blasphemer; you would be defiled if you gazed on his countenance! . . .Which one, which one of the three? . . . The first, just behind the two Romans on horseback. Quick, push forward through the crowd, close enough to spit on his face. It's your duty. Hide your eyes, but spit to signify you have no part in his guilt. Don't touch him, he's all bloody, the filthy dog! And look (it's all right, if you don't look on his face) there's a dog following him!

The dog had appeared out of nowhere, and was trotting along beside him, nuzzling Jesus whenever he sagged or fell, baring his teeth and snapping at the guards who must prod his master back into action. They went after Ben, too, with their lances, but he always came darting back.

It's the heretic all right, the one who's claiming to be the Messiah, wants to overthrow the Temple, get rid of the priests. . . .

It must be that mad prophet from Galilee, the one that preached from the Temple porch. The teacher, the healer, the miracle worker! Preaching and healing. Often a dog was with him, a brown dog like this. . . .

Some people were sobbing, reaching out their hands to Jesus, though he was too blinded with spittle and blood and the buzzing, stinging flies to see them. He could not even lift his hands to drive the torments away.

He saved my life. . . . He saved my child. . . . I am walking because of him. . . . Jesus, son of God, don't let this happen. Save yourself—don't let them do this to you!

Why are they killing him? others were asking. *The priests are jealous of him, Herod's afraid of him. He's John the Baptist's cousin, he might cause an uprising, another slaughter. . . .*

A young man fought his way forward, fell into step beside the accompanying soldiers, who were trying to keep back the crowd. "See here," he reasoned desperately, "your prisoner brought me back from the dead, I tell you! You could ask my mother, if she were here—she lives in Nain, my widowed mother. I was already dead and on my bier when Jesus saw us and took pity on us, came to my side and touched me—"

"Stand back," the soldier warned curtly, staring straight ahead. "We must keep order. We do not judge him. We are simply carrying out the execution; we have nothing to do with his guilt or innocence."

"Stop this, stop this!" a woman was moaning hysterically. "My little girl was blind from birth—look at her now!" She shoved the bright-eyed youngster forward. "He healed her, he made her see. . . . Jesus, dear Jesus, stop them, don't let them. Save yourself! We need you—don't leave us, don't leave us!"

Trying to hush and comfort her, friends led the woman away. "Don't," they were pleading. "It will only make things harder for his mother." They gestured in compassion and embarrassment. "See, she is standing over there."

Jesus became aware of Mary then; he knew she was standing not far away, between Magdalene and John. They were supporting her, their arms about her as the horses clumped slowly toward them, under the arched entrance of the canopied street. He could not see her at first, but he felt her agony and knew that she was pressing one hand against her mouth. . . . That she should see her son like this, his hair and beard matted with blood, his face savaged, his back bent, staggering, half crawling along under his disgraceful burden, like a worm. . . . He had fallen twice; she must not see him fall again. Gritting his teeth, Jesus strained to lift his chin, to pull himself upright, his back a little more upright, that he might walk before her with some dignity, like a man.

And as he drew closer he turned his tormented head in an effort to make out her face. The figures loomed and receded through the blur of blood and slime. He halted, struggling to see them. One eye was swollen shut now; insects swarmed about his face, maddened by the blood and the sweat. He was powerless to brush them off, he could not wipe his eyes. He could only stare in the direction of those he loved, trying desperately to convey his love.

Magdalene's face was a blur, large, white; John, he sensed, was weeping. But Mary's face emerged, small and bittersweet, gazing back with her heart in her eyes.

Jesus' puffed lips were struggling. His teeth had been loosened, his wounded tongue was swollen with heat and thirst. He could barely speak. But as he saw her thus at last, the words were torn from him. *"Mo-ther!* . . . O-o-o-o-h, *Mother!"*

A little way beyond, Jesus fell again. For the third time. The crowds were growing more sympathetic. There were hoots of derision for the soldiers, cheers for the fiercely protective dog. Cries of "Help him, help him!" More women were weeping. The commander in charge was growing impatient—and concerned. He pulled his horse to a stop, to discuss the situation with the officer beside him.

These delays were getting serious—past noon and not yet even to the Ephraim Gate. These men had to be crucified within the hour or there would be trouble to pay with the Jews. Probably trouble already: The priests and other dignitaries who were to observe the execution had left for the site long ago. It was hot out there, very hot and stinking—they would be fuming.

And if their prize was dead before they even nailed him up for an example—! Or if they got him up so late he wasn't dead by sunset—

Gaius, the legate, dismounted to inquire of the soldiers who were both coping with the dog and trying to get Jesus back onto his feet.

"What do you think?"

"Very weak, sir," said the one kneeling beside him. "He can't carry this load much longer."

"Untie him, give him a drink of water. We'll have to get somebody else." Pushing back his helmet, Gaius surveyed the crowd, quickly spotted a candidate, and beckoned with an imperious wave.

The man who strode forward in response was husky, tall, bull-necked. His face was grim. His name was Simon. He had come all the way from Cyrene in Libya, bringing his two small sons for their first Passover. This was their final day of the happy week. He had taken them out this morning for another glimpse of the Temple, shining like a jewel in the sun. A procession was just turning the corner, heading toward the city gates. The crowds were so great they had run toward it jubilant, never expecting anything like this. He had tried to shield his sons' eyes, had hurried the boys back to their mother, yet returned himself, drawn by some compulsion he could not explain.

Simon nodded at the Roman's request. Without a word, he went to the prostrate man, helped loosen his bonds, and picked up the heavy crossbeam. He was a very strong man, a woodcutter; he had eaten well and slept all night; he had not been beaten, had lost no blood. With only a few grunts, he shouldered the beam, and gripping it firmly with his big hairy hands, stalked ahead with it through the gate and on up the sloping path toward Calvary.

The place was a deserted field just outside Jerusalem: rocky, weed-grown, its lower levels used for the burning of refuse; its broad upper area for crucifixions, for the knoll on which the crosses stood could be seen by travelers passing along the highway to the west. A grisly warning.

Toward its top, a grotesque, empty-eyed rock formation gave it also the Aramaic name Golgotha—"The Skull." Vultures and buzzards circled endlessly overhead, or plummeted suddenly to snatch at scraps of flesh. Hopeful, half-starved dogs prowled the heaps of smoldering garbage, which gave off an acrid blue haze. On days of execution the dogs lay in wait, panting, their yellow eyes on the dying. On these days too, from a clump of trees not far from the knoll, the witches hovered. Very old women, or sometimes young ones, secretly clutching small vessels in which they might catch a few drops of the victims' blood for their rites.

Striping the sky like a bleak and barren forest were the permanent vertical *stipites* to which the crossbars would be fastened: shorter stakes for petty criminals, taller ones for the more important—any person who should be lifted up plainly for all to see and revile. The three supports selected for today were perfect: a high central pole, flanked by two shorter ones. (It would be easy to hoist the thieves. They would have to use a ladder for the Galilean.) All provided an excellent view for the court of observers, who would be watching from the hillock, and all were highly visible from the road.

The soldiers who had been sent out early to make preparations were pleased with their choice, but hot, half drunk, and growing nervous at the delay. It was a relief when at last they saw the procession come toiling up the hill, but something of a shock. For a few paces in the lead, ahead of even the horses, a big man was stalking, carrying the crosspiece for one of the accused.

Simon flung the huge beam down. It landed with an explosion of dust at the soldiers' feet. He was very hot, breathing hard, angry, very angry, consumed with some helpless rage. He could smell the tarred wood on his hands, the rank wild sweetness of spring weeds. He saw the huge mallets lying in the dirt or propped against the posts. He saw the buckets of sharp, glittering three-cornered nails. Saw also a pail of the slop called *posca*, made of vinegar and beaten eggs, with which the guards refreshed themselves while waiting for the victim to die.

He felt sick to his stomach. He knew he could not witness the brutality to come. The air was sultry, leaden; it was hard to breathe. An ominous rumbling came from the mountains, the sky was overcast, a few dark clouds were forming. A storm could be brewing. Rare for this time of year. Could be a bad one. Good thing, though—might wash things clean. This filthy place! He had to get out of here fast, get back to the decency of his wife and sons. But he could not leave without another look at that poor wretch. Glad he had helped him, spared him at least that much more torture.

Jesus was standing upright now, and Simon was astonished to see how tall he was, shocked to discover his dignity and beauty. The hair and beard, blood-matted though they were, the bruised and battered face—yet this was a man of unusual beauty. A nobleman perhaps; it was evident in the way he strove to bear himself even now, in the sheer power of personality that still poured from him, jolting Simon.

His robe too, dirty and bloodstained, yet it still glistened faintly, white and silver—an excellent robe, a robe without seams. Two soldiers had leapt forward and were beginning to strip it from him. Simon shuddered; a little cry of protest escaped him. They had recognized its value—he would not be allowed to die in it. They would probably roll the dice for it as he hung above them. This was the way of soldiers, to be expected. . . . But no more, Simon thought ferociously. *No more!*

The other prisoners, naked from the beginning, and no longer shielded by the crowds, were being paraded across the field. Simon could hear the roars of laughter, the shouting and jeering, along with a few shrill screams from horrified women.

Simon's jaw tightened; he clenched his fists. Gaius, who was overseeing the preparation of Jesus, was draping his robe, with some distaste because of the blood, over his arm. They were ripping Jesus' tunic off now and casting it on the ground. But when they reached for his last remaining cover, that piece of linen which was wrapped around his loins, Simon heard himself uttering one curt command.

"Stop. No more!" His voice was not loud, only hard with the authority born of outrage.

Astounded, the soldiers halted, turned to regard him. "Who are you?" the officer asked.

"Simon of Cyrene. The one who carried his cross. Have the decency not to expose this innocent man. His mother may be in the crowd."

Gaius' cheeks burned; he was affronted, defensive, yet ashamed. We are not monsters, he thought. We, too, have wives and mothers. And now he remembered Simon. "Very well. You did me a favor. I owe you one." He made a reluctant but restraining gesture to the guards. "No more," he ordered. "That's enough."

Simon plunged through the surrounding confusion of men, horses and equipment—ladders, ropes, pulleys—tripping and nearly falling over one of the ugly black crossbeams lying on the ground. "Stand back, stand back!" soldiers were warning people who were trying to get close enough to watch the nailing, sometimes adding they'd actually get a better view from higher ground. Dogs barked, flies buzzed, vultures circles, acrid smoke drifted from the incessant fires. Excited or grieving spectators were still trailing up the path, though not as many as might have been expected; some had already seen enough, and the day was so hot and sultry, a storm threatening.

Perched on a semicircle of rocks which formed a natural amphitheater, robed priests and well-dressed personages were mopping their brows, cursing the heat, and occasionally bellowing at the Romans. A few Pharisees, deciding they had more important things to do, were rising in obvious disgust and about to depart. Passing them, Simon surmised they must be members of the court responsible for the coming travesty. Pompous, self-righteous, annoyed at the inconvenience, they would go back to their day's business, pray loudly on street corners and make another sacrifice at the Temple.

Nearby, a small group of women, obviously frightened and bewildered, huddled together conferring, and then took refuge in the shade of a clump of trees. All were weeping; no doubt friends or relatives of the condemned, Simon thought. And again he was assailed by that blind, debilitating rage.

Last of all he encountered the three. Magdalene and John were supporting Mary as they came slowly across the trampled grass. Simon halted; his heart stopped. For he knew the minute he saw the small woman between them that this could only be the mother of Jesus, the man whose cross he had borne. That same mysterious beauty. That same poise and dignity of bearing. Even in these circumstances of utter degradation, an absolute purity and perfection that seemed to eradicate, even to glorify for an instant, the ugly squalor of this scene.

Simon was drawn to her, blocking their path. He gazed at Mary in awe, feeling the same piercing thrill of wonder he had just experienced in the presence of her son. Though not a demonstrative man, he had to curb a preposterous impulse to throw himself at her feet.

Yet she was human; that small sweet face, however brave, was already agony-scarred. How much could she bear? The ultimate agony lay ahead . . . *but some things she must not bear.* Simon's eyes signaled quickly to Magdalene and John. Frowning and shaking his head, he indicated the direction he had just left. "I wouldn't advise—" he whispered. "There is a grotto just beyond. Take her there to wait. Come, I'll show you."

Both nodded. But as they started to follow his lead, Mary pulled back, protesting. "Where are we going? No, no, I must be with him!"

"In a little while." John's hand was firm on her arm. "Please, Mary, this is best."

"Don't do this, don't keep me from him!"

"For his sake, Mary," Magdalene kept saying. "Jesus wouldn't want you there—not yet, not yet."

Simon prayed desperately that he still could find it. A cool cleft, half hidden by vines. He'd played there with his Jerusalem friends on visits as a boy. It had been their secret place. Incredibly, it was still there, actually an arch, with openings that revealed the sky, but its thick rock walls would mute the sounds from below. Within, all was silent except for small birds chirping.

Simon urged them to wait there. He didn't say why, but their anguished faces told him they understood. Mary's eyes were closed; she was rocking back and forth, murmuring her son's name in a little singsong, as to a child. Instinctively, with a pathos that tore Simon, she had covered her ears.

There was a moment of awkwardness as Simon turned to leave. He knew he could not stay with them; it would be an intrusion. And he was desperate to get back to his wife and sons. Yet he had another strange, strong feeling—the longing to remain.

A curious silence greeted him when he burst back out into the light. The crowd seemed to be waiting, expectant. There was only a low murmuring, which seemed at first one with the faint thunder from the mountains—then, piercing the air, came the first bloodcurdling screams. . . .

Simon refused to look back; he couldn't. But he knew, as he ran furiously, blindly, from Golgotha, that the deed was done.

Waiting there with the women in the grotto, John fixed his mind on James. Both women were trembling; he had an arm around each of them to steady them, but his own knees were weak and his heart faint. Frantically, desperately, to drown out the sounds and the horror ahead, John focused his thoughts on his brother. What had happened to him? And the other apostles. Had they met with trouble? All night he had expected at least some of them to appear, searched for them in the crowd. Especially James! Where were they now, on this critical day? . . . Peter's absence he could understand; Peter had been beside himself last night, on the point of collapse. But James, and the others . . . Where were Jesus' men?

The women, amazingly, were out there, John remembered. Those who had served the Master, and others, huddled together on the hillside some distance from the knoll. Looking up, in his distraction, John had seen them as he and Magdalene led Mary across the field. . . . But James—they had never been apart, not in a single adventure or hour of trouble. Surely James would come running to join him; it seemed to John he could not, literally could not, lift his eyes to that cross without him. . . .

The crowd was roaring, shouting wildly. Its noise reached the three clinging to each other for comfort in the small enclosure. It was time now. Whatever was happening was beginning and they could not escape it; they could hide here no longer.

Mary was the first to speak. "Come," she said tightly. "We must go."

She freed herself from their embracing arms, moved quickly to the doorway and began to claw away the entangling vines. She was strong with a sudden tigerish strength. She began to run ahead of them down the path.

"Wait, Mary, wait!" they cried, for the path was rutted and stony. They followed, alarmed lest she stumble and fall. The brambles tore at her skirts—they had to free her. The thorns scratched her legs, pierced her sandals. She was weeping desperately, yet making no sound; never had they been aware of such utter, heartrending weeping. And as they paused, while John knelt to draw a thorn from her foot, her eyes were straining in the direction of the knoll. *"Tinoki, tinoki*—my little one, my precious boy . . . Jesus . . . *Jesus!"* she was crying, with such passion it seemed her very love might release some power to bring him down.

And through John's consciousness flashed a staggering thought: Was it possible, was it possible? At the last minute, even now! Beneath the sweetness, gentleness and beauty of this tiny woman ran a strength beyond anything he had ever known. The apostles had been granted the power to perform miracles—why not Mary, his own mother? The one who had first given life to this Son of God. Might not God grant her the power to save that precious life now?

Around them rained the clamor, the shouting frenzy of the crowd. Some were shaking their fists toward the three crosses that could be glimpsed above the heads of the soldiers, mounted or on foot, who were keeping people at a distance. Some were laughing, others weeping. But a kind of angry jubilation prevailed, which became a chant, accompanied by stamping staves:

"Come down, come down!" the people chanted, as they swayed. "King of the Jews, come down! Miracle worker, son of God, heal yourself!" *Bam, bam, bam!* went the staves. "Come down, come down!"

The Roman commander came riding up to the three. "Go back. We have strict orders—you can't come nearer." Then he saw Mary's white, determined face.

"This is his mother," Magdalene said grimly, before John could speak. "He deserves at least that comfort. Let us through!"

Gaius caught his breath. So the Cyrenian was right. The man's mother was here. Sweat poured down his scarlet face. "Follow me," he said, cursing and heartsick that he could do no more.

The soldiers assigned to do the job had picked up their tools and been dismissed. One of the thieves had put up a savage fight; it had taken four of them to hold him down. Spikes were still scattered all over the ground. The commander had commended the soldiers and said they needn't linger to hear the screaming. Those forced to remain on guard stood leaning on their spears, backs to the crosses, or wandered about visiting quietly, trying not to listen.

Two, as required by law, were dipping sponges in mixtures of vinegar, gall and myrrh, preparing to offer them up on reeds when the hideous muscle cramps began and the pains and the yelling became intolerable.

A little group of four was squatting, rattling dice in a leather cup. The thieves were naked, but they could gamble for the tall one's garments. A pitiful, bloody heap, but the robe was worth something—a truly fine robe, without seams. One of them held it up to be examined. The highest roll of the dice would win it.

"What's he up there for?" one of them asked. Nobody seemed to know. Then they noticed the sign of ridicule above his head: *Jesus of Nazareth, King of the Jews*. A seditionist, evidently. They regarded each other, puzzled, and shrugged. "The Jews will try to put the blame on us."

"Let them. Anyway, we're forgiven. Didn't you hear what he said? Asked his God to forgive us, claimed we didn't know what we were doing."

They laughed doubtfully. The youth who was rolling the dice paused, cocked his head. "I'll say one thing for him—he's brave. Not like the others. Not a peep out of him." He snapped his fingers: a pair of fives! He had won the robe. "Look." He shifted around to observe. "He's even refusing the sponge."

The violent muscle contractions had set in. Unbearable cramps that traveled from the arms down through the back, belly, legs, the clawing nailed feet, set the victims mad with pain. This was the best time to offer the balm; it stupefied them somewhat, and sometimes hastened their asphyxiation. Which was an act of mercy for everybody; otherwise the thing could go on for hours. They were anxious to get out of here, catch the games at the coliseum, if it didn't storm—the skies looked threatening.

The writhing, moaning criminals were sucking the sponge greedily and begging for more. Jesus, elevated between them, only shook his head, though his face was contorted and his lips nearly bitten through. . . . He must keep his senses as long as he could. In his own agony he must try to comfort the two who were suffering with him: the thief who was reviling and cursing him for not performing a miracle that would save them all; and the other one, pleading piteously, "Remember me, please remember me when you come into your kingdom!" Jesus must utter such words as he could from his tortured mouth, to help them.

But he could not help himself; he sagged and rose, sagged and rose, strangling, fighting for breath. Fighting to remain conscious. He could not die without seeing Mary once more, and she was coming, she was coming. . . . Through Jesus' anguish he sensed their approach—his precious mother, with Magdalene, the women he loved above all others except his blessed lost Tamara. And John, the apostle dearest to his heart.

Ben, lying forlornly at the foot of the cross, confirmed it. Suddenly raising his head, he began to bark and darted out to meet them. The soldiers had given up trying to drive him off with the other dogs. Let him stay, he was obviously attached to his master. Let him lie there, head on his paws, grieving. He would keep away the scavengers that were sure to come prowling.

Jesus strove to lift his head as the three figures swam dimly into focus. Though moaning now, he could not greet them, he could only form the shape of their names with his broken lips. He could not gesture: His crossed feet were nailed to the post; huge spikes had been driven through his wrists. He could only hang there helpless, while the blood ran down his arms. He could move only his head and his great loving, pleading eyes. But the shadow of a smile flickered. And at last, with an effort, he managed to speak:

"Moth-er . . . behold . . . *your son!*"

Mary clutched her aching throat, but her chin was high, as thus at last she beheld him—as she had always known that one day she would: The baby she had borne and suckled at her breast. The beautiful boy she had raised. The youth, beloved of all who knew him, who would be tempted as other men are tempted, that he might be totally one with man. But overcoming temptation, to walk the earth as shepherd, teacher, prophet, healer. Above all, as the fulfillment of God's promise—Messiah, Son of God.

Again and again the sword had pierced her heart, or so she thought. But now that he hung before her, dirty, bruised and beaten, naked except for the bloody scrap that barely covered his loins, pinioned to those stakes like some massive bird that can no longer fly—sagging and rising, sagging and rising in order to breathe, to sustain itself—Mary knew the sword had only scratched the surface of her heart: perhaps to test the true depth to which it could finally be plunged. Savagely, blindly, with a pain too intense for tears or sound, she suffered it now. Every lash that had torn his flesh, every blow that struck, every nail that had been driven through gristle and vein, Mary felt them now . . . she hung on the cross with her son. But for his sake she could not, would not, cry.

Mary nodded. Setting her teeth, summoning all her strength, her own lips smiled faintly back. "I am proud of you," she cried softly. "Oh, my darling, no mother on earth will ever be prouder of her son."

Deeply moved, Jesus turned his head to John. "Behold . . . your . . . mother!" he panted.

John gripped Mary's hand. "I will take care of her for you," he promised brokenly. "From this day on she will be as my own."

On a great shudder of love, Jesus became aware of Magdalene, who had come forward, and taking the hem of her gown, was wiping the blood from his feet. Her shoulders were shaking, her dark head was bent. There was no basin with which to wash them, but leaning her cheek against them as she had once long ago, she bathed his feet with her tears and kissed them. She looked up then, and stood gazing at him, desolate in her adoration, drinking in the sight of him, the sweet and terrible sight of him. Helpless, bereft, she could only stare at him, while the things she longed to say to him seemed almost to burst her heart.

There was a snarl of thunder, a stab of lightning that brought the startled soldiers to their feet. Some came running, thinking it had struck the cross. Most of the watching crowd had already fled before the storm. Hurling only a few taunts and insults behind them, they had gathered up their skirts and departed. The hillside was almost empty, except for the little huddle of distraught women, who still kept vigil among the suddenly lashing trees. There was no longer need for the mounted soldiers; the knoll itself had cleared, except for a handful of essential guards, who stared anxiously at the darkening skies.

Jesus rolled his eyes upward. His suffering was growing monstrous, every nerve and muscle cramped into knots—hard, stony, cruel—enough to tear teeth from their sockets; the unquenchable thirst was beginning. He could not bear for them to see him in such torture. "Please . . . please!" They must go. Leave quickly. His parched lips strove to form the words, his eyes were pleading. A terrible storm was coming, it would be dark soon, they couldn't find their way. . . . These things he conveyed.

"But we love you!" John wept in desperation. "We want to stay with you."

No, no, no—Jesus was violently shaking his head. His gaze fell on the cowering dog. Benjamin was so afraid of storms. "Ben . . . Benjy . . ." Jesus turned his face toward his mother, eyes streaming, and she knew he was bestowing the animal's care to her.

"Come," John said. "Ben's frightened. He wants us to take the dog and leave."

"I can't, I can't," Mary said fiercely. "Never! You take the dog and go. I will stay and die with him."

"You must come with us." Magdalene's arms were about her, warm, sweet, strong. "We will go only a little way, just up the hill; we will join the women on the hill."

The greenish light had turned gray, an unnatural dusk was falling, darkness coming fast. They had to grope their way, John carrying Benjy, who kept whimpering, struggling, his head peering over John's shoulders. Suddenly, at a clap of thunder, the dog broke free; before they could catch him he was running back through the storm to the cross. The skies were exploding. Lightning flashed, spearing the ground; it was their only illumination, guiding them around the rocks and thorns. The very earth shook beneath their feet. It helped Mary to know that Ben had raced back to be with Jesus. Screaming, she had tried to break free herself; she would have run back through the storm to him too, if she could. John and Magdalene had restrained her.

At last they found the sheltering thicket where the women stood fast. Weeping, they held out their arms to her, drawing her in. To Mary's amazement, her sister, also named Salome, was among them. "Hush, hush, hush," she was soothing, "I am with you. Our mother sends her love. . . . And you have other sons—"

"They have abandoned their brother," Mary heard herself moaning. "They don't believe in him."

"Not all of them," Salome tried to comfort. "James does. And Jude, I'm sure. They are in Jerusalem. They arrived only this morning and are even now with Elizabeth."

The trees thrashed, lightning stabbed the leaves. "Your sons have come to take you home," Salome told her. "They had hoped to take Jesus with them."

"They are too late, too late!" Mary sobbed wildly, sinking to her knees. "Their brother's body will be buried by sunset."

Though there would be no sunset this night. It was night already; the skies were black, the sun hiding its face. The wind calmed suddenly, and the stars came out, blandly twinkling. An eclipse, the women about them were saying. But Mary knew better: God himself had died, and the whole world had gone into mourning.

The women came to kneel beside her, to hold her hand and press wine to her lips, to try to comfort her. It didn't matter; she knew them and she knew them not; she hung on the cross with her son. . . . At last, John was drawing Mary to her feet. The sky was growing lighter; the eclipse seemed to be over. Three hours, they said, it had been dark, but she knew that for her it would be dark forever.

"Come," Magdalene and John were saying, along with Mary's sister, on whom she leaned. "We will go. We must go back—there are men there asking to see you."

Gaius, the officer who had led them in, came up to Mary and held her hands, though he could not meet her eyes. "Our soldiers did their best," he said tightly. "They offered him balm again, and at the last he took it."

"Did he say anything?" Mary pleaded.

"Yes. It was—I'm not sure of the language and he was very weak, though at that time the guards say he rallied, and spoke clearly—"

"What did he *say*?" she demanded.

"I believe it was—" He hesitated. "Forgive me, it was—that he cried out in a loud voice asking why his god had forsaken him."

Another soldier spoke up "*Eli, Eli, lama sabachthani,*" he offered. "Those were his exact words. I know the language and I heard them clearly."

"*My God, my God, why have you forsaken me?*" Mary whispered. She swayed, was steadied by Magdalene, twisted free. She must brace herself. Her fists clenched. Her face lifted. Small and fierce she stood, dry-eyed, beyond tears, staring at her son hanging there in this cruel, seeming ignominy. Torn, savaged, smeared in his own blood, his magnificent head no longer struggling to remain upright, but lying at last on his breast, rejected, defeated, submissive.

Yet more—something more. . . . In forgiveness and dignity!

For she saw that those arms, still nailed to the cross, were outstretched in blessing. *Eternal blessing,* it came to her in a thrill of revelation. *The blessing of the suffering savior.* Jesus, in his anguish, was but quoting the famous twenty-second psalm of David, which so vividly portrayed him:

The enemy, this gang of evil men, surrounds me like a pack of dogs. They have pierced my hands and feet, they have exposed my bones with their whips, they gloat and stare, they divide my garments among them and cast lots for them. . . .

"My God, my God," Mary cried out softly, in awe and thanksgiving. "He was confirming for us that he *is* the promised One!"

The soldiers regarded her curiously, surprised at her words, not understanding. How could they? His executioners were Romans; they knew nothing of psalms and prophecies. Most of them were young, wretched, detesting this job. She pitied them, even the one exhibiting Jesus' robe to the others; it glistened in the sun even now . . . that last proud gift of his grandmother. And though Mary's heart broke, she was also comforted, remembering, as her son had:

But even in my affliction the Lord has not despised me, nor hidden his face from me. . . . I will trust him; I will stand and praise him before all the people, I will fulfill my vows . . . our children, too, shall hear from us about the wonders of the Lord, generations yet unborn shall hear of his miracles. . . .

Jesus knew—he had always known—this was not defeat but triumph!

No, she could not convey this to the Romans. She couldn't even proclaim it to those who had condemned him, nor to those who so viciously mocked and reviled him during his torture. The crowd of spectators had fled before the coming storm. Only the women still weeping on the hill would understand; and the two who had watched beside her. But soon, very soon, all who remembered that psalm would start up in horror at the events of this day.

For they would realize a truth that would haunt them forever: They had murdered their own Messiah.

"Your son also said, 'It is finished,' " another guard stepped up to inform her. "I, too, speak the language, and heard it. Your son submitted his spirit to his god."

Mary nodded, grateful. "Yes. It is accomplished." At last a tear darted down her cheek; she brushed it away with a finger. "He has fulfilled his mission."

John approached with the two men. He introduced them. Nicodemus, a tall, dignified gray man with sober eyes. One of Jesus' first converts, Mary remembered. The other, squat, plump, blunt, deeply shaken: Joseph of Arimathea, a scribe. "Both of us heard your boy speak one time at the Temple, when he was twelve. You had lost him, remember? We were so impressed—" The phlegmy voice broke; he paused to wipe his eyes. "We followed his career, we did everything we could to save him. And now . . ." They had gone to the authorities for permission to bury Jesus, they told her.

They glanced at the skies. The sun was a glowing disk on the horizon. "There isn't much time," said Joseph. "I have an unused tomb in a nearby garden. We would like to carry him there now, if you approve."

Mary drew her hand down from her eyes. It was trembling. She stared at them for a minute, and pointed feebly to the cross. Soldiers were already hastily setting up their ladders, pulling and wrenching at the spikes that had impaled him. "I . . . you will bring him to me first?"

"Of course." They conferred with John a minute, looking for a place where she could sit down. Gently, then, they led her to a fallen log.

The body of Jesus had collapsed into the soldiers' arms. His legs had not been broken to assure death, but blood and water spurted from his pierced side. They stanched the flow as best they could with a towel. Then, moving carefully, the soldiers carried Jesus to his mother and laid him across her lap.

Chapter 28

*M*AGDALENE lay in torment, listening for the first crowing of the cocks. All night, it seemed to her, she had lain thus listening, in the house to which she had returned with the other women.

From time to time she had gone to the window and scanned the skies, praying for the first gray signs of morning. Only then would she dare to rise and slip away, back out to the garden. She knew she must go, yet she could never find her way in the dark. She knew only that she must see Jesus once more. Make her way somehow into the place where they had laid him. Untie the napkin from his face and gaze upon him; touch him, anoint his body with the spices and oils there had been so little time for during that frantic and devastating hour when the men—with all those women following, wailing and weeping—had carried his poor tortured body to the tomb.

It had all been so rushed, so confusing. What to do about Jesus' mother? Mary had been unable to stand, once they took her son from her; she could only cling desperately to her sister. John, running up from where they were wrapping the Lord, had told the two to wait; litters were being summoned to take both of them to Ein Karem. He, John, would stay with them and see them safely there.

Magdalene had realized she was no longer needed. She had hurried to join the others; but the precious body was already being wrapped; curious people stood about watching—the soldiers, one or two officials, servants, and all the distraught women. No time to embrace him, to tell him goodbye; too late to say the things she had longed to while there was still time. What had locked her lips? Why hadn't she had the courage to cry out to him the true depth and

⟨ 385 ⟩

breadth of her love while he hung above them on the cross? The presence of his mother—of John?

Magdalene bit her fingers, tormented by frustration and regret. She had been last in the procession. She wanted to be the first to go to him now. Mad as it might seem, she would make her way alone to the garden, and be alone with him at least a few minutes, in tenderness and caring. How she would roll away the stone she didn't know. Although it occurred to her that by sunrise a gardener might be about, and willing to help her. Or one of the guards. There would be guards before the entrance.

Nicodemus and Joseph of Arimathea had spoken of the guards before they left the tomb. Turning to regard the immense wheel now rolled before its door, they had remarked that the place would be safe. Dusk was falling, jackals howling, the awful ordeal of night's loneliness descending; yet they agreed there would surely be soldiers arriving soon. Pilate, Herod, the high priest—if necessary the whole Sanhedrin—would be sure to send armed men to guard the tomb, lest the body disappear.

"They can't risk having the apostles break in and steal it," said Nicodemus. "As they might try—and you know what they'd claim."

Joseph of Arimathea had snorted. "I wouldn't worry about that. By now that loyal band of his is probably back home safe in Galilee!" Sardonic, grieving, he motioned to the dog that now lay, head on his paws, before the stone. Joseph's thick lips quivered. "Jesus has his own guard," he muttered brokenly, and bent to pet him. "Well, Benjamin, you followed him this far. Now stay and guard him well."

Magdalene was concerned about the dog. She prayed that the guards, exasperated by his stubborn vigil, had not killed him. Or even succeeded in driving him away. She must somehow get him back to Mary. She would carry him, if necessary. . . .

Magdalene got up once more, creeping around the women whose pallets lay beside hers, and scanned the skies. A few scattered stars still shone, but the skies were paling. The moon, still beaming but fragile, floated like a bubble on the topmost spires of the Temple. A Temple still intact, she noticed. Wild stories had been circulating—all during the Sabbath. About the eclipse, the darkness, the earthquake: It had shaken the very foundations of the Temple, people were saying at the synagogues and in their homes—worshipers there had screamed and fled; the very Holy of Holies was threatened, the veil before it had been suddenly rent. There were even claims that some tombs had burst open, graves given up their dead. Superstitious frenzy, the kind of talk that followed any unusual event, especially at festival time, when emotions ran high. Magdalene dismissed them.

It would soon be daybreak; the first roosters were crowing. Carefully, Magdalene dressed, pulled on her cloak. The garden would be cold. Trying not to waken anyone, she crouched to find her sack, and fumbled in it for the small bag of myrrh and aloes she had assembled. One of the women rolled over, groaning. Magdalene held her breath. She must hurry. Soon they would all be stirring, anxious to go with her. She did not want them. She loved them, they had become her family, her sisters, but this was something she must do alone. For she knew that however deep and genuine their sorrow, they could not love Jesus as she did; none of them owed him as much as she did.

Few women had been abused by men as she had—used, degraded and nearly murdered by men in the street. Jesus had more than saved her life, he had restored her virtue, her dignity, her self-respect. Of them all, only Adah, who had been like a mother to her, could even begin to understand. And Adah had Peter. Adah, who had been frantic at his absence, was asleep even now in another chamber, in her husband's arms.

Peter had returned last night, shortly after sunset, when the Sabbath was over. John was with him; he had found Peter, exhausted and bereft, back at the upper room where the apostles were hiding. Their arrival here had been a tremendous relief to everyone. James was all right, John told his desperately worried mother. Confused, shocked, distraught—yes, like all the other men. But unharmed. The apostles were taking counsel about what to do next. It would not be safe to show themselves just yet. Nicodemus and Joseph of Arimathea were keeping them informed.

"We, too, could be targets," John said, "at least for the next few days. The council wants to be sure we won't cause trouble." He hesitated. "Or try to steal the body of our Lord." The women gasped. "They are very uneasy about Jesus' statement 'I will rise up again in three days.' " John had spoken calmly, trying not to alarm them. "Pilate has ordered extra guards at the tomb; but only until there's no danger we will try to claim that he has risen from the dead."

Both Peter and John urged the women to be patient until this blew over. It wouldn't be safe to start home just yet, as other pilgrims would be doing. In a few days the apostles would come forth and form a caravan to get them all back to Galilee. . . .

Magdalene hurried along the still-dark streets. Here and there a few lamps burned; there was the glimmer of a lantern swinging, the glow of a torch lighting the underside of arches and awnings. She shrank into a doorway, heart pounding; the old scenes of her ravishing rose to haunt her . . . a woman alone before daylight on the streets of Jerusalem. But it was only a few families herding sleepy children toward caravans making an early departure. She could hear the jingling of harness, donkeys braying, the patter of hooves. But mostly the crowing of the cocks, and the first chirping and trilling of the birds. The moist, chill air made the city's smell more pungent—dung, straw, spices, dyes and dust, all mingling with the ever-present scent of burning from the Temple. Beyond the northern wall, a mist hung over the Kidron, giving off its own rank wet odor.

In the wall was the gate that led to Golgotha.

Magdalene shuddered at the thought of crossing that field alone. But there was no way to avoid it. The garden lay on the opposite side. Bracing herself, she pressed on, past the caves and hovels of the poor who lived near that dreadful place, and crept through the gate. When she came out, the ghost of a moon still floated overhead, the sky was growing pink. And there, emerging through the mists, silhouetted against the sky, were the three black crosses. Horror struck her . . . and suddenly the staggering impact of her loss. Magdalene bent double, clutching herself. It seemed for a moment she could not climb that hill. She could not pass those crosses. But she must find him, she must reach him somehow, to perform for him this one last act of love.

Magdalene surveyed her surroundings. She could skirt the edges of the field. It would take longer, but she need not go directly past that knoll. She clutched her cloak around her; careful not to look up, she began to pick her way through the wet weeds and grasses, cluttered with trash and bones, and around the rocks that were beginning to glisten in the light.

The sun was just rising when at last she reached the lane of willows that led into the garden place of the tombs. The lacy green branches swayed tentlike above her. The delicate new light rained through. Birds were in full cry now, trilling and chirring, ringing their little golden bells. There was the heady fragrance of many flowers, a final burst of color and sweetness, before the walls of gray rock into which the tombs were cut took over. Magdalene's heart was beating hard. Could she find him? There had been so much haste and noise and anguish—where had they laid him?

She paused, searching the bewildering masses of rock formations. Then it came back to her: It had been down a short flight of steps. The men had to be careful with their burden; two of the women following had stumbled. She remembered now—it had been the first tomb just beyond the steps. . . . And it would be guarded.

Closing her eyes for a second, Magdalene drew a deep, prayerful breath. Then she descended the steps.

At first she thought she had been mistaken . . . another tomb perhaps, a different flight of steps. For the sepulcher before her was open. No stone sealed its door; its great wheel was leaning against the side. And no one was standing guard. In her dismay, she looked around, anxiously searching the garden. But no—these were the only steps; and she remembered now, quite clearly, these same scarlet flowers were spilling from the deep crevice above it.

The tomb was obviously empty. Magdalene stood frozen, white and still. Then she began to shake. *He was not there! Someone had taken him away.* But where? Who had rolled away the stone? Where were the guards? Who could possibly have done this senseless thing? Some of the apostles? Peter and John had said nothing of this last night. Yet, as she trembled there in those first shocked moments, it was the only explanation that came to her. Some of them must actually have attempted the very thing their enemies had predicted. Incredible, insane! What could be accomplished? It would only bring certain disaster on them all.

In terror and panic, Magdalene ran back up the steps. She must get word as fast as possible to Peter and John. Surely they did not know of this; they must see for themselves. They would know what to do. Heedless of rocks and thorns, she raced from the garden and up the path, directly across the field, darting among the grisly forest of waiting poles. There was no way to avoid passing the knoll. The three crosses were still there, one higher than the others, as if stretching its arms out to the world. The rising sun glistened on its tarred surface; it seemed to shed a special light of its own. And now, for the first time, Magdalene cried out: "Jesus, Jesus, precious Lord! Where have you gone?"

She was weeping when at last she reached the city wall. Her skirts were torn from the brambles; she had fallen, one knee was bruised, it was hard to walk. People were stirring now, carts beginning to rumble toward the markets. A few people gazed at her curiously as she half hobbled, half ran down the narrow winding street toward the house. To her great relief, she saw Peter and John just coming from there, looking concerned. The women had missed her, and sent them out to look for her.

"Thank heaven, thank heaven," she sobbed, grabbing Peter's arm. "Come quickly. They have taken the Lord out of the sepulcher. Someone has taken him away and I don't know where to find him!"

"Are you sure?" They were staring at her, aghast.

"I was there. The tomb is empty!"

"Go then," Peter barked. "Go back to the house; stay with the women."

"No, I will go with you! Only don't wait for me; I have hurt my knee. I will follow. Run as fast as you can!"

The men raced off together. But John was younger and faster; he reached the tomb first and, stooping, looked inside. Peter, who came lumbering up, found him pale and shaken, leaning against the open door. Peter was flushed, panting, his eyes large with the unspoken question.

John made a weak gesture, "See for youself," he whispered.

Without hesitation, Peter squatted and maneuvered his big body through the entrance. Inside the small low-ceilinged chamber, he straightened as much as he could. The linen wrappings were there on the stone bench—bloodstained, smelling of the spices that had been hastily scattered among their folds. On a ledge a few feet away lay the napkin, neatly rolled.

Astounded, Peter stared, his throat working. Then he beckoned dumbly to John to come inside. Together, stunned, they looked about, trying to take it in. "Why would they take him without his bindings?" Peter whispered. "Would they bury his naked body? Why wouldn't they carry him away as we left him?"

Their eyes locked. Both were breathing hard. They hardly dared to speak as the first inklings of the incredible truth began to dawn. "Isn't it possible," John ventured, "that he freed *himself*? That Jesus was not stolen but freed himself, as he said!"

Peter continued to stare about, dazed. He had seen many miracles; why should this stagger him? His heart was pounding too hard for him to respond.

"We have seen him conquer death," John went on carefully, though his voice shook with hope. "Again and again we saw it. Lazarus . . . that little girl . . . the man in Nain . . ."

"And he promised," Peter choked. "He could have risen! Yes, yes, he could have risen. . . . *Jesus has risen as he said!*"

They were delirious. Dumbfounded. Bewildered. They only knew they must carry this news to the other apostles. Assure them it was true, it had to be true, and beg them to believe. To rejoice and also believe. Yet warn them. This news, however glorious, would bring about a crisis. Create new problems, new dangers. The authorities might arrest them, all of them, for they would be immediately suspect. They would have to decide what to do. Whether to remain in hiding until Jesus showed himself to them—came to their rescue—or to flee.

In their excitement and confusion, they were halfway down the hill by a different path, before they remembered Magdalene. But then she had injured her knee; surely she had taken Peter's advice and gone on home to the women. She needed to have it tended, she needed rest. Magdalene had been with Mary throughout the whole ordeal; she was exhausted, grief-stricken.

They hesitated. No, don't wait or go back for her; surely she hadn't tried to follow.

Sobbing, Magdalene huddled on the steps before the tomb. Her bruised knee was swelling; she must have twisted it when she fell against the jagged rock. The pain was intense. It was nothing, she realized, as nothing compared to the suffering on the cross, or what many other people suffered every day—but compounded by the agony of this utter loneliness . . . Jesus was *gone*! The one she loved so much had vanished, she knew not where.

Even Peter and John were not here, and she needed the comfort of their presence, their reaction to this appalling thing: What had happened to their Lord? Where now could they turn?

The sun was nearly risen now, its colors flooding the sky beyond these bleak gray rocks. How could the day dawn with such brilliance and bird song, when all hope was gone? Through her tears Magdalene stared at the open tomb. Its entrance was tinged with a light she had not seen before. . . . Natural light, she thought at first, a baptism from the rising sun. . . . But as she watched, the radiance increased—became so bright the doorway seemed almost to be ablaze. Perhaps, she thought wildly, there had been some mistake! She had not looked within. What if, by some miracle, it was *not* empty, as she had supposed, but still filled with his blessed presence?

Magdalene sprang up, trembling. Now she, too, crouched, and dared to look within. But the sight was so dazzling she cried out and had to shield her eyes. She, too, saw the abandoned grave clothes, the napkin neatly rolled and lying on a shelf. But upon the bench where the precious body had been so carefully laid sat two presences. Their raiment was glistening, their beautiful faces serene.

"Woman, why do you weep?" one of them asked gently.

"I weep for the one who was here!" she cried. "I weep for my beloved Master, whom I have come to anoint."

"He is not here," they told her. "Go and seek him in the garden."

Beside herself, Magdalene turned and hobbled as fast as she could up the steps. The pain didn't matter. If he had been moved, she must find the place. The gardener might know! Gardeners rose early; the man who tended the gardens would also know about the tombs. Seeing a figure in the distance, she ran toward him.

"Help me," she pleaded, even before he turned. "Have you seen anything amiss? They have taken away my Lord, and I don't know where to find him!"

"Who is he?" the man's voice asked. "Who is it that you seek?"

"Jesus of Nazareth, my Lord and my God. Sir, if you know who has carried him away, tell me where they have laid him."

"*Magdalene.*" She heard her own name spoken. "*Magdalene.*"

Jesus turned then and she saw him, in all his radiant beauty, once again she saw him, clad in purest white like the angels. And her legs failed her. She sank at his feet, weeping.

"*Rabboni!*" she cried, reaching up to him. "Dearest Jesus, my Lord . . . *Rab-boni!*"

"Magdalene," he said again. But he drew away a little and lifted his hand to restrain her. "Do not touch me," he said gently. "Do not hold me, for I have not yet ascended to my Father."

She felt the very power of his presence drawing her to her feet. She stood before him, amazed, exalted. He lived, he lived! Though in a different dimension.

"Go to my mother and my brothers and tell them what you have seen. Go to my apostles and all my disciples and tell them, 'I have seen the Lord.'"

The women were all up now, and busy making their own preparations. A strong odor of myrrh, oil and spices filled the house. They looked up in astonishment as Magdalene burst in, breathless. They had never seen such ecstasy and wonder on a face.

"He is risen, he is risen! I have seen the Lord!"

They gazed at her, astounded. In disbelief. "We were just coming to join you," Adah said. She made a bewildered gesture to the jars and packets on the table. "See, we are ready—we want to help—"

"It's too late. . . . *I* was too late! Put those things away. Jesus doesn't need them! The door was open, the stone was rolled away. He is not there. But he is *alive*, I tell you. I saw him and spoke with him!"

The women gasped. "Then . . . where *is* he?"

"You will see him soon. He promised! He told me simply to spread the word. I am going on now to Elizabeth's to tell Mary."

"Magdalene, please—" Adah put out her hand, concerned. "You didn't sleep well; you were restless all night—I could hear you. Please lie down awhile and rest."

"No, no, I must go. When I've seen Mary, I will go on to the house where the apostles are staying."

"Didn't you see Peter and John? They went out to look for you."

"Yes, yes, I encountered them on the road. They went on to the tomb, I told them to hurry, they could run faster, I had already been there but I would follow. They must have seen what I saw—the empty place, perhaps even the angels, I don't know." Magdalene halted. She was being incoherent; they must think her mad. They were staring at her open-mouthed. It didn't matter; she was eager to leave, to spread the news, above all to bring this tremendous joy to Mary.

The women looked at each other in dismay when she had gone.

Then, murmuring among themselves, they returned to their spices. "Poor Magdalene, this has been too much for her," Adah said, deeply troubled. "Some of us had better wait here, in case she comes back and needs help."

This was agreed. Adah herself would stay—she was closer to Magdalene; the others would go on without her.

Thus the little group set off, taking the path across Calvary that led most directly to the place where Jesus had been laid.

And behold, when they were halfway there, almost to the very knoll where Jesus had been crucified, they froze. For he was coming toward them. Bright in the morning sunrise, with a faint smile on his lips, was the man they had followed so far, and served. Loved as a son, father, brother, friend, but above all, as Lord.

He was clad in garments whiter than any they could ever achieve with their washing. His hair and beard were no longer blood-matted, his face was no longer savaged, but beautiful, incandescent. Only his wounded feet and the wrists he held out to them bore evidence of the brutal murder they themselves had seen.

"Hail!" he said. And seeing their pale, shocked faces: "Don't be afraid. . . . Put away your spices. Go and tell my apostles I will soon be with them again, both here in Jerusalem and in Galilee."

And they came up to him, weeping in their astonishment and joy, and fell at his feet and worshiped him.

Epilogue

---

*A*ND now for a little while Jesus lived and moved on his beautiful earth again. This body he occupied now as real as the one before, able to feel all he had ever known and enjoyed on earth. But transcendent, moving about without effort, at will.

Three times he appeared to his apostles in the upper room, asking them why they were troubled. Letting them examine his hands and feet, that they might believe and turn their anguish into rejoicing. And when they went briefly back to Galilee, twice he joined them there, eating and drinking with them, even the newly caught fish broiled over a charcoal fire. And commissioning them to carry on after his departure.

"Feed my sheep," he told them—Peter especially, over and over. "Go and make disciples of all nations, baptizing them in the name of the Father and of the Son and of the Holy Spirit, teaching them to observe all that I have commanded you; and lo, I am with you always, even to the end of the world."

He walked beside Cleophas on the road to Emmaus, and broke bread with him, comforting him, and assuring him he had not failed. . . . And he visited his mother and Elizabeth, holding their hands and telling them many things as they sat together on the roof, with his dog Ben's head resting against his knee. Loving and praising them— two selfless women whom God honored above all women.

And when the apostles returned to Jerusalem, he instructed them further, opening their minds to an even greater understanding of all that had been written concerning his own birth, death and resurrection. "Stay on in the city, and when the Holy Spirit has come upon you, you will receive power to testify about all this with great effect."

No longer must he attack the priests and scribes and Pharisees for the cruel and selfish hypocrisy of selling and sacrifice at the Temple:

That had been done. Never again would he be on trial for preaching the truth as God's son: That had been done. No more would he be tortured in prison, or on the cross. That, too, had been accomplished. He had been in hell and risen; he had been with the Father and returned. Soon now he would have to go back to the Father.

Finally, when forty days had passed, he led them out as far as Bethany—his mother and his two brothers with them, for they, too, had stayed on in the city, and all of them believed. And Cleo, too, was with them, holding fast to Jesus' dog. And Martha and Mary and Lazarus were there too, near their house where the little group gathered, and the beautiful Magdalene. And although they had anticipated why they had come, that he was once more going to leave them, their hearts were not sad. Though they were weeping as he bade each of them goodbye and lifted his hands to bless them, they were comforted. For he also promised that within a few days they would have a remarkable experience: The power of the Holy Spirit would come upon them, and they would be his witnesses unto the uttermost parts of the world.

And even as he spoke, in that rich sweet musical voice they would remember forever, Ben began to bark and strain, lifting his head like the others to watch as his master disappeared. For before their eyes Jesus was being lifted up to heaven, and a cloud received him out of their sight.

And behold, two men in white clothing appeared before them, asking, "Why are you gazing up into heaven? This same Jesus, who has just been taken up from you, will come again in the same way as you have watched him depart."

And they returned to Jerusalem, in wonder, rejoicing.

Ten days later, during the Feast of Pentecost, they were all assembled at the Temple Mount when suddenly there came a sound from heaven, as of a rushing mighty wind, filling all the house where they were sitting. And they were filled with the Power of his Holy Spirit, as he had promised! A power that transformed them, molding them, this first small band of followers, into a great army that would move from Jerusalem into all the world, to conquer it, not by the sword but by the victorious news of his kingdom.

And from that day to this, all who love and follow him anxiously await his return.